INTO A
DARK FRONTIER

INTO A
DARK FRONTIER
A THRILLER

JOHN MANGAN

OCEANVIEW PUBLISHING
SARASOTA, FLORIDA

ISBN 978-1-60809-310-6

Published in the United States of America by Oceanview Publishing
Sarasota, Florida
www.oceanviewpub.com

10 9 8 7 6 5 4 3 2

PRINTED IN THE UNITED STATES OF AMERICA

This book is dedicated to those who serve something greater than themselves.

ACKNOWLEDGMENTS

FIRST, I WOULD like to recognize my wife for her support and patience as, month after month, I vanished into the study to write this story. Being new to the world of professional writing, I owe much to Sally Kim and Joshua Hood, who offered their advice, encouragement, and got me pointed in the right direction.

As for the story itself, as I struggled to patch it together, friends such as Matt Tieman and Tisha McGarry labored through the early versions, critiquing it and guiding its development. However, it was my editor, John Paine, who helped trim away the deadwood and unearthed the true story line within. A special thanks goes out to Simon O'Neill who helped me with the Kiwi slang and also Reid Mangan and David Raymond for their technical advice.

Thank you to my agent, Bob Deforio, for taking a chance on an unknown author.

I would most like to thank the men and women of the US, and allied, Armed Forces whom it was such an honor to serve beside. Your humor, courage, and selfless devotion to a higher calling inspired me to begin writing, hoping that, in some way, I could share you with the world. Although the story itself is fiction, the valor and sacrifice depicted within it is not. Thank you all. I hope you enjoy the story.

INTO A
DARK FRONTIER

IN THE NEAR FUTURE

CHAPTER ONE

NEW JERSEY

SLADE CRAWFORD RAN for his life, heart thudding, legs failing. He looked back over his shoulder to where his stolen truck burned like a funeral pyre, sending trembling bands of light through the trees. Defeat, dark and leaden, lay in his chest whispering that he'd lost, that his escape had failed and that the end was inevitable. His cadence broke and for a moment his run became a shambling trot. But then, summoning his grit, Slade willed the doubting part of his mind blank and allowed himself to know only one thing: that he had to continue running.

Placing the North Star off his left shoulder, Slade labored across a series of open fields, his feet heavy with mud, then he scratched through a fold of trees until he found a dirt road. Aiming toward glowing horizon lights, he covered the miles as best he could, pushing his body deep into nausea, hobbling and sprinting through the darkness. When he reached the concrete lanes of a quiet suburb, he slowed his pace to a walk, then turned into a children's playground, and seated himself on a wooden bench, sick with fatigue. As the lung spasms subsided, he ran a hand across his face and cleared the sweat from his eyes.

So this is how it feels.

Slade was no stranger to manhunts, but he had always experienced them as the predator—never the prey.

He gave himself a pat-down; he still had a burner phone, a multi-tool, headlamp, and most importantly, his treasured Sig Sauer P220, the engraved pistol that Bravo Platoon had presented to him on the day he was awarded the Navy Cross.

Back when they still called him a hero.

He checked his watch.

Despair hammered his gut. Right now, the freighter that would carry him to freedom was scheduled to depart and he still had fifty miles to go. He powered up the burner phone and called Abe Howard, his only contact on the freighter.

The phone's ringer droned on without answer. "Come on, pick up, pick up, dammit."

As the seconds ticked by, Slade was acutely aware that in the darkness that surrounded him, a great and inescapable trap was closing. With the realization that a domestic terrorist was on the run, the FBI, DHS, and local law enforcement would be creating concentric rings of checkpoints, roadblocks, and roving patrols. Overhead, armed drones were converging on the area, their unblinking eyes scanning and probing.

The line opened. "Hello?"

"Abe! Abe, this is Bradshaw. Don't—"

"Where in the name of God are you? We're casting off now."

Slade bolted back to his feet and started across the park at a run, the phone still pressed to his ear. "Listen, you've got to stop the ship. Understand? I can make it. Just don't leave yet."

"But how long will you be? We're about to push back from the dock."

"Do what you have to, Abe. I'll be there in an hour. Just stop that ship." Breaking the connection, he pocketed the phone and continued his sprint.

Weaving his way through children's playground equipment, Slade gritted his teeth in anger; his life lay in ruin, his escape plan had been reduced to ash, but as long as he was alive, he had only one option.

Run.

CHAPTER TWO

48 HOURS EARLIER, NORTHERN IDAHO

WITH THE WINDOW for his escape fully open, Slade had sawed through the GPS tracking device that was bolted to his wrist, then taken to the highway in a stolen Tacoma pickup truck. Infused with the desperate energy of a fugitive, he'd left Sandpoint and headed south, knowing that alarm bells were already ringing throughout the Department of Homeland Security.

From the day that he was released on parole, Slade had planned for this moment. Using the precision ingrained in him during two decades at Special Operations Command, he'd weighed risks, analyzed threats, and prepared for contingencies. None of that did anything to ease his looming sense of dread; he was off the grid now, but the problem with this grid was—it would kill to get him back.

Passing through Coeur d'Alene, he turned east on Highway 90 and crossed the vast plains of Montana, stopping every four hours to relieve himself beside the road and refuel the truck from five-gallon jerry cans stocked in the bed. Traveling as he was, there had been no gas station receipts to flag his route, nor rest stop surveillance cameras to record his stops.

He drove without incident through the first night and into the following day, eating plastic-wrapped food and downing amphetamines. But turning south outside of Sioux Falls he ran into an early winter storm. He pressed on, faster than he should, hunched over the wheel, wipers clacking, staring hypnotized at the endless snow streaks that sped out from some dark other-where and then back again into nothing.

With the pale dawn came clear skies and numb exhaustion after a night spent on edge. But the back roads that he used to skirt Indianapolis were old, rutted, and covered in black ice. Losing control, he fishtailed, left the road, and blew a tire in a forlorn, husk-stubbled cornfield.

Slade was fine and the truck was fine, but crouched there amongst the whispering corn stalks, trying to raise the vehicle, he found that the jack sank repeatedly into the muddy earth, confounding his designs. Hands raw and numb in the blowing cold, he laid down rocks and debris, jacked again and failed. He tried to goad the lamed vehicle forward and onto the road, but it spat and trundled, the blown tire flapping. He tried again and again, but there was no limit to how much of his effort the earth could consume.

The farmer who found Slade waving a jacket beside the road, mud-coated and wild-eyed, paused to help the stranger. Hesitating, the farmer left his vehicle, offered assistance, and had the Tacoma pulled onto the road within the hour. He then helped Slade jack the truck up, change the tire, and go on his way.

Already hours late, his margin for error consumed, Slade pressed his speed as fast as he dared, knowing that another delay would end his new life before it had begun.

* * *

He was five miles past the New Jersey border and drunk with fatigue when he blew through a speed trap and woke a sleeping cop.

With red and blue strobes coloring the interior of his cab, Slade slowed the Tacoma and pulled to the side of the road. The cop coasted to a stop five meters back but stayed in his cruiser, running a vehicle license check.

Rigid in his seat, Slade weighed all, holding his life in the calculations. It had been forty-eight hours since he'd destroyed the GPS wrist monitor, more than enough time for the Department of Homeland Security to issue an arrest warrant. Had his stolen Tacoma already been reported?

Slade squinted through the rearview mirror, trying to determine if the cop had a partner. He drew the Sig. He fingered the seat belt release.

The clock on the dashboard marked the agonizing flow of lost minutes.

As the cruiser's door swung open and the cop lifted himself out, Slade dropped the transmission into reverse and hammered the gas pedal to the floor.

The pickup lurched backward, tires spinning, closed the distance, and powered into the cruiser with a metallic *crunk*, knocking the cop down and both vehicles askew.

Slade unbuckled his seat belt and was out the door, sprinting, Sig rising as the downed officer struggled to stand and draw his weapon.

Slade clacked two deafening rounds high over the fumbling officer's head, closed the distance, leaped, pinned him, then buttstroked him across his jaw. The officer went limp.

He was searching for the cop's handcuffs when the screaming of locked tires sent him scrambling for the shoulder, dragging the unconscious officer behind him. A skidding car sluiced past and powered into the Tacoma in an explosion of glass and debris.

More screeching. More cars slamming into the pileup. Legs pumping, Slade hauled the dead weight of the officer until they were safe and clear of the road. Battling a wave of guilt, he checked the unconscious cop; he was bleeding heavily from a crushed lip but was breathing well. Slade positioned him so that his mouth would drain of blood, swept a loose tooth from his mouth, whispered an apology, then turned back toward the car accident.

The Tacoma was overturned in the middle of the road, blue flames spreading around it. People limped from their wrecks. Slade ran to and checked the crumpled vehicles, helped a stunned woman from her car and away from the growing flames. He ran back to his vehicle, but the interior was already engulfed.

Red and blue police lights flashed in the distance. Turning from the wreckage, his path lit by the burning Tacoma, Slade bolted into the tree line.

CHAPTER THREE

NEW JERSEY

"Do what you have to, Abe. I'll be there in an hour. Just stop that ship!" Breaking the connection, Slade pocketed the phone and continued his sprint across the playground.

Entering the surrounding neighborhood, Slade combed the streets looking for another car to steal. Hell, he'd already jumped parole, stolen a truck, and shot at a cop. One more theft wouldn't hurt.

He didn't have to look long; the blue Chevy Impala was old, pre-blackbox with no security system. The window yielded to the butt of his pistol, the steering column and ignition yielded to his multi-tool.

With the minutes ticking by, Slade sped down darkened streets, knuckles white against the steering wheel. The path ahead was murky, his assets laughable, and with each passing second, his chances of success moved toward zero.

His heart leaped at the sound of a cell phone chime: a text message had arrived.

Couldn't stop them. We have departed. Clearing the harbor now. Best of luck to you.

Slamming his fist against the steering wheel, Slade braked to a halt and screamed in frustration, watching as the best of his rage blew from his lungs and vanished into nothing.

He hung his head and sat unmoving, the idling engine the only sound in the cold night air. The door for his escape had just slammed shut, but goddamn if he wasn't going to kick it back open. What were his options? Jack a boat and chase the freighter down? He'd have to find a speedboat to overcome the freighter's head start. Then what? Perform an underway boarding with no boarding equipment? It wouldn't work. His mind turned . . . He couldn't catch the freighter by land or by sea . . . that left only air.

Utilizing his burner phone, he trolled the Internet. Three minutes later, having found what he needed, Slade hammered his foot on the gas and blasted back into the night.

*   *   *

Twenty minutes later, Slade pulled to a stop in a dark parking lot at the end of a heavily forested road, his headlights illuminating a cluster of buildings, aircraft hangars, and a sign that welcomed visitors to the Central Jersey Skydiving School.

Target in sight, he drove onto the grass, angled toward the school, then accelerated forward, smashing the car directly into the building's front door. There was a pop of exploding headlights and crumpling metal as the door swung inward. Slade backed up, exited the vehicle, then entered the building, headlamp splaying.

He found himself in a large room decorated with pictures of happy skydivers, grinning mid-fall and on the drop zone. Slade walked to the back of the room and kicked his way through another locked door. The room was lined with neat rows of packed parachutes. When he found one that suited his purposes, he pulled it from the rack and slung it over his shoulder.

Slade then ransacked the school until he found his prize: a small brass key chained to a pink rabbit's foot—the ignition key to an airplane. He pocketed it and grabbed a pair of aviator headphones off a wall hook.

Back in the main room, Slade scoured the pictures hanging on the walls. There it was, in over a dozen pictures—a blue Cessna-172, tail number N39676. After memorizing the number, Slade switched off his headlamp, then turned and bolted from the building.

As he labored toward the parked aircraft, with crisp winter stubble crunching underfoot, Slade heard police sirens blowing on the night wind and saw the flicker of blue strobes breaking through the trees.

Hurrying, he crossed onto the concrete apron, flipped down the red filter on his headlamp, and risked a dim glow. The third aircraft that he came to was a blue Cessna, tail number N39676. Ducking under the Cessna's wing, Slade rapped his knuckles against the metal skin. The response was solid and dull; the fuel tanks were full. He opened the cockpit door and flashed his light inside. All of the seats had been removed save the pilot's, leaving enough room for a handful of jumpers. Slade tossed the parachute and headphones inside then moved to the wings and unhooked the tie down cables, the cold metal clasps sticking to his fingers. With the aircraft unchained, he yanked the wooden chocks from beneath the wheels and pulled the nylon covers from the pitot tube and engine cowling.

As he lifted himself into the cockpit, Slade's nostrils filled with the smell of plastic upholstery, aviation fuel, and the tang of stale puke. Through the rear window he saw a fleet of tactical vehicles as they streamed into the parking lot, tires squealing, sirens moaning, men dismounting. Fighting the urge to rush, Slade swung his headlamp over the instrument panel. He was not a licensed pilot but had paid for enough lessons to get his solo certificate.

Slade brushed his fingers over the forest of knobs, found the battery switch, clicked it on, activated the instrument lights, then began the starting checklist as best he could remember.

Battery. Fuel. Avionics. Flaps. Throttle. Fuel mixture. Master switch. Ignition!

The electric starter wined, the cylinders coughed, the plane shook, and the engine came to life with a clattering roar. Slade scanned the gauges as they jumped to life.

A brilliant light dazzled Slade's eyes from twenty feet out the right door. "Slade Crawford! DHS! Hands up! Hands up now!" a voice screamed.

The Sig came into Slade's hand and extended across the cockpit, bucking and exploding, deafening in the enclosed space. The passenger window evaporated in a white fog and the dazzling light disappeared. Slade worked the trigger until the gun fell silent then dropped it to the floor. He jammed the throttle full forward, but the aircraft shook and roared and went nowhere as gunfire erupted behind him and bullets *tick-ticked* through the aircraft's aluminum skin.

"Parking brake's on!" Slade screamed at himself as he slapped the brake lever off. Suddenly loosed, the Cessna bolted forward at a cockeyed angle and nearly tipped. Working the rudder pedals, Slade straightened his course and trundled across the parking apron and into the grass, still accelerating.

Fumbling in the darkened cockpit, he clicked on the landing light, careened past a windsock, then crossed over the runway at a right angle, still accelerating. Nearing takeoff speed, the airframe chattering as it jolted across the rough terrain, he struck a small rut and bounced into the air, but floundered and settled back to the grass.

Peering forward into the rushing lightpool, Slade glanced down at the airspeed indicator, waited through an agonizing chain of heartbeats, then pulled back on the yoke, lifting the aircraft smoothly away from the great black mass of the earth below.

CHAPTER FOUR

SLADE WIPED AT the bloody groove that a bullet had opened on the back of his neck. The wound did not penetrate muscle, and his neck still moved freely, but he could feel a sodden mess growing down the length of his back. He pressed at the flowing gash, wiped his eyes to clear the stinging fuel vapors, then swung his headlamp to confirm what he already knew: that his right-wing fuel tank had been severely holed and was blowing raw misted fuel through the shattered passenger window.

He reached for the fuel tank selector and turned the lever to "Left," ensuring that the engine would receive its fuel from the undamaged fuel tank.

Gritting his teeth, Slade replayed the brief encounter back at the airport. What had tipped the DHS to his escape route? Did they know about the freighter? Would they be waiting for him there? Knowing that he would find no answers, he turned his attention back to the task at hand.

He wiped at his eyes again, spit against the gagging petroleum, and peered forward through the cockpit window. Before him stretched the endless never-dark of East Coast suburban sprawl, the length of which was lit by cul-de-sac neighborhoods, pulsing freeways, strip mall colonies, and big-box mega-hives. Flying at 500 feet over the halogen lightscape was as simple as flying in daylight. Slade adjusted the trim wheel, then kept only two fingers on the control yoke. True to its design, the sturdy Cessna tracked straight and level.

Slade glanced at the compass; he was headed south. Slight pressure on the yoke brought the aircraft into a gentle left turn, which he maintained until he was headed east toward the Atlantic Ocean. With the aircraft on course, Slade flashed his headlamp around the cabin. Finding the aviator headphones, he slipped them on to deaden the bellowing engine. He then pulled out the burner phone, activated it, and sent another text message to Abe Howard, his contact on the freighter.

Ask ship captain, what is your magnetic bearing FROM the Verrazano Bridge. Please turn on all ship lights n put strobe light on aft deck. What is wind strength n speed?

With the message sent, Slade turned his attention skyward and found that the overcast was thinning. Easing back on the yoke, he put the aircraft into a climb and ascended into the broken star field above.

Suddenly an unintelligible voice scratched in his headset. Slade reached for the VHF radio and turned up the volume.

"Unidentified aircraft over Middlesex, bearing 0-9-0, altitude 1,500 feet, this is Newark Control on Guard, you are in violation of class Charlie airspace. Contact me on 1-3-5-7-5, reset your transponder and ident."

Slade knew that the situation was rapidly deteriorating. A terror suspect was at large, a federal agent had been fired upon, and a stolen aircraft had just been spotted heading in the direction of New York City. It was only a matter of time until the Air Force interceptors arrived.

Focused forward, Slade saw that he was approaching the convergence of the Raritan River and the Arthur Kill channel. As he crossed over the southernmost tip of Staten Island, he turned north, following the glowing constellation of the eastern shore. The arching necklace lights of the Verrazano Bridge lay directly ahead, and beyond that, the galactic blaze of New York City rose into view.

To his right lurked the void of the Atlantic Ocean, lightless and starless, a place empty of all perspective, depth, or distance. To Slade, it looked like world's end, a cliff as stark and infinite as the one that once haunted the dreams of ancient mariners.

Somewhere in that black hole lay his freighter.

Stabilized on the new course, Slade grabbed a handhold and eased himself from the pilot seat. Then, kneeling in the wind-blasted cabin, he set to strapping on the parachute.

With the chute firmly in place, Slade reseated himself behind the flight controls. He made a course correction. The aircraft was starting to wander as the leaking tank emptied and the fuel load became unbalanced.

"Attention on Guard. Unidentified aircraft over Great Kills Harbor, heading 0-4-0, altitude 5,100 feet, this is Newark Control, contact me on 1-3-5-7-5, squawk 5-7-3-2, reset your transponder and ident. You are in violation of class Bravo airspace, turn left to 2-7-0 immediately or be subject to interception."

Slade ignored the radio and checked his phone. There was a new text message.

Captain says magnetic bearing is 170 FROM the Verrazano bridge. Range six miles. Winds variable. Strobe light on. Why?

Slade yelled in triumph and pounded his fist against his thigh. Then calming, he began to calculate a dead reckoning solution to the ship. According to the text, if Slade crossed over the Verrazano Bridge on a heading of 170 degrees then flew for six miles he would end up directly over the ship. As for the six miles . . . he was flying at 110 knots, roughly two miles every minute. If he held his course for three minutes past the bridge, that would give him the necessary range. But his target was moving, so it would be farther out to sea by the time he arrived. Slade added another thirty seconds to his calculations.

Droning minutes passed.

Slade ignored the increasingly urgent demands coming over the radio.

The lights, arches, and steel cables of the Verrazano Bridge slid beneath the Cessna's nose. Slade banked the aircraft to the right, held the turn, then stabilized on a heading of 170 degrees. He hacked his stopwatch, starting a three-minute-and-thirty-second countdown.

As he turned away from the lights of New York City, the unlit chasm of the Atlantic yawned open before him. He checked his timing—forty-five seconds had passed. He peered forward again, squinting into the black void that had swallowed the whole of the world. There was no horizon, no up, no down, just a cavernous pit with a scattering of depthless lights. He found a distant ship. No, it was Venus. No—

The frigid wind blast was increasing, the howl of the slipstream now deafening. Something was wrong. Slade leaned back in his seat and looked at the instruments. The artificial horizon showed a steep, descending left turn. The instrument must be malfunctioning—

Suddenly, a memory surfaced: a flight instructor, wearing aviator sunglasses and headphones was sitting next to Slade, his face awash in high-altitude sunshine. The man tapped the instrument panel. "Trust your instruments, Slade, trust them with your life. At night, in the clouds, over dark water . . . the seat of your pants will lie . . . lie like a Pattaya whore. Trust your instruments, Slade."

Trusting his instructor and fighting against his every instinct, Slade rolled the artificial horizon level and pulled back on the yoke.

When the instruments stabilized, he glanced at the compass; he was 45 degrees off course. Cursing violently, he turned the nose of the Cessna back to heading 170. But it was too late—he'd ruined the dead reckoning course to the ship. He would have to search blindly now.

"Single engine Cessna, three miles southeast of Staten Island at 6,000 feet, heading 1-7-0, not squawking, this is Viper 1-3 on Guard, make an immediate right turn to heading 2-7-0."

The voice coming through the radio sounded forced and nasal, as if spoken by someone with a strong head cold. Slade recognized it as a man talking through a pressurized oxygen mask.

The F-16s had arrived.

Ignoring the interceptors, Slade tried to stabilize on the 170 heading but found it impossible. His instincts said that the aircraft was in a steep right bank, while the instruments indicated the exact opposite. The aircraft was growing progressively more unstable, and Slade's ability to control it was slipping away. The Cessna now climbed and dove, rolled back and forth, opposing and amplifying Slade's every control input. He gripped the control yoke with both fists, shoulders hunched as a growing panic constricted his throat. The Cessna was in a dive again, engine howling. G-forces crushed Slade into the seat as the aircraft seemingly rolled upside down, through the vertical, then pitched into a death spiral.

Panic veered into abject terror.

A blazing horizon rolled into view. New York City! Slade wasn't upside down; he was in a steep dive and turning left again. But with the appearance of a distinct horizon, the spatial disorientation vanished, and he was able to control the aircraft. Watching the city lights, clinging to them like a raft, Slade rolled the wings level and pulled the Cessna's nose away from the Atlantic, heart convulsing beneath his ribs. He'd turned the aircraft all the way around and hadn't even known it.

"Single engine Cessna, this is Viper 1-3 on Guard, you are headed into the New York City restricted area, turn back out to sea or you *will* be fired upon. I repeat, you *will* be fired upon."

Slade grimaced. He was incapable of controlling the aircraft in complete darkness. If he turned out to sea as instructed, he would lose control again and spin into the water. But if he stayed on course toward New York City, the F-16s would turn his Cessna into a cloud of metallic confetti.

Faced with only one option, Slade leaned across the cockpit and popped the handle on the jump door. Dread building, he pulled himself from the seat and knelt before the yawning, wind-blasted chasm. He swept the floor of the Cessna with his headlamp, found and holstered his Sig, then clenched his fists and hurled himself into the void.

CHAPTER FIVE

One Thousand

A river of liquid ice flooded through Slade's clothing and wrapped him in a blanket of agony.

Two Thousand

Spread-eagled, back arched.

Look thousand

He looked for the ripcord handle and snapped his hand to it.

Pull thousand

He punched the ripcord away from his body. There was a moment of nothing, then the opening shock snapped his chin to his sternum and yanked the crotch straps deep into his groin.

The windblast stopped.

A cold, gasping, empty silence.

Slade raised his hands and fumbled in the darkness, trying to find the parachute's riser cables. He found them, grasped the rearmost ones, then pulled down to flatten the parachute's natural glide path, slowing his descent.

He'd heard the F-16 call his altitude at 6,000 feet just before he jumped. A parachute's sink rate was roughly 600 feet per minute… that meant he had ten minutes to save his life.

Craning his neck, Slade looked around, trying to find a boat, any boat, someplace that would keep him from the freezing water. He pulled harder on the left riser bundle, guided himself through a full turn, and scanned the ocean in all directions.

There. An oil tanker less than a mile away, lit up like a small city, headed toward New York Bay. He could reach the ship, and landing on its mammoth deck would be little challenge.

Slade was banking in the direction of the oil tanker when he heard the sharp thunderclap of a detonating warhead off to his right. He turned in time to see a pathetic bundle of flaming debris and sparks that had once been his airplane tumble from the sky. Instinctively, he craned his neck and looked for the F-16 that had just downed the Cessna. But something else caught his eye, far out in the Atlantic, a strobe light blinking in the darkness.

Hauling on the risers, Slade changed course toward the strobe. Was it his freighter? Was it within range? He strained his eyes trying to find clues to its distance, anything to indicate how far away the ship was. But there was nothing, no wake, running lights, or reflections on the water, nothing but a single strobe, blinking in the deep. He tried to judge its angle below the horizon, but there was no horizon to see. Did the light move? Drop lower as he approached? It remained absolutely motionless.

Twice, Slade began to turn back for the oil tanker, but twice, he stopped himself. Landing on the oil tanker would save his life but would sentence him to a concrete broom closet for the remainder of it.

Long minutes ticked by with no change save the complete numbing of his hands, face, and the stiffening of his blood-slicked shirt. He could see no water, no whitecaps, no reflections, just that one strobe silently calling him to his doom.

Slade looked back at the oil tanker. It was out of range now. He had chosen his fate.

Looking to the strobe again, he realized there were other faint lights surrounding it. They were the ship's mast lights. He imagined he could see the form of the freighter itself, the size of a nail head held at arm's reach.

Slade's biceps trembled in exhaustion, but he kept pressure on the back risers, pulling for every extra inch of glide distance, willing the boat closer. Slowly the light blob grew and began to drift lower in his field of view. Then the masthead and running lights became distinct—red on the ship's right side, green on the left, white on the front and back. Slade read the lights and their meaning. He was off the boat's stern with a 40-degree crossing angle. He pulled harder on the right riser and swung his vector into lead pursuit. He needed to aim his parachute not at the point where the freighter currently was, but at the point where it would be minutes from now.

The ship was now the size of a man's thumb, its length a mess of antennas, cranes, exhaust stacks, guy wires, and railings, all threatening to block his descent, snag his chute, snap his bones, or hurl him back into the waiting sea. The flag snapping from the transom indicated a crosswind of 5 knots.

A minute later Slade was looking down at the freighter between his dangling feet. He had made the distance but still needed to land on the rolling deck. He estimated the approach variables.

Altitude: 300 feet.

Time to touchdown: 30 seconds.

Ship speed: 15 knots.

Wind: 5 knots from port.

Touchdown point: 50 square meters, steel railings, flag pole, milling people.

Slade alternately increased and decreased pressure on the risers, guiding himself through a series of S-turns, eyes padlocked on the freighter as he bled off altitude, aligned his glide path, adjusted his descent angle, and gauged his closure, attempting to orchestrate for one perfect moment the union of falling man and moving ship.

Fifteen seconds from impact, now directly behind the freighter and sensing that he was overshooting, Slade pulled into another deep S-turn. But as he pulled out of the turn, the numbed fingers of his left hand slipped free from the riser. He snapped his hand back into place and corrected onto course, but the damage had been done—his point of impact was now behind the boat.

Slade popped his chest strap free to prepare for a water landing. But it was pointless. He would be a mile behind the boat before they could bring it about. If they did return for him, it would be to retrieve a frozen corpse.

The only chance to win back the extra distance was *ground effect*, the aerodynamic phenomenon that increases the glide distance of a wing being flown in close proximity to the ground.

Throat tightening, Slade moved his hands to the front risers and pulled down, diving the chute directly toward the black hole of the Atlantic Ocean. Listening to the rising hiss of air sluicing through the risers, he turned his eyes to the approaching ship, desperate for clues to his altitude. As he sank below the freighter's deck, he began a slow, steady pull on the back risers, trying to level his flight path and skim along, inches above the invisible surface.

If he pulled too early, he would run out of speed, stall, and settle into the water.

If he pulled too late, he would slam at full speed directly into the frigid ocean.

Eyes glued to the deck railing, Slade continued his final pull, bleeding off the last of his airspeed. The freighter loomed above him. He could hear the chug of its diesels and the splash of its bow wave.

Slade's leg snapped up behind him, his boot caught by the crest of an invisible wave. Spasming with fear, he did a complete pull-up against the risers, pulled his knees to his chest, and flared the parachute, clawing for altitude as the steel hull rushed toward him.

He ballooned away from the water, lifted his feet, and sailed up and over the railing. People scattered and screamed as he smashed into the deck and tumbled in a ball, limbs exploding in pain. Then he was being dragged, pulled toward the railing, his chute inflated by the moving freighter's induced winds. Slade clawed at the release latches, but his left hand refused to work, the fingers twisted into impossible shapes. The deck slid past, bodies piled on top of him, strong arms pulled, the risers popped free, and the chute collapsed at last.

Slade lay on the deck panting, the pain of impact lost in the rush of impossible success. Startled faces filled his vision, mouths frozen in "O." He pushed himself up on an elbow and took in the stunned crowd that had congealed around him. He offered a Hollywood smile. "Crawford. Slade Crawford. Permission to come aboard?"

CHAPTER SIX

STRIPPED TO THE waist, Slade sat in a small, poorly lit infirmary amidst the stink of marine paint, rusting steel, and nervous men. A woman claiming to be a nurse cleaned and stitched at his neck wound. The pale, thinly haired matron was rough with the needle and had shown no hesitation as she popped his fingers back into joint. His hand still held a faint tremble from the pain of it, the joints humming like tuning forks beneath the bandage and splint.

Slade ran his eyes over the group of men clustered on the far side of the cabin. Their clothes were made of homespun fabric, their beards were neck length, and their vocabulary laced with biblical syntax. The men were Judeans, a fundamentalist Christian community fleeing from America to resettle in Africa in order to live and worship as they pleased.

Slade had first heard about them from his best friend and former SEAL teammate, Mike Albertson, who currently worked for a South African security agency. In between numerous jokes about Mormon wives and Jonestown Kool-Aid, Mike explained that the Judeans had contracted with his outfit to provide a professional Security Advisor. In the spirit of frogman comradery, Mike had tossed Slade the contract. Slade fit the bill perfectly, and his phone and e-mail conversations with the Judeans had gone smoothly with one small exception: Slade hadn't told the Judeans that he'd been placed on the Terrorist Watch List, the No-Fly list, and stripped of his passport. Or that he had to notify the DHS if he left Sandpoint for more than twenty-four hours. Or that his real name was actually Slade Crawford. Small oversights in his opinion.

The Judeans argued amongst themselves over the ramifications of Slade's untimely arrival.

Slade listened to their discussion and struggled to contrive a cover story that would explain his unconventional boarding technique as well as the Terror Alerts that would be blasting across the airwaves. He could think of none. His only option was the complete truth.

"My name is Slade Crawford," he interrupted loudly. The room fell silent, and the Judeans turned as though surprised to discover the blood-slicked stranger in their midst. "I'm the Security Advisor that was hired to ride with you to South Africa, train you, and then escort you into the interior. I've been corresponding with your Chief of Security, Mr. Abe Howard."

A gangly fellow with a patchy beard and sandy blond hair stepped from the crowd. "I'm Abe Howard. But . . . but the man we hired, the man I've been in contact with, was Mr. *Bradshaw*, not Crawford."

"Bradshaw was me. I was operating under a false name."

Mr. Howard was visibly taken aback. "Why?"

"Because I was being monitored by the federal government and I couldn't afford to have them track me."

"The federal government? Are you a fugitive?"

"I am now."

"For what?"

"I was wrongfully accused of being involved in the DC car bombings, for which I was imprisoned and tortured for over two years. I was eventually released but on the condition that I surrender my passport and wear a GPS monitor." Slade held up his arm and displayed the bandaged wrist where the device had been. "The monitor tracked my every movement and recorded everything I said, every conversation that I was a part of. I couldn't live like that . . ."

"What about your bullet wound?"

"I wanted to leave. They wanted me to stay."

"And the parachuting?"

"I was late. You left on time."

"So they'll be searching for you. That means they'll come here. Come after us!"

"No. They launched interceptors and shot down my aircraft. They think I'm dead in the water."

Slade's admission did nothing to lighten the mood in the cramped cabin.

Another man raised his voice. He was a corpulent fellow, his face rimmed by a mane of jowls and wattles that quivered like raw liver. "You concealed your identity from us. Are on the run from the federal government. Were involved in a gunfight. And had your aircraft *shot down* before parachuting onto our boat!"

Slade shrugged apologetically.

Quivering Jowls conferred with his companions; they made no effort to lower their voices.

"Do we now turn our backs on somebody who is being persecuted? That has never been our way."

"How do you know it's persecution, Brother? He could very well be a terrorist—"

"We will become accomplice to his crimes. We *must* radio the Coast Guard."

Slade stood and faced them. "And what then?" he interrupted loudly. "After the Coast Guard takes me in, do you imagine they'll let you continue on your way?" Slade looked each of the men in the eye. "They'll want to investigate your relationship with me. Am I one of you? Did you know about my past? They'll have a thousand questions and none of them can be answered if they allow you to leave.

"If you make that radio call, the Coast Guard will direct you back to port. They'll impound the vessel, search every hold, detain every person, and then the FBI and DHS will go through your lives with a fine-toothed comb. They'll go through your e-mails, phone logs, Internet histories, bank records, everything. They'll find the taxes you failed to pay, the sedition you spoke of, and the mistresses you've kept. They'll catalogue every detail of your lives then manufacture suspicions that serve their own ends. I know this because they did it to me. Twenty-four years of honorable military service to my country meant nothing to them. If you turn me in, the new lives you were hoping to build in Africa will end before they have even begun."

Silence reigned in the small room. The ship labored through a series of abrupt peaks and troughs. The men struggled to stay on their feet.

"He speaks the truth, brethren," came a voice from the back of the group. "If we give him up, our chance for freedom will be lost."

Another man spoke in disagreement. An argument broke out, then grew in intensity.

Suddenly, the crowd hushed as a black-clad man with dried-apple skin and a stringy beard stepped forward. "Brothers, I have long suspected that this moment would come. The moment when the Devil himself would send one of his agents into our midst. One meant to divide us and weaken our resolve."

"Look, I'm not trying to divide anybody—"

"We have allowed a viper into our midst!" The man hurled his finger at Slade with the violence of a spear. "See how he endangers all that we have worked for, and turns us against each other? Let us silence this serpent's tongue! Seize him, and cast him into the holding cell while we decide his fate!"

Most of the men murmured in disagreement, but a small party coalesced around Slade's accuser where they formed a tight, whispering knot and glanced repeatedly at Slade with narrowed eyes.

Slade shook his head in refusal. "Listen, nobody's seizing anybody." He then lowered his voice in warning. "And I sure as hell ain't going into a cage." He turned then for the surgeon's cabinet and opened it drawer by drawer with the casual air of one hunting for a snack. Reaching, he drew forth a surgical blade, bright as a mirror, then set it on the table, resting six inches from his fingers.

The assembling war party regarded the stone weight of his gaze and the broad sweep of his rugby scrum chassis, overwritten in part by a vulgar intertwining of tattoos and knotted scars.

The whispering alliance faltered.

Slade eyed the men assembling against him—they were inexperienced and afraid. Slashing them down in the cramped confines of the infirmary would make for short work. But then what? Hijack the entire ship and steam to Africa? With hundreds of other Judeans still on board? Slade recognized that the moment he spilled blood, he was finished. He stood and moved away from the knife. "I am sorry that I brought this upon you. But like you, I was only trying to live my life in freedom." Slade knew that he had to drive the discussion away from himself and his untimely arrival. He needed to play on the fear that he knew was gnawing at the heart of every man in the room. He needed to offer himself as a solution to that fear.

"When you and your families reach Africa you will face dangers unlike any you have seen before. I am Chief Petty Officer Slade Crawford, and I have spent the last two decades fighting in some of the worst places on Earth, many of them African. I have spent months living with African tribes, training them, equipping them, learning their ways. I am well acquainted with the land, the clans, the weapons, and the diseases. If you will allow me to ride with you to Africa, I will spend the voyage training you, teaching you how to protect your families and how to succeed. If you will give me this chance at a new life, I will be eternally grateful."

"More lies from the Deceiver! Listen not to—"

"Brother Mantis, that's enough," Jowls said, silencing the spitting old crow. He stepped forward and addressed Slade directly. "I do not know who you are, but I know that you speak the truth. It has never been our way to turn away a stranger in need, even one such as you. You may remain with us and sail to South Africa." He looked over his shoulder. "Brother Howard, see that our guest is given proper food and clothing. I believe there was a stateroom already set aside for him. If it is taken, then give him mine." Jowls turned and left the cabin.

CHAPTER SEVEN

THE SOUND OF diesel engines rumbled up from below deck, shaking the freighter from its battered keel to its rusting forecastle. Wrapped in a course wool blanket, Slade stood on the aft deck watching a blaze of city lights recede in the distance as the ship's screws boiled the ocean below.

In his open hand lay a military shoulder badge: an American flag, its threads worn through, it's colors dimmed by decades of grime and sweat. The wind trembled the flag, threatening to blow it from his grasp. He stood for long moments, watching it, gathering the courage to release it. But finding himself lacking, he balled his hand into a fist and returned the flag to his pocket.

Shivering now, Slade turned from the railing and started inside, turning his back on the land of his birth. But as he entered the ship's hatch, he paused and looked over his shoulder. On the distant horizon, a statue of a robed woman striding forward, holding aloft a golden beacon. Battling a flash of anguish, Slade watched as the last of her disappeared into the gathering night.

* * *

Freshly showered and with a full stomach, Slade lay on his bunk unable to sleep, pale green blossoms firing along the back of his eyelids, the dislocated fingers humming in the dark. He knew he had not escaped the DHS and FBI. The last six hours had transformed him from a simple parole jumper into an armed enemy of the state. And even though they hadn't tracked him as far as the freighter, they would soon enough.

Electronic surveillance archives would be used to identify his burner phone. They would check the records and see his last text message to Abe Howard. They would find out who Abe was. They would track him to the harbor. They would get the name of the freighter and its South African destination. They would find that a parachute had been stolen. They would divine Slade's escape plan. The F-16 pilots, equipped with night vision goggles, may have seen his parachute. It would take time and legwork, but they would figure it out. Would they divert a Navy ship to intercept the freighter? Would a rendition team be waiting for him in South Africa?

He searched for answers but found none.

As he descended into troubled sleep, Slade felt frigid air cutting at his face and hands. He heard wind humming through a parachute shroud and the chugging of diesel engines. He saw a black waterline rushing up to consume him. He saw the face of a child peering over a deck railing, watching as Slade sank from this world, leaving only endless ripples on a becalmed mirror sea.

* * *

For Slade, sleep brought no comfort. In his dreams he saw the ruins of his life, like the flotsam of a shipwreck washing past.

He saw a long line of men, his men, standing shoulder to shoulder, dressed in camouflage, burdened by automatic rifles and body armor. He studied their faces, spoke their names, and saw their funerals.

He saw a young boy with eyes much like his own, playing beside a pond. He heard people yelling, calling for help. He heard his wife screaming as their son was pulled from the water, beautiful and empty. He saw his wife curled beside the headstone, her face as lifeless as the corpse interred beneath her.

He stood in the doorway of his house, divorce papers crumpled in his fist, staring at the empty rooms, empty closets, and empty bed.

And then came the great betrayal, the moment when the country he'd served for over two decades turned on him, came for him in the night: he heard the front door splintering, the flash-bangs detonating, felt the boot hammering his face into the floor, and then the steel manacles as they clacked over his wrists.

He saw himself chained naked to a wooden board, his frozen skin a bloodless blue, water being poured over his face and the endless questions to which he had no answer.

He clawed at his eyes to stop the seeing.

CHAPTER EIGHT

STRUGGLING AGAINST THE iron stiffness in his neck wound and the nausea of the amphetamine hangover, Slade leaned over the deck railing and watched the depthless blue sliding past his feet. He breathed deeply of the salt spray that flowed up from the sapphire bow wave and across the decks, but the beauty of his surroundings brought no comfort. To Slade, every shadow on the horizon concealed a US frigate, every cloud a surveillance drone and their destination a rendition team. The doorway to freedom had been opened, but he still had to get through it.

Absent the adrenal rush of flight, Slade now faced the magnitude of what he'd just done and what he'd left behind. Worst of all was the memory of his final confrontation with his sister, of what she'd said and what his leaving had done to her.

* * *

As his last act before he fled Sandpoint, Slade had made a late-night call at his sister's house.

Blowing his hands against the cold, he crossed the lawn beneath autumn-yellowed oaks and skirted around to the rear of the house. Standing on tiptoes he unscrewed the porch light and then knocked on the back door with raw knuckles.

The window curtain jumped and the face of his sister peered out into the gloom. Seeing the broad silhouette of her brother standing

on the porch, she immediately opened the door. Although still energetic and bright eyed, Summer was a beautiful woman to whom time
had not been kind. Once flawless, her face now bore the deep frac-
ture lines of a young widow struggling to raise three daughters alone.

"Hey, Slade! Come in, come in, it's freezing!" she said, clutching
her arms around herself and motioning him inside. "Gosh it's cold.
What are you doing out so late?" As Slade entered, surrounded in a
rush of frigid autumn air, Summer's eyes scrolled over her brother,
taking in the changes that had crept in since his troubles began;
since the false accusations of domestic terrorism, since the brutal
interrogations and two years of confinement. Slade's shoulders still
retained the spread and bulk of a defensive lineman, but his presence was somehow diminished, withered by the ordeal. His curly
black hair and beard were unkempt, shot through with wisps of
gray. Summer remembered him in his collegiate prime, the shining charisma, the weight and gravity of him, the mass that moved
across the playing field with such terrifying speed. She remembered
the day he'd returned from SEAL Qualification Training smiling
from ear-to-ear, squeezed into that ridiculous sailor outfit the Navy
made him wear. During his two decades with the SEALs, Slade's
strength had lent itself to his job; he was a breacher and pointman,
using sledgehammers, cutting torches and explosives to undo the
creations of other men, to make passage where there was none. He
was the one who set the explosive charge, stood closest to the blast
and was first through the smoldering breach, wreathed in smoke
and embers . . .

As Slade turned to face her, the look in his eyes cemented Summer
in place. "What's wrong?" she asked.

Slade pursed his lips, his throat constricting with emotion.

Summer's eyes fell upon the bandage encircling Slade's wrist
where the GPS and audio monitor had been. Horror bloomed in
her eyes like a red sunrise. "Oh no! What did you do!"

"What I had to," Slade said quietly.

Panicking, she slammed the door shut and snatched the window drapes closed. Her voice sank to a strangled whisper. "They'll know it's off! They'll come for you! You'll have to . . ." She studied his eyes and saw the truth within them. "You're leaving."

Slade nodded.

"But . . . Where will you go?"

"South Africa. There's no extradition treaty, and I know the area. I've arranged a contract job and—"

Summer held up her palms as if trying to stop a speeding vehicle. "Slade. You don't have to run. I know you're upset. But don't throw away what you still have."

Slade pointed to where the monitoring device had been. "You think that being imprisoned and tortured for two years *upset* me? Is that what I should call it?"

"I know. Christ, I know how angry you must be." She put her hand to her forehead. "You gave them everything . . . And then they took everything. I know how deeply that wounded you but don't let that drive you into a stupid decision."

"It's the only decision."

"No it's not! Stay here with the last of your family! Be here for me and my daughters. Stay with the people that actually care about you!" She waited for a response, for him to acknowledge the truth of her words. When there was none, she erupted, "Slade, you gave everything to your country, gave everything for people that don't give a damn about you. And now you're about to make another mistake, throw away the only family you've got left. You always talked about duty . . . what about your duty to us?"

Slade wiped his nose and hung his head. "I gave them everything, didn't I?" Unconsciously, his right hand moved to cover his naked ring finger.

"Yes." Summer's voice began to tremble as long-suppressed words began to rip themselves free. "Christ, eight months after little Nick drowned you were out the door again. Right when Vanesa needed you most." Summer knew that she was on forbidden ground but she pressed ahead, unable to stop herself. "The Navy would have given you a desk job, given you a chance to stay home. But instead, you went back to war and left your grieving wife in an empty house."

A flash of genuine rage contorted Slade's face. "Goddammit, woman!" he thundered, fists white at his side. "You bring the death of my son into this. And criticize me because I have a sense of duty? My nation was at war. The lives of my men depended on me. That's not something you walk away from."

"I'm not the one you need to be angry at, Slade," Summer countered. She waited for him to retreat before continuing. "You gave them everything, and in the end, they treated you worse than trash." She shrugged her shoulders and laughed bitterly. "What can I say? You're a fool."

Slade's head drooped and he nodded wordlessly as he pressed at his shimmering eyes. "I'm sorry." He pointed to his bandaged wrist. "But it's already done. They'll send me back."

"Then suck it up, do the time, and then come back to us."

"I can't go back." He shook his head. "I'm sorry but I can't. They'll have to kill me."

Summer forced herself calm and searched Slade's face. "You're really going to leave us . . ."

When there was no response, Summer's shoulders slumped in resignation. Surrendering, she dried her cheeks, stepped forward, and put her arms around his neck, pulling him close. She held him for long moments, whispering the familiar goodbyes, needing no response.

Slade struggled to speak, his breath coming in ragged surges, fractures of doubt spreading through the granite face of his resolve. He wanted so badly to stay, to bathe in the warmth of the people who loved him. His eyes swept over the house in which they stood—the children's toys in the corner, the quilted blanket on the couch, the flames flickering in the fireplace.

Summer pulled away, hugged herself, and dabbed at her eyes. "Do you have to go right now?" she asked.

He nodded wordlessly.

"Okay. Let me get you some things." Summer broke away from him, went into the kitchen, and returned moments later with three colorful metal boxes. "Here are the girls' lunches for tomorrow. You can take them. And these, too." She offered up a handful of family pictures, shuffling them into order. "Keep them someplace safe."

Seeing the small lunch boxes, Slade couldn't stop the tears. He shook his head, refusing, but took the pictures instead. He unzipped his jacket and pulled out a billfold, strung around his neck with a length of para-chord. "I'm so sorry. I'm so sorry," he sniffed, as he tucked the photos away.

She kissed him on the cheek one last time, smoothed his jacket, checked the buttons, and patted his chest. "Go do what you have to do." She hugged him close. "Go find a world you can live in."

CHAPTER NINE

GRIPPING THE DECK railing of the freighter and looking backward toward the following horizon, Slade's thoughts lingered on his sister and the terrible dread that must be hers. Summer would have seen the terror alerts and the manhunt for her brother, but ultimately had the media reported him dead? Or left the possibility that he was still alive? Slade's natural instinct was to get a message to her, to let her know that he was well. But even the most discreet attempt to contact her might tip the authorities that he was alive. Barcoded mail, phone calls, and Internet messages could be traced to their source. Paper letters could be analyzed for contact DNA and syntax patterns. No matter how clever Slade might be, the mere existence of a message of unknown origin might be enough to alert the authorities. If they did think him dead, a complete information blackout was Slade's only chance of maintaining the illusion. Eventually, he would find a way to contact Summer, but for now he had to run silent and deep.

Standing at the railing beside him, Abe Howard leaned on his forearms, eyes holding on the distant horizon. Looking for a distraction from the thoughts roiling his mind, Slade turned to his companion. "Abe, you mind if I ask you a few questions?"

"Shoot."

"I'd like to get a better feel for you and your people so that I can integrate smoothly."

"Okay."

"So, why are you doing this?" Slade gestured toward the freighter. "Uprooting everything and moving to Africa? Seems a bit drastic."

Abe nodded his head in understanding. "We had no choice. The situation in America had become impossible for us."

"Got tired of baking gay wedding cakes?"

"What? Oh . . . No, they didn't force us to bake any wedding cakes." Abe grinned at the joke, but turned serious again. "But if we stood up for our biblical beliefs, we were accused of hate-speech. Many of us lost our jobs. They shouted us down, picketed our businesses, called us bigots because we wouldn't let grown men into the restrooms with our little girls. Our youth couldn't get into universities or start careers. It's like the whole world had gone mad, turned upside down.

"But the final straw was when they came for our children." Obviously upset, Abe took a deep breath and forged ahead. "We refused to homeschool our children with the curriculum the government instructed, or to inject them with poisonous vaccines. So, they came in the night, men with guns, and seized our little ones. Our children were returned after a lengthy court battle, but only after they had been exposed to immoral ways of life. And several of them . . . Several had even been abused while in state custody." Abe swallowed a lump and lowered his eyes. "What would you do if that happened to your children? Would you not go to the ends of the earth to protect them, Mr. Crawford?"

Slade nodded wordlessly, concealing a flash of pain.

"So we decided to resettle our community, to move to a place where we could live according to God's law. We had decided to move but we didn't know where . . ." Abe raised his head and looked to the east. "And that was when Africa fell apart, when the great famines and plagues struck. We heard about it but couldn't quite believe what people were telling us. So many millions dead. All the nations cast down and broken."

"We all thought that," Slade agreed.

"But eventually the African turmoil subsided, and our Elders received a revelation; God told us that Africa had been cleansed of sinners, as was Gomorrah, and that we should go there and re-found Zion. Our church has done extensive missionary work in Tanzania over the last fifty years. The revelation instructed us to go to the shores of Lake Malawi and live there among the people that we know. The farmland is rich, the water clean, many good Christians there to receive us." Abe stood erect, a smile on his face as a surge of optimism swelled his chest. "We have closed our accounts, sold the last of our possessions, and are ready to start our lives anew, four hundred faithful Saints, secure in the hands of Christ."

Appalled, Slade searched the Judean's face, but to his dismay, he saw only naked sincerity. "Abe, what exactly do you think happened in Africa over the last three years?"

"We know that there was a great upheaval—famines, plagues. It was cleansed of sinners."

Slade's eyes narrowed. "And . . ."

"And that the Lord has commanded us to resettle there."

"That's all you know?" Slade stifled a curse. "Abe . . . Don't you watch the news? Read the Internet?"

"No." Abe shook his head. "No, we do not. Like the Amish before us, television, Internet, and all electronic media are forbidden in our community."

"So you think Africa was 'cleansed of sinners', and that's the limit of your understanding?"

"God reveals to us what we need to know."

Suppressing a flash of anger, Slade turned to face Abe and raised both his hands as if bracketing something of immense importance.

"Okay, let's back up a few years so you can grasp the magnitude of the shit-show you're walking into."

Abe froze at Slade's unpolished candor.

"You ever hear of Boko Haram over in Nigeria? The African off-shoot of ISIS?"

"They were kidnapping schoolgirls, right?"

"Among other things, yes. Three years ago they decided to up their game, so they attacked Nigeria's Independence Day celebrations. They managed to capture the Nigerian president, his family, and most of the senior cabinet whom they subsequently tortured and executed live on the Internet."

"We did hear about that."

"Yeah, so did Planet Earth. The Nigerian government responded with a formal declaration of war and began a genocidal purge against Nigeria's Muslim north. But the purge pissed off the rest of the Muslim world, so the Sunni Gulf States began pumping in weapons and fighters, just like they did for ISIS in Syria. After that, things got really bad."

"Goodness, how could it get any worse?"

"NATO showed up."

"Oh."

"Following the templates perfected in Afghanistan, Iraq, Libya, Yemen, and Syria, NATO bombed the living hell out of Nigeria and started airdropping crates of weapons to anybody that could fog a mirror and wave a US flag. The ensuing chaos quickly spilled over the borders and ignited a general Muslim-Christian war that stretched from Liberia in the west, to Kenya in the east."

Abe stood wide-eyed.

"And then it got really serious. You see, Africans pump plenty of oil out of the ground, but they refine only a small fraction of it—they have to import almost all of their diesel and gasoline. And there are only a few deepwater ports in Africa that can offload fuel tankers on an industrial scale. So guess what happened."

"Uhhh..."

"That's right—the fuel terminals were destroyed by fighting. With no fuel, all of sub-Saharan Africa's industrial economies came to a halt, full stop. No electricity, farming, transportation, water, sanitation, or communications. Civilization ended.

"Over the next year, all of sub-Saharan Africa became an enormous failed state. Famine, ebola, cholera, and Rwanda-style genocide killed over *400 million* people. The greatest loss of life in human history. The only country that survived was South Africa as they still had functioning fuel terminals and a robust army.

"Abe, the place you plan on settling got hit hard; the Christians who lived there were only a small minority to begin with. I'm sorry, but they're gone. There will be nobody to welcome you and help you play pioneer. The people who remain in Africa are the worst of the worst—the psychopaths and apex predators." Slade pointed at Abe's chest. "Civilization breeds soft, civilized men." He then pointed toward their destination. "Africa breeds Africans. I'm not saying this to scare you, Abe, I'm doing it to wake you up. You, and all of your people, are going to be targets twenty-four hours a day until the day you die."

Abe's face had turned a shade that reflected the pale blue of the sky above them. He swallowed thickly. "I appreciate your honesty, Mr. Crawford. But we have been through trials and tribulations before."

"Not like this." Slade glanced in the direction in which they sailed. "Unless you lived through the Old Testament ... Not like this."

Abe turned back to the railing and looked out to sea, stricken. Slade sensed that perhaps he had pushed his new charge too far.

Destroying the man's confidence and planting the seeds of fear would help nothing. "Hey, I didn't mean to rain on your parade there. We've got some work to do but we'll get through just fine. I'm going to train you and your people like I used to train my SEALs. We're going to get you top-notch equipment and come up with a plan that keeps you and your people safe," Slade said with artificial confidence.

Abe turned back toward Slade, but it was clear that his confidence hadn't been restored. "Yeah, about that . . . Uhhh . . . Have you actually been to Africa? Like you told us?"

Slade saw his meaning and hung his head in embarrassment. "I lied to you about my name but not my resume. I'm a retired Senior Chief, did twenty-four years in Naval Special Warfare, SEALs. Cumulatively, I've spent several years in Djibouti, Somalia, Kenya, Nigeria, Sudan, and South Africa. From a military standpoint, I know the place as well as any Westerner."

"That's an impressive resume," Abe said. "So why . . . Why were you accused of being a terrorist? Why did you have to run?"

Slade hunched over the railing and his face clouded. "Wrong place, wrong time." He drew a deep breath. "Three years ago some buddies and I went out for drinks at a bar in town. Turns out a man was there that had been involved in the DC car bombings. The FBI did a records search of all the cell phones that were in the bar that night. I'm a demolition expert. They saw that I was there at the same time as the bomber. They don't believe in coincidences, figured I was in cahoots, was plotting the next attack."

"I still don't get it. You're one of the good guys. Why would they suspect you?"

Slade shook his head. "My military record proves that I'm willing to take extreme risks. I've made statements critical of government policies. That was enough for them to serve a no-knock, hi-risk warrant at my house. They used all their toys for the takedown: drones, MRAPs, snipers, flashbangs. Killed my dogs." As he spoke, Slade's voice became crisp with anger.

"But still, you hadn't broken any laws. How were you imprisoned?"

"I didn't know who was smashing in my front door at two a.m. so I roughed up one of their agents." Slade shrugged apologetically. "Wasn't anything a good oral surgeon couldn't fix."

"Oh."

"So that got me confined under domestic terrorism auspices. And once you're in, it's damn near impossible to get out; secret courts, secret evidence, secret judges, suspended rights."

"Gosh, I'm so sorry. That must have been terrible."

Slade looked away, embarrassed by Abe's naked sincerity. "Shit happens."

"Well, on the bright side, I'm thinking we picked the right man for the job," Abe said, trying to lighten the mood.

"I'll give you my best," Slade responded truthfully.

Relaxing, Abe slumped back onto his forearms. "So, tell me more about yourself, Mr. Crawford. Any family back home? Children?"

Slade shook his head. "A sister and her kids is all I've got left. I was married for a while. Met her in Cape Town during a training deployment." Slade pursed his lips. "She did the best she could, stuck it out for eight years . . ."

Detecting the residue of regret in Slade's voice, Abe stroked his beard thoughtfully and attempted to offer consolation. "I imagine that military life is very difficult . . . And that for men such as you it rarely ends well."

Slade smiled at the Judean's unintentional insult. He looked toward a distant place. "No . . . No, it doesn't."

CHAPTER TEN

"My name is Slade Crawford," Slade said, projecting his voice to fill every corner of the dank cargo hold, "and I am a killer." He looked at his audience; 150 men, ranging from bald-faced boys to withered grandfathers, sat, stood, and crouched in every corner of the echoing chamber. They shifted nervously, glancing at each other.

"All of Africa has become a failed state. There are no longer any nations, no longer any governments. There is no one to oppress you and no one to protect you. If you are to remain safe . . . if your families are to remain safe, you must learn to do the unthinkable. In Africa you will find the freedom you are seeking, but you will also find that the only law is the law of the gun. It is my intent to make you students of that law and teach you to deliver its terrible justice." Slade ceased his measured pacing. He looked at his audience, at the hunched old men, round-bellied fathers, and stubble-lipped boys. All appeared uncomfortable.

It was time to begin.

* * *

The days passed quickly. Confined as they were to the ship, the men and boys proved eager to lose themselves in the novelty and rigor of Slade's training regimen. They developed a martial vocabulary, practiced taking orders, and learned the basics of soldiering and tactical teamwork. He required that they camp and live on the deck of the ship, forsaking meals and sleep, holding watch, patrolling and perfecting the basics of small-unit security.

They established a grappling ring on the fantail and trained in martial arts and physical confrontation. Slade had them fashion mock weapons, then trained them to place a human form in their sights and pull a trigger. He repeated the drills until they were numb with exhaustion, then trained them for hours more. And although he drove them hard, Slade made sure to never browbeat or belittle the Judeans. He held no illusions that he could create soldiers in two weeks. Instead, his goal was to build confidence, camaraderie, and coherent teams.

Throughout the exercises, flocks of women watched from the upper railings. The young women and girls giggled and pointed at the men in their labors. The mothers, knowing the meaning of the exercises, creased their brows in worry.

One girl stood apart from the others, late teens or early twenties, tall and slender with a sharp angular beauty and a porcelain complexion framed by Indian ink hair. Her eyes were steadier than those of the other girls; they didn't dart away when Slade looked at her. In fact, she met Slade's gaze and returned it with a smirk of suppressed laughter. Or was it scorn? Slade was still trying to decipher the expressions when a gust of sea wind pressed the thin fabric of her prairie dress against her body, revealing in intimate detail the curved forms beneath. Caught looking, it was now Slade's turn to lower his eyes.

"Best not be ogling the children, now," Slade said to himself. Clearing his throat and finding his center, he returned to the tasks at hand. There was no time for distractions. Africa was approaching, the Judeans were unprepared, and their future was as clouded and unknowable as Slade's own.

CHAPTER ELEVEN

ON THE SIXTEENTH night under way, the freighter made landfall under a brilliant arch of stars, calm seas, and a following wind. Slade stood among a jostling, animated crowd that pressed against the deck railings, watching as the brilliant lights of Cape Town drew near.

Three miles out, a pilot vessel pulled alongside the freighter and boarded a customs officer, harbor pilot, and security team. Slade moved to the stern of the freighter and spent tense moments waiting to see if the captain would call his name and summon him to the bridge. He eyed the life preserver, backpack, and rappel rope that he had covertly attached to a side railing. He gauged the miles to shore and the frigid waters.

An hour ticked by, marked by the slow rocking of the freighter.

In time, the inspection team returned to their pilot vessel and departed, the freighter's engines grew louder, and the ship resumed course toward her waiting berth.

Slowly, the lights of the harbor drew closer and surrounded them, the engines slowed to a faint thrumming, the bow thrusters hummed, and the heavy freighter came to rest against the dock. Within minutes, the mooring lines were attached and the ship held fast.

Slade stood on the deck, alone in the silence, standing on the cusp of a new life, daring to hope that he was free. Those around him shook hands and embraced, welcoming each other to Africa.

* * *

Unable to sleep, Slade spent the remainder of the evening walking the decks, talking with his fellow travelers. Dawn found him sitting cross-legged, taking a light breakfast atop the pilot house as sunrise cast violet and gold streamers across the towering mass of Table Mountain, Devil's Peak, and Lion's Head.

Tucked into a natural amphitheater of rocky green slopes, the glimmering towers of Cape Town stood over an active and energetic city; cars moved along freeways, aircraft descended from the sky at regular intervals, and cargo ships lay at the docks beneath towering cranes.

Slade alternated his attention between the beauty of the surrounding countryside and the cluttered industrial playground of the dockyard, eagerly looking for signs of his friend Mike Albertson. He was interrupted by the sound of someone climbing the pilot-house ladder and a shock of rusty blond hair rising into view.

"Mr. Crawford, if you would finish your breakfast, the representatives from Kruger Industries and Executive Outcomes will be here in a few minutes," Abe said. "As Chief of Security I want you along to advise on all weapons and equipment purchases."

Slade set down his breakfast, rose to his feet, and spread his arms as broadly as his grin. "Ready!"

* * *

At precisely 0800, a white VIP bus pulled alongside the ship and a plump fireplug of a man disembarked. Well groomed and dressed in a white linen suit, the African approached the small Judean delegation that had assembled on the dock.

Slade eyeballed the newcomer and the interior of the bus looking for the familiar profile of Mike Albertson, but his friend was nowhere in sight. Slade's pulse rose a notch—the first thing a rendition team would do is isolate him from potential allies.

Instinctively, he scanned the surrounding wharf, its maze of cranes, forklifts, and shipping containers, searching for signs of a developing trap. The dock would be a perfect place to grab a fugitive; there were infinite places to conceal a team, few bystanders to interfere, and the ocean made an ideal barrier to escape. Even as he mapped out possible evasion routes, Slade was fully aware that the pistol tucked into his belt would do little to deter a well-equipped team of professionals.

As the Kruger rep approached, Brother Hendrik stepped forward and extended his hand, jowls quivering with excitement. "Mr. Khune?"

The South African took Hendrik's hand in both of his and offered a slight bow. "Mr. Hendrik, I presume? Baruti Khune. I am so pleased to finally meet you."

"Ah, the pleasure is mine, Mr. Khune."

"Welcome to Cape Town, Mr. Hendrik. I hope your voyage was…" Khune glanced toward the rust-covered freighter. "Pleasant?" The man's voice was soft, his Afrikaan accent clipped and precise.

When the exchange of pleasantries was concluded, Mr. Khune stepped aside and gestured toward the waiting bus. "I'm sure you are impatient to get started. Let's be on our way, shall we? I have some wonderful equipment ready for you to review."

But as the group began to shuffle toward the bus, Khune clapped his pudgy hands together and interlaced his fingers. "I'm dreadfully sorry, but if you'll excuse me, I must bring up a spot of business." His eyes zeroed in on the broad-shouldered athlete who stood among the Judeans. "Is there a *Jacob Bradshaw* among you?" he asked, utilizing Slade's alternate identity.

Slade hesitated a moment, and his eyes darted toward his flanks before he stepped forward. "That would be me. You can call me Slade."

"Slade it is, then." Khune pumped Slade's hand vigorously. "Welcome, sir, welcome. Your colleague Mr. Albertson gave us a full briefing on your rather impressive resume. I've been looking forward to bringing you on board our team."

"Pleased to meet you, too, sir."

"As for our personal business, we can attend to the administrivia later this afternoon," Khune continued. "But for now, I imagine you would like to remain with your charges?"

"Yes, sir, that's exactly what we'd planned."

"Excellent! Let's be on our way, then." Khune turned to board the bus, but Slade stopped him.

"Mr. Khune, I thought that Mr. Albertson was going to meet me here. Do you know where he is?"

Khune glanced over his shoulder to ensure that all of the Judeans were aboard the bus. When he spoke, his voice had dropped several decibels. "To be perfectly honest, in regard to your colleague, we have something of a Dr. Livingstone situation on our hands."

"Dr. Livingstone situation?"

"Well… Quite frankly… We don't know where Mr. Albertson is. Nor the twenty men who were traveling with him for that matter."

Slade's eyebrows rose in alarm.

"Mr. Albertson was leading a resupply convoy, trying to reach a settlement north of the Niassa region. They were supposed to return two weeks ago, but I'm afraid there's been no word of them."

"Is that common?" Slade asked.

"It does happen. But no, it isn't common, particularly for groups as well armed as Mr. Albertson's. We've been attempting to contact the settlement that he was trying to resupply, but I'm afraid we haven't had any success with that either."

"Christ."

"I'll fill you in on the details this afternoon. But for now, let's take care of the day's business, shall we?" With that, Mr. Khune turned and entered the bus.

Slade remained outside, mind churning. Aside from his intense concern for Mike's life, he'd just been isolated from his one trusted ally. And now he was being lured into the confines of a vehicle over which he had no control. Slade's eyes darted toward cover. Was this the trap? He scanned the nearby docks but saw nothing suspicious, and dammit, he didn't have much choice. Gritting his teeth, Slade climbed aboard.

As he climbed the steps into the interior, his eyes found the emergency exits and the mechanisms that operated them. He seated himself within arm's reach of the driver and gave the man a visual pat-down, looking for a weapon, an earpiece, or anything that might indicate he was something other than a bored, out-of-shape chauffeur.

When the last of the passengers was settled, Khune gave the signal, and the driver put the bus in gear, accelerating through a labyrinth of docks, cranes, and shipping containers. Slade waited through anxious moments, expecting to see a swarm of cars block their path and marksmen rise into position.

When no ambush appeared, his mind turned back to his missing friend. He played through scenarios that would explain a convoy dropping off the grid for two weeks. None of them were good, but Mike Albertson was a professional without peer and could survive in the bush indefinitely. And for now, Slade had too little information to make even the shallowest of judgments. He would grill Mr. Khune later, but for the time being, he had to deep-six the issue and focus on the tasks at hand.

As the bus left the harbor and passed through the heart of Cape Town, their route briefly grazed the Long Street district where he had met his wife, so many years earlier. Slade looked down the passing surface streets, eyes lingering on the sidewalks where he'd once walked, the bars where he'd once drank, and the cafés where he'd sat in sunshine.

Flickers of happiness like blown embers.

He found himself surprised by the impact of it all, by the immediacy, by confirmation that these places actually existed. But he was surprised more by the young man that had once walked these streets with a smile on his face, drunk on whiskey, life, and the smell of the beautiful woman on his arm. He realized that he missed not only her, but the person that he was back then—young, cocksure, unburdened by loss and failure. He wondered what he would do if he saw her on the street. If—

Slade cursed and snapped himself back to reality. There could be a rendition team closing in and he was acting like a lovestruck teenager. He'd blasted the locks on the doorway to freedom, but getting through it was by no means assured. He had to remain focused and professional if he was going to pull this off.

Clearing the central district, the bus accelerated onto an expressway. Merging with light traffic, they skirted the colonial architecture of the city center then plunged through the steel and glass canyons of the financial district.

Slade maintained his vigil, watching the surrounding traffic, looking for cars that stayed with the bus through interchanges, followed too closely, or repeatedly surfaced in the traffic flow. He saw nothing suspicious but knew that a well-trained team with multiple vehicles would be undetectable.

After a lengthy drive, the bus left the expressway, pulled into a sprawling industrial park, and stopped before a heavily guarded gate. Mr. Khune leaned from a window, spoke with a guard, and submitted to a retinal scan. A second guard boarded the bus, inspected the length of the interior, then motioned for the gate to open. Moments later the bus parked in front of an enormous warehouse. As the brakes hissed, the door swung open, and Khune bounded down the stairs.

Slade began to relax. If South African officials had wanted to turn him over to the US, it would have happened already.

Dismounting the bus, Slade stayed with the Judeans as they followed their guide into the warehouse.

With his polished shoes clicking over freshly waxed floors, Khune paused before a large set of doors, made sure that all of the party had caught up, then cleared his throat theatrically. "Welcome, my friends . . . to the Cave of Wonders!" he said, opening the doors with a flourish.

The settlers were not disappointed; arrayed before them was a vast hall, filled with the pride of the South African military industry. Immediately in front of them crouched a bristling Rooivalk attack helicopter. Beyond that, the hulking form of wheeled tanks, mobile artillery pieces, and endless exhibits displaying mortars, rockets, heavy machine guns, rifles, pistols, and hand grenades.

Khune started down the row of vehicles, waving his hands, motioning for his group to follow. "Right this way, my friends, right this way," he said, raising his voice to be heard in the cavernous hall.

After a brief walk, he stopped in front of a large cargo truck outfitted with raised suspension and heavy studded tires. He leaned and patted the side of the vehicle. "This little lady is what we call the Wheeled Cargo Vehicle 5, of which your party has already purchased twenty. The WCV-5 is our newest offering and it is designed to carry fifty-seven tons of cargo, or fifty passengers, deep into the African interior. It is off-road capable and possesses the latest in hydrogen fuel cell technology. What makes this vehicle special is that it possesses its own solar-powered, hydrogen generation system. This means that as long as you have the sun, a water source, and a few days' time, you can generate your own hydrogen fuel. Its speed will not win any awards back home, but given there are no petrol stations where you are heading, I think you will find its performance more than agreeable." Khune wagged a finger. "So, no complaining!"

The Judeans murmured approvingly as Khune answered their questions. When he had exhausted their curiosity, the South African guided them to the next display where it appeared as if a heavily armored submarine had been hoisted onto a six-wheel, all-terrain chassis.

"A Cougar!" Slade said upon seeing the vehicle. "Where'd you get this old MRAP?"

"Where can't you?" Khune chuckled. "Your War Department seems to have a policy of scattering them across the globe. We salvage them for pennies from your former allies, retrofit them, then sell them back to the Yanks fleeing America. Ironic, no?"

Turning back to the vehicle, Khune made a show of straining to reach the raised underbelly. "While the WCV-5 is designed to carry you and all of your goodies, the Cougar is designed to ensure that all those goodies remain firmly in your possession. It has run-flat tires, a V-hull to deflect mine blasts, and enough armor to defeat small arms, RPGs, and 23 mm rounds. It can carry ten combat-equipped troops and mounts its own 14.5 mm cannon in the cupola on top. Your group has purchased two of these configured as fighting units. The third is configured as a command vehicle, providing you with satellite Internet access, sat-com radios, reconnaissance quad-copters, and audio-visual links to your ground parties."

After answering their questions, he led them further into the hall, toward a cluster of small-arms displays. "If you'll come right this way, gentlemen, I'd like to introduce you to a rifle that is particularly suited for your unique situation." Khune straightened his tie and swept his arm over a display that held dozens of battle rifles. "This, gentlemen, is the CR-30." Khune picked up one of the weapons, unfolded its stock, and held it high for all to see.

"It looks much like the FN SCAR, yes? Basically, it is, but with a few modifications to adapt it to your environment. First and foremost, it uses the same bullets and magazines that the AK-47 uses. I know it's not the optimal cartridge, but it allows you to scavenge a resupply from anywhere on the continent. The barrel has an integrated sound suppressor, and if you should find yourself in the wrong neighborhood after dark"—Khune pointed to the grenade launcher that was slung under the barrel—"just lob a time-fused 40 mm grenade, and the local chaps will remember that they have pressing engagements elsewhere." Khune tossed the rifle to Slade. "When facing a problem that can only be solved with kinetic energy . . . this will solve it."

Slade examined the rifle, peered through its optics, thumbed the ranging laser, and examined the targeting display. He nodded in approval and looked toward Abe, a smile spreading across his face. "Last time I felt like this, I was twelve years old. I'd just found my dad's porn stash."

Abe suppressed a grin as Brother Mantis turned and scowled.

Khune cleared his throat. "I know that all of this can be overwhelming for those who are unfamiliar with firearms, but I assure you that over the next week our instructors will make you experts at these weapons. And now, I'd like to show you something else. Something . . ." His voice trailed off as he searched for just the right word . . . "Extraordinary. Right this way, my friends."

* * *

After a short drive in the VIP bus, the Judeans found themselves at a stable, standing beside a fenced-in corral. A dozen horses stood on the far side of the enclosure, drinking from a trough. The ammonia tang of manure drifted on the afternoon air.

Turning toward the distant horses, Khune emitted an ear-piercing whistle, then waived a large carrot above his head. Hearing the summons, the herd turned as one, then started over at a gallop.

There was a collective gasp as the horses arrived in a cloud of dust and jockeyed for position opposite Mr. Khune. The animals' shoulders were level with the top of Slade's head, their skulls as broad as carry-on suitcases, their hooves the size of buckets.

Brother Hendrik took a step backward, his chin retreating into a protective fold of jowls.

"Them's some biiiig bastards." Slade whistled.

Khune tossed carrots in strategic directions, spread the herd out, then turned back to his human audience. "Fifteen years ago, Kruger Industries anticipated that Africa would need reliable transportation that doesn't depend upon hydrocarbons." Khune lured in one of the horses with an offered apple. "We call this the African Horse," he stated with obvious pride. The animal woofed, extended its neck over the fence, and vanished the fruit.

"Using advanced genetic modification techniques we've bred them specifically to the African environment. In addition, we spent a great deal of time studying the immune systems of the Burchell's zebra. Consequentially, we've developed a series of vaccines, which makes these horses completely immune to the African diseases that prove so troublesome to Eurasian breeds."

"Uhhh," one of the Judeans interrupted, "what does this have to do with us?"

"It has everything to do with you. You see, there are no petrol stations where you are going. And the small amount of hydrogen fuel that you generate will be consumed by your trucks and electrical generators. There won't be enough surplus fuel for you to go hot-rodding about in those SUVs you Americans are so fond of. But not to worry," the South African continued, "your cargo trucks will carry the equipment and bulk of your people, while your scouts range ahead on horseback and keep the convoy secure. These horses are the natural choice. They can cover over forty miles per day and cross terrain impassable to wheeled vehicles, particularly during the wet season. Horses give you mobility, range, stealth, and most importantly, they don't run out of petrol."

"That's ridiculous," the Judean stammered. "Nobody uses horses anymore. They're too . . . too . . ."

"Too sensible?" Khune glanced toward Slade. "Mr. Crawford, what is your opinion on the matter?"

"Horses are legit." Slade shrugged. "American Spec Ops used them extensively in Afghanistan. Horses were used to great effect during the Angolan and Rhodesian wars of the 1970s. For our purposes, they're ideal."

"But few of us know how to ride! We—"

"Listen to Mr. Khune," Slade interrupted. "He's trying to keep you alive. We have no logistics train to resupply us. What happens when our fuel generators break down? Would you prefer the rescue party covers a thousand miles on foot, or on horseback?" Slade said, ending the debate.

"Don't worry, my friend," Khune added, "these horses are extremely easy to work with, and our equestrian center will have you up and riding within a few days." He grinned and lowered his voice. "Somewhat competently."

CHAPTER TWELVE

LATER THAT AFTERNOON, after the Judeans had retired to their freighter, Mr. Khune escorted Slade to a nondescript office building. Inside, he was introduced to Executive Outcomes reps who quickly formalized their working relationship. In less than thirty minutes, Slade had submitted to a biometric survey, signed their documents, opened a numbered bank account, and scheduled himself for a series of additional briefings.

With the formalities completed, Slade turned to Mr. Khune and began digging for more information on Mike Albertson. Citing his lack of expertise on the issue, Mr. Khune directed Slade toward the EO Operations Center.

Stepping over bundles of electrical wire and fiber optic cables, Slade entered a small, windowless trailer. Inside, seated at a desk strewn with empty soda cans and surrounded by corkboards and sticky notes, a single attendant monitored a series of chat windows, spreadsheets, and digital maps.

After introductions, Slade turned to the issue at hand. His questions about Mike Albertson came rapid fire, the answers came back halting and incomplete. Many were met with a blank stare or shrugged shoulders.

What was the convoy's planned route? What type of vehicles were they traveling in? How were they equipped and armed? What was the emergency recovery plan? Where were the nearest friendly settlements? What radio frequencies did they monitor?

"This is ya first rodeo, init?" the attendant said as he buried his arm in a jumbo bag of Cheetos.

"No. It's not."

"First with EO I mean." The man pronounced EO as ee-oh.

"Yes"

"EO don't run things like ya Yanks is used ta, with all the pomp 'n polish. EO likes to keep it simple. They gives ya the chickens to look afta . . . and if ya make it back in six months, they gives ya the money. That's about it.

"I will tell ya this." The man rotated in his chair then pointed at a digital map with a Cheetos-stained finger. "You see all these little dots scattered about?"

"Yeah." Slade leaned forward and studied the constellation of green and red dots spread across the map.

"Them's the settlements we've been supplying. Chinese, Indian, and Paki mostly."

"Why all those countries?"

"There's a land grab on! But lots of 'em's just dumped here by their governments to ease population pressure back home. Go west young Mohamed. Ha!"

"Okay."

"But see all them dots that's colored red? Them's the settlements that's gone."

"Gone?"

"Gone. Massacred. Dead. Burnt. Didn't fit into the new neighborhood. Need more?"

"No." Slade ran a hand through his beard. He'd known things would be difficult, but he hadn't anticipated it would be this bad.

The man buried his arm in the Cheetos bag again. "I's you, mate, I'd pack it up and call it a day." He dragged his finger along the screen like a child playing connect the dots. "From the looks of all these new red ones, I'd guess a pro has got in on the game. Look, he's just rollin' along gobblin' up all the chickens."

Slade leaned in closer to study the map. The attendant was right, there was a string of over a dozen red dots, strung together in sequence.

An hour later, Slade left the Ops Center with a few scraps of information, a growing sense of dread, and little else. In his left pocket, he held Mike's scheduled route, the frequency to his survival radio, and the number to his sat-phone. In his right pocket, he held maps of the destroyed settlements. On one matter, the attendant in the Ops Center had been perfectly clear: there would be no rescue for Mike Albertson. EO was a business and it was cheaper to hire new contractors than to maintain an expensive search and rescue program. The men who went into the bush did so knowing that if things went sideways, their ticket to safety was printed on the soles of their boots.

And in this case, a pair of spare boots would be required. A map study revealed that Niassa, Mike's last reported position, was over 800 miles from the South African border. Mr. Khune had not been exaggerating when he said that they faced a Dr. Livingstone situation; a rescue expedition could be months in the making.

As for doing the job himself, Slade had few options. His advance salary would be just enough to get himself into trouble but not enough to mount a credible search and recovery mission. The best Slade could do for Mike was to continue on with the Judeans. The Lake Malawi region where they intended to settle was just over 100 miles from Niassa. That would put Slade within striking distance, give him time to develop a credible plan, and perform a thorough search. As excruciating as the wait was going to be, it was the only option that had a chance of success.

After departing the Ops Center, Slade's first act was to withdraw half of his advance salary and convert it into 1/10th-ounce gold

Krugerrand coins. The following morning, he commissioned a tailor to sew the fingernail-sized coins into a nylon web belt. The loaded belt was stiff, heavy, and a poor fit, but it ensured that Slade would never be caught without means.

CHAPTER THIRTEEN

THAT NIGHT, LONG after the sun sank into the western sea, Slade left the freighter and made his way north through the docks, the sound of Judean hymns chasing at his heels. Crossing out of the dreary shipyard, he passed into the colorful and brightly lit streets of old-town city center, electric with movement, sound, and color. There, he explored its neon-lit caverns and raised his drinks from polished teak bars, seeking out the men with sun-weathered faces, stained boots, and calloused hands.

When chatting up a new friend, Slade inevitably steered the conversation to their experiences in the African interior. More than happy to accommodate him, the men would talk of its roadways, settlements, currencies, communication networks, and dangers. He listened to stories of fortunes won and friends lost. But always he dug into the boasts and tall tales, asking subtle but revealing questions, peeling back the layers of varnish to uncover the slivers of truth within. He bought drinks by the dozen and developed a network of contacts but always kept an eye over his shoulder, a clear path to the exit, and his Sig close at hand. Intensely wary of a rendition team, Slade trusted no one, accepted no invitations, and made a plan to kill every person that he met. He had made it through the door, cleared the breach, and goddamn if he would let somebody claw him back through.

* * *

It was near three a.m. and his fourth night in Cape Town when Slade's eye locked onto a woman shouldering her way through the smoky gloom of his favorite pub. Heads turned and followed her. The woman took a seat at the bar, ordered a drink, and produced a coin. She drummed her fingers as she waited for her drink then spun on the stool to take in the local color. Slade muttered a curse—it was the Judean teen from the boat, the girl with the dark hair. He finished his whiskey Coke, set it down, rose, and worked his way through the crowd. By the time he reached her, there was already a player at bat, leaning in on his elbow, chatting her up. Slade tapped the man on the shoulder. "I need a word with my niece."

The man turned with anger, looked Slade over, nodded his head, and quit the field.

Slade took the open stool and ordered a fresh whiskey Coke. He raised his voice for the girl to hear him over the din. "Out a bit late for a school night, aren't you?"

The girl turned and studied him. She took a sip of her drink. "A bit old to be out babysitting, aren't you?"

Slade thumbed toward the crowd at their backs. "The education these gents will give you ain't the kind you want. Bad place to be."

"Is that so?"

"It is." Slade swiveled his stool to face her. "Look, just because you spent a weekend partying in Peoria with a fake ID doesn't mean you know what you're doing. Coming here alone was a bad, bad decision."

She snickered, clearly enjoying the confrontation. "You want to compare bad decisions, Grandpa?" She met Slade's gaze and leaned forward conspiratorially as if discussing something of great importance. "I'm not the one who got myself shot, and then had to parachute onto a boat, and all for the privilege of babysitting a bunch of religious nutjobs on the far side of the world. Men who have their shit together don't have to do such things, now do they?" She slid her straw between her lips and took a long sip, watching Slade's eyes as her barb struck home.

Pride stinging, Slade studied her closely for the first time, noticing the rare symmetry of her face, radiant with defiance, and the sweep of hair that fell across her shoulders like a pair of glossy raven's wings. For Slade, it was a Herculean test of will to keep his eyes from traveling down to the swell of her chest. He swallowed thickly, then nodded toward the door. "Cute, but it doesn't change the fact that we're leaving and going straight back to the ship."

She laughed again. "Not gonna happen, Grandpa."

Slade grabbed onto her slender wrist. "You're coming with me."

The girl remained unimpressed. "I'll scream."

"They'll laugh."

"At you," she countered.

Tired of the banter, Slade changed his tone. "This is no place for a young girl, and I'm not taking any more shit. Playtime's over."

The girl glanced about, took in the pressing crowd of roughnecks, and seemed to think better of being there. Her shoulders slumped, and she nodded in acquiescence. "Okay. Take me back."

Slade turned to rise. "Good girl, now let's get—"

Using her free hand, the girl pushed off of the bar, spun toward the crowd, pivoted quick as lightning, and delivered a vicious kick to the back of a man's knee. The man's leg folded beneath him, and he toppled backward into Slade's lap. As Slade reflexively raised his hands to protect himself, he felt the girl yank free of his grip. Shoving the man aside, Slade stumbled to his feet and pushed his way after her. He circled the interior of the pub, searched the bathrooms and exits, but she was gone, lost in the cigarette-hazed gloom.

Cursing, Slade returned to the bar, took his seat, reached for his drink, and found nothing but a ring of moisture where his glass had been. He turned at the sound of somebody tapping loudly on a glass window. The girl stood outside of the pub, peering in at Slade. She raised a brimming whiskey Coke in mock salute, downed it in a single go, smashed the glass to the pavement, then darted away.

Slade's cheeks reddened at the laughter growing around him.

* * *

The next week passed in a blur of activity as the settlers familiarized themselves with their horses, weapons, vehicles, and communication equipment. Slade shared all his intelligence with the Judeans, telling them of the other settlements that had been destroyed or gone dark. The information did nothing to deter them, but they did invest more in weapons and armament as a result.

As their departure date approached, the cargo trucks were loaded with supplies, the final stores laid in, and the new equipment hoisted back aboard the freighter.

* * *

In a gated residential neighborhood high on the green slopes of Table Mountain, Slade stood naked before a broad, plate-glass window, the chill morning air raising gooseflesh along his spine.

Far below him, the first half-light of dawn brought color and form to the ghost shapes of the city. His eye tracked to the pale band of surf that rimmed Cape Town's shores and then beyond to the infinite plane of the southern ocean: dark, unknowable, and filled with hidden danger. In the harbor below, the Judeans would be turning from their bunks, kneeling in prayer, and raising their voices in song. Their ship would depart with the rising of the sun.

Slade glanced at his watch and reached for his clothing. But hearing a gentle sigh behind him, he turned and looked to the curved figure stirring beneath satin sheets. He paused, glanced at his watch, and looked back toward the bed. A tousle of blond hair shifted, exposing the graceful curve of a feminine neck.

He dropped the clothing. There was time enough . . .

CHAPTER FOURTEEN

PANTING HEAVILY AND wiping at the sweat that ran down his face, Slade climbed the swaying boarding ladder. His trip back to the ship had been delayed longer than expected, requiring him to run the last few miles through the dockyards.

To his relief, he found the Judeans behind schedule as well, and, although the freighter's decks were covered with those who'd come to see the departure, its mooring lines were still tied and its engines silent.

Stepping onto the crowded and lively deck, Slade's smile of relief faded as he found himself confronted by a dark figure with a waist-length beard and a perpetual scowl. It was the man that had wanted to attack Slade his first night on the ship.

"Good morning, *Mr.* Crawford," the man said with unmasked hostility.

Slade took a moment to catch his breath. "Good morning, *Mr.* Mantis."

The elder Judean leaned forward and sniffed, breathing in the rich scent of expensive bourbon and cheap perfume that emanated from Slade's person. "I trust you had a pleasant evening in town."

"It went well," Slade admitted.

Mantis' eyes scrolled over Slade's disheveled hair, unshaven face, and the purple hickey printed on his neck. He extended a gnarled hand and brushed away the glitter that sparkled in the fabric of Slade's shirt. "It would appear that you are not one to shy away from . . . worldly pleasures," Mantis said, stepping deep into Slade's personal space. "The eyes of the Lord are upon you, Mr. Crawford. Remember that always." Mantis then clasped his hands behind his back, turned, and strode into the crowd.

"And a merry Christmas to you, too, sir," Slade murmured. After taking a few deep breaths, Slade worked his way to the bow of the ship and took a seat atop the deck railing, caught up in the carnival atmosphere.

There was a sudden round of cheers as Elder Hendrik appeared on the elevated deck of the pilot house. Crowded shoulder to shoulder, the Judeans jostled for position, craned their necks, and hoisted children atop their shoulders. Smiling broadly, Hendrik called for the crowd to quiet, then stepped forward and raised his voice to be heard.

"Brothers and Sisters! On this blessed morning, we embark on the next leg of our exodus, bringing us one step closer to New Zion. Today, we will reembark and sail up the eastern coast of Africa. In four days' time, we will make landfall in the port of Mtwara—on the coast of what was once Tanzania. There, we will unload our provisions and proceed westward toward Lake Malawi!"

The speech was interrupted by a violent shuddering and the sound of 1000 horsepower diesel engines rumbling to life. The crowd broke into spirited cheers; it was time to depart.

* * *

Two hours later, the mountains of Cape Town had been reduced to a cluster of shadows on the following horizon. Slade stood on the bow of the freighter, face into the wind, eyes squinted against the morning sun, each thrum of the engines driving him closer to his missing friend.

CHAPTER FIFTEEN

SLADE RAISED HIMSELF in the stirrups and stretched his legs, the new saddle leather groaning softly beneath his weight. Lowering himself back into the saddle, he squirmed uncomfortably, still unaccustomed to straddling an animal as broad as a refrigerator. Leaning forward, he patted the horse's neck and ran his hand along its hide, which was the color of a midnight sea strewn with white storm foam. The horse snorted, shifted lazily, and scuffed its hooves over the moldering concrete of the Mtwara wharf.

After adjusting his sweat-stained boonie hat, Slade drew his canteen and used it to soak the camouflage shemagh that he wore around his neck. He then scanned the wharf and its debris, his eyes straying over the rust-pocked shipping containers, toppled cranes, and fire-blackened fuel depot. The prow of a sunken ship jutted from the water, an oil sheen spreading from its leaking hold. Along the perimeter of the wharf stood a rickety barbed-wire fence and a solitary gate guard. Beyond the fence lay a road of matted trash and a field of tin-roofed shanties punctuated with shocks of head-high elephant grass and leaning date palms.

A little girl stood at the fence, naked, her belly distended as though pregnant, head perched atop an impossibly thin neck. Utterly motionless, the child's eyes remained fixed on points unknown.

Abe Howard sat rigid in his saddle next to Slade, watching as their freighter made its way back out to sea, the muted chugging of its engines fading in the distance. There was no wind, no motion, nothing stirred save their ship, sailing now toward another horizon.

Surrounding the two men, four dozen armed and intensely nervous Judeans sat upon their mounts, heads turning, hands resting on their weapons. The convoy of cargo trucks, passenger vehicles, and the three Cougars stretched along the dock beside them, immobile and silent.

As the ship passed from sight around a bend in the coastline, the silence that replaced its mechanical heartbeat was the silence of the void, momentous and deep. The crowd shuffled anxiously, reacting to the subtle yet immense shift in the rhythms that governed their lives.

Slade turned toward Mr. Howard and noted that the Judean seemed unable to pull his eyes from the turquoise ocean, his last bridge to the world they'd left behind.

"Trying to recall the last time you made a mistake this big?" Slade asked.

The joke found its mark. "Something like that," Abe said with a smile.

"Well, heck! Let's get these cowpokes on the road!" someone yelled. The forced enthusiasm stumbled and died in the unnatural silence.

Nobody moved.

"What's everybody waiting on?" Abe asked.

"You," Slade replied.

"Hmm?"

Slade lowered his voice. "Abe, if you haven't figured it out yet, Hendrik and Mantis are leaders *inside* the church . . . *You* are the leader out here. So, put the spurs to that horse, head toward that gate, and watch what happens."

With visible effort, Abe moved the reins and applied slight pressure with his heels, turning his horse toward the gate. Urging his horse forward, he startled at the loud clopping of the animal's stride. From behind him came the sounds of more hooves, then the soft whine of hydrogen drives and the crunch of gravel beneath knobbed tires. Trailed by fifty armed riders and the vehicle convoy, Abe crossed the quay then reined to a halt before the gate.

Crouched on his haunches, a solitary African blocked their path. He was dressed in a gold tracksuit and battered shower shoes. His eyes were curry-yellow with jaundice and one of his cheeks bulged as though it concealed a goose egg. A clotted stew of green spittle and chewed khat leaves stained the ground in front of him. The man rose and shuffled forward, accompanied by a constellation of flies that circled him like errant satellites. A battered AK-47 hung from his shoulder, slung by a length of t-shirt fabric knotted around the barrel and stock.

He looked up at the foreigners with unconcealed contempt, raised a hand, and rubbed his thumb and forefinger together, demanding his due. There was a long, awkward moment as Abe searched his empty pockets for the toll.

Growing impatient, Slade whistled, got the man's attention, and flicked him a small silver coin. The man's hand struck at the coin, pulled it from the air, and held it close for examination. He crouched and bounced it off the concrete, listening to the authenticity of its ring. Satisfied, he pocketed the offering, shuffled to the gate, and pulled it open on shrieking hinges.

The Americans sat motionless atop their horses, framed by the rusted iron gateposts, weapons laid across their thighs. Before them opened the vast expanse of the African continent, shimmering and unformed in the day's heat.

CHAPTER SIXTEEN

THE LAND THEY rode into lay as it had for millennia, painted with an ancient web of game trails, paths, and roads that offered passage to destinations unlearned of and gone. The Americans traveled these underfoot with their own destination hazy and remote, the red clay soil clinging to their tires, boots, and hooves.

Within the day their world expanded into a vast billiard plain, choked with stands of brush, banana trees, palm and umbrella Acacia, atop which falcons perched like ink-black commas. As they left the coastlands behind, the land swelled into gentle hills and seized into violent outcroppings of rock that stood against a fractured azure sky through which clouds of vultures drifted endless and without aim. In the underbrush that scratched past their legs, lesser things scurried and fled while rainbow-snouted baboons slank among the limbs, barking at the otherworld strangers like enraged gnome-men.

Beholding these wonders, the Judean children pointed open mouthed and pressed their faces against the windows of their vehicles, while the horsemen, backs rigid, squinted against the beating sun, their knuckles pale against the black of their rifles. Heads turning, the scouts probed for danger but found nothing other than shadows of themselves as they wound through deep, shaded forests and crossed plains bald before the sun.

Guiding their course, Slade kept the convoy clear of population centers and major roads. The villages they did pass through proved to be motley collections of ramshackle mud huts interspersed with dilapidated cinder block houses. Along their mud streets and alley-ways lay the bones of their people, filling ditches and piled in drifts, mixed and moldering, thick as litter on a carnival lawn. Where people had once lived, plants swayed and grass stood while the ancient dirt wattles and cheap buildings faded into the browning bone mud.

Laboring each day under the sun, Slade's face tanned, his legs strengthened, and his saddle took on the polished sheen of heavy use. As he and his fellow horsemen gained confidence, their gaits gradually changed from a walk, to a trot, to a canter, and the convoy began to cover the miles more quickly. Eager to reach their destination, they no longer stopped to investigate villages, for at each, they found nothing but the same empty ruins and yellowed bone fields. Twice, Slade was sure that he caught sight of distant figures moving among the trees, but twice, his binoculars proved them shadows thrown by the aging day.

* * *

The Judeans followed him along the shifting roads and trails, their pace steady and sure, their passage marked by a thin curtain of raised dust, the soft whine of hydrogen drives, and the sound of wavering hymns.

During the fifth day of their journey, the Judeans stared in wonder at the abrupt rock faces and jagged peaks thrusting up from the green expanse of the Selous Niassa plains. Mealtime found them sitting at tables laden with the meat of gazelle and antelope and their dessert plates lined with mango and banana pulled from the forests.

After dark, the Judeans spent time with their families, singing, reading, and praying. Slade spent his evenings alone beside deadwood fires, staring long hours into the shifting embers, the faded flag cupped in his palm, running his thumb over it like a braille talisman. Each night he remained there long after the flames had died, leafing through the pictures that Summer had given him, jaw clenching and unclenching, surrounded by his nightlands.

CHAPTER SEVENTEEN

SLADE REINED TO a stop, took a pull from his canteen, wiped the sweat from his face, and flexed his healing fingers. He drew his binoculars, glassed the terrain ahead, and saw the unmistakable lines of human structures lying in the distance.

Abe pulled up next to him, swatted at the following insects, and smiled at the horizon. "Smooth sailing so far. I think we'll reach tonight's campsite a few hours early."

Slade shook his head, then pointed down the road. "There's a village ahead."

"So? We'll press through. Just like all the others." Abe shrugged and began to spur forward.

"Wait." Slade snapped his hand out and stopped the Judean. "Something's different."

Abe's brow creased. He raised his lenses again and peered through them. "It's just another village. Burned cars. Empty buildings. Overgrown fields."

"Look at the buildings."

"Prefab trailers. So what?"

"Even spacing, straight lines, ninety-degree intersections."

"So?"

"It's not African."

Abe squinted and chewed his lip. "You're right."

"Look past the buildings, on the far side. The burned-out trucks."

"Mmm . . . Looks like a bunch of cargo trucks . . . Oh . . . Just like *our* trucks."

Slade lowered his binoculars. "It's a foreign settlement. What's your plan?"

Abe glanced back at the armored bulk of the Cougar, 300 meters behind him. "Mmm . . . how about we just press on through," he said with a shrug. "If something happens, we'll just fall back behind the vehicles."

"Bad plan." Slade adjusted his seat and tried to relieve the pressure on his saddle sores. "Abe, you know what the worst thing about life is?"

"What's that?"

Slade leaned and spit. "There's no theme music."

Abe blinked in confusion.

"So you never know when something really shitty is about to happen." He searched for Abe's eyes and made sure that he had his complete attention. "You're only a few days into this and you're already getting cocky. Let's halt the convoy and send a few scouts forward. If everything is kosher, we drive on through. Cautiously."

"Okay." Abe fidgeted, adjusted his earpiece, and tapped on the communications computer he wore on his wrist. Tinkering with the settings, he activated the radio net that allowed him to address the entire convoy. "All stations, this is Brother Howard—go ahead and halt the convoy. Team leaders, set up a 360-degree perimeter. Then meet me at the command vehicle."

Slade nodded in genuine approval. "Good. Let's go."

* * *

Abe, Slade, and the four team leaders stood in a loose circle, their horses shifting beneath them. Immediately behind them the command vehicle sat astride the road like a metallic whale, its surveillance periscope extending skyward, its air-conditioning fans humming. The windows of the vehicle revealed the scowling mug of Elder Mantis and a concerned-looking Elder Hendrik.

Abe wiped at the sweat trickling down his face. "Okay, brethren. We've got some structures up ahead. Looks like it might be one of those foreign settlements. I want to take a scout party forward, check things out, and determine if we can drive the convoy through."

"Who are you going to take?" a team leader asked.

Abe turned toward Slade. "Who would you recommend, Mr. Crawford?"

"No need to go heavy. You, me, and two others that can handle their horse well."

"Okay." Abe turned back toward his team leaders. "Who are our best riders?"

There was an immediate answer. "The Brightman kids. Been riding since they were pups, very skilled. The best among us."

"But they're still teenagers . . ." Abe turned toward Slade. "What do you think?"

"If they can ride and follow directions, I'm game. But it's your decision."

"Alright. We're just scouting. Have them come up. The rest of you hold things down until we return. Any questions?"

"Who's in command while we're gone?" Slade asked.

"Uhm . . . I guess . . . Brother Maynard, you're in charge while I'm gone."

"Me?"

"Yes. Just keep things quiet. Let the children out to stretch their legs. Keep them near the vehicles and implement the recall plan if things get dangerous. Any questions?"

There were none. The team leaders turned their horses, some with difficulty, and trotted back to their positions.

When the team leaders were clear, Slade urged his horse forward and pulled in close to Abe. He glanced down to ensure that both of their radios were inactive.

"Abe, did you even look at your men? None of them know what the procedures are. They don't have a clue what they're doing. You've got to get your people squared away!" Slade's voice held a sharp edge. "If you don't, you will pay for it in blood."

Abe swallowed but raised his chin. "The Lord protects the faithful. He looks down—"

"No!" Slade's sudden anger took even him by surprise. "You will not fall into that *inshallah*, God-willing bullshit!"

Abe froze in his saddle.

"What will keep you alive out here is the sweat and pain you put into your training, not your *faith*." Slade stabbed his finger toward Abe's chest. "Trust no one. Not your God. Not me. No one!"

Abe sat stunned.

"And you sure as hell shouldn't trust your men. Did you get a look at their equipment? Gleason's radio was set to the wrong net, and he wasn't even wearing his sidearm. Carlisle had his weapon on full auto and his scabbard was unbuckled. It's only a matter of time until he kills somebody."

"Well, hold on now, some of the brothers felt that they needed to be able to draw their weapons and shoot quickly if they are set upon by wild—"

"Abe, new guys giving each other advice is like siblings fucking; all you end up with is bigger retards. Now get their kit squared away like I showed you. You're going to have to step on some toes, crush some nuts, and hurt some feelings. That's your role as a leader. Your responsibility is to them first, your faith second. Got it?"

Abe's throat bobbed as he swallowed a lump.

Slade pressed in closer, unable to control the chaotic anger that surged through him like a loosed freight train. "Do you know what the worst moment of your life will be, Abe?" he continued, his voice suddenly hoarse and labored. "It will be the moment you stand over the grave of someone you love, knowing that you could have prevented it . . ." Slade struggled to speak through a constricted windpipe. . . "if only you'd done . . . done the right thing." His voice seized up and he raised a hand to cover his face.

"Mr. Crawford?" Abe asked, suddenly concerned. "Mr. Crawford?"

Slade turned away and ran his palm over his face, pressed at his eyes.

Abe waited in silence, mouth hanging slack.

After his breathing slowed, Slade wiped at his nose, took a deep breath, and turned back to his companion. "Sorry about that . . . I'm way out of line," he said, his voice barely audible. "We have a lot of work to do. But it's nothing we can't fix." He leaned across the divide and slapped Abe on the shoulder. "Alright, enough of that." Raising his head, he pointed toward the distant village. "Let's get this done. Where's our riders?"

One minute later, a breathless fourteen-year-old boy reined his horse to a stop beside the two men. The boy's chestnut hair was mussed, his eyes wide, his excitement palpable. "You wanted to see me, sir?"

"Yes, Isaac. We're going to scout a village," Abe said. "Would you like to come along?"

"Scouting?" The boy's jaw dropped then reclosed. "Of course, sir!"

Slade pulled up next to the boy and inspected his kit, checking the pockets, tugging on his straps. "Got extra water?"

"Three liters, sir."

"Radio?"

"Channel 5, sir."

"Let me see your weapon."

The boy reached and unsnapped the retention strap, pulled his rifle from its scabbard, and handed it to Slade, keeping the muzzle clear of them both. Slade checked the safety, cracked the bolt to ensure a round was chambered, then tugged on the magazine. "They tell me you can ride. That true?"

"I won first place in the county barrel racing competition two years ago. Charlie Gailer beat me last year, but that was because my horse threw a shoe. Everybody says that if—"

"You know how to follow instructions?"

"Yes, sir." Impressed with the boy's conduct and demeanor, Slade nodded his approval. "I hear you have a brother who's coming with us. Where is he?"

"Right here, Grandpa," a feminine voice cooed.

Slade hung his head and suppressed a groan. Gathering his strength, he turned in his saddle and confronted the lopsided smirk of the raven-haired girl. Reigning to a stop beside him, she met Slade's eyes without hesitation and leaned forward to whisper, "Pardon my *insufferable* manners, but I never thanked you for the drink."

Slade ignored the taunt and looked her over. Her tight riding pants were sun-faded, her boots scuffed, her hat salt-rimmed, and her saddle polished lacquer-smooth from years of use. What caught Slade's eye, though, was the Government Issue, Colt 1911, .45 caliber pistol holstered on her waist. The weapon was old, sixty years or more, the dark-blue finish worn down to raw steel. Slade had a dozen questions about the weapon and where she had gotten it, but he feared the verbal exchange that would be required to answer them. The girl looked like she could ride and her kit appeared to be in order.

"Can you follow instr—"

"Your girth strap is loose," she interrupted.

"What?"

She pointed to the belly of his horse. "Your girth strap needs to be tightened a notch. That's why your saddle's slipping around." She pointed toward his feet. "And you need to raise your stirrups an inch. That'll keep your heels down and smooth out your bounce. Your horse will thank me for it."

"Anything else?" Slade deadpanned.

"Yup." She pointed toward the horse's bridle, and she began to open her mouth when Abe interrupted.

"That's enough for now, Elizabeth. There'll be plenty of time for that when we get back."

"Alright . . ." Elizabeth shrugged in indifference, folded her hands on her saddle horn, and waited patiently.

When he was certain that nothing more was forthcoming, Slade directed them down the road. "Alright then . . . Let's do some scouting. Lead on, Mr. Howard."

Slade took the rear as the four scouts rode forward through the convoy. Abe waved and smiled at the young faces pressed against the caravan windows. Isaac's chest swelled and he sat erect as they passed a crowd of teens spilling from a passenger truck. The teens surged forward, gawking up at the riders. "Where are you going? What's going on? Is there trouble?"

Elizabeth urged her horse forward to escape the teens, but Isaac slowed, adopted an air of bored repose, and reached a hand forward to rest casually on his weapon. "Headed up the road a few miles. Going to scout a village."

"When will you be back? Are you guys going alone? Isn't it dangerous?"

"We'll get back when we get back," Isaac replied.

Suppressing a smile, Slade watched as Isaac's gaze passed over the buzzing crowd and settled upon a girl who stood by herself. She was strawberry-blond, with cello curves and a light dusting of freckles across her cheeks and nose. When she saw Isaac looking at her, she feigned interest in something in the opposite direction. Isaac's head followed her as they passed.

As they continued forward and cleared the convoy, Slade spurred forward to take the lead. As he passed Isaac, Slade caught the boy's attention. "Don't worry, son." He turned in his saddle and glanced back toward the teens. "She noticed."

The boy's face reddened.

CHAPTER EIGHTEEN

THE FOUR SCOUTS stood silent. Around them, the ruins of the settlement lay naked before the morning sun. Looking over the charcoaled buildings, puddled plastics, and heaped bones, Slade raised his arm and pointed, cataloging the chapters of the tragedy.

Hand-dug trenches, blockaded streets, and barricaded doors: Siege.

Mounds of spent bullet casings: Resistance.

Ragged holes blasted through walls: Heavy weapons.

Bullet-holed skulls and rows of clothed skeletons: Executions.

Wire-bound wrists and hacked bones: Torture.

Dismounted and crouched, weapon slung across his back, Slade leafed through a pile of household debris. He picked up a battered magazine and turned the pages. "Everything is in Mandarin. The shell casings are 5.8 millimeter. This was a Chinese settlement."

"Wh . . . what happened to them?" Abe's face was pale.

"They got their asses handed to them is what. Sometime within the last few weeks." Slade toed an intact spine and rib cage. "There's a lot of connective tissue left. It still reeks. This wasn't too long ago."

"Who did this?"

"Someone who didn't like Chinese."

"What uh . . . What do you think . . . Could this happen to us?"

"I don't know, but these guys weren't prepared. All those trucks out back are diesels and their weapons were all small caliber, just rifles and pistols. They didn't have any heavy weapons or armor."

"Oh."

"And there's something else, Abe. I didn't mention it before because I wasn't sure, but now I am."

"What?"

"Whoever did this"—Slade thumbed toward the heart of the ruin—"has been in every village we've passed through."

"What do you mean? You said all the other empty villages... The people died years ago, during the big collapse."

"They did. But someone came through afterwards and did a bit more." Slade walked toward one of the trailers and entered it. He returned a moment later carrying a cooking pot. He tossed it up to Abe. "The pots, pans, cups, and bowls in every town we've passed through have been holed. Thousands. Every single one."

Abe examined the pot. A hole had been hammered through the bottom with a sharp object.

"Out here, if you can't boil water, you can't drink, you can't cook, you can't live. Also, all the wells have been filled in, the orchards cut down, and anything of use has been burned. It's scorched earth. I saw it in Sudan. It's a campaign to drive people out. And to do that across such a big area... It would take an army. Thousands of men. This is bad. Really bad."

As he vocalized the situation, Slade felt a growing sense of dread, suspecting that he had confirmed the reason for Mike Albertson's radio silence. Mike's convoy had been trying to resupply a foreign settlement, a prime target for somebody waging a scorched-earth campaign. Fending off bandits was one thing, but outlasting a disciplined army was another entirely.

"I've no idea how far these guys are ranging," Slade continued, "but this region is too hot, you can't settle here."

"The people who did this? Who are they?"

"I don't know. You take the convoy and the kids on ahead. I'll stay behind, see what I can find. I'll catch up by nightfall."

CHAPTER NINETEEN

SLADE KNELT BESIDE piles of spent brass and scanned the surroundings, seeing what the doomed gunners had seen. He peered through aligned bullet holes, finding the source of the fire. He examined the buildings, terrain, and skeletons, collecting evidence.

He realized that he was not alone.

Isaac and Elizabeth watched from atop their horses.

Slade motioned them closer with a quick angry movement. "What in God's name are you two doing here?"

"Thought we'd stay and help out," Elizabeth said.

Slade pursed his lips in frustration, raised his binoculars, and glassed in the direction of the retreating convoy. The image refused to focus in the wavering heat. "Did you tell Brother Howard you were staying behind?"

"No, sir," Isaac said.

Slade looked down at his wrist computer. It indicated that the convoy was out of radio range. He struggled to hide the frustration that contorted his face. Two unaccounted-for-personnel could wreak havoc on a unit. He couldn't let this pass. "You said you want to help, right?"

"Yes, sir."

"Okay then. Come with me." Slade turned his mount and led the two teens a short distance to an open field behind the settlement. He reigned to a stop and dismounted beside a pile of burnt corpses, mounded waist high. He motioned for the siblings to dismount and join him beside the contorted pile of charcoaled flesh.

He turned to Elizabeth and looked into her now shimmering eyes as he pointed a thumb toward the pile behind him. "These gents are going to give you an education . . . And you're not going to like it."

Slade crouched down next to the cindered bodies and examined them. "You notice anything odd about this, Elizabeth? Anything seem out of place, Isaac?"

The two teens shook their heads but kept their eyes averted.

"Look at it, goddammit!" Slade's voice rose in anger. "Start looking at the world you live in, or you'll end up in one of these goddamn piles. Now look at it!"

Elizabeth raised her head.

"What do you see!"

"Bodies," she said meekly.

"Bodies," Slade repeated, his voice calming. "Good. Does that strike you as odd? Why are there bodies, and not skeletons?" Slade pointed back toward the settlement. "All the other corpses have been picked clean. But here in this pile, and only this pile, there are still intact bodies. Why?"

The teens avoided his gaze and shook their heads.

"Because the scavengers refused to eat them," Slade continued. "Why is that?"

"Because they were burnt?"

"No." Slade shook his head. "There were plenty of picked-over skeletons back in those burned buildings. Char won't stop a hungry vulture." Slade then tightened his gloves, turned back to the pile, put a boot on it, grasped a protruding arm, and heaved. With the sound of popping gristle, the arm separated and pulled free. Slade dropped it, grabbed a torso, and muscled it out piecemeal. From behind him came the sound of violent retching, and then vomit splashing across the ground.

"Isaac." Slade attacked the pile again. "Does liquid gasoline burn?"

More heaving. More splashing.

"No, it doesn't," Slade said. "Gasoline *vapor* is what burns after it has mixed with oxygen. So, if you were to pour, say, fifty-five gallons of gasoline atop a pile of living humans and light it on fire, the people at the bottom of the pile wouldn't actually burn now, would they? No gasoline vapor. No oxygen. No fire." Slade rolled more corpses from the pile. "The people at the bottom would actually die of asphyxiation. And the gasoline that seeped to the middle, having never burned, would still be there, wouldn't it? The gas smell at least, you can never get that out. Ahhh, there it is; come on over and smell it."

The teens remained bent over, hands on their knees, straining against their gorge.

Slade tromped out of the pile, wiped his gloves and boots on the grass, approached them, and held up his hands, the gasoline reek surrounding them. "That's why scavengers wouldn't touch the corpses—they were soaked in gasoline."

"Why are you doing this!" Elizabeth cried, tears working down her cheeks, vomit dripping from her chin. "What the fuck is wrong with you!"

"Elizabeth . . . We're a thousand miles from anyplace that sells gasoline. It's more valuable than gold out here. So, who in the hell has enough of it to waste on a pile of Chinese schlubs who don't mean a damn thing? And look at this." Slade reached into his cargo pocket and produced an unfired shell as large as a banana. "I found this up on the hill. Twenty-three-millimeter cannon, high explosive, armor piercing. Vehicle mounted." Slade tipped it and pointed to the numerals stamped on its base. "It's brand new, straight from the factory in Serbia. That means it wasn't scavenged from an abandoned military depot, it was recently imported." Slade turned toward the ruined settlement and studied it, hands on his hips. "They've got vehicles, gobs of fuel, and heavy weapons. That means they have an international supply line and a logistics system. That means they have funding, bank accounts, leadership, communications networks, international contacts. That means they have a mission. And you know what that means, kids? It means you have to get the hell out of here, as far away from this region as you possibly can. New Zion is finished."

Elizabeth stood erect, eyes wide. She wiped her chin. "Oh."

"I'm sorry for these things I had to show you." Slade pointed a thumb toward the pile. "But you don't have the luxury of not knowing. This is your world now, and you must be able to read it."

Drying their faces, both teens nodded in numb comprehension.

"And if you ride off again without telling somebody—"

"Won't happen again, sir."

"Good. Lesson's over. Let's catch up with the others."

Slade led one last sweep through the devastated settlement before turning to follow the convoy. Passing the last of the burned trailers, he reined to a stop, gaze fixed on a series of tall wooden poles, more than a hundred, standing vertically on both sides of the road.

Isaac stopped and followed his gaze. "What are those?"

Slade pointed down the road. "Go on ahead, son."

Isaac remained rooted in his spot.

Slade turned away from the boy and inspected the poles. Each was a rough, five-meter shaft as thick as a forearm, the top ends sharpened to a wicked point. One meter from the top, a crossbar and sweeping crescent shape had been nailed to each.

"Is it some sort of symbol? Chinese?" Isaac asked.

Slade stared intently at the base of the nearest pole. He dismounted, knelt, and pushed back the weeds and grass that obscured the base. He found the jumbled remains of a human skeleton there.

He reached and pulled up an irregular lump of material that was ringing the pole. He examined it briefly before dropping it back into the grass and wiping his hands on his pants. Then he mounted his horse.

"What was that?" Isaac asked.

"Nothing. Move along," Slade answered curtly, the sharp edge in his voice goading the boy into motion.

As he settled in his saddle and spurred forward, Slade glanced back at the object that ringed the pole. It was a human pelvis.

CHAPTER TWENTY

THIRTY MILES PAST the ruined settlement, the convoy halted for
the night. Concealed in the shade of a mango grove, the trucks
parked in a protective circle and unfolded their awnings. As the
tents rose, the camp came alive with the clang of dishware, the
screams of playing children, and the confused energy of a camp
newly pitched. Slade stayed by Abe's side until long after dark, ensuring that the surveillance nets were established, patrols sent out,
sentries stood-to, and equipment stowed.

When the clang and rattle of camp had faded to silence and the
last quiet hymns had died with the campfires, all that remained was
the sound of uncounted eons moving across the African plains.

Abe Howard stood watch atop one of the cargo trucks, slowly
scanning the horizon with night vision lenses. The surrounding
world was full of living things, but nothing larger than a house cat
approached the camp. Beside him, Slade sat in a fabric beach chair
performing his nightly ritual, calling each of the sat-phones that
had been in Mike Albertson's convoy. The raw violence they had
uncovered at the Chinese settlement lent a sense of urgency to the
ritual and tonight, as on all the others, each of his calls went straight
to voice mail. Muttering a curse under his breath, Slade dropped his
sat-phone, rose, and paced the length of the truck, hands on his hips.

Sensing his companion's frustration, Abe approached. "Beautiful
night, isn't it, Mr. Crawford?"

"What's that?" Slade responded.

Abe craned his neck back and pointed to the dome of stars and planets circling overhead. "Take a look."

Slade stopped his pacing and looked up to take in the sublime view. After a long silence the tension drained from his stance. "Thanks, Abe."

Abe shrugged. "Don't thank me. I wasn't the one who made it. Our creator was the one who—"

"Ahhh, don't go all missionary on me now," Slade said. He slapped Abe on the back. "You know I ain't the type to suddenly find Jesus."

Abe chuckled. "Don't worry, Slade. We wouldn't accept you into our church even if you wanted to join us."

Slade's eyebrows rose in surprise.

"If you joined our church"—a look of deep concern spread across Abe's face—"with the way the single ladies have been looking at you, and talking about you . . . I'm afraid that fights would break out."

Slade's eyebrows rose even further. "The single ladies? Talking about me? Really?" he asked hopefully.

There was a long pause as Abe struggled unsuccessfully to contain himself. "No . . . Not really."

Slade hung his head and listened to the erupting laughter, his face reddening in the dark. "Christ, I walked right into that one."

Abe struggled to catch his breath, wiped at his tearing eyes, and slapped his companion on the back. "I didn't mean any harm, Slade. But good grief. For a man your age, ain't no eligible ladies here except a few old widows in their seventies. Talk about desperate." More laughter.

"Yeah, you got me, Abe, got me pretty good . . ." Slade grinned sheepishly, finding himself genuinely liking the man standing beside him.

With Abe's breathing restored to normal, his voice returned to a more serious tone. "So, after today . . . The Chinese settlement . . . What do you think we should do?"

Slade let the air from his lungs. "We'll be crossing a river tomorrow. I recommend we stop there, set up the hydrogen generators, and refuel. Can't ever let the tanks get below 50 percent. While the convoy is refueling, we'll send out scouting parties in all directions. See what information we can glean, perhaps find some Chinese survivors, mine them for information. In the meantime, we need to get on the Internet and search for intel on the raiders. Check the news, UN reports, and NGO chat rooms. We need to find an area where you can settle in peace."

"I agree that we should send out scouting parties, but our ultimate destination is not in question, Mr. Crawford. We are continuing on to Lake Malawi and New Zion. That much is settled."

Slade grudgingly withheld his opinion on New Zion and elected to change the subject instead. "There's something else I'd like to bring up," he said, examining the space between his boots.

"Shoot."

"I want to apologize for this afternoon, Abe. I had no business attacking your faith. And as for your men, I should have said what I did in a more accommodating manner."

Abe shook his head. "Think nothing of it, Mr. Crawford. I had it coming."

"No. I know that you're doing your best. This would be an overwhelming situation for anybody. I should have been more tactful."

"Apology accepted, Mr. Crawford. Thank you."

Slade smiled with relief. "Good. Got any questions? Need any more fiery speeches?"

"No. Not right now." Abe chuckled. "Maybe later."

"Alright." Slade moved to the ladder and began to climb down. "It looks like you've got things under control. I'm going to get a few hours' sleep."

"See you in the morning, Slade." Abe paused for a long dramatic moment. "And say hi to all the single ladies for me."

* * *

Slade was still laughing when he reached the bottom of the ladder and turned toward his quarters. He had not taken his first step when he paused in the pitch dark . . . something was wrong.

There came the crunch of a boot on dry grass. A shadow pressed in toward him. "Good evening, Mr. Crawford," the shadow hissed.

It was Mantis. Slade took a step backward, creating distance between himself and the Judean. "Good evening," Slade replied, intensely aware of the other shadows, other men, converging around him.

"Enjoying your chat with Brother Howard?"

"Always," Slade said, as he quietly drew his Sig.

"Good. But I'm sure you're aware that I'm not here for a social call," Mantis continued.

Slade took a step sideways and turned his body, placing himself in a position to see all of the assembling shadows.

"I've come calling"—Mantis' voice took on the aggressive cadence of a prosecuting attorney—"because I've known exactly what you are since the moment you dropped from the sky and landed on our vessel."

"And what would that be?" Slade asked, measuring the angles and distances to the shadows arrayed against him.

"A deceiver! A polluter! A clouder of men's minds! You are the very hand of the Adversary, sent to divide us and turn us away from New Zion. Something that I cannot allow to happen." Sensing Slade's defensive positioning, Mantis chuckled. "You are in no danger, Mr. Crawford. No danger for now."

"That's comforting."

Mantis attempted to press closer, but Slade straight-armed him in the chest, maintaining the distance. Unfazed, Mantis continued his speech. "I did not travel eight thousand miles for my people to be subjected to the same perversions and doubts that afflicted them in America. I will not stand idly by and watch as the Whore of Babylon whispers in the ears of my flock. So, know this, Mr. Crawford. There is no bottom to the cup of wrath that God will pour down upon the head of one who deceives his children. Do you understand me?"

But before Slade could form a reply, Mantis and his host of shadows had vanished back into the night.

Slade scanned his flanks, then holstered his Sig. "Perfectly," he replied.

CHAPTER TWENTY-ONE

THE STARS HAD faded from the eastern horizon when Slade awoke stiff and kinked, the previous day's ride throbbing in his bones and his confrontation with Mantis knocking around his skull. Slade pulled back the mosquito netting, swung his legs from the cot, and dressed in the fading darkness, pondering the new developments.

He'd known there would be conflicts between himself and the settlers, but this was not mere friction, it was opposition, quite possibly violent opposition. Mantis was drawing sides, had muscle, and in time, would use it to enforce his will.

And, if things got ugly, Slade could not simply leave. He was depending on the Judeans to get him within striking distance of Niassa. Mike Albertson's life depended on it.

But weighing more heavily on Slade's mind was the fact that, although he had escaped from his old life, little had changed. He was still surrounded by the web of violence and conflict that had defined his world for the last two decades. Although the specifics and the scale had changed, Slade Crawford was still at war.

* * *

When Slade arrived at the makeshift stables, he found a pair of dark forms standing beside his horse, talking and giggling as they worked curry brushes over the animal.

Isaac and Elizabeth.

Slade listened for a few moments, then took an overly loud slurp of his coffee.

The teens looked up. "Good morning, sir!" Isaac said.

"Morning, kids. You're up early."

"Good morning, Mr. Crawford," Elizabeth said with a soft confidence.

Isaac pointed toward the saddle. "You had some problems with your rig yesterday. Figured we'd get it fixed for you if that's okay."

"Absolutely."

"Just watch and we'll show you how to set it up." Standing on an overturned bucket, Isaac threw a blanket across the horse, then waited for Elizabeth to heave the saddle into place.

Slade found his eyes following the curvature of Elizabeth's form as she lifted the saddle and positioned it onto the horse, then knelt to pass the girth strap under the belly.

When they had applied the saddle, bit, and bridle, Isaac patted the animal on the shoulder. "There you go, sir. He's all ready and will be a lot easier to ride now."

Slade nodded his head in appreciation. "Thanks."

"So what'd you name him?" Elizabeth asked.

"Who?" Slade replied.

"Your horse. What'd you name him?"

"Oh . . ." Slade scratched his head. "I hadn't really thought about it."

"Come on, you have to have a name for him," she said, her voice gilded with laughter.

Slade stepped back, crossed his arms, and looked his animal over. "How about . . . Maurice?"

"Ha! A big guy like this? No way."

"Alright then, a big guy needs a big name. I'll call him . . . Big."

"Big? That's like, wow, pathetic. But if that's the best you can do." She shook her head and put her hands on her cocked hips.

"Big it is," Slade said, forcing his gaze away from the girl. He looked toward their unsaddled horses. "You two riding with me today?"

"Can we?" they asked in unison.

Slade pointed toward the west. "I'm scouting up the road a ways and I need partners who know how to ride. Clear it with Brother Howard first."

"Holy cow." Isaac turned immediately and dashed away, calling for Brother Howard.

"You sure you want me along?" Elizabeth asked with exaggerated concern as she shifted her weight to her other hip. "I'd hate to be a source of distraction for you."

Slade ignored the bait. "You two are the best riders here. As long as you give me pointers on my riding, I'd love to have you along. I need all the help I can get."

"Yes, you do." Elizabeth nodded in sage agreement. "Yes . . . You . . . Do."

His patience at an end, Slade lowered his voice to a panther's growl. "Stow that shit. I ain't one of those blushing church boys you're used to toying with."

It was Elizabeth's turn to stammer a non-response.

Slade took a step forward, deep into her personal space. "You're playing a dangerous game, little girl." His voice sank to a whisper. "Because I guarantee you can't handle the prize."

More shocked silence.

Mission complete, Slade decided to offer her an escape. He stepped back and motioned toward her holster. "So, what's the story on your piece?"

"Uhhh . . ." Blinking, she looked down at the weathered 1911 holstered on her hip. " I . . . I got it from my dad."

"Heirloom?"

"Yeah. Passed down from Great Granddad."

"He in the War?"

"Company commander. First Infantry Division."

"The Big Red One. Impressive. You know how to use it?"

"Dad wouldn't have given it to me if I didn't."

"Sounds like a good man."

"He was."

"Brother Howard says we can go!" Isaac shouted from across the clearing. "Come on, Liz, come on, let's saddle up!"

She glanced toward her brother. "Uhhh . . . I'll be back . . . I guess." Still stunned, Elizabeth turned haltingly and walked toward Isaac, leaving the alien scent of freshly washed skin and shampooed hair drifting on the morning breeze.

Slade turned away from her receding figure and shook his head. "You dirty old lech," he chuckled to himself. He then approached his horse, slid his rifle into the scabbard, put his foot into the stirrup, and grunted himself aboard, wincing as his raw groin settled into the unforgiving saddle. The blaring heat of day was just beginning to rise as he popped the reins and eased Big into a trot.

CHAPTER TWENTY-TWO

THE FOLLOWING DAY, Isaac did not report for the morning ride. When Slade inquired after the boy, nobody would say where he was. Slade pressed the issue and Abe informed him that Isaac was not well and would be indisposed for several days.

That evening after dark, as Slade went about his chores, a soft voice called to him. "Pssst! Mr. Crawford! Gramps!"

Slade turned. Elizabeth stood behind one of the trucks, concealed from the rest of the camp. She motioned him closer.

Slade approached. "Hey, what's up? Have you seen Isaac today?"

She nodded and glanced over her shoulder. "He's in the medical trailer."

"Medical? Is he okay?"

"Not really. You need to go see him."

"Absolutely, I'll go right now," Slade said, concern growing. He noticed that Elizabeth was holding her head at an unnatural angle, concealing the left side of her face from him. He shifted to see, but she shied away. He reached his hand and turned her face. The left cheek was swollen and bruised, the lip split.

She pushed his hand away. "I'm fine. But Isaac . . . could you just look after him? He needs somebody on his side. And nobody . . ." She gestured angrily toward the rest of the camp. "None of these assholes has the guts to help him." She lowered her eyes and turned her bruised cheek away. "I tried . . ."

"Elizabeth, what the hell's going on?"

"Since the Chinese settlement, people have been arguing. There's been trouble. Lots of folks want to go back, but everybody's afraid of Mantis and those goons he runs around with. Just go help Isaac, okay? He's in the medical trailer." Turning, she darted away.

* * *

Slade found Isaac on a cot in the medical trailer, facedown, his back covered in bandages. The boy avoided Slade's eyes and would not answer his questions. When Slade lifted the spotted dressings, he found rows of swollen welts raised on the pale flesh. In places, the skin was broken. The attending nurse would tell him nothing. When Isaac still refused to speak, Slade went in search of answers.

* * *

Slade knocked on the door to Abe Howard's trailer.

"Come in."

Wiping his boots on a metal grate, he entered and found Abe typing on a foldout desk in the cramped cubicle he called home.

"What happened to Isaac?" Slade demanded, his anger barely controlled.

The Judean looked up from his work. "He is not well."

"*Not well*, and *got the shit whipped out of him* are two different things! Now what's happened!"

The tall Judean pushed himself back from the keyboard, crossed his arms, and shifted uncomfortably. He pretended to gaze out a window. "It is an internal matter. It is not your concern, Mr. Crawford," he said in a soft voice.

"If my best scout can't ride, then it is my concern. What happened? Who did it?"

"It's complicated."

"I've got time."

Abe pursed his lips and took a deep breath. "It was Elder Mantis."

"Mantis did that to him? And slapped Elizabeth around, too?"

"Yes."

"And what do their parents have to say about it?"

"Isaac and Elizabeth's father was killed in an accident several years ago. Their mother remarried. Elder Mantis has been their stepfather since."

Slade stood speechless. He eased himself into a cheap plastic chair and softened his tone. "It's not my place to tell you how to treat your children, but follow-on effects are different out here. You've lost one of your best scouts and are using up medical supplies. Isaac also has a chance of developing an infection, which—"

"You don't have to convince me on any of those issues, Mr. Crawford." Abe rose and began to pace the room. "We're horrified by the punishment Isaac received. But Elder Mantis is of the fundamentalist sect. They have different views on the discipline of their children . . ." His voice trailed off in futility.

"So what did Isaac do?" Slade asked. "He seems like a polite young fellow."

"Elder Mantis disapproves of a relationship that Isaac has been cultivating with a young woman."

"That strawberry-blond gal he's always making eyes at? The little porker with all the freckles?"

"Yes. Elder Mantis has seen their growing friendship and claims the lad is flirting with temptation."

Slade leaned forward. "Isaac was whipped for being friends with a girl?"

"There are complicating factors, Mr. Crawford," Abe interrupted. "It is a delicate situation."

"Like what? Mantis wants her as a second wife for himself?" Slade smirked, trying to lighten the mood.

A stricken look flashed across Abe's face.

"Christ, I was only joking," Slade gaped. "Mantis wants that gal for himself, and Isaac is his competition? She can't be more than sixteen."

"Fifteen."

"Ah, hell . . ." Slade hung his head and dug his fingers into his temples. His eyes stayed on the floor for a long time. When he finally spoke, his voice carried the tone of one treading in a place he did not belong. "Abe, Mantis has resorted to violence in a schoolyard squabble over a girl." Slade sat erect and locked eyes with the Judean. "What do you think he'll do when the conflict is over something serious?"

Abe remained silent.

"Abe, you're a peaceful, nonconfrontational man, and that has served you well over the years. But you now live in a world where that trait will be your undoing. You must find the strength to change."

The Judean looked down at his hands and said nothing.

"I'm sorry, I've said more than I should." Slade rose and walked to the door but paused while pulling it open. "Abe, on the day that you go head to head with Mantis . . . and your God won't tell you what to do . . . come talk to me."

Slade stood outside of Abe's trailer, cooling his temper, letting his eyes adjust to the glow of the crescent moon that hung overhead. As the surrounding shadows began to take on form and meaning, he looked to the nearby river, a ribbon seemingly made of the palest shades of silver. There on the banks of the glowing water he beheld the eye-shine of an enormous crocodile, its gaze upon him, bloodless and unblinking.

From a darkening sky, a gust front stalked across the water, churning roughshod its oily surface.

CHAPTER TWENTY-THREE

MIDNIGHT CAME BLACK and stilled, the night's moon lost beyond the western horizon. Slade sat in his beach chair atop a cargo truck, a data slate in his lap, listening to the witchlike howls of wild dogs as they hunted through the surrounding night. He tapped on the slate and manipulated a satellite map of the route they had been following, placing icons on every destroyed village he and the scouts had encountered. He studied the trail of scorched earth and found nothing to give him hope. The mark of the destroyers was everywhere and their path pointed straight toward the heart of Niassa, the area where Mike Albertson had gone missing.

Slade had hoped to find an intact settlement by now, to have talked with locals and gotten hard intel. Instead, after two weeks in the field, he had nothing to show but a trail of ashes.

Frustrated, he rose, then checked the video feeds on his wrist computer; nothing of note stirred except the other guards. He jogged in place, pushed back mental cobwebs, then seated himself. He lifted his coffee cup and took a long pull of his pleasantly bitter brew, relishing its aroma.

He breathed in the night air.

Something was wrong.

Slade set his cup down and picked up his rifle, breathing stilled.

The wild dogs had gone silent.

He rechecked the video feeds, found nothing out of the ordinary. He reached down to retrieve his coffee. His hand missed the cup and contacted the truck's metal roof, pausing there.

A slight vibration rose through his fingertips. He let both hands fall to the metal surface. The metal was vibrating. An electric motor? An air conditioner? A cooling fan? He tried to discern the source of the vibration, but the truck and its electronics were stone dead.

Slade rose, lifted his night vision binoculars, and scanned the perimeter. He raised his computer to his mouth. "Bill? Gary? Everything good on your side?"

"Doing peachy," came the sleepy reply. "Got some big ol' bats flyin' around over here."

Slade lowered the binoculars and stood listening.

Then it came, carried on the cooling night air—a faint, rhythmic thrumming. Something mechanical was out there, thrashing and moaning in the black. Slade came fully awake now, ears cocked, eyes darting. The sound grew stronger, building in intensity along with his heart rate. Still swelling, it took on a disturbing, impossible familiarity.

Slinging his weapon across his back, Slade climbed down from the truck, clicked on his headlamp, and set a rapid pace toward the center of the convoy.

"All security teams, fall back! Fall back to the command vehicle. Fall back now!" Slade barked into his computer.

By the time he reached the command vehicle, he was at a dead sprint, the noise thrumming in his chest, building to a deafening staccato roar, vibrating his teeth and filling his chest with a sense of impending doom.

Slade knew with terrible certainty that only one machine in the world made that terrible noise—the Osprey.

* * *

Four CV-22 Osprey tilt-rotors plunged from the night sky, prop-rotors blasting great rivers of air toward the quaking savannah, turboprop engines screaming. The first two Ospreys landed just past the convoy, lashing the trucks with a typhoon of dust, rocks, and uprooted brush. The second two machines touched down abeam the convoy, dark shadows sprinting from their tail ramps before they had fully settled.

Slade struggled to stand against the biting gale of dirt and debris, hands vainly shielding his eyes. "All teams! Drop your weapons!" he screamed. "All teams, drop your weapons and lie facedown! Don't fight! Don't fight!"

Over the shrieking mechanical gale, Slade heard a single gunshot. Turning, he saw another sentry, Elijah, crouched in terror, pointing his rifle skyward. Slade bolted toward him, sprinting to save the Judean's life. Diving, he clawed the rifle from Elijah's hands and drove him to the ground, tumbling in a heap.

"Stay down! Stay down!" Slade screamed.

Elijah struggled and struck at Slade in his confusion, but Slade remained spread-eagled atop him, hands extended far from his body, fingers spread. "Stop moving, stop moving!"

An eye-searing light erupted around them, and a rifle barrel was hammered into the center of Slade's back, knocking the wind from him.

A voice came from above. An American voice. "Smart move, motherfucker."

CHAPTER TWENTY-FOUR

Slade lay with his face to the earth, hands flex-cuffed behind his back. Forty heavily armored soldiers ransacked the campsite, while others guarded rows of prone, flex-cuffed Judeans. They searched the trucks, their war dogs barking, emptying the vehicles' contents, flashlights sweeping as they cataloged and videotaped the details. They spoke little, calling out to each other only as their tasks required. From overhead came the dull clatter of the orbiting Ospreys. From around them came the shrill cries of terrified women and sobbing children.

A gloved hand clamped onto Slade's shoulder, rolled him over, grabbed his jaw, and tilted his face upward. A lensed device hovered in front of his iris. There was a blink of light. The device emitted a series of electronic chirps. The soldier released Slade, then spoke into a radio, "X-Ray 5-7 has the bird in hand."

Released, Slade let his face sink into the thorns and stony grit. He knew these men and their methods well enough. There would be no escape, no reprieve. He had made it through the doorway to freedom . . . But not far enough.

And worse still, the sting of betrayal. The boot in the back, the bite of the cuffs. These men had once been his brothers. He'd stood by them, bled with them, and now he was nothing more than their prey. Better to have died in the cold waters of New York Bay.

When they hauled Slade to his feet, his arms had gone numb behind him. Iron hands steadied him, half carried him into the mess tent, and placed him at the table where he had eaten his dinner earlier that night.

Seated at the table across from Slade, a giant of a man reviewed a series of handwritten notes, his hairless dome gleaming in the overhead lights. His eyes shone black, set deep within a time-weathered face so sharp and barren that it appeared skeletal. He wore faded camouflage fatigues and colonel's birds, but displayed no name tag or unit patches.

Standing in the far corner, an out of shape, balding gentleman was polishing a pair of wire-rim spectacles. He wore nondescript civilian clothes and watched Slade intently.

A spook?

Beside the spook, in Slade's beach chair, sat a man in freshly ironed 5.11 tactical cargo pants and a button-up khaki shirt emblazoned with the letters D.H.S. Beneath the impeccable dome of his gelled hair he wore a shit-eating grin. The man raised his hand and offered a friendly wave. "How's it going, Slade? Long time, no see."

Slade choked back a bolus of rage; DHS Agent Stanley Cooper had been Slade's chief antagonist during his confinement. Back then, Cooper had been a low-level functionary desperate to make the big time, and his overly zealous pursuit of Slade had been his ticket up the ladder. Given his presence here in Africa, it appeared that Cooper was not one to walk away from a gift horse.

"FYI, that was me at Jersey Airport," Cooper continued with mock sympathy. "Gave you your shot . . . You missed."

Slade ignored the taunt. In spite of the totality of his defeat and the inevitability of his fate, he found some part of himself unable to quit the fight. He gauged the force arrayed against him; AFSOC Ospreys . . . Army Delta . . . DHS . . . CIA . . . And oddly, a full colonel in the field. It was a formidable task force, but there could be conflicting motives among the many players . . . perhaps something to exploit . . .

The colonel looked up from his notes and placed Slade in an eye lock. "Can we remove the flex-cuffs, Mr. Crawford?" His voice was flat, precise, like a straight razor.

Slade nodded.

The colonel studied Slade's eyes for a moment longer, then nodded his head almost imperceptibly. Slade heard the metallic scrape of a blade being drawn behind him. The flex-cuffs fell free. Slade leaned back into his chair, placed his hands atop the table, and rubbed at the welts that encircled his wrists.

The colonel picked up a tablet, tapped on it, and browsed through several pages, narrating as he read, "Senior Chief Petty Officer Slade Crawford, United States Navy, retired . . . Forty-five years old . . . Son of a Methodist minister . . . Graduated University of Idaho as a varsity lineman with a Bachelor's in Political Science .. . Turned down Officer Candidate School, enlisted instead . . . Made it through SEAL pipeline and all specialized training without incident . . . Psychological profile indicated aptitude as a breacher and pointman, positions to which you were assigned and at which you excelled . . . Spent last twelve years of your career at Dev Gru where you accrued numerous awards and citations to include a Distinguished Service Cross for your actions at Suez. Retired with an Honorable Discharge. Sole next of kin is a younger sister . . . Parents deceased . . . Wife divorced, currently living abroad . . . Male child deceased . . ." The colonel set the tablet down and fixed his eyes on Slade. "You have a rather unremarkable dossier, Mr. Crawford. Even your brush with the FBI and DHS two years ago was decidedly pedestrian, more circumstantial than anything else." The colonel leaned back and folded his arms across his hay bale chest. "So, imagine my surprise when the DHS told me that you had fled to Africa to establish a terrorist training camp. A camp from which you and your fellow travelers would seek to inflict injury upon the United States."

Slade refused to look toward the DHS agent, fearing that the man's smirk would push him beyond control.

"That's a serious charge," the colonel continued, "serious enough that I felt it necessary to make a house call."

Slade forced himself to sit as a stone, eyes forward.

The colonel picked up the handwritten notes he had been reading. "But I now have before me an inventory of the equipment found in your encampment. It reveals that you have assorted power generators, irrigation, and farm equipment. Seed, pesticides, livestock, food, medicine, and living arrangements for the 392 people in your group, 267 of which are children under the age of eighteen. Your armory consists of small arms, a few vehicle-mounted weapons, and a small number of RPGs. There are no bomb-making materials or components. The people in your company have no record of military training and only a smattering of legal infractions, none of them violent." The colonel put the notes down, leveled his gaze at Slade, and folded his hands on the table before him. "If you were an outside observer, Mr. Crawford, what would all that lead you to conclude?"

Gaining control of his anger, Slade glanced back and forth between the agent, the spook, and the colonel, trying to take measure of the dynamic between the men.

The spook was unreadable.

Agent Cooper was nervous, his bullshit intel exposed.

The colonel was pissed, having been played by an agency he didn't respect.

Slade realized that there was a significant wedge between the colonel and the DHS agent. What Slade needed to do was tap on that wedge and see if he could drive it deeper. If the split became wide enough, perhaps something would develop.

Slade licked his lips. "If I'd been told all of that? And found out that reality was the exact opposite? I'd conclude that I'd been used by an incompetent clown trying to make a name for himself," he said, nodding toward Cooper.

Visibly annoyed, the agent sat upright. "I don't see any point to this conversation, Colonel. The man is a known terrorist. Let's bag him and RTB."

The colonel's head swung like a ponderous turret, came to bear on the agent, paused, then swung back toward Slade.

Slade felt a glimmer of hope, because Cooper was right, standard operating procedure called for minimum time in the target area. The fact that the colonel was bothering with a field interrogation spoke to a pressing, time-sensitive motive that the DHS agent wasn't party to. The colonel needed something from Slade. But what was it? And how could Slade turn that to his advantage?

"You are accused of serious crimes, Mr. Crawford," the colonel said, "including the attempted murder of a federal agent. How would you answer to those charges?"

Slade realized that if something was going to develop, it would have to come from the wedge. Some situations required a delicate touch, others required a hammer. "You would have done no different, Colonel. The only thing I did wrong . . ." Slade lifted his hand, formed it into an imaginary pistol, and sighted on Cooper . . . "was miss that nancing little faggot."

The agent bolted to his feet. "I don't have to take this shit!" Fist cocking back, he advanced on Slade, but one of the Delta boys stopped him with an arm to the chest. The agent tried unsuccessfully to shoulder past the guard.

The colonel turned toward the scuffle. "Be seated, Agent Cooper!"

The DHS agent looked stunned. "Colonel Kraven, this man is a confirmed terrorist! He fired upon a—"

"You are here at my pleasure. Be seated or be removed."

"But, sir! I—"

The colonel pointed toward the door. A second guard advanced, and within seconds, the sputtering agent had been hauled from the mess tent.

Slade sat stunned. His little stunt had earned him a nugget of information: the colonel's name was Kraven.

The colonel turned back toward Slade. "I apologize, that was appallingly unprofessional, but as you know, we are sometimes required to work with outside agencies."

"Understood."

Kraven abruptly shifted gears. "So . . . Mr. Crawford . . . You have been on the ground for several weeks now. What is your evaluation of the region?"

"Sir?"

Kraven leaned forward on his elbows and spread his hands. "You're a security contractor. What is your assessment of the local environment?"

Slade shifted in his seat. The questions had lost the authoritative edge of an interrogation. The colonel seemed genuinely interested in Slade's response.

"It's troubling, sir."

"How so?"

"I've found evidence of a scorched-earth campaign. Similar to Darfur and Chad back in the day." Slade shrugged. "Massacres, filling in wells, cutting down orchards, holing the pots and pans, burning tools and stock."

"Specifics."

"Two days east of here, we came across a Chinese settlement, about two thousand people. They'd been slaughtered by a well-armed force equipped with 23 mike-mike, RPGs, mortars, small arms." Slade noticed the spook cock his head forward. "The attackers weren't particularly disciplined, used khat, they get paid in Yuan, the new gold-backed ones. There was also evidence of . . . rituals . . . standard blood-cult shit."

Kraven and the spook shared a glance.

"And their ammo was manufactured this year," Slade continued. "The Privi Partisan factory in Serbia. Which raises the question: How did they get ammunition that was manufactured *after* the collapse?"

"Continue."

"Everything points to these guys having an international logistics system, which means they are highly organized and well funded. Which doesn't fit the blood-cult theme."

"Did you collect any artifacts, Mr. Crawford?"

Slade leaned back in his chair and crossed his arms. "I found a dead raider. Got a few bills off of him. Shell casings, the serial number off his rifle. A cell phone."

"Where are they?"

Slade hesitated, gauging his leverage.

Kraven's face let him know that he had none.

"Under the cot in my quarters, in a black plastic bag."

A soldier moved to the door and left.

Kraven steepled his fingers. "My time here is limited, Mr. Crawford. I'll cut to the chase. I have no interest in the Judeans. They are free to go. As for you, I have three options: Capture you . . . kill you . . . or employ you."

Slade blinked.

"I am lacking many things in this region, most of all human intelligence. You have two options: you work for me and collect the intel I need . . . Or I turn you over to the authorities." The colonel waited, hands folded. "Choose."

Slade struggled to assimilate the turn of events. "You're going to let me go free?"

"You will not be free. You will do what I say without question. Failure to obey will have lethal consequences."

"And when would this arrangement end?"

"When I determine that I no longer require your services."

"And my legal status at that time?"

"Alive."

"You're saying that you're just going to turn me loose." Slade shook his head, incredulous. "I've sat on the other side of this table before. What's your hook?"

Kraven reached for the tablet. He tapped on it several times then laid it back on the table. The audio recording was scratchy and distorted, but the voice was unmistakable. It was Summer . . .

"I'm so worried about Slade. I'm not sure about this, this Africa thing. Are you sure he'll be safe? Can the authorities track him there? Can they go after him there . . . Okay, if you say so . . . Alright, thank you so much. You've been such a help."

Kraven studied Slade's face as the recording played. He tapped the tablet off and locked eyes with his captive. "Aiding and Abetting—Conspiracy to Commit—Rendering Aid and Assistance. And as you are acutely aware, Mr. Crawford, terrorism charges are referred directly to Homeland Security Courts; secret trials, secret evidence, suspended rights. And I've got enough evidence to put your sister in a concrete box for the next decade. And her little girls? They'll end up in foster homes."

Slade sat ashen, the last remnants of his world crumbling.

The colonel pointed to the tablet. "I secured this data file through my own channels. It belongs to me and me alone. If you try to run or fail to perform as instructed, your sister will go to jail. That's my hook."

Slade fought for composure, looking for a way to get Summer off the chopping block, to take her out of play. "I don't buy it. That DHS agent has seen me," Slade said, pointing to Agent Cooper's empty chair. "He'll testify that I'm alive and at large. They won't care that I'm working for you. They'll go after my family with a vengeance. They'll manufacture something and grab her regardless of your tape. It's irrelevant." Slade knew that his argument doomed himself, for without leverage, Kraven had every reason to turn Slade over to the DHS and wash his hands of the incident. But if it could take the heat off Summer . . .

"No," Kraven said. "Agent Cooper will go home in disgrace. My report will say that the Judeans had no knowledge of you and that Agent Cooper fabricated intelligence in pursuit of a personal agenda. I will conclude that you perished in New York Bay. With this embarrassment on the record, the FBI and DHS will find markedly less appetite for pursuing a case that was, quite obviously, never a genuine threat to begin with. Unless, of course, a tape was to surface which linked your sister to your cross-country shoot-'em-up. So, your fate—and your sister's fate"—Kraven tapped a finger against his own chest—"rests solely with me."

Slade looked for a way to escape the checkmate but found none. "Alright then. What do you want?"

"The force that attacked the Chinese settlement—I want you to collect as much intel on them as you possibly can. I need to know who they are, where they're from, who leads them, how they recruit, their supply chain, their finance trail, everything. When I have a specific location that I need looked at, I'll notify you to move. Right now, you don't have to leave the convoy. Keep doing what you're doing. If recent history serves, the raiders will come to you." The colonel rose as if lifted by hidden cables and began collecting his effects.

Slade stood up with the colonel. "What's that mean? What else do you know about these raiders?"

"Nothing that you have a need to know."

"I need every scrap of intel you've got!" Slade's voice rose. "There are hundreds of women and children here. Entire convoys have gone missing in this region. Another SEAL went comm-out a few weeks ago, just west of here, he was trying to—"

"Mike Albertson?"

Slade felt his world shift again. "Yes . . . What do you know? I've been trying to find—"

The colonel drew his tablet, tapped on the screen, then slid it across the table for Slade to view. "Mike Albertson," he said.

The corpse lay as a disheveled pile of black-crusted clothing and yawning machete wounds. The tattoos were unmistakable. The face, only partially decomposed, was clearly visible. In the background, behind the corpse, overturned and burnt-out trucks could be seen.

Slade slumped into his chair and moved past numb. The colonel's mouth continued to move without sound. Slade stared unseeing, his heart hammering in his ears, watching as images of his dead friend flashed in front of him.

Through the cloud of pain and disbelief, he heard a droning buzz. He looked around. The colonel was still speaking.

"If it's any consolation, it appeared that Mr. Albertson died quickly," he said. "That's more than could be said for the others in his group." Preparing to leave, the colonel retrieved his tablet. "As for our business . . . my men will give you the necessary comm gear and will fit you with a GPS tracking tag. You have your orders, now—"

Mainlining a volatile cocktail of rage and grief, Slade slammed back into his surroundings, bolted to his feet, eyes wet, nostrils flaring like an enraged bull. "Not a chance in hell," he snarled.

Kraven froze. The spook did a double take.

"Think you can get that tag on me? Just try it." The challenge hung in the silent mess tent. "I will not wear your fucking *dog collar*."

Kraven stood in granite silence, studied his captive and the murder written on his face. He turned and walked for the door, his back rigid. Slade watched him go, not caring that he had sealed his fate. He glanced toward the nearest soldier, the one that he would force to gun him down.

But Kraven stopped in the door, turned back, and leveled a long blade of a finger at Slade's throat. "If you make me regret this"—the blade retracted into a tight fist—"I won't hesitate to call the rain."

CHAPTER TWENTY-FIVE

DAWN CAME WITHOUT glory, bled of all color and life. Slade watched as the four Ospreys clattered down from their orbit, four drops of midnight black set against the rising dawn. The aircraft turned, slowed, then settled to the ground within their own windstorms.

As the engines howled down, the soldiers rose in ordered columns, heads bent against the lingering gale, and filed into the Ospreys without looking back. Kraven was the last soldier to board, with Agent Cooper circling at his heels, shouting frantically over the din, pointing back toward Slade. With the cargo ramp motoring shut, Cooper finally boarded, whereupon the Ospreys' engines built to a banshee scream, and they vaulted into the air atop tornadoes of swirling debris.

Slade fought against the buffeting winds, hand shielding his eyes as the blast receded. Then with the last echo of their departure still fading, he turned and stood blinking on the empty plains. Returning to the ransacked convoy, he walked through the chaos as though sleepwalking, picking up scattered articles, righting toppled containers, collecting panicked livestock, and apologizing again and again to the people around him.

* * *

Come nightfall, he accepted a plate of food and seated himself at a quiet place outside of the convoy. But spooning at the mush, Slade found himself unable to eat, nauseous over the death of his friend, the violation of his forced servitude, and of seeing his sister thrown into jeopardy as casually as a poker chip. His stomach churned, sick with the realization that he'd been clawed back, that the best of his efforts had been undone and that men unknown to him had decreed that his life was not his own. And worse, that the country he had given everything for still saw him as nothing more noble than a condom, a scrap of trash to be fucked and then discarded.

Setting the stew down, he lifted a silver flask to his lips and swallowed a thick slug of whiskey, the sting of it welcome and needed. As the drink settled into his belly, the menagerie of shadows before him moved out of focus and became something other than an African forest. Instead, he saw Mike Albertson during their time together in Basic Underwater Demolition School, his face a comical mask of sand and mud, screaming as he struggled to lift a rubber raiding boat over his head.

And then he saw Mike rotting in the sun, crumpled and torn, his spark vanished.

Slade took another deep pull on the flask, thirsting for its offered oblivion. He turned at the sound of someone approaching. Abe Howard stood beside him.

"Evening, Slade. You doing alright?"

Shaking off the visions, Slade struggled to rise from the ground, mumbling a reply.

"No, don't get up. I'm sorry to intrude," Abe said. "I just thought that maybe—"

"No, Abe, it's me who needs to apologize. God, I'm sorry. I brought all this down on you. It's all my fault. I'll leave in the morning."

Abe shook his head and held up his hands. "Nobody is asking you to leave, Mr. Crawford. We knew the risks when we asked you to stay with us. The Elders have already discussed the matter and they would like you to remain. Although, there were those who did agitate for you to be cast out."

"I don't blame them."

"I do have a question though," Abe said.

"What?"

"Why did they come for you? Then let you go?"

Slade told Abe about the confrontation in the mess tent and about the deal the colonel had forced upon him.

"Why would this colonel care about a group of raiders?" Abe asked.

"I don't know. And why did he need me?" Extending the train of thought, Slade began to wonder how Kraven had known about Mike Albertson. Had Kraven gone after him as well but arrived too late? Or was Mike already working for Kraven? From the beginning?

"Perhaps to men such as the colonel," Abe said, "you're easy to use and cast away. If they lose you, it is of no consequence."

"Expendable and deniable, yes."

"I fear you may have cut a deal with the devil, Mr. Crawford."

"True. And, Abe, there's something else."

"Yes?"

"Before he left, the colonel implied that the raiders . . . would come to us. Soon."

Abe scuffed at the ground then looked at the mark, trying to hide the fear that trembled his voice. "That is what I and the Elders had feared. And to return your honesty, that is the sole reason they have allowed you to stay."

"I understand," Slade said. "How is everybody holding up? After seeing the Chinese settlement . . . And then last night . . ."

"We are holding up, Mr. Crawford. We are not as fragile as you may imagine."

Slade shook his head in wonder. "Where do you get the strength, Abe?"

"From our faith, Mr. Crawford."

Seeing the doubt in his companion's eyes, Abe lowered himself to the ground and took a seat next to Slade. He then reached and took the flask from Slade's hand, tilted his head back, and downed a stiff bolt without hesitation. He looked at the flask, nodded his approval, and handed it back. "You have excellent taste, Mr. Crawford."

Slade's eyebrows peaked in surprised admiration.

When Abe spoke again, his voice carried a tone that Slade had not heard before.

"Four years ago we had a disagreement with the national authorities. They demanded that we send our children to government schools. We refused. The situation escalated. Then one day they sent men with guns to remove our children. But my wife . . ." The air left his lungs. "My wife . . . She moved to block their way as any mother would, tried to prevent her child's abduction. So, they shot her, Slade. Three times in the chest. The officer said he felt threatened by a ninety-five-pound woman. She bled out on the floor, at the feet of the children she was trying to protect. And I couldn't . . . I couldn't stop it. I was right there . . ." Abe closed his eyes, unable to continue.

Slade waited in anguished silence.

"And that destroyed me. The loss. The guilt. The hatred of the men who did that to us. It destroyed me. But ultimately, I was saved by faith." Abe chuckled and broke into a smile. "But not in the way that you're thinking. I didn't expect a winged angel to descend from the heavens and fix everything." He looked at Slade and addressed him directly. "What saved me was the understanding that I exist in order to serve something infinitely greater than myself. Within that context, my suffering is insignificant and short-lived." Abe rested his hand upon Slade's shoulder. "I know that you carry a heavy burden, Mr. Crawford. For there is pain enough in this world to break even the strongest of men. And to be released from that pain . . . to rise above it . . . a man must risk everything, let go, and trust in something greater than himself."

CHAPTER TWENTY-SIX

FOR SLADE, THE gentle rhythm of saddle and hoof had grown comforting and melodic. Now, two days into an overnight scouting sortie, he found that his eyes scanned the horizon but saw little and that his ears, cocked into the wind, heard only the previous day's conversation. Abe's words had struck home in more ways than one. Slade tried to look at himself from afar, as would a stranger. Was he that transparent? Did he carry his wounds so openly? And what truth was there in Abe's belief that—

"So, what's your story, old man?" Elizabeth asked, suddenly riding beside him.

"What's that?" Slade responded. He glanced around, Isaac was still riding 100 meters off his left, scanning the horizon, but Elizabeth had closed the distance without him even noticing. Damn.

"Your story . . ." Elizabeth repeated. "I presume you have one. That colonel didn't fly to the ass end of the world just to have a conversation with any old schmuck. He came for something important. Something that you had to offer . . ."

"He was lonely," Slade dodged. "Needed somebody to share his feelings with."

"So that's how it's gonna be?" Elizabeth responded. "In the few weeks that I've known of you, you've been gunshot, blasted out of the sky, parachuted onto a boat, publicly humiliated by a teenage girl, and then kidnapped and released by a military task force. I'd guess there's some interesting backstory in there. I'd guess you used to be somebody important . . . but then you screwed it all up, pissed off some bigwigs, and now you're hiding down here with us."

"You're a good guesser."

"So what laid you low, Slade? Fast women? Gambling? What brought you down?"

"Too much liquor and jazz."

"Liquor . . . and . . . jazz?" Elizabeth's eyebrows narrowed and her nose crinkled. "Did you just quote a musical? *Chicago*?"

Slade was betrayed by the smile that spread unbidden across his face.

"Holy shit!" Elizabeth slapped her thigh and leaned forward over her saddle, bent double with spasms of laughter. "Mr. Bad Ass himself is into musicals! O! M! G!"

Slade felt a stab of embarrassment at how good her laughter made him feel. He waited until she had recovered, then changed the subject. "So what about yourself, Elizabeth? What's your story? You don't strike me as the Judean's model citizen."

"Them?" She pointed a thumb back toward their distant convoy. "My mother got into the religion after she remarried with Mantis. I was fifteen, never bit off on the whole Jesus thing. Worshiping a level-eight Magic User always struck me as somewhat odd."

"Magic what?"

"Magic User." Elizabeth waved a hand dramatically. "Walks on water, resurrects, heals, feeds masses. Smiting moneychangers is a cool power, but I just couldn't worship the guy."

Slade bent his neck back in laughter. "Oh man, Mantis must have loooved you."

"Yeah, it got pretty rough at times."

"So why are you here? You're old enough to leave home, right?"

"I'm twenty next month. I could have left." Elizabeth's face darkened. "But I couldn't leave Isaac alone with that asshole, Mantis. You saw what happened the other day."

Slade glanced at the bruise on her cheek. "I'm sorry for that." He lowered his voice. "Look, if you ever need—"

"I also enjoy it here," she interrupted, diverting the conversation. "I've been to Tanzania four times on missions with the church. This place suits me. Life here is more . . . consequential. Also, I've got a good handle on Swahili and a smattering of Chaga. It'd be a shame to let it go to waste."

"You speak Swahili?" Slade asked, genuinely impressed.

"Yeah, pretty well. I've always been good with languages. It's my thing."

"Wow. Show me a little. Say something."

"Okay, okay . . . How about . . ." Elizabeth's voice deepened into a strained imitation of an aggressive male. "*Unataka kufanya ngono! Ni lazima kufanya hivyo sasa!*"

"Ha! What the heck was that?"

"I'm not sure." She shrugged innocently. "But the local boys kept saying it to me whenever the adults weren't around. Something about a gift they wanted to give me in private. It was the strangest thing."

Slade laughed deeply, his spirits buoyed more than they'd been in months.

"What's so funny?" Isaac asked, now riding beside him.

Slade startled again. Jesus, he was getting sloppy. Isaac had ridden up on their conversation, and Slade hadn't even noticed.

Isaac guided his horse in closer to Slade's. "What were you guys talking about?"

"Old-people stuff—escrow, variable rate annuities, things like that."

"Okay. Hey, Mr. Crawford, mind if I ask you a question?"

"Shoot."

"Why don't you pray?"

"What?"

"It's just that I've never seen you pray."

"Man, I'm getting tag-teamed here," Slade muttered under his breath. "No, Isaac, I don't pray."

"Never?" Isaac asked, incredulous.

"I've done some praying in my day. Spent many a Sunday in the pews. But I don't anymore."

Isaac's face clouded with confusion. "Why not?"

Slade glanced toward Elizabeth, hoping for a lifeline, but received only an amused smile. "Well . . . I guess I don't have anything to ask for," he replied.

Isaac scratched at his faintly stubbled lip. "You don't have to *ask* for things. You can *tell* things, too, you know."

Slade nodded. "Yeah, I know. I've done some telling before."

"Really? To God? Like what?"

There was a long moment of silence before Slade answered, "That he and I had to part ways."

Isaac's brow furrowed. "Why'd you have to do that?"

"Because." Slade paused in answering, intensely self-conscious of the eyes upon him. "If everything in this world is what God intended . . . and if I hated this world . . . then that means I hated his intent . . . So I hated him."

The trio rode in silence for long moments.

"What got you so mad? Did you lose somebody?" Isaac asked.

Slade did not answer.

"Was it Nicholas?"

Slade's face blackened at the name.

"Sorry." Isaac pointed to the bramble of tattoos on Slade's forearms. "I can read."

Slade rode for several more beats, eyes locked forward. "Yes. He was my son."

"What happened?"

The paralysis that descended on Slade's face was enough to warn Isaac away. The boy said, "I'm sorry," then nothing more.

*   *   *

An hour later, Elizabeth slowed her horse to a walk and then to a halt. She turned her head from side to side, looking in all directions. "You hear that?" she asked.

Slade halted his breathing and listened. "No."

"Really?"

"I worked with explosives for twenty-four years."

"Drums," she said, "from the other side of that ridgeline."

Slade halted, looked in all directions, and gauged their exposure. He tapped his wrist computer and consulted its map. "Looks like there's a small town on the other side. Used to be called Ngongo. If you're hearing drums, there must be people. Let's check it out."

The siblings' eyes widened with excitement. They turned their mounts and within minutes were climbing the backside of the ridgeline, leaning forward in their saddles, working around trees and knots of brush. Slade could hear the drums now, pulsing through the air, holding a steady beat, a marching cadence.

Nearing the crest, they halted, dismounted, and hobbled their horses inside a sheltered clutch of trees. Weapon slung across his back, Slade approached his companions and inspected their kit. "Let's have a look at you—No loose flaps—Everything closed." He lifted their weapons. "Round in the chamber—Safety on—Sights open—Excellent. Now stick by my side and do what I say. If things go sideways, get back to the horses and ride like hell. First rally point is the rock outcropping we passed at noon. Simple enough?"

They nodded.

"Alright, let's go."

Slade led them forward. As they approached the crest of the ridge, he lowered himself onto his belly, crawled forward into a stand of brush, and found an opening through which the entire breadth of the plains beyond rose into view.

Below them, a two-lane asphalt highway stretched unbroken from horizon to horizon, its length strewn with derelict vehicles, its shoulders matted with debris. To their left lay the picked bones of Ngongo—a stunted dwarf town in the best of times, now a pushed-together trash heap of stained concrete buildings, corrugated shanties, and mud wattles sprouting like earthen boils.

And approaching the village along the highway came a procession, one thousand strong, marching in unison to a pounding drum section, clapping, chanting, and wailing, caught up in the contortions of ecstasy and despair. At the center of the procession stood a litter, borne aloft by raw-shouldered slaves, a tribal priest sat ramrod straight atop a backless throne, his painted skin gleaming like boiled leather newly drawn from the tanning vats.

Marching before the royal person, five hundred Penitents, stripped to the waist, struck at themselves with polished swords and hooked flails. Rivulets of blood and shredded flesh flowed down their faces and backs while clouds of flies spotted their skin. Leading the procession, standard bearers held aloft a field of desiccated human corpses that had been impaled on rough wooden poles, anus to mouth. These unfortunate ones, their arms and legs dangling limply, heads thrown back, mouths caught in wood-choked screams, stared up with fly blown eyes past the looming emblem of the cross and crescent.

CHAPTER TWENTY-SEVEN

SLADE REACHED INTO his pack, pulled out a recorder, and began filming the procession, narrating the details as he observed them. "Fifteen January, 10:26 Zulu, two kilometers east of Ngongo on highway 284. Approximately a thousand individuals, all African, westbound on foot at a slow march." Slade panned the camera over the crowd, lingering and zooming in on specific details. "All participants appear to have a cross and crescent brand on their chest. All are wearing traditional African tribal garb." Slade panned his lens over the grizzly standards. "All impaled corpses appear to be foreign races, no Africans. The flanks of the column are guarded by two squads, each man armed with an AK-47 and two spare magazines. Squad leaders are equipped with handheld radios. Security detail maintains a traveling overwatch and does not participate in the ceremonial marching."

Slade swung his camera further down the road to where a small convoy of pickup trucks trailed 500 meters behind the procession. "Looks like a vehicle-mounted security element. Antennas on the trucks indicate that they have a command-and-control system in place." Slade swung the camera back to the procession. "Center of the column has some sort of . . . a witch doctor or . . . a tribal priest on a raised litter." Slade zoomed in and held his hands steady as the priest filled the screen. He panned over the intricate runes and symbols inked on his face, the chest brand and the coal-black skin beading in the afternoon sun.

Slade pulled back from the video recorder and took in the whole of the procession before him. Here was a chance to collect hard intel on the raiders, and in doing so, a chance to peel back the layers of the Kraven enigma.

Slade returned to his recorder and glassed the edge of Ngongo where a large crowd of locals had gathered. Some appeared enthusiastic and began dancing to the approaching beat, others milled nervously. The village elders and their muscle, three hundred strong, blocked the highway in front of the procession. A few of them were armed with battered rifles, the rest spears and machetes.

As the procession approached, the drums sped up, pulsing relentlessly, building to a thunderous crescendo, then stopped. The thousand-man procession halted as one.

The village muscle shifted nervously and fingered their weapons.

At the center of the procession the royal litter was lowered to the ground. The Priest rose, gathered his skin robes, and strode forward, his followers parting and prostrating themselves as he passed. The Priest advanced, flanked by polemen holding aloft their grizzly standards, dead limbs swinging like fly-swarmed marionettes.

He approached the Ngongo village elders. There was a verbal exchange, which became heated but eventually cooled. In time, an agreement was reached. The village muscle pulled back, the drums resumed, and the Priest led his followers into the center of town.

Slade, Isaac, and Elizabeth watched as the procession made its way to an open space in the center of the village. There, the column of bleeding Penitents formed themselves into a large ring, at the center of which their colleagues assembled a small stage. When the stage was complete, the Priest's backless throne was placed atop it. The Penitents standing in their ring began to circle the throne, clapping and chanting to the continuing drumbeat. The local villagers flocked in their hundreds, then over a thousand, drawn by the drums and growing spectacle.

"What the hell is this," Slade murmured to himself, "a roadshow?"

Suddenly, the Priest vaulted onto the stage adorned in a yellow-feathered headdress and wielding an ornamental bone scepter. He raised the staff and launched into an animated tirade, his speech fierce, his movements violent. The gathered locals warmed and pressed in closer. Within minutes they were mimicking the Priest's enthusiasm, jumping in time with his movements and the driving drums. The Priest goaded them on, shouting at them, pumping his scepter with the beat. Suddenly, the Priest froze in place. Then slowly, he lowered the scepter and pointed toward stage left.

A man hunching on all fours spidered onto the stage. The newcomer's body was covered in white paint, his face demon masked. The crowd hissed and shook their fists. More actors appeared onstage; a young teenager with a father and mother figure.

The parents began to lecture the teenager, their fingers wagging. The boy was contrite and bashful, head hanging low. Then the white man came forward and whispered in the teen's ear. The teen abruptly assumed a hostile pose, and began back-talking the parents, head popping, fist shaking. The parents recoiled. The crowd booed. The Priest then rose before the crowd, turned, and leveled a finger in judgment upon the teen. Two men seized the youth and pinned him shirtless across the Priest's black-stained throne. The Priest uncoiled an immense bullwhip, then reared back, the length of it snaking off behind him in a long sinuous coil. The crowd grew deathly quiet in that moment of pause before he spasmed forward and brought the whip down in a tight arc that popped like a gunshot and flaying a length of wet flesh from the teen's back. The Priest then fell into a rhythm, sawing back and forth, the whip flicking like a serpent's tongue.

High on the ridgeline above, the Americans flinched in time with the gasping crowd and the distant popping of the whip.

"That poor kid is one of his own people!" Isaac gasped.

"You're right," Slade said, deeply disturbed. "To take a whipping like that, just for some street theatre? He must be drugged."

When the whipping was complete and the insolent boy had been dragged away unconscious, the next act took the stage: two good friends talking and laughing. The white spider slank to one of them, embraced him, and urged him into pick-pocketing his unsuspecting companion. But the thief was caught, and again, the Priest pronounced judgment. However, this time the offender's arm was lashed to the throne, a long blade flashed chrome in the sunlight, and the sinner fell back, hand-stump spurting. The Priest picked up the severed hand like an offending insect and tossed it from the stage. The crowd shrieked and stampeded away from the appendage but within seconds swarmed back over it, kicking and stomping, pumping their arms in time with the accelerating drumbeat.

"Jesus," Elizabeth breathed, her face paling, "that guy put his hand on the chopping block without a struggle. What kind of drugs do they—"

Slade abruptly pushed himself back and spun to face their rear, his weapon raised. "Quiet!" he hissed. "Someone's coming." He pointed toward a small depression surrounded by thick brush. "Quick, follow me!"

CHAPTER TWENTY-EIGHT

PUSHING ELIZABETH IN front of him, Slade sprinted across a small stretch of open ground, then slid into a deep thicket, branches scraping against his cheeks. He was turning to hold the branches open for Isaac when his heart stopped; the boy was not behind him. Instead, Isaac remained frozen on the far side of the small clearing, staring after Slade with panicked eyes. Slade glanced in the direction of the approaching noise then back at the boy, held up his palms and made a shushing motion, indicating to Isaac that he should remain in place, lie down, and stay quiet. Isaac did so.

The hushed silence that followed was deafening. Slade remained in a crouch, eyes scanning, the stock of his rifle pulled into his shoulder. Beside him, Elizabeth did likewise, mimicking his actions. Across the clearing, Isaac lay open-mouthed, flies settling on his skin, knuckles white against his weapon, the muzzle bobbing in time with his heartbeat.

More crackling came from the far side of the clearing. The murmur of several men talking to each other. Fifty meters to their front, an African emerged from the brush; he wore only tattered camouflage pants and sneakers. A battered AK was slung across his back. On his chest stood the angry boil of a freshly healed brand: a cross and crescent. Three more men and a boy appeared. They talked among themselves while pointing at the surrounding vegetation and forest. One of them walked in a wide circle, head down, examining the ground beneath his feet. He crouched, pulled up a plant, and examined a break in its stem. He tasted it, then he lowered himself onto all fours, pressed his nose to the crushed vegetation, and drew a deep breath. Rising, he spoke to his companions and fanned them out across the clearing, searching for more signs.

Slade grimaced. They were being tracked. He and Elizabeth had a clear escape route, but it was too late for Isaac to reach it. They were trapped in place. Slade held himself motionless as the tracking party slowly worked in their direction. Rivulets of sweat coursed down his face and formed a running puddle between his shoulder blades.

A potbellied boy of no more than ten years wandered toward Isaac's position, dragging his AK behind him like a sleepy child would a teddy bear. He stopped six feet away from Isaac, lit a crumpled cigarette, dug a finger into his belly button, then flicked away the found refuse. The boy drew a deep puff, glanced at a bird circling overhead, then allowed his eyes to fall upon Isaac's hide. Before the boy's brain could assign meaning to the collection of lines and shadows crouched before him, Slade's bullet had entered and then left his skull.

Slade erupted from the brush, rifle cracking, bullets slapping through the trackers, cutting them down in a spray of lead, brass, blood, and bone. He continued to advance, muzzle tracking from target to target until all of the party lay in sodden heaps. An unseen boy rose from the tall grass, terror stricken. He dropped his rifle, turned, and ran. Slade pivoted toward him without pause, tracked and hammered a bullet through his spine. He then circled the small clearing, rifle raised, searching for more targets, checking the dead, finishing the wounded.

Satisfied, he loaded a fresh magazine into his rifle, then returned to his companions. Elizabeth stood on the edge of the clearing, eyes saucer-wide, her rifle raised but unfired. Slade grabbed Isaac's arm and pulled him to standing, but the boy's feet remained frozen in place. "Come on, gotta move." Slade was about to grow angry when he realized that Isaac's horrified gaze was focused on him. He softened his tone and put his eyes directly in front of the boy's. "Isaac. I know some serious shit just went down, but I need you to pull it together and come with me. Okay?" He reached forward and gently slapped Isaac on the cheek. "Time to move."

"Isaac, come on! Move!" Elizabeth hissed.

Hearing his sister's voice, Isaac nodded numbly and began to trudge forward, zombie-like, eyes locked on the bleeding corpses before him, the snapped limbs, exposed innards, and disassembled faces.

As they cleared the massacre, Isaac's senses seemed to return and he was able to break into a jog, followed closely by his sister. Slade led the way, rifle half raised, covering their advance. When they reached the horses, Slade swung himself atop Big, waited for his companions, then spurred hard into the surrounding brush.

CHAPTER TWENTY-NINE

As the sun set over the western hills, Slade found a copse of trees where a natural weep had created a shallow pool and a rich garden of life. He guided Big into the secluded hide as a tribe of irate monkeys swung and howled through the shaded dome. He made sure that his companions were comfortable, set their horses to drinking, then retrieved Kraven's sat-phone from his saddle bags.

The device chirped as it made the satellite connection. After a brief delay the line opened, and a digitally masked voice answered the call. "I show you encrypted." The disguised voice was unrecognizable, but the clipped cadence was distinctly Kraven's.

"I've got an intel dump for you," Slade said. "I had a little run-in with the boys you're looking for."

"Copy. Send it."

Slade told Kraven about the encounter with the raiders.

"What was your take on them?"

"It's definitely the guys that are tearing up the countryside and wiped out the Chinese. They have the same cross and crescent emblems and the same impaling practice. They appear to be poorly disciplined at the squad level, typical African, but well organized on a macro scale. They had centralized command and control as well as coordinated overwatch security and roving patrols. They look like a cult, but they have people working with them that are pros. Most likely foreign."

"Explain."

"Take a look at this." Slade tapped on the sat-phone's screen. "I'm sending a video. Let me know when it comes through."

"Alright, I've got the file open," Kraven said. There was a minutes-long pause as the colonel skimmed through the video. "What's your take on it?"

Slade scratched at his beard. "It wasn't a raiding party. I think they were . . . recruiting. But their religion looks like it was made up by a foreigner."

"Explain."

"It's a mish-mash of local animism, Christianity, and Shiite Islam. Their symbol is a cross and a crescent moon, Christian and Muslim in one. And their parade was a blend of religions, too. Looked like Irish marching season crashed into Ashura."

"Marching what?"

"Marching season in Northern Ireland—when the Micks get all boozed up and parade around waving their dicks at each other. But it also had elements of the Ashura pilgrimage—the one where the Shiites go full-retard, whip themselves with razors, and bang swords against their faces."

"You're right, it did look like Ashura."

"Yes . . . But African Muslims are Sunni. They see Shiite rituals as blasphemy, worthy of death. And then the Penitents all gathered around that black cube, the throne, started walking in a big circle, counterclockwise, like the Hajj pilgrimage in Mecca."

"Okay."

"And then the street theatre bit—they were acting out the Ten Commandments but using punishments from the Koran. If we'd stuck around, I think we'd have seen a beheading or two. So, taken as a whole, it makes no sense . . . Protestantism and Shi'ism . . . In a place where there aren't any Protestants or Shiites. Throw in the fact that these guys have competent leadership and recently manu-factured munitions . . . looks like foreign involvement. In summary, it appears that foreigners are using locals to kill foreigners." Slade shook his head at the improbability. "Anything to add, Colonel?"

"Negative. Keep up the good work." The digital voice masking could not conceal the colonel's lack of surprise.

CHAPTER THIRTY

As HE STOOD watch over the siblings that night, Slade caught a glimmer of starlight reflecting from Elizabeth's eyes.

"Can't sleep?" he asked softly.

There was no response.

"Worried about getting home? Don't sweat it. The convoy is only a few hours ahead. We'll be back before lunch tomorrow."

Elizabeth refused to acknowledge Slade, but her breathing became deep and labored.

"What's wrong?" Slade asked, though he already knew the answer.

Struggling to maintain her composure, Elizabeth rolled to face Slade. "I never saw anybody killed before."

Slade studied the varied shadows that comprised the girl's face. "I know. I'm sorry you had to see that." He seated himself beside her, but she turned her back.

"Does it bother you what I did today?" he asked.

The response was long in coming but spoken with conviction. "Yes."

"We wouldn't be alive if I hadn't," Slade replied gently.

"I know. I tried to shoot, too, to protect Isaac . . ." Her breathing quickened and her words spilled rapidly. "But I couldn't! Killing is the worst thing you can do and we just . . . We slaughtered them like animals."

Slade nodded. "Yes. That's true. But your's and Isaac's lives are worth more than theirs so—"

"It's not a question of *worth*!"

"To me it was. As human beings, you two are worth more than them. All of them."

A sob threatened to free itself. "So they died because of Isaac and me."

"No. The decision was mine. They would have harmed something greater than themselves. I chose not to let that happen."

"But some of them were just kids! One was running away for Christ's sake!"

"And he would have returned . . . with hundreds of men in trucks."

"But what if he was . . . I don't know . . . good! What if he was there because . . . because he was forced to? I saw his face . . . he was so terrified. God, that was evil."

"Do you believe I'm evil then?"

Elizabeth thought for a long time. "No . . . But what you did was." She shifted back to face Slade. "Have you done that before? Killed people like that?"

Slade looked at his hands though he could not see them. "Yes."

"Why?"

"I had good reason."

"Like what?" Elizabeth's voice held a hostile edge. "Somebody in the military told you to?"

"No. Again, it was my choice." Slade spoke slowly, choosing his words and their meaning carefully. "The people I killed—before— were building a world that requires the destruction of mine, of everything I value."

"Muslims?"

"Yes, they were Muslims. And I believed my society and its values were worth preserving. Just as I believed your life was worth preserving."

"So that made killing okay," she spat.

"No. It made it necessary."

"So you killed to protect your society. The same society we're all running from? That's the people you killed for?" Elizabeth waited for a response. After receiving none, it became her turn to study the shadowed form before her. "Does that change the meaning of the things you did?" she asked, her voice softening.

Slade searched for his answer. "I don't know. At first I was doing it to protect something I valued. Then one day . . ."

"Yes?" she pressed.

"It was just killing."

"So all those things you did in the military, it was for no reason?" Slade didn't answer.

"But you stopped then, right?"

"No."

"But . . . I don't understand. What were you doing it for?" Elizabeth asked.

When there was no answer forthcoming, she turned away from Slade. "I'm sorry," she whispered.

Slade rose, brushed off his hands, and moved to stand sentry. "Yeah . . . So am I."

* * *

The girl lay unsleeping. In time, she opened her eyes to behold the star-fields turning on their ancient migration and the man-shaped void that stood among them.

CHAPTER THIRTY-ONE

THE FOLLOWING MORNING Slade and his party overrode a series of fresh vehicle tracks. He dismounted and crouched on the trail, his fingers grazing over the freshly turned earth. Shallow and faint on the hard-packed soil, they offered few truths. Walking slowly, head bowed, he scouted down the trail until he found softer earth, the better to read them. Two light vehicles had moved through this place, the dust of their passing still fresh upon the surrounding brush and grass. They had been moving quickly, throwing up debris on the outside of their turn radius. The treads were old and worn, bald in places with differing tires on each axle.

Slade stood, lips thinning as he scanned the horizon, then hurried his small party along the trail. They followed the vehicle tracks until they intersected the main road where the Judean convoy had passed the day prior. Deep ridges stood upon Slade's brow as he saw the vehicle tracks skidding to follow in the convoy's wake.

Disaster weighed like a stone in his heart.

He hurried from the road at Elizabeth's frenzied waving. Standing in her stirrups, the girl pointed toward the horizon. There, in three separate places, curtains of dust rose from the trees, vehicles on the move, converging toward the distant convoy.

Slade pushed his radio to maximum transmission power. "Abe! Abe, come in. This is Slade!"

The radio link crackled as though open, but there was no response.

"Abe, this is Slade. I'm nine miles east of your position. You've got multiple vehicles converging on you. Do you copy?"

Distant yelling over the radio link, barely audible.

"Abe, this is Slade, you've got—"

Over the crackling static Slade heard the unmistakable sound of gunfire.

Cursing, he mounted Big with a leap and spurred forward at a gallop.

CHAPTER THIRTY-TWO

ELIZABETH LOWERED HER binoculars. "Why don't they just cross the river?"

"I don't know," Slade replied. "Maybe there's something wrong with the bridge." He raised his lenses again. A mile in front of them, the Judean convoy sat motionless, logjammed at the mouth of a metal bridge. Positioned on the flanks and rear of the convoy, the three Cougars fended off a swarm of battered pickup trucks that stalked through the brush like mechanical sharks.

Seemingly at random, one of the attacking trucks would break from cover and dart toward the Judeans, the Penitents in the truck bed firing wildly, only to veer away as the Cougars' turrets swung upon them. The Cougars would loose sustained bursts of cannon fire in response, felling trees and raising long divots of red earth but nothing more. The attackers' movements were chaotic, thus perfect, leading the inexperienced Judean gunners to fire continually and ineffectually at the darting school. Eventually the Cougars' magazines would run empty, the guns would fall silent, and the trucks would close for the slaughter.

"You're right," Isaac said. "There's something wrong with the bridge. Look on the near side where the metal meets the concrete. Somebody's welding."

Slade refocused his lenses, saw the pinprick of blue light and a cascade of sparks. "Good eyes, son. So, if the bridge is out"—Slade cast his lenses farther afield—"the only good escape is to the south. And it looks like those cult bastards are already digging in to block that."

"Where?"

"Look to the south, they're already in position to block any escape. They're thinking two moves ahead. Not good." Slade panned his glasses over the blocking force—eleven vehicles, over a hundred men on foot. And the Priest, still adorned in his feathers and body paint, pointing and shouting, barking orders into a handheld radio.

Slade lowered his glasses then looked to his rear at another column of dust converging on their location. "More dust trails."

Elizabeth turned in her saddle. "More coming?"

"Yeah. That means they have over-the-horizon communications. These guys have their act together."

"So what do we do?"

Slade pointed toward the Judean convoy. "We go in."

"Really? Can't we wait out here?" Isaac asked.

"I need to get in there. The longer we wait, the harder it'll be to get inside." Slade tapped on his computer and brought up the command radio net; it was a confused jumble of static, gunfire, and panicked men shouting back and forth.

"Attention on Command Net. This is Scout Party Five. We're approaching from the east on horseback," Slade said. "Hold your fire. I repeat, hold your fire."

Slade then sheathed his rifle, snapped the restraint strap closed, put both hands on the reins, and worked his feet deeper into the stirrups. "We go hard. We go fast. We don't stop. The biggest danger will be those Cougar gunners. They're panicked, and they'll shoot anything that moves. Don't stop until you're past them and in the middle of the convoy."

Elizabeth nodded, narrowed her eyes, tightened her gloves, and reseated her boots in the stirrups.

When he was sure that both teens were ready, Slade relaxed his reins and applied stiff pressure with his knees and heels. "Follow me."

Flanks trembling with excitement, his breath already coming in sharp huffs, Big began to gather speed. His stride transitioned from a bumping trot, to a canter, then a gallop, his beat accelerating, flowing, becoming smooth and rhythmic. Slade raised himself in the stirrups, hunched forward over Big's heaving neck, and felt the animal's chest expanding like a bellows as the wind built from a whistling stream to a pressing river. He gave the enormous animal free reign, shouted encouragement, and leaned into the curves as Big charged through the brush. Speed panic rose in his throat, tears whipped back from Slade's eyes, and his clothing snapped the air behind him.

There was a flash of colored movement in the brush to the right. Slade leaned left and blasted through a stand of trees while young boys with rifles scattered like frightened birds and terrain flew past in a blur.

Isaac and Elizabeth pulled abreast, their horses' necks stroking like pistons, the explosive huffing of their breath mixing with sporadic gunshots from their rear. With opening terrain, Big stretched into a long, loping gallop like a freight train at full steam while Slade's thighs and back muscles seemingly caught fire.

Suddenly, a Cougar stood among the trees like a metallic elephant, its turret swinging toward them. Slade dug the last of his strength into his heels and leaned forward till his face pressed against Big's lathered neck and the cannon leveled its terrible bore, turret motor whining. But the cannon didn't fire, and the three riders darted past in a flash and continued onward, unstoppable until at last they reined to a halt in a shower of clodded earth in the center of the panicked convoy.

CHAPTER THIRTY-THREE

SLADE HEAVED HIMSELF up the ladder and into the command vehicle, the chilled air hitting him like an electric shock. He found Abe Howard, Hendrik, Mantis, and a number of other men clustered around the bank of video screens.

"Get your guys to stop firing," Slade ordered. "At this rate you'll be out of ammo in an hour."

They looked up as one, panicked faces smoothing into a flood of relief.

"Mr. Crawford! Praise God you made it safely. We're under attack from three sides! We've already had two men nearly wounded and one vehicle has—"

"Those pickup trucks can't do a damn thing at these ranges. They can't hit crap while they're moving, and their guns won't penetrate thick armor." Slade made a poking motion in the air. "The only thing they'll do to your Cougars is spiderweb a windshield."

Slade shouldered through the crowd and scanned the bank of digital maps and screens. Five of the screens displayed the jumpy, nausea-inducing video feeds from men on foot. Two showed the frantic interiors of the other Cougars, where a motley collection of middle-aged men called out enemy sightings and yelled vague instructions to the turret gunners. Bedlam was general and spent brass fell like rain.

"Get them to cease fire," Slade instructed.

"I've tried but no one will listen!"

Slade thrust out his open palm and snapped his fingers. "Headset. Now." Abe gratefully relinquished the headset and slid his chair back from the communication suite. Slade leaned forward over the console, face filling the camera feed, lips pulled back in a snarl, nostrils flared. He spit into the microphone, "The next one of you bloody cunts that so much as breathes on a trigger is going to get his ass widened three sizes. By this." Slade brandished his ham fist and filled the camera's field of view with the scarred bludgeon. "If you doubt me, then touch that trigger and see what happens."

Silence descended upon the savannah.

With order restored, Slade continued his broadcast in an overly genteel voice. "Now that I have your attention . . . You will fire only if a vehicle comes within five hundred meters. Or if gunfire actually begins to hit you. Two-second burst maximum. Questions?"

There were none.

Slade moved away from the camera's field of view and lowered the microphone, his face transforming from a mask of distilled hatred to one of deep satisfaction. He looked at his frozen companions and shrugged apologetically. "They'll get over it."

The cooling fans hummed quietly.

Slade rubbed his hands together enthusiastically. "Alright, Abe, now show me exactly what you have going on here."

Abe pointed toward the digital maps. "There's not much to show. We're here, jammed up against the river to our west. They're here, arrayed in an arc around us. We're boxed in."

Elder Hendrik wove his fingers together and leaned over Slade's shoulder. "Are these the same bandits that attacked the Chinese?"

"Yes," Slade confirmed.

The assembled Judeans groaned. One buried his face in his hands, shoulders quaking.

Turning away from the screens, Slade pulled Abe, Mantis, and Hendrik to the side. "First off, you're doing great. We need to tighten up a few details, but for now you're solid."

Abe accepted the praise humbly.

"But there's something else we need to talk about."

"Yes?"

Slade lowered his voice to a whisper. "You can't settle here. It's too dangerous and you're isolated from resupply. That leaves two options: punch through the encirclement and escape to the south, twelve hundred miles back toward Johannesburg; or fight your way back to the coast, link up with the freighter, sail back to Cape Town, and start over with a different plan. Those are your options."

Mantis struck like a coiled snake. "I have long known this moment would come! When the Adversary would seek to lead us away from New Zion! Do you imagine that the Saints would forsake God's plan at the first hint of adversity?"

"You don't have to abandon your plan; you just have to change it." Slade pointed toward the perimeter. "These guys have found you and will follow you to Lake Malawi. You can't settle here."

Mantis drew himself up. "God has proclaimed that we will continue westward across the bridge. That is final."

"Alright." Slade picked his words carefully, shifting his attack. "So when will the bridge be repaired?"

"Our engineer says three days."

"Three days? Guys, we don't have one day. Now that they've pinned you down, they'll call in the big stuff: twenty-three-millimeter cannon with armor-piercing ammo, heavy mortars. We've got to keep moving. If we act now, tonight, we can break through the encirclement and escape."

"God has proclaimed that within three days' time the Saints will be delivered in safety to the other side of the river."

"Now you're just making shit up—" Slade stopped himself, ran his hands through his hair, eased his breathing, then continued softly, "Are there any other options that have been explored?"

"No."

"So start exploring them." Slade looked to Hendrik for support, but the man was paralyzed. In spite of the air-conditioning, rivulets of sweat coursed through the folds of his chins and beaded onto his chest.

"It is a test of *faith*, Mr. Crawford, something which you would not understand."

Slade clenched his fists in frustration. "Faith is your suicide note."

Mantis cooled and grew calm. "Mr. Crawford, the counsel of your forked tongue is no longer required. You are relieved of your responsibilities and will take leave of us immediately."

Slade stepped forward and leaned in close enough for Mantis to smell the stink of his breath. "This ain't about me. It's about you and the people you are responsible for protecting. Because if you continue to sit here, three days from now the crocs will be crawling from the river to feed on your dead children."

Abe paled visibly. Hendrik still dripped. Mantis didn't flinch.

"That's it? That's the final decision?" Slade asked, glancing around the group.

"Yes," Mantis answered.

Slade drew back and placed his hands on his hips. "You may have spoken, but I haven't. I'm calling a powwow tonight, all hands on deck."

CHAPTER THIRTY-FOUR

SLADE RETURNED TO his quarters, steam cooling. The sat-phone Kraven had left him was chirping softly. A conversation request was waiting for him. He picked up the phone and accepted the request. Twenty seconds later the line opened.

"I show you encrypted," a digitally altered voice said.

"What do you want?" Slade barked.

It sounded like Kraven was shuffling papers. "Proceed to Nairobi immediately."

"Kenya? That's six hundred miles north of here."

"Yes. Contact me when you're outside Nairobi, and I'll outfit you with urban ops gear."

"Negative, I'm pinned in place by your buddies. Time to roll in the air support. Give me uplink freqs, and I'll talk your assets onto target. Hostiles have unarmored trucks and dismounted infantry; 114Ks and airburst GBU-31s will do the trick. I can have these guys cleaned up in an hour once the strikers arrive."

"The data you collected from the Chinese massacre points to Nairobi. When you arrive, I'll need you to locate the Penitents' logistics hub then track and identify their organizational structure. I need to know their—"

"You're not hearing me, Colonel. I said that I can't move. I've got four hundred civilians surrounded by two dozen gun trucks and more are on the way. Now get your aircraft on scene, and I'll take care of this problem."

"The Judeans are not my concern. Nor are they yours. Proceed to Nairobi and—"

Slade broke the connection, dropped the phone, and clenched his fists in frustration. "Jesus, I'm surrounded by assholes."

* * *

With nightfall came an extended lull in the fighting, but the crowd of Judeans who assembled to hear Slade speak still milled like nervous horses, eyes darting toward the occasional burst of gunfire that crashed through the night. The men stood in tight clusters and clutched their rifles like totems for fending off evil spirits. A small campfire had been lit and the smoke blew in stinging, unpredictable gusts. The distant sound of women and children singing hymns shifted in the smoky air.

Slade turned toward his companion. "Your light discipline is crap, Abe. I told you to get all the lights out, especially the fires."

"I know, I know. But the Saints were so filled with fear that I authorized this small one. We have it well blocked off with the trucks. It can't be seen from outside the camp."

Slade bit his lip in frustration. "How many people are going to show up?"

"I don't know, but Elder Mantis has forbidden any of his flock from attending."

"Then what are they doing here?" Slade pointed to a group of fundamentalists.

"It would appear that some have chosen not to heed his counsel."

A man approached, eyes brimming. He clasped Slade's hand and pumped it furiously. "The Brethren have been praying mightily for you, Mr. Crawford. We look forward to hearing what words you would share with us. Thank you for staying, sir, thank you!"

Slade returned the man's two-handed shake. "I'll do what I can."

With that, Slade checked his watch and moved to address the men that had assembled. He told them what he had seen in the Chinese settlement and of the terrible calculus that doomed their quest for New Zion. He told them that they needed to break through the encirclement tonight or they would die in place. The crowd murmured and buzzed, debated back and forth, Slade answered their questions as best he could. The exchanges grew in intensity with some of the men shouting at each other. A brief shoving match broke out but was quickly subdued. The men in favor of breaking out began to gain the upper hand.

"And then what!" came a shouted challenge.

The crowd fell into silence as a black-clad Elder Mantis strode to the fire and stood there amongst the drifting embers, eyes glittering. His right hand stretched to the sky, his left clutched a leather-bound Bible to his breast.

"God has declared that he will deliver us to New Zion as surely as he led Moses out of Egypt!" Mantis' voice dropped and he leveled a finger at the crowd. "I ask you: What will you find when you follow Mr. Crawford to the south and you reach your *new location*? You will find only that you have betrayed your faith, abandoned your God, and left yourself naked before the fangs of the world!"

"The fangs are already here, Mantis, and they're hours away from slaughtering you. You must break out and find a different place to settle."

Mantis stuck out his chin. "We are continuing onward, Mr. Crawford. The Saints are unshakable in that conviction. A divine revelation is not to be overturned by these"—he gestured violently toward the perimeter—"these Sons of Cain."

"Those Sons of Cain will follow you to Lake Malawi. You need—"

"Heed not his counsel, Brothers and Sisters! For he—"

"Shut the fuck up and don't interrupt me," Slade spat.

Mantis recoiled as though struck.

"And while we're on the subject," Slade continued, "next time you feel like beating children . . . come try it on me first. We'll see how it goes."

Mantis stood unspeaking, his Adam's apple bobbing. Two of his thugs moved to bracket him, facing Slade with hunched shoulders and tight fists. One rested his hand on his holstered pistol.

Slade turned back toward the crowd. "Bottom line: if you wait any longer you'll be out of ammunition and options. You must escape . . . or die."

A man in the crowd stepped forward. "Crawford is right! You saw what they did to that Chinese settlement! And they had many times our number!"

Cries of agreement rose and spread.

Mantis struggled to regain his momentum, faced the crowd, and raised his hands. "I ask you this, Brothers and Sisters: Who exactly is *Mr.* Slade Crawford? He is an unbeliever who has given his life to the folly of strong drink, whore flesh, and the way of the gun! He wallows in iniquity and—"

There came then a gentle whickering sound from above as something unseen took passage through the night. Slade threw himself to the ground, dragging Abe with him as a deafening blast concussed through the camp, shattering glass and lifting people off the ground. Screams pierced the darkness.

The shell had burst near one of the passenger transports, and the vehicle listed to one side, tires shredded, windows shattered. A high-pitched wailing of confusion and pain came from the interior. A mob of people instantly swarmed toward the vehicle, parents blind with panic pulled bleeding children free. Cries for the medics went up.

Ears ringing, Slade climbed to his feet as a chaotic crowd dashed in every direction, each man calling for the lights to be extinguished, for people to move to cover.

Slade dragged Abe to his feet, brushed him off, and straightened his clothes. "Alright, they're already lobbing mortars. Debate Club is closed. We're breaking out tonight. If we're still here come daylight, we'll be dead before lunch." As he talked, Slade led his companion toward one of the armored trucks and crouched down beside it, using it for cover. "You'll lead a breakout," he said, glancing at his watch, "in roughly four hours."

Abe nodded his head as hard resolve congealed in his belly. "Okay. I can do it. I'm sure the Brothers will agree to the plan."

"Good."

Crhump! Another shell detonated, like an immense door slamming in the distance.

Abe's eyes flicked toward the sound, but he remained focused. "Breakout in which direction? How?"

"Due south."

"But that's where they are massed. They've blocked it off."

Slade nodded. "I'll remedy that."

"How?"

"I'll ride out. Jack them up. Draw them away. Then you punch through the hole and escape south."

"Who . . . Who will go with you?"

"Nobody."

"You're going to leave us alone? And how'll you catch up?"

"It'll be a while—best case several weeks."

Genuine fear rose in Abe's eyes. "Is that the right thing to do?"

Slade's shoulders slumped and his face sagged. With that one question, his confidence evaporated. "Abe . . . I'm just stumbling through this," Slade said in a voice that was barely audible. "I've fucked up everything that a man possibly can. Ask your God what to do and I'll do it."

"I don't know what to do either, Slade. You saw us back there at the meeting, we've got a civil war on our hands. I need somebody here on my side!"

"Yeah, about that meeting . . ." Slade's eyes narrowed. "Frankly, Mantis is going to get you all killed." He leaned in close to Abe, glanced over both shoulders, and lowered his voice. "If Mantis were to no longer be *a factor*—" Slade placed his hand atop his Sig and popped the button on its retaining strap. "Would that help things?"

Abe recoiled, a nervous smile flickering across his mouth.

"I'm serious," Slade continued. "All you have to do is nod your head. Problem's solved."

Abe's smile fled. His eyelids fluttered. "N- no that shouldn't be done."

"You sure?"

"Yes."

"Alright. Sorry. Would've been impolite not to ask."

Slade drew a single deep breath, looked at the surrounding chaos, and listened to the *crhump* of another explosion. "Abe, I don't know much, but there is one thing I'm certain of." He dusted off his hands and pointed toward the darkness beyond the perimeter. "It's high time somebody stabbed these pricks—right in the neck."

CHAPTER THIRTY-FIVE

Slade stood next to Big, checking the saddle and bridle. He turned to the two mechanics who had been assigned to help him. At Slade's direction, they had found a wheeled handcart and fitted it with poles and straps so that it could be pulled behind Big. He supervised as they set the poles on either side of his saddle and secured it via flexible nylon webbing. Big snorted, tossed his head, and stamped the ground, still spooked by the occasional explosion that boomed through the night. Slade attempted to soothe the nervous animal, stroking his glossy neck while the mechanics shied away, wary of an errant kick.

"Looks like this rig will do just fine," Slade said to the mechanics. "All I need now is a dozen blankets and some guns. Lots of guns."

"The armory truck is right this way, sir."

* * *

After stocking the handcart with ammunition, PKM machine guns, and RPGs, Slade turned Big toward the command vehicle. He found Abe waiting outside.

"Have you swept my route with the drones?" Slade asked as he dismounted.

"Yes. The raiders are clustered around their campfires. Most are sleeping. They don't have any patrols that we could see." He tapped on his wrist computer and downloaded the data directly to Slade's device. "So what's your plan again?"

Slade pointed to Abe's video screen. "I'll ride out through their perimeter then circle back and take out their mortar crew and some of their fuel trucks. When the guys that are blocking the southern road see all the fireworks, they'll come charging to the rescue, opening up the road for you to punch through."

"Looks pretty simple." Abe nodded.

"All good plans are. After you break the encirclement, just keep blasting south. You'll pass through a small town called Ngongo thirty miles south of here. You may run into a few Penitents but nothing the Cougars can't handle. Shoot first, stop for nothing. Got it?"

"Got it." Abe offered his hand. "I guess it's goodbye until you are able to catch up. Take care of yourself, Mr. Crawford, I know you were sent to us by God."

Slade shook the offered hand and looked at his feet as he choked back a lump. "Thanks for trusting in me, Abe, even when I didn't deserve it."

"Brother Crawford? Where are you going?" a woman's voice asked. Slade turned. A figure appeared out of the shadows. Elizabeth Brightman stood wide-eyed, her automatic rifle gripped in her hands, the weapon cartoonishly large against her slender frame. Her eyes flickered over the surrounding darkness, her face animated by the raw fear that flowed through the besieged camp.

Isaac materialized beside her, his rifle slung across his back. "You're leaving?" he asked.

Slade approached the two. "Yes, for a while."

"I'm coming with you," Isaac said.

"The hell you are! You're both staying here!" Elizabeth countered. She leveled a finger at Slade. "I don't know what kind of shit you're thinking of pulling but—"

Slade held up his palms in protest. "I'm not deserting you. I'm breaking us out of this trap. And, Isaac, I'm sorry, but you're needed here with your family."

Slade turned to speak with Elizabeth, but she cut him off. "This is an epic bad idea. You saw Mantis back there at the meeting. You're the only thing that's keeping him from steamrolling everybody and—"

"Elizabeth, Brother Howard has everything under control—"

"No he doesn't, he's—"

"Elizabeth, I'm sorry, but I don't have time for this. I have to go." Slade then addressed them both. "You're going to stay together and not let the other out of your sight, you hear?"

The siblings nodded their heads.

"And if anybody threatens your loved ones"—Slade turned and locked eyes with Elizabeth—"then you'll do what needs to be done. And let neither God nor man stop you."

Elizabeth looked at her younger brother. Slade watched as the fear and uncertainty written on her face transformed, channeling itself into hard resolve and purpose.

"Now you understand," Slade said. "And now I have to go."

Elizabeth nodded her head in grudging acceptance. But as Slade turned to leave, she stepped forward and grabbed his shoulders, leaned, and placed her lips next to his ear. "Thank you for standing up for us when nobody else would. And get back to us, I owe you a drink." Then turning on her heel, she vanished into the night.

Though she was gone, Slade could not stop seeing her, feeling the heat of her presence, the strength of the feminine, refusing to submit in the face of overwhelming force.

CHAPTER THIRTY-SIX

THE ILLUMINATED DIALS of Slade's watch read 0315. Penetrating the raiders' cordon had not been difficult, but backtracking and coming in from their rear had taken more time than he'd anticipated. He was twenty minutes behind schedule.

Dropping to one knee, he wiped his sodden face, drew his canteen, drank heavily, and cleared his gritty throat. When the canteen was stowed, he completed the final equipment check. Feeling in the darkness, his fingers found the rough metal of an RPG lying on the grass. Next to it, in perfect order, lay another RPG and two PKM light machine guns, 500 rounds each.

Slade fished in his chest pocket, pulled out a set of earplugs, and worked them into his ears. He then pulled on his gloves, hefted the RPG to his shoulder, and set his face against the cheek rest. Two hundred meters to his front, the raiders' campsite lay quiet, its trucks dark, its mortar tube silent.

Slade breathed deeply, eyes closed, expanding his mind into total presence and total calm. Grass rustled in a gentle northern breeze, trees scraped against each other, insects buzzed, and men snored softly around a dying campfire.

His right eye opened behind the RPG's iron sight and framed the dim silhouette of a fuel truck.

The thumb hammer clicked into place. His finger tensed the stiff trigger. Further. Further.

Back-blast slapped through the night and a brilliant flash strobed against the trees followed by a chest-thumping concussion and a roaring mushroom cloud of flame.

Slade tossed the launcher away, hoisted the second launcher to his shoulder, and cocked the thumb hammer. Flaming scarecrows danced hysteric in his sights.

Squeeze . . . Back-blast!

Slade tossed away the second RPG launcher, crab-shuffled to his right, and belly-flopped behind the first PKM machine gun. He cracked back the charging handle, set the stock into his shoulder, and crushed the trigger. The weapon exploded to life in his gloved fists, bucking and thrashing like an animal hooked to a live wire. He swept the muzzle slowly back and forth, working ruby tracer fire over the blazing campsite, chasing the rickety shadows that scrambled through the firelight, dashing and toppling in their dozens.

At twenty seconds, the barrel began to glow a dull cherry red. Slade continued to lash the campsite, setting more brush and trucks afire. At thirty seconds, heat like an open oven began to pucker the skin of his face. At forty, the white-glowing barrel began to droop and surrounding grass sparked into flame. At fifty seconds, there was a loud bang and the weapon's barrel ruptured in a spray of smoking metal.

With the gun abruptly silent, Slade rolled to his right, racked the bolt on the second gun, and smashed the trigger, resuming the deafening staccato chatter.

Slade raked the burning campsite for fifteen seconds, set another two trucks ablaze, then ceased fire, and looked to the south. One kilometer away, on the road astride the Judeans' escape route, the main blocking force was springing to life, awakened by the spectacle of Slade's attack. Slade swung his barrel in their direction and loosed a long ballistic arc of tracers, peppering the blocking force, ensuring that any sound sleepers would be fully roused.

When the second gun fell silent, Slade sank to his knees, eyes stinging from the heat and smoke. He pulled a fragmentation grenade from his belt, wedged it snuggly beneath the sixteen-pound weapon, then pulled its arming pin and carefully backed away. The weight of the weapon held the grenade's triggering mechanism in place, preventing detonation. As a final measure, Slade snap-activated a chemical light, wedged the glowing tube into the crotch of a nearby tree, then turned and ran to the east.

* * *

Minutes later, Slade lay on his belly at his second hide-site, watching the dim green glow of the chemical stick, 300 meters away. Beside him lay six thermobaric RPGs and two PKM machine guns, 500 rounds each.

There had initially been no response from the shell-shocked camp, but eventually, sporadic return fire flickered to life. Illuminated by burning trees and brush, Slade could see a man pushing and clubbing his men into action, shoving them out into the darkness to search for their attacker.

Slade swung his lenses a kilometer to the south where the blocking force was now fully mobilized and reacting to the attack. A dozen sets of headlights had flared to life and were now bumping through the brush, beams swinging wildly. The southern blocking force was on the move, coming to support their besieged comrades.

With reinforcements en route, the campsite defenders became bolder, venturing toward Slade's previous firing position.

Suddenly there was excited shouting and pointing, full magazines were emptied, an RPG was loosed flaming into the night. The glowing chemical light was working like a charm, drawing the raiders in.

As the first of the reinforcing gun-trucks arrived, the hunters seemed to gather courage and charged the chemical light in a pack, hacking, spearing, and shooting at their own shadows.

Slade waited, breath held.

Boom!

The booby-trapped grenade exploded among the frenzied attackers, hurling them to the ground in a blossom of yellow flame and silver sparks. The survivors fled wailing, and the arriving gun-trucks opened up, spraying fire randomly, killing many of their own. Slade cursed and hunkered down as ricochets slapped past his hide.

As more gun-trucks arrived, the men's courage and bravado returned. A man wearing a beret and camouflage uniform leaped from one of the vehicles, shouting curses at the men. Underlings approached him and pointed in different directions, gesturing wildly. The man then pulled out a whistle and began blowing on it between shouted commands. His cadre of fifty men responded with some semblance of order, springing to attention in a ragged formation. Cohesion was slowly gaining the upper hand.

The last of the gun-trucks arrived and parked beside the others in a perfect cluster, their headlights illuminating the yelling, pointing man.

Slade pulled himself to one knee and hoisted an RPG to his shoulder, the headlights of the nearest vehicle centered in its sights.

The night was rent by a tremendous flash and the hell-heat of a thermobaric detonation.

Slade picked up a steady rhythm. Hoist-cock-fire. Hoist-cock-fire . . .

Seven detonations tore through the scrambling raiders in quick succession, then an unending stream of tracers lashed the terror-stricken men, scything them down as they scattered away from their burning vehicles.

With his weapons empty and a dozen gun-trucks alight, Slade turned, trotted to his final hide-site, picked up the remaining weapons, exhausted them in short order, then made for his last rendezvous.

Upon reaching his horse, Slade climbed into the saddle and spurred forward, the guttural roar of the Judean cannon reverberating in the distance. He rode without stopping through the growing dawn, keeping to forested low ground and deep vegetation, putting distance between himself and the morning's action.

As the sun broke free of the horizon, Slade halted his flight, dismounted, and climbed the backside of a stone karst. Glassing the terrain to the south, he found a long dust cloud climbing the morning sky. He counted two dozen Judean vehicles fleeing down the southern road. They were not being pursued.

For the next four hours, Slade rode perpendicular to the Judeans escape route before finally turning south to parallel their course. Throughout his flight he kept his radio tuned to the Judeans tactical control frequency, listening to them as they made their way southbound. As the distance between them grew and terrain intruded, the radio traffic became broken and incomplete with long bursts of static and intermittent periods of silence.

But the fragments of conversations that did come through were becoming increasingly strained. Men began to shout back and forth across the net. Slade turned Big toward the nearest hill and galloped to the crest looking to find better radio reception. As he gained the peak, he heard a transmission as clear and sharp as the horror that bloomed in his heart.

"Mantis has the Cougars! He's taken them and is heading back to the bridge—"

Before the transmission was even finished, Slade had turned directly toward the Judeans and broken into a hard gallop, his course guided by a curtain of black smoke climbing the southern sky.

* * *

It was just past sunset by the time Slade reached the base of the smoke columns, their fires casting wavering beams of light through the forest canopy. The stench of burning rubber and plastics made the air difficult to breathe.

He counted five cargo trucks, three passenger vehicles, and the three Cougars, all burned down to frames of warped and charred steel. Mantis and his followers had broken from the main convoy and headed back toward New Zion, running themselves directly into the pursuing Penitents. The destroyed vehicles showed that their blind faith in the Cougars' firepower and their God had been misplaced.

Slade rode among the burning vehicles, counting the mutilated bodies that littered the roadway. There were more than a dozen corpses, all men, but not the hundred or more people that the passenger trucks could have carried.

Flashlight burning, Slade searched for a sign. He found a confused trampling of footsteps leading away from the passenger vehicles. The shoe marks of children and women. Slade imagined the horror as the Judeans had been herded along, the terror screams, the red-faced crying, the Penitents striking at them, drunk on a cocktail of power and their victims' fear.

A cluster of women's tracks led toward a clearing on the side of the road. Clothing and underwear were strewn about, the grass trampled flat. Another trail of footsteps led to a collection of tire tracks then disappeared. Over a hundred people had been herded into vehicles and then driven toward Ngongo.

With dread twisting in his stomach, Slade turned and rode after them, a long necklace of burning vehicles reaching to the horizon before him.

CHAPTER THIRTY-SEVEN

IT WAS THREE hours past nightfall when Slade crested the ridge-line above Ngongo, Big blowing and panting, Slade's face a mass of welts and scratches from the branch strikes he'd sustained in the dark. Blinking past sweat-stung eyes, Slade raised his binoculars and scanned the city below.

Enter hell.

Bonfires had been set throughout the town and in every corner of the commons, turning the entire settlement into a flickering battle of shadows, light, and writhing shapes. At the center of the commons lay a wailing crowd of Judeans; the women in various stages of disheveled undress, the men broken and bloody, all hemmed in by a pen made of trench fires, gunmen, and a dozen trucks, their headlights illuminating the cowering mass. And around the pen, already dozens of vertical poles, the forms atop them like bleached worms impaled, staring upward in their final scream. Beyond them, shovel teams were digging the postholes for a hundred more.

At intervals, one or two of the surrounding Penitents would charge the Judeans like predators darting into a school of prey, laughing, making a game of it, the loser of which was beaten to the ground and dragged away weeping. And beside the pen, driven by drums and loudspeaker hip-hop, the townsfolk screamed and leaped in a feverish blood rave. At the center of the maelstrom, the Priest stood upon his stage, pumping his scepter and shouting, feather headdress trembling as he conducted a sacrament of mass murder.

Slade tried to lower his binoculars as the next Judean was dragged to the stage, a withered old man, his waist-length beard his only modesty. The man fell to his knees, shouted toward the sky, and clasped his hands in prayer. Mantis.

Slade watched as Mantis was dragged up the stairs and across the stage that now glistened liquid black, his feet leaving drag marks in the thickening blood. At the top of the stage he was bent over the throne and his limbs restrained. Directly in front of Mantis, the Priest reached the apex of his dance, spittle and sweat flying from his beat-driven gyrations while feathers shaken from his headdress fell like technicolor snow. Four men dressed in tribal costume entered the commons, holding upright a sharpened wooden pole, twenty feet in length. The men advanced through the hysteric crowd, pole raised for all to see, while Mantis bucked and screamed and pissed himself in terror. The men climbed the stage, stopped behind Mantis, lowered the pole into alignment, set the tip, braced their feet then paused, waiting for the final command. Strutting across the stage the Priest put a cupped hand behind his ear and motioned for the crowd to make more noise. He feigned disappointment and demanded more enthusiasm. When at last he was satisfied, he dropped his hand in a chopping motion. The four impalers lunged forward, heaving on the shaft as Mantis went rigid and blew out his final scream. As he attempted to draw breath, the impalers heaved a second time and blood erupted from the Judean's mouth like a gargoyle rainspout.

The crowd went berserk.

The Priest approached Mantis' still thrashing body, grasped the stringy hair, lifted the head to properly align the throat, conferred advice upon his team, and then signaled for the final thrust whereupon Mantis' teeth hinged outwards and the pointed wooden shaft sprouted from his mouth, glistening and foreign.

Slade watched as the pole was then dragged to the impaling forest and raised to vertical, Mantis atop it dripping, arms and legs swinging like a disjointed puppet. Slade's lenses strayed along the forest of murdered Judeans, stark and pale in their final humiliation. He gazed in horror at the grotesque, distorted faces of those who had taken him in, carried him to freedom, and placed their trust in him. There, dangling nude, the nurse who had set his fingers. And Brother Hendrik, who had allowed him to stay. And there, the woman who handed Slade his meal every morning.

Dropping the binoculars, Slade clenched his fists till the knuckles popped. "No. No. No. Nooo!" Eyes tearing with shame and rage, eager to meet what end he could, Slade abandoned the last of his caution and started down the hill at a gallop.

Crashing across the flats and past the outermost shanties of the town, his nostrils filling with the stink of decaying garbage and human waste, Slade continued forward through a maze of crumbling cinder block buildings, all empty save for snarling gutter dogs. With the pressure of the drumbeat swelling in his chest, Slade advanced until he caught site of the baying crowd, its colors mixing and roiling like a slaughterhouse stew.

He couldn't continue forward on Big. He would be seen by every eye in the commons and shot or dragged off his mount within seconds. But in the churning darkness and the chaos of the moment, a man on foot might go unnoticed.

After a brief search, Slade found an abandoned car repair shop. He rode into the vehicle bay, dismounted, tied Big to a hydraulic lift, then hurrying, rifled through his saddlebags. The first 100-round drum magazine that he withdrew he slapped into his weapon. The second drum he clipped to his belt. He then pulled a fragmentation grenade from his vest and fed it into the underslung launcher. The rifle weighed in his hands ponderous and heavy, pregnant with dark potential. Next, he searched the building, found a filthy, threadbare blanket and threw it over his shoulders like a poncho, covering his clothing. Slade then unrolled the shemagh from around his neck, wrapped it around his head and face, drew his pistol, and bolted toward the commons.

The drumbeat was speeding up again, goading the mob into a higher frenzy as another Judean was led to the slaughter. The drums, the crowd, and celebratory gunfire were now deafening. Slade moved along the outskirts of the mob, weapons hidden beneath the blanket, keeping his speed up, angling toward the pen where the Judeans were held. Other than the direction in which he was heading, Slade had no plan—no plan other than the introduction of acute chaos.

He began to press his way through the crowd's outer rings, looking for a way through the stinking mass, but it was packed too tightly. He couldn't reach the pen this way. Searching for another avenue, he noticed a dilapidated two-story building standing on the shore of the churning sea. Children hung from its windows, gawking, dancing, and cheering at the spectacle. Turning on a new angle, Slade made his way toward the building, but a man did a double take, shouted, and grabbed Slade by the shoulder and tried to pull him around. Slade spun, gut shot the man with his pistol, and was on his way before the body hit the ground.

Reaching the building, Slade shouldered his way through the front door, found the stairs, and took them three at a time. The upper story was a looted office, the window crowded with hooting teenagers all jostling for a better view of the slaughter. Slade approached the first teen and delivered a vicious front kick that sent the kid sprawling into the others like a bowling pin. He then waded into their confused midst kicking and striking with the butt of his rifle, clearing them out. The confounded teens shrieked and ran, scrambling over each other to escape down the stairs. Within seconds, the floor had been emptied and not a shot fired.

Slade moved to the window and looked out over the crowd. The pen lay to his left. To his right, another Judean was being strapped to the sodden throne. It was Abe Howard.

For Slade, there were no more choices to be made, no path but one.

He retreated from the window a single step, lowered himself to one knee, set the rifle in his shoulder, straightened his spine, and pulled his arms tight against the rifle sling. His breathing slowed, then paused, and his finger fell toward the trigger.

CHAPTER THIRTY-EIGHT

CALM. BUDDHA CALM. The animal roar of the crowd ebbed. Colors flared, lines sharpened, and distance faded. The scope ranged the target, the red aim point glowing crimson on the nearest impaler.

Silence without end.

Crack! Crack! Crack! Crack! Crack!

The stage stood empty, the Priest's yellow headdress lay crumpled and blood-spattered on the ground. Slade shifted aim to one of the gun-trucks and moved his finger to the grenade trigger.

Mule kick to the shoulder.

The rifle came back down from its recoil as the detonation smashed through the commons and the truck's fuel tank ignited. The roaring crowd veered into panic and sporadic gunfire erupted as spears were hurled in all directions. The Penitents attacked the village muscle in confusion, their machetes flashing. The village muscle returned the favor and set against the Penitents with spear, club, and rifle. There was a frantic rush as the crowd exploded away like a flock of scattering birds.

A knifeman mounted the stage and advanced toward Abe, blade drawn. Slade tracked on him. Crack!

Fingers pointed up at Slade's window. Eyes turned on him. The jig was up. He descended the stairs at a sprint, feeding another grenade into the launcher.

Crouched in the door, he sought a clear path to the stage. A phalanx of bloodied Penitents armed with their swords and razor whips charged him in a frenzy. He brought the rifle to his shoulder, touched off the grenade, selected full-auto, then leaned into the stuttering weapon as it emptied its magazine and carved bloody gaps in the approaching wall. But they charged fearless and painless, limbs blown free, blood gushing, entrails hanging. Slade fell back into the building, the empty drum magazine dropping free. He hoisted the second drum into place, shouldered the rifle, smashed the trigger, and leaned into the wave as they funneled through the door like a tide, suiciding on his muzzle. As the last of them fell, Slade advanced, climbing up and over the moaning pile, face stomping the ones that still snarled and clawed at him.

As he cleared the building, men with guns advanced across the commons, spraying wildly. He cut them down then rose and sprinted forward through a blur of confusion, leaping over gibbering mounds, the rifle slapping against his shoulder.

He vaulted onto the stage, slick with a patina of gore, pulled his knife, and began to cut Abe free. "Where are the kids! Where are they!"

Abe worked his mouth but could produce no answer. Suddenly, the Priest, risen from the dead, charged across the stage directly at Slade, eyes red-rimmed with rage. Slade spun, drew his pistol as he fell back, and fanned the trigger. The Priest's head snapped to the side in a spray of blood, and he tumbled from the stage.

Recovering, setting to work on Abe's bonds, Slade looked toward the Judeans' pen. The jailors were caught up in the chaos, the trucks pulling away, gunning point blank into the Ngongo crowd. Some of the Judeans scrambled and ran into the darkness, others sat and wept.

"Ruuuuuun!" Slade bellowed. "Ruuuuuun!"

With his bonds cut, Abe staggered to his feet, eyes riven with fear and confusion. Slade pointed the way, then pushed and dragged Abe back across the commons. Within seconds they found themselves lost in the alleys now spinning with panicked mobs fighting both the Penitents and each other. Spears clattered against concrete. Slade spun and toppled a spearman with a burst.

They found the auto garage, guided by the sound of Big screaming and kicking at a clamoring mob. Slade charged into their midst, clubbing, smashing, and yelling until the room was clear. Calming the horse, Slade pushed Abe up into the saddle leaving a smear of blood on the polished leather. He gave Abe the reigns then led them into the alley, gun stuttering, sweeping and smoking, clearing the foot traffic. The magazine dropped away empty; he slapped a new one into place.

Gaining his bearings, Slade pointed Abe in the right direction and followed after him on foot, turning and hacking at the pursuing Penitents. With the alley cleared and with a moment's respite, he tried repeatedly to mount the horse with Abe, but repeatedly slipped and fell.

Just run, dammit.

Darting between the mud wattles, they cleared the village and bolted across open ground, trying to reach the ridgeline as a swarm of Penitents converged around them. Unable to mount, Slade slapped the horse forward up the hill then turned on their pursuers, fired another grenade, emptied another magazine and then another. He sprinted up the hill after Abe, stumbling in the dark, legs numb, throat caustic, chest imploding as he climbed the never-ending slope. Turning at the sound of gunfire, finding his rifle empty, he drew his pistol and punched down three more at close range.

Lungs searing, clutching at empty magazine pockets, Slade's legs began to buckle and cave. Suddenly, Big was beside him with Abe reaching down, grabbing him by the hair. Slade leaped, got a hand onto the far side of the saddle, and levered himself aboard as Abe popped the reins, yelled, and bolted them forward.

The shouting behind them faded to silence, drowned out by the sounds of galloping hooves, beats bringing life as clear and sweet as water.

CHAPTER THIRTY-NINE

NAVIGATING BY THE dim red glow of Slade's headlamp, they put two miles of thick forest between themselves and the Penitents before they halted. Slade dismounted gingerly, legs trembling, sick with fatigue. Abe slid to the ground in a heap, a steady runnel of blood flowing from under his shirt.

Slade knelt in front of Abe, put his hand on his shoulder, and looked him in the eye. "Stay with me, buddy. We've got five minutes then we're moving again."

Abe's chin began to tremble, his hands rose to cover his face, and a guttural sob escaped his lips.

"No! Not now!" Slade grabbed Abe's face and fixed his eyes with an intensity that was indistinguishable from rage. "Nothing exists except the next ten seconds. Understand?"

Abe nodded dumbly.

"Okay, lie back, let me have a look at you." Slade eased Abe to the ground then gently pulled the Judean's hands away from his abdomen to reveal the bubbling spring from which blood ran black as engine oil. He broke open the med kit he kept in his cargo pocket, pulled out a Kerlix bandage, and tore the sterile plastic packaging. The bandage was a narrow ribbon of fabric that when unrolled was over twelve feet long. As Slade unrolled the bandage, he fed it directly into the bullet hole, pressing it in with his finger, three knuckles deep. "Sorry, bro, this is gonna suck."

"What are you doing?" Abe gasped, spasming away from Slade's touch.

"What I got to."

"Oh, Lord! Oh, dear Lord!" Abe wailed as Slade fed foot after foot of the bandage into his innards. When the bandage was gone, Slade found the exit wound on Abe's back, packed in another twelve feet of Kerlix, then sealed both punctures with tape.

Slade checked his watch. "That's five minutes. Time to move." Ignoring Abe's ragged sobs, he helped the Judean to his feet, pushed him up into the saddle, climbed on with him, then set off into the night.

* * *

An hour later, Slade could no longer ignore Abe's desperate pleas to stop. Dismounting, he laid Abe down beneath a flowering tree that still dripped from a newly passed storm. Abe's voice was frail and weak, his breathing shallow, his face pale as plaster. Slade inspected the wound; it was still sealed, but Abe's belly was grossly distended and turgid. The wound was bleeding internally, slowly filling Abe's abdomen with blood. There was nothing more Slade could do.

When Slade extinguished the headlamp, they could see nothing in the utter-dark, and so, spoke to each other's shadow-self, their words halting and incomplete.

"Did anybody . . . get away?" Slade asked.

Abe's head shook back and forth. "I don't know."

Slade formed two words in his mouth and regretted it the moment that he spoke them: "Isaac? Elizabeth?"

A sob came in the darkness. "I tried . . . I tried . . . I'm so sorry . . ." The remaining words were lost in strangled agony.

Slade covered his face and the air left him. "You idiot! You fucking idiot. You let Mantis kill you all!" Slade then spoke to himself. "I should have stopped him. I was supposed to do it. I was the one."

"No," Abe gasped, "you're not a murderer. God gave us choices, Slade. I made mine as I had to. So did you. This was God's plan."

"God's plan! Everyone's dead, Abe! Everyone! Your family is dead!"

Abe wept without reserve, his body contorting with sobs of purest anguish. In time, he grew too weak to cry and his breathing slowed. "It's okay, Slade. It's okay. Their suffering is at an end. With God's blessing, I'll be with them soon enough."

Slade pointed back toward Ngongo. "He doesn't *bless*, Abe, he *punishes*. He exacts retribution! Fuck your God and damn you for trusting him. He—" Slade's voice cracked and he covered his eyes and could go no further.

In the following silence, there was only the sound of Slade's erratic breathing and the patter of water dripping from the tree overhead. Abe raised a wavering hand and placed it on Slade's arm. His voice was weak, barely audible, and strangely peaceful. "What was it, Slade . . . What was it that made you so angry?"

Slade struggled for long moments, attempting to utter words that would not come. When he finally did speak, the sounds that his mouth issued seemed alien and incomprehensible, as if forming words never spoken by man during the whole of the earth's turning.

"We . . . we were in Turkey, watching the Syrian border, chasing HVTs northeast of Kobani . . . Trying to locate the facilitators and money men that were smuggling Jihadis across . . . My recon team was set up in a good location, recording the local pattern of life."

Slade raised his head and looked into the surrounding darkness, seeing before him the rolling hills and dusty plains of northern Syria. "We could see for twenty miles across the flats, clusters of

cinder block hovels, the orchards, the dry fields plowed but un-
planted. I could never figure out how they watered the fields. That
always stuck with me... We watched the firefights, the vehicle movements, the Jihadis chasing and slaughtering the refugees whenever
they made a dash for Turkey. Entire families were cut down in front
of us—parents, grandparents, kids, uncles, cousins. We watched it
for days; it looked like they were playing a game of hide-and-seek.
We grew numb to it, made jokes, kept score.

"On the fourth night, we left our hide on foot and headed back
to base. Our route took us past a section of the border where the
fence had been torn up—border was nothing but an idea in that
place. We heard a noise coming from the other side, over in Syria. I
saw something through my night vision goggles." Slade pointed to
the darkness in front of him. "It was a pile of shapes and bundles,
ragged lumps strewn about, a refugee family that almost made it.
About fifteen people." Slade drew a deep breath. "What we'd heard
was a kid . . . sobbing quietly, still alive. She was whispering . . .
Saedny ya Allah, over and over. *Saedny ya Allah* . . . She was praying,
asking God for help. Asking him to send somebody..." Slade wiped
at his face and covered his eyes. "And there I stood . . ."

Abe squeezed Slade's arm, offering encouragement.

"My guys wanted to go get her, step across the border, take her
back to our hospital. But we had orders not to enter Syria, so I told
them no. They kept pushing, said nobody would know which side
we got her from. I stood there for... I don't know how long. I knew
what the right thing was, what I should do, but . . . I couldn't.

"So I gave the order, told my men to shut the hell up and get back
in file. Then I led them back to base. Debriefed. Took a shower. Ate
a hot meal. Watched a movie." Slade went silent.

When there was nothing more forthcoming, Abe struggled to
raise his head. "You're a good man, Slade. Something stopped you.
What was it?"

"I was . . ." Slade pressed at his eyes until he saw sunspots. "I was afraid of what I would find over there. That I would find those people, the refugees, were . . . No different from me . . . No different from the people I love. If I found that out, saw it with my own eyes, picked up that little girl and saw her loss . . . That would change the meaning . . ."

"Of what?"

"Of everything."

Abe squeezed Slade's arm weakly, the last of his strength ebbing.

"Abe, God didn't put me there so that I might show mercy. Mercy means nothing to him. He put me there so that I might understand his world and therefore understand him. But I was a coward, turned my back, and walked away so that I could continue living in a world I knew." Slade sat up straight, his eyes liquid. "So he killed my son in return. Next day I found out that Nicholas had drowned at a birthday party back home." With the words finally spoken, Slade placed his hand on Abe's chest and let it rest there, feeling the absolute stillness that had taken hold within. "And that's how I met God."

Alone, utterly alone, Slade rose and paced back and forth, tearing at his hair, wandering, lost.

CHAPTER FORTY

Crouched in the darkness, without family, friend, or country, Slade Crawford had arrived at his road's end. In his right hand his finger rested on the trigger of his final salvation. He turned the pistol in the red lamplight and examined the intricate mechanisms and pathways that comprised its form. He tested its weight, read the lines rendered in steel, and held in regard its only truth—that man desired above all things the power to destroy that which God had made. In that respect the pistol was no different than he—useless in the pursuit of all enterprise or designs, save one.

He peered down its shaded bore like one gazing upon a seer-stone, took sightless inventory of his world, and saw that it was littered with loss, missteps, and betrayal. Flexing the trigger, trembling, he pressed further and looked upon the whole of his life, the sum total of his days and found only a legacy written in blood and chaos, one of trespass and ruptured forms.

And in that moment of ultimate despair, he found himself able to look upon the terrible question that still squirmed in the depths of his self-loathing: What if his son, Nicolas, had instead lived and grown to manhood? What was the boy's inheritance? What knowledge and understandings would Slade have gifted? How to extinguish men and undo their works? That it was as easy as pinching out a candle flame?

And if his son had asked him *why*? Could Slade say that he had served some greater good, that there existed some just and noble machine that required a cog such as he?

The answer lay deeper in the darkness if he pressed but further ...

Slade startled at the sound of the hammer snapping home on an empty chamber. Dropping the pistol, he sagged forward and wept into his hands.

CHAPTER FORTY-ONE

KRAVEN'S SAT-PHONE CHIMED from inside of the saddlebag. Slade waited until his breathing slowed before he removed his hands from his face. He glanced to his right where the phone pulsed like a slow-beating heart inside the bag. He made no move to answer it. In time the chiming ceased, but the message light continued to pulse softly in the darkness, a dim reminder that the world still stood, that the grand machine ground on without pause. Slade drew his sleeve across his running nose. He was not free to end his life, there was still work required of him. But first he had to attend to the task at hand. Not rage—Not revenge—

Retribution.

* * *

Small groups of Penitents roamed the forests and plains searching for Judeans and Ngongo villagers. They made no effort to conceal themselves, talking and laughing as they searched with flashlights and torches, still drunk on the night's slaughter. Slade found an isolated band and stalked them at a distance. When they had tired of the night's entertainment, they lit a small fire and laid down beside it, whereupon Slade fell on them and slew them while they slept. Walking among their ragged forms, he stooped to each in turn, opened their throats, and then carved the brands from their chests, placing his boot against their necks as they sobbed and thrashed beneath him. When the task was completed, Slade turned his gaze toward another campfire flickering in the distance.

* * *

Dawn broke over the horizon to reveal six Penitents facedown in the dirt. Two of them dead in their own blood puddles, the remaining four still moaning and crying, their hands zip-tied behind them, each of their Achilles and hamstring tendons cut through to the bone, leaving garish smiles spread across the backs of their legs.

Slade wiped the blood from his knife, sheathed it, and crouched over a pile of their belongings. He lifted a backpack and shook out its contents: candy bars, a knife, narcotics, a cell phone, a bottle of water. Slade set the cell phone aside and moved onto the next bag. As he lifted the pack and shook out its contents, his heart stumbled then took off at a sprint.

A US Government Issue, 1911, .45 caliber pistol. Well worn.

There wasn't another like it for 5,000 miles. Slade lifted the pistol and examined it, checked the chamber and magazine. It was empty, all rounds having been fired.

Moving quickly, Slade combed through the remaining packs and gathered up six cell phones. He opened them, gained access with the Penitents' thumbprints, then began paging through the media files. All contained jostling videos of the Judeans during their capture. Slade gritted his teeth and watched, jaw flexing, sweat beading on his forehead as he took in a vile collage of murder and rape. He noticed a shock of jet black hair in the background of a picture. He expanded the image. Elizabeth. Slade picked up the other cell phones and began comparing the media. He read the time stamps,

studied the locations, vantage points, and people present, tying together the broken threads of the story: The adults had been herded
into pickups then driven to Ngongo for slaughter. Elizabeth and
some of the other teens had been herded into a large cargo truck,
but that vehicle did not reappear in any videos taken at Ngongo. It
had gone elsewhere.

Slade walked to the four remaining Penitents and lowered himself to one knee where they could clearly see him. He dropped the
magazine from his Sig, thumbed out four bullets, and used them
to reload and charge the 1911. He then showed the Penitents pictures of Elizabeth and the cargo truck on their cell phones, then a
map of Tanzania on his wrist computer. "Where?" he asked slowly.
"Where did the truck with the girl go?"

He knelt beside the first Penitent, pressed the barrel of the 1911
against the man's eye, and repeated the question.

"Fuck you!" The man raised his nose in a sneer and pursed his
lips to spit as the .45 detonated.

Slade wiped his face clean and moved onto the next Penitent, positioned the dripping pistol against the man's eyeball, and repeated
the question.

"Where? Where did the truck with the girl go?"

"Nairobi! Girls go Nairobi!"

"Nairobi, Kenya?"

"Yes! Nairobi, girls go Nairobi!"

"Why Nairobi?"

"Sell them kids. Sell them for good moneys."

"Sell them kids?"

"Yes, sell them kids, very good moneys."

"Looks like I'm going to Nairobi," Slade whispered to himself.

Before he mounted Big and rode from the site, Slade secured the
1911 in his saddlebags, its magazine empty.

Slade studied the maps on his wrist computer. He would follow the eastern branch of the Great Rift Valley, due north across Tanzania, traversing terrain as rugged and varied as anywhere on earth; bone-dry deserts, open savannah, rain-forested mountains, glaciers, and active volcanoes, over 600 miles of rough, unknowable terrain. The battery on his wrist computer was fading and he would have no maps showing where to find shelter, food, or water.

He would be there in ten days.

* * *

Taking a bearing off his compass, Slade set his shoulders north toward Nairobi. Hips sawing steadily, he kept a brisk pace, taking rest when needed and drinking when thirsty. Days passed full of azure skies, emerald plains, heat, sweat, and the taste of wild game.

Over a muddy river, brown and laconic, Big's hooves rang the iron bridge, flaking great scabs of rust like stricken butterflies into the water below.

Through the following days, Slade rode on highways split by trees and through the remains of failed cities, the dead citizenry scattered and intertwined in the sweet spring grass, their skulls popping and snapping beneath Big's hooves. Here the nights were star-choked and fragrant, filled with night birds and moonshine orbs reflected from hyena-pack eyes that slouched and cackled through the night like black witchlings.

He rode down into and through a fire-stormed land of gray ash drifted so deep that his horse became mired in the thick talcum, then across a flat plain where a following wind swept their dust along with them till man and horse were obscured in the haze of their own going like some great jinn conjured forth across the plains.

On the eighth day, man and horse rested among the thatched huts, zebra rugs, and ivory tusks of an abandoned safari lodge. Returning from a hunt, Slade hung the rusted meat hooks with fresh game, dripping crimson, and stared sightless into the brazier as lard sizzled and spat upon coals resurrected.

Roaming the dusty halls and empty rooms, he dressed himself in salvaged clothing, polished a mahogany dining table, straightened its chairs, set its places, and lit its candles. Clattering through the pantry, he unearthed a Sapphire gin bottle then poured the stemware full. When each place was served and the chair pushed in, he took his seat beneath the glittering stares of mounted beast heads then used his teeth to pull chunks of flesh from a platter of steaming shanks. When he was sated, he ran a napkin over his wet hands and dripping beard, then raised a glass to the empty seats and toasted by name each of the beloved ghosts seated there.

With the bottle drained of its spirits and the china smashed to shimmering dust, he lifted a fire of his own making to the thatched roof huts and set the world ablaze while above him an immense storm thundered and strobed. Driven by buffeting winds, the flames flowed around him in a luminous river then surged out across the savannah, setting it alight and driving before it everything that lived.

Slade stood atop his quaking shadow, naked and raving, anchored to this world by the barest of threads, calling out across the burning plains for the ones forever lost to him.

Were his own name called openly, he would have reckoned it for that of a stranger.

CHAPTER FORTY-TWO

VIEWED THROUGH SLADE'S binoculars, Nairobi appeared as two distinct cities, neither of which lay entirely comfortable with the other. The western half of the city reclined among forested hills, its red tiled roofs and neatly trimmed gardens slowly succumbing to a riot of resplendent trees and creeping vines while herds of cattle grazed where white-clad golfers once roamed.

In stark contrast, Nairobi's eastern reaches were a congested industrial slum, pocked with an acne of alkali strip mines, cavernous warehouses, flooded gravel pits, and fields of tin-roofed shanties. Even now, nothing save rot grew among the cramped housing projects and sprawling trash fields while rusting iron piled in drifts along its twisting footpaths.

Straddling the divide between these two worlds rose a cluster of skyscrapers, conference centers, hotels, and sports stadiums. And from the very center of that glass-and-steel garden rose the Asubuhi Tower. Yearning to be the tallest in the world, the Asubuhi Tower was supposed to have been the exclamation point announcing Africa's birth into the modern age. Now, a perfect epitaph, it stood as an unfinished skeleton of spiraling columns draped in a veil of collapsed gantries, toppled cranes, and shattered windows.

Crouched in the shaded reaches of the surrounding hills, Slade watched as the lowering sun set the tower afire and clouds of night birds took flight from its cavernous hollows. He panned his binoculars over the city, watching sporadic vehicle traffic flow along its roads and smoke drift from its chimneys. A familiar droning sound turned his face skyward. Overhead, a white C-130 cargo plane drifted past, landing gear extended, flaps lowered, the "UN" painted on its tail clearly visible.

Civilization lived.

* * *

Slade drew Kraven's sat-phone and powered it up, battling against the rage that clouded his vision, and set his hands to trembling. There was a special place reserved in hell for Colonel Kraven and Slade intended to send him there. But for now, he would play Kraven's game and milk him for equipment and resources as he searched for Elizabeth. Slade would settle their score at a later date. Kraven had said that the evidence against Summer belonged to him and him alone. That meant that it would die with him.

Slade pressed Kraven's speed dial.

The line opened.

"I show you encrypted," a digitized voice said.

Slade moved to speak but failed.

"I show you encrypted," Kraven repeated. "Go ahead."

Slade's fingernails pressed deep grooves in his palm. "I'm here," he said.

"Understood."

"Who's my on-scene contact?"

"There is none."

"You're kidding."

"No."

"You have no assets to receive me?"

"None that you can tap."

"Christ." Slade shook his head in frustration. "I also need a better vector on my objective. What level of intel are you looking for?"

"The info you gleaned from the Chinese settlement pointed toward Nairobi as the Penitents' base of operations. Find them. Map their leadership pyramid. Find their money trail, logistics train, weapons pipeline, recruitment pool. All of it."

"And you want that from a one-man operation that has no cover story, no equipment, no contacts, and stands out like a hard-on in church?"

"Affirmative."

"It'll cost you," Slade snorted. "I'll need high-end equipment: giga-pixel network cams, e-snoops, night optics, cash, iron, security, the works. I'm running a CR-30 rifle and Sig 45 compact, I'll need a suppressor for the .45 and subsonic ammo for both."

"Copy all. Give me a drop location. I'll get a package to you."

Slade looked over his shoulder. The edge of the clearing where he was sitting was as good as any. "Point Of Impact, two hundred meters north of my current location. Run in heading . . . 0-4-5 degrees. And don't skimp, Colonel. Make sure the computer has an industrial-strength web crawler with strong artificial intelligence and voice interface. I can't program for shit."

"Understood."

"And one other thing," Slade said. "Who are these guys and why do you care?"

The line was already dead.

*　*　*

Slade lay on his back, binoculars in hand, watching for passing satellites in the clear night sky. Big pawed the ground beside him, grazing contentedly, uprooting long mouthfuls of greenery. The scent of cut grass, warm leather, and horse drifted on the evening air.

Slade chewed on the conversation with Kraven. The colonel's lack of candor was understandable. The more Slade knew, the more of a liability he became, the more damage he could do if he talked to the wrong people. As long as Kraven didn't actually tell him anything, and only gave him tasks, Slade would be nothing more than an international fugitive with a wild story. That part made sense, but why the inability to commit normal military resources? If he ordered it, Kraven could have a platoon of skilled operators walking the streets of Nairobi within hours. With a little more planning, he could ensure that the men were of African descent, skilled in local languages, and dressed in local garb. With a little more effort, they could be backed up by National Intelligence Assets, a Cyber Warfare unit, and a squadron of surveillance drones operating above 30,000 feet. Those assets already existed and the channels for using them were well established—

Slade's train of thought was derailed by a faint rushing sound followed by snapping brush and a light *tump*.

He rose to his feet and brushed off his clothing. Weapon slung across his back, Slade crossed the open field, grass swishing between his knees. Big followed, sniffing cautiously. In the faint starlight, he was able to make out an irregular shape lying flaccid in the grass; it was a large, fabric parawing, collapsed, and wavering. Taking the slick fabric in hand, Slade pulled on it until he found one of the nylon risers then followed it down to where it attached to a carbon fiber fuselage the size of a large bathtub. The object was cold to the touch. Feeling in the dark, he located sturdy plastic locks, popped them open, and raised the lid. Freezing air fogged from the interior.

The device was a JAV-47 Wind Drifter, designed to covertly resupply American forces operating in hostile environments. Dropped from high altitude, the device deployed its nylon parawing then autonomously steered itself to a predetermined location. With the right altitude and winds, the Wind Drifter could deliver a thousand-pound payload more than fifty miles. The freezing air trapped in the fuselage betrayed this vehicle's high-altitude, long-distance flight.

Slade risked a dim light and scanned the interior. Strapped to the bottom of the tub was a large military backpack and two gray objects similar to soda cans. Slade freed the backpack, braced a foot against the fuselage, and grunted it up onto his shoulders. It was surprisingly heavy. He then hoisted up the gray cylinders. They were AN-M14 thermite grenades. Kraven wanted no evidence left behind.

Gathering up the parawing, Slade piled the black fabric next to the fuselage. He then tucked one grenade into his utility belt and grasped the other in his right hand, ensuring that the metal spoon was firmly pinned beneath his fingers. With his free hand, he yanked out the stiff safety pin, extended his arm, and dropped the grenade into the Wind Drifter. There was an instantaneous *pop* followed by brash hissing and an acrid plume of smoke. He repeated the procedure for the second grenade, then grabbed Big's reins and walked rapidly from the site, eyes averted. Behind him the two grenades flashed to life, flickering with an unearthly orange light, splashing raw heat over the back of his exposed neck and hands. Burning at over 4,500 degrees Fahrenheit, the thermite grenades could convert rocks into flowing red mush or an engine block into a bubbling puddle of liquid steel. Within seconds the parawing and fuselage were blazing cinders as was the brush and small stand of trees it had landed near. His path lit by the roaring inferno, long shadows trembling, Slade rode from the valley and into the sheltering darkness.

For Slade, the arrival of the Wind Drifter raised more questions. Why hadn't the cargo aircraft just flown to Slade's position to deliver the goods using a conventional parachute drop? It would have been a lot cheaper, simpler, and more reliable. Instead, the cargo aircraft had flown to within fifty miles of him but then chosen *not* to over-fly Slade's location. Kraven preferred to throw away an expensive Wind Drifter rather than have his cargo aircraft approach Nairobi. And given that there was no Kenyan government to file a protest, then who was this operation being concealed from? Watching Kraven tiptoe around Nairobi was like watching the Yankees refuse to play ball in New York.

Everything indicated that normal military ops in Nairobi were forbidden. The colonel was handcuffed, and Slade was his work-around. And who could handcuff a man like Kraven?

Washington, DC.

A smile opened a bloody fissure in Slade's chapped lips. He had just found Kraven's pulsing jugular. All he needed was a way to open it.

CHAPTER FORTY-THREE

SLADE SAT ON a shaded bluff, chewing on the last of his sun-dried antelope jerky. In the distance the morning sun threw copper gild across the slums and gleaming towers of Nairobi while the smoke from breakfast cook-fires lent an ivory haze to the vision.

He unzipped the upper compartment of his new backpack and inspected its contents. The bag contained four multicolored bricks of currency sealed in plastic wrapping, prepaid debit cards, and a false ID that claimed his name was Thomas Molton. There was also electronic intrusion gear, ultra hi-resolution cameras, frequency monitors, modem parasites, card readers, a ruggedized tablet computer, compact VR goggles, memory chips, and equipment for analyzing biometric and DNA evidence.

The backpack's lower compartment contained a pair of faceted "fly-eye" synthetic vision goggles, batteries, concealable gel armor, intrusion alarms, micro trip-mines, and an urban ops man-purse. Packed beneath that was a suppressor, boxes of sub-sonic ammunition, tools, night optics, and infrared targeting lasers.

Slade lifted the suppressor out and rolled it back and forth in his palm, feeling its weight. A new idea surfaced, causing the sweat on his forehead to chill. Perhaps American boots on the ground were *not* forbidden. Perhaps Kraven, under orders, simply needed a deniable assassin. It would explain the presence of the CIA spook back at the Judean mess tent. The CIA was no doubt neck deep in their endless shadow wars, particularly now while Africa's future was so fluid. There would inevitably be people whose views of that future ran counter to the CIA's. People would have to be eliminated . . .

Slade felt sick as, one by one, the pieces clicked into place and the immense, grinding machine revealed itself. Taking pictures and filing reconnaissance reports was one thing, becoming Kraven's personal assassin was another entirely. Slade would not be alone in Nairobi. Kraven's men would be there to watch over him, ensure that he did his job, and when the time came, dispose of him.

He fisted the silencer back into the backpack, stood, then lashed the gear onto Big's saddle with abrupt, violent movements. He pulled himself into the saddle and popped the reins.

His fate awaited.

CHAPTER FORTY-FOUR

WEAPON RESTING ACROSS his knees, Slade entered the sprawling outskirts of Nairobi and passed through its shaded suburbs. Smelling woodsmoke, he rode cautiously through a neighborhood where laughing children played soccer.

Skirting a planted field, its crops sprouting emerald and gold, he passed a column of brightly clothed women chattering gaily, teeth aglow, water jugs balanced atop their heads. All eyes turned to follow him, but life continued on uninterrupted.

Still cautious, he avoided an intersection where blue-helmeted soldiers sat lazily around a checkpoint. If the UN soldiers noticed him, they gave no indication.

As the city rose to surround him, swaying green life and the calls of songbirds gave way to rusting steel and the sound of Big's hoofs scratching over sanded concrete. Small children stalked the American, palms outstretched. Beautiful women dressed in colorful *kitenge* smiled at him, flashing rows of glossy pearls and polished gold. Other women, their hair covered in black *hijab,* slunk away, eyes averted. The ammonia stink of piss mixed with the smell of woodsmoke and cooking meat.

A small company of turbaned riders trotted past, their yellow-stained eyes scrolling over the strange arrival, their threadbare mounts shying and stamping. The riders continued on, their weapons untouched.

A withered old man crutched toward Slade and offered up some ragged bundle for barter. Big swung his massive head and struck at the man like a cobra, jaws popping like a sprung trap. The man recoiled. Slade tipped his hat in apology and rode on.

Around him now small shops offered their polished garbage wares and the city became confused and eclectic, taking on the feel of a mushroom trip and Burning Man dream.

In the streets, a honking flow of tuk-tuks, stretch limousines, buses, tractors, livestock, and exotic sports cars, some pulled by donkeys, many bedecked in Christmas lights and nightclub strobes. Sharing the thoroughfares were crowds of locals bedecked in a menagerie of Western casual, haute couture, military camouflage, wedding gowns, and tribal skins; a Dr. Seuss playground, the plundered riches of a dead world raised like Lazarus and sent spinning down the streets and alleys of an alien planet.

As night approached, the last of the shops closed, their metal shades clacking down from rollers while derelict bus hulks were pushed in front of doors like medieval barricades. Riding quickly, Slade entered the steel-and-glass plateau of the city center as the last crimson shades of daylight retreated up shattered skyscrapers and thick shadows puddled in the alleyways. Women vanished from the streets, and the shopkeepers followed soon thereafter while knots of young men, increasingly raucous, dragged rubbish into piles for burning.

Up ahead was a growing blaze of electric light and noise: music— like dull pounding from inside clubs; shrieks of laughter growing; the incessant background hum of diesel generators. Slade spurred toward the growing light pool where UN soldiers dressed in mishmash uniforms stood ragged at its rim, as though to keep both the night and its citizens at bay. The dull glow of their cigarettes bobbed lazily as they waved him through.

Crossing the terminator between darkness and light, Slade found himself in another world. Here, gaudily appointed nightclubs and restaurants lined the streets, spilling their thick beats and rich smells into now crowded streets. Neon signs sputtered and flickered in time with techno and hard rock while whore-dressed women beckoned and hooted at loose knots of Western men, luring them into bars and clubs.

Slade dismounted and continued on foot, leading Big in such a way that his face was largely obscured behind his mount. He noted fresh horse dung scattered along the streets. Man and horse garnered an occasional glance but no direct scrutiny; rough men were not uncommon in these parts.

He approached a man wearing riding boots and asked him where both he and Big could obtain accommodations. The man pointed down the street and stated that the Grand Regency could accommodate both man and horse.

Continuing on, Slade found the Grand Regency hotel, a soot-stained ivory tower, its upper floors cloaked by the descending ceiling of night. At the hotel's entrance, lit by flickering torch and pale klieg lights, a dozen ramshackle taxis and tuk-tuks queued to service groups of men who strolled at regular intervals from its glass and marble interior. Most of the men wore sidearms.

Approaching the hotel directly was not optimal; the fewer details that people knew about his arrival, the better. He looked for an opportunity to present itself and found it in a pair of billy-club guards who stood on a street corner. A small bribe sent one of them to fetch a hotel bellhop. While the man was gone, Slade engaged the remaining guard. The man was former Kenyan military and was now employed as a night watchman for the central district. He was under strict orders not to interfere with foreigners and was tasked with keeping local Africans in order. Slade was still pumping him for information when the other guard returned, a uniformed bell-hop in tow.

Slade asked the young bellhop if the hotel offered stable services for its guests. The boy said yes and pointed toward a cluster of buildings on the edge of Uhuru Park. Slade instructed the boy to lead him there, and within thirty minutes, Big was comfortably stabled with a week's board paid up front. Slade then gave the boy a stack of small bills and instructed him to fetch a baggage cart, three large suitcases, and a blanket.

Twenty minutes later, the boy returned with the requested gear. Slade placed his personal equipment and rifle into the luggage. He then heaved Kraven's backpack onto the luggage cart, covered it with the blanket, and stacked the suitcases atop it. Retaining only his belt and holstered Sig, Slade turned toward the hotel.

The interior of the Grand Regency hotel was an ivory-columned atrium, choked with potted trees and flowering plants. Along the walls of the lobby, torches and gas lamps had been placed at regular intervals. The torches were dead now, but the soot marks above them spoke to frequent usage during power outages.

The bellhop gestured toward a polished mahogany reception desk, behind which stood well-groomed attendants. Beside the counter a large chalkboard announced the hours during which electricity would be available. Beside that stood a refrigerator from which bottled water could be obtained.

Slade moved toward the desk, noting that the armed guards inside the atrium were discreet, well equipped, and Western. Slade looked them over, wondering which ones were in Kraven's employ, which ones would be reporting his arrival, and which ones would be assigned to silence him. Slade gave each of the guards a pet name based upon a distinguishing physical characteristic. He would have to be able to identify them on site, for if he ever encountered one of these men in a dark hallway, it would not be a coincidence.

An attractive African woman with a brilliant smile looked up from her work. "Good evening, sir. Welcome to the Grand Regency. How may I help you this evening?" She spoke with a crisp accent that betrayed Kenya's colonial past.

Slade's response was polite, brief, and without detail. After checking in and receiving his room key, he found the concierge and gave the man a list of supplies he needed for immediate delivery. The concierge said that the merchants would not be available at this hour. Slade gave him enough money to ensure that they would.

Key in hand, Slade climbed the stairs, two bellhops struggling behind with his luggage. The second-floor hallway was dim and smelled of urine and bleach. Stopping outside his door, he tipped the bellhops then motioned for the boys to leave. When they were clear of the hallway, he drew his pistol, flicked on the targeting light, then let himself in. The interior lights worked. Slade kept the targeting light on as he cleared the room, closet, kitchenette, and bathroom. Satisfied that the room was empty, he pulled his bags inside and locked the door. The once luxurious room was thoroughly worn but well cared for. The carpet was stained but swept, the sheets bone-yellow but ironed smooth.

Clicking off the overhead lights, Slade moved to the window and opened the curtains. His window was sturdy, locked from the inside, and offered a quick escape should it be required. The view from the window overlooked a lush courtyard, in the center of which lay a sapphire pool and open-air restaurant, both empty at this late hour. Closing the curtains, he looked about his room, shoulders slumping, overcome by a wave of crushing fatigue. He holstered his pistol, moved to the bed, sat heavily upon it, and massaged his temples. He leaned back, spine popping, descending slowly, submerging himself in the foreign comfort of the bed. His eyes drooped in the soothing darkness.

A light tapping sound.

Slade rolled from the bed, weapon extending, targeting light on, blinking rapidly. He'd been asleep. Damn.

Knocking at the door again, slightly louder this time. He rose, moved to the door, opened the lock, then backed away, his weapon still raised. "Come in."

The door creaked open timidly. "Your parcels for you, suh."

"Set them down inside the door."

The concierge stepped into the room, visibly nervous, one hand shielding his eyes from the targeting light. He set down a number of bulging plastic shopping bags before backing away.

"Before you go . . ." Slade moved to the blinded man and slid a bill into his hand. "For your trouble."

"Yes, suh." The man nodded and left. He would be more than pleased when his sight returned.

Barring the door again, Slade turned on the room lights. He then pulled the blankets and sheets off the bed, manhandled the mattress across the room, and stood it against the door. It was followed in short order by both box springs. Anybody coming through the door would be slowed substantially. He then unbuckled his belt and holster and set them within arm's reach. He piled the blankets in the corner and lay atop them, fully dressed, feet toward the barricade. A thrown pillow knocked off the light switch and darkness descended upon his world.

CHAPTER FORTY-FIVE

THE FOLLOWING DAY was already spent and fading when Slade awoke, his back throbbing and kinked. Groaning softly, joints popping, he levered himself from the floor, stretched his back, and glanced about the room as if seeing it for the first time. Through sleep-smeared eyes his watch told him that he had been asleep for fifteen hours.

He bent and retrieved his pistol belt, secured it to his waist, then shuffled to the window and pulled back the curtains. A small crowd had already formed in the courtyard and was taking drinks and dinner at the poolside bar. His eyes tracked a waiter pushing a tray of food. He had his vector, but first the details . . .

Slade opened the bags the concierge had delivered and pawed through their contents. Everything he'd requested was there: a fresh change of clothes, soap, shears, razor, floss, brush, paste, and first aid kit. He turned toward the mirror. Normally, he would have inspected his face, the better to gauge the ordeal he'd just endured. He would have examined the grime-clogged pores, waxy teeth, debris-matted beard, and xylophone ribs. Instead, he kept his gaze averted, avoiding his own eyes, not wanting to see what lived within them.

After forty-five minutes of showering, abrading, shearing, and clipping, he'd unearthed a form that was passably human. Another ten minutes were spent lancing the blisters and bandaging the saddle sores that decorated his inner thighs. Finished there, he tried on the clothes he'd ordered; the socks, cargo pants, and collared shirt were an acceptable fit. He smoothed at his hair, checked his teeth, smelled his armpits, then turned for the door.

* * *

Minutes later, Slade sat poolside taking an early dinner. The steak, promptly served, was bloody, the fruit fragrant, the coffee bitter. He found that he had to restrain himself from shoveling the food directly into his mouth with both hands.

He shared the pool deck with a smattering of patrons and sunbathers taking in the last of the day's sun. The sight of tropical drinks and neon bikinis was jarring after so many days of want and filth. As cosmopolitan as it appeared, barbed wire and an armed guard on the containment wall were stark reminders of what lurked beyond.

Slade stayed at the restaurant for an hour, finished off another complete entrée, then moved on to the bar. His senses dulled by the mammoth dinner, he passed on the alcohol and ordered tonic water instead. As night fell, the crowd grew steadily, cheered on by Euro-lounge beats, tiki torches, and a steady flow of international liquors and beers. Slade remained aloof from the holiday atmosphere, listened to conversations, identified accents, judged clothing, and appraised jewelry.

Standing at the bar, locked in a running battle with the hotel's liquor cabinet, tattooed and heavily muscled security contractors laughed, caroused, and backslapped. The cowboys.

Sitting in the corners, long-haired activists tapped furiously on their iPads, updating their blogs, Instagram, and Facebook profiles. At the table next to Slade, a sullen hipster sipped a slushy fruit drink, ate the cherry from the umbrella, adjusted his man bun, then posted a teary-eyed dispatch from the hot zone.

Less in numbers, but more liberal with the cash and bottle service, was a knot of balding banker types with soft skin and heavy watches. They spoke with American, Asian, and European accents. Slade pegged them as bureaucrats from the various UN agencies in town. Many of the softies had corporate logos stitched on their polo shirts, no doubt the midlevel managers overseeing fat construction contracts.

The bar's three tribes had little in common except for their collective interest in a small clutch of women that held court at the center of the patio; young, photogenic, and supremely confident, they were the television reporters, glam-aid workers, and celebrities passing through town, all eager to get a head-shot of themselves feeding black people.

Slade read the groups as the typical well-heeled, post-conflict crowd. The bulk of the bloodletting was over and the first wave of vultures and do-gooders had begun to descend, all wanting a piece of the agony and glory.

Nursing his tonic, Slade pieced together what little he knew about Nairobi's power players, the ones who might possibly lead him to the Penitents. The most obvious player, but surely one of the weakest, was the United Nations contingent that lounged about the city. The UN was famous for doing jack shit, but they had money, and UN soldiers had a long history of involvement in the sex trade. Were they possible buyers?

What about the security contractors? The cowboys? Many were less-than-reputable ex-soldiers working with no adult supervision. As of this moment, the cowboys topped Slade's list of suspects for weapons trafficking. They might be bringing in the toys but they sure as hell weren't controlling the devils who used them. As for the flesh trade, the cowboys would be johns and nothing more.

But who was running Nairobi, holding it all together? The city was remarkably peaceful, given what was going on in the countryside. And in Africa, peace only came about when somebody with serious balls managed to kill all of his competition. So, who was the Big Chief in town? Whoever he was, he would be neck deep in the flesh trade and would also be getting a cut of the Penitents' weapons trade. If Slade could find the Big Chief, he would find the Penitents.

The surest way to find the Big Chief would be to find the levers of power. In this place, power was expressed by the control of food, water, fuel, weapons, and flesh. Slade needed to find where people lived, how they traveled, communicated, and traded. He needed to map Nairobi's human terrain, electrical tides, food markets, vehicle traffic, and the currents of commerce. When he found who controlled all of those, he would have found the Big Chief and his clan. Then he would find their flesh trade. Then he would find Elizabeth.

Again, the Big Chief was the key.

He would start by walking the streets, developing contacts, and placing key areas under surveillance. But Nairobi was a city that stretched across 300 square miles. Pointing Kraven's cameras at a few buildings would be like trying to map the Milky Way by studying a dozen stars. He needed a broader picture before he could focus on details.

Slade rocked back in his chair and looked up at the sky, contemplating his ludicrous task. His eye fell upon the looming shadow of the Asubuhi Tower, leaning 1,200 meters overhead.

Now there was distance, there was perspective. Slade pursed his lips and rubbed the muscles on the back of his neck. It was going to be one hell of a long night.

CHAPTER FORTY-SIX

STANDING IN THE moon-shadow of a crumbling building, Slade pulled at the cinch straps of his waist belt and shifted the backpack's heavy load off his shoulders. Firming his balance, he craned his neck back and beheld the impossible mirrored bulk of the Asubuhi Tower as it rose before him like a vertical highway. His eyes traveled its length, straying over the twisted lattices, the missing windows, the gaping floors, and the toppled cranes hanging by their own cables, twisting and gonging in the wind like grotesque wind chimes.

Descending, his eyes came to where the tower's base jutted from a rubble field of shattered glass and twisted metal, a cratered moonscape scarred by the meteoric impact of debris shed from the upper floors.

He lowered himself to one knee and adjusted the display of his synthetic vision goggles. The honeycombed image peeled back the dark of night but revealed no sign of life in either the infrared or visible spectrums. He shifted to the ultraviolet spectrum and scanned for the glimmering reflections of human spoor. There were faintly glowing patches of piss and excrement but nothing bright enough to indicate continual activity.

Slade glanced skyward one more time, then rising, brought his weapon to port arms and shuffled out into open ground. Bent beneath the weight of his pack, he picked his way through the debris field, clambering over bent I-beams and ducking under twisted girders. Feet crunching over glass drifts, he skirted the crumpled Jurassic skeleton of a fallen crane, its limbs and inner workings compressed to ruin. Panting, weapon coming to a half raise, Slade padded through the tower's arched entrance, under its looming steel horizon, and into the echoing cathedral of the central atrium.

Gaze pivoting, weapon raised, Slade backed himself into a corner. He dropped to one knee, looking, smelling, and listening; jaw slackening as he became aware of the immensity of the hall that surrounded him, the great pillars, looming sculptures, and soaring arches. And inside that vaulted hollow, planted at the very heart of the tower, rose the bloated trunk of a giant boab tree, its upper branches extending as though to hold aloft the dying steel colossus. And above the boab, a rising column of empty space, infinite and dark, penetrated upward floor by open floor, upward and upward through to the very crown of the tower—a passive cooling tube, open at both ends, drawing in chilled air from high altitudes, the perpetual flow cooling the building. Slade remained in shadow and listened to the building breathe and hum while drops of water pattered down from atmospheric water condensers.

Moving through the vast hall, Slade searched for and found the tower's service stairs. He then took hold of the railing, drew breath, and started to climb.

Advancing with caution, he crouched at each landing and searched for movement or signs of life written in the all-coating dust. He found rodent tracks, bird sign, and corpses withered these many years, but nothing more.

In time the air grew cool against the free running sweat that darkened his clothing and matted the hair along his forehead. His steps turned to bent-back plodding and his breathing to labored gasps. He paused often and sometimes lowered himself to a knee but invariably he straightened himself beneath his burden and continued upward.

As the air thinned around him, the floors became raw concrete and strewn with finishing equipment—spools of cabling and wires, plumbing, rolls of carpeting, cabinetry, and paneling. Then the exterior cladding disappeared from the windows, and the night winds moved with him through vacant spaces while dozing bird colonies squawked above their guano piles.

Then further up, up into a realm of rusting steel timbers and barren gratings strewn with power saws, concrete mixers, welders, and snarls of electrical wiring.

Dawn was approaching when the stairwell ended and he emerged at last into the upper spires of the tower's crown. Here the wind moved with a whisper, being drawn down into the cooling tube. Slade lay his pack down at last, straightened his spine with an audible crack, then stretched against the muscle spasms that writhed the length of his back and legs. He seated himself, weapon across his thighs, complete in his exhaustion, wiped at his face and pressed at his neck. He looked about. All was black sky. He then turned and lay in wait for those who would have strength to follow.

As he crouched in waiting, thousands of feet below him the first morning cook fires flickered to life and the scattered constellation of watch-fires slipped into extinction.

Sipping at his water, Slade watched as the dawn revealed a curiously rounded horizon that swayed in rhythm with the bending of the tower's steel. When daylight was full upon him, he surveyed his vantage point with narrowed eyes. The uppermost level of the tower was unsuitable for his purposes. Shouldering his pack, weapon ready, Slade down-climbed the tower until he reached the levels that still had exterior cladding.

There, he pushed through a heavy door into a space resplendent with hanging art, marble statues, and hardwood engravings. The walls were hung with hand-woven Persians and the halls echoed with the sound of his dusty boots treading on polished teak. Slade pushed again through a heavy steel door and found himself in sunlight, standing before a broad concrete pad, its edges dropping to infinity. A helicopter lay on its side in the center of the pad, debris scattered, blade stumps bent like the fingers of one caught cheating at cards.

Back inside the tower, Slade found a high-ceilinged luxury suite where he tried out the satin-sheeted mattress, then stood to admire the view. Entering the business office, he found a dried corpse slumped over a mahogany desk, its white silk shirt stained to black. Slade pulled the chromed revolver from its spider hand and used the barrel to push the corpse erect in its leather chair, skull stump lolling. He then wheeled the body into a corner, returned to the executive desk, brushed away the skull fragments, took off his backpack, and emptied its contents onto the dusted surface.

*　*　*

Slade spent the remainder of the day turning the crown of the Asubuhi Tower into a hi-tech observation post. For electrical power, he deployed a solar array on the roof, camouflaging it with construction debris. He placed multi-spectrum sensors with overlapping fields of view, ran their wires back to the business suite, then spliced their feeds into a tablet computer. When he was finished, the tower was wired to provide twenty-four-hour visual and electronic surveillance of the city.

Seated in a high-backed executive chair, Slade activated the system, then calibrated and integrated the different sensors. He then fed the output to a pair of virtual reality goggles, giving him a synthetic 360-degree view of the city.

Donning the goggles, Slade turned his head to take in the city, its mottled patchwork of red-roofed houses, green fields, and sprawling industrial slums.

He activated the magnification function and zoomed from 1,200 meters, straight down to street level where he read the license plates on moving cars, counted individual leafs on plants, and watched the lips of men locked in conversation.

Turning back to his system controls, Slade activated the electronic emission detectors that would enable him to track cell phones, radios, and Wi-Fi networks. Over the coming days, his system would record all physical and electronic activity in Nairobi, building a picture of its currents and the rhythms that defined it.

He spent the remainder of the day flying over the city, learning its layout, reading its street signs, and watching its citizens and traffic. He mapped vehicle routes, gas stations, water distribution centers, living areas, and open-air markets. He paid special attention to the location of UN security outposts; clustered near the city center, the blue-helmeted soldiers motored through packs of cigarettes, helmet straps dangling, their weapons untended. They interacted with no one, and when their replacements arrived, they exchanged places without speaking. Most notably there was not a single UN outpost east of the Asubuhi Tower. In fact, east of the Asubuhi there were no traces of Westerners—it was a no-go zone. The area was heavily populated but was a trash-strewn maze of slums, alleys, and gutted buildings.

That was where the Penitents would be.

As the hours of surveillance ground on and his fatigue grew, Slade felt his discipline fading along with a growing inability to stick to the script. He found himself repeatedly wasting time, peering into windows and courtyards, probing the shadows, searching for a girl with raven hair, for a shock of pale skin among a sea of black. Or was he looking for something else? A vanished wife? Or was it a son he couldn't protect? Was it something he'd lost or something he'd never had?

Absolution?

Slade slapped the VR goggles from his forehead, stood, and paced the darkening suite, massaged the knotted flesh around his eyes and listened to the tower groan and breathe around him.

Sleep. Damn, he needed sleep.

With slumping shoulders and a shuffling walk, Slade double-checked the motion detectors and trip mines he had placed in the stairwells. He then set his weapon within arm's reach and fell unconscious upon the satin-sheeted bed.

* * *

Deep in the night, Slade was startled awake by the sound of a support girder giving way, its joints snapping, its great weight clanging and gonging down the endless well of an elevator shaft and the tower itself groaning and trembling as its terrible mass realigned.

Blinking in the dark, he rose and walked the echoing labyrinth until he found himself lost, wandering without compass or light, trapped in a hollow shell, adrift in a sea of ruin. Surrendering to his fate, he lowered himself to the floor and spent long hours staring into the void with eyes that could not see.

With the arrival of dawn, he rose, found his way, returned to his observation suite, donned the VR goggles, and turned his chair to the southeast. There, the sprawl of the international airport was already alive with UN construction teams and a churning concrete plant. He spent the morning studying the immense UN compound being built there, Camp Annan.

Come afternoon, he lowered his goggles, rubbed at his eyes, stretched his back, and walked the slow swaying tower, inspecting his equipment and double-checking his security arrangements.

Exploring the tower, three floors down, his eye fell upon a shock of green movement, a stand of trees rustling in the wind. He moved toward the trees and found a sky terrace jutting out into open space, planted with a flourishing orchard and rioting garden. He walked out into the green and sunlit canopy.

The smell of wet earth and open spaces.

There, in that impossible forest, tiger-striped shadows swayed beneath the trees and all was silent save the moving of wind and the chirping of birds that lofted among limbs hanging pregnant with fruit. Slade seated himself on the edge of an empty stone fountain, cupped his hands beneath a dripping pipe, and pulled in the cool water. He drew down a peach and pressed his teeth into its skin. When he was finished, he wiped at his mouth and tucked the wet pit into his pocket. He took and ate another, then sat among the trees and watched as the sun retreated up the tower face and the shadows rose from the streets below and all was covered and still.

With the rise of full dark, Slade secured his observation post, double-checked the trip mines, lifted his weapon, and climbed down the tower, limping through the endless spiral, hands scuffing along red painted railings. As he descended, the air became dank and oppressive, the heat growing in intensity until it matched the smoldering coals lodged in his calves, back, and thighs. It was three a.m. before he escaped the endless stairs and exchanged the tower's incredible over-weight for a sweltering dark sky.

Back in his hotel room, he took a cold shower and scrubbed himself clean before falling into sleep.

CHAPTER FORTY-SEVEN

SLADE GRITTED HIS teeth and shouldered through the pressing crowd of babbling street vendors and open-handed children, keeping one hand over his billfold and the other on his pistol. The sun had barely cleared the horizon, yet a crowd of urchins and street vendors had already formed a perimeter around the hotel. The crush was so thick that he was considering a return to the hotel and a second breakfast when the sound of wooden staffs smacking against flesh announced the arrival of hotel security. There was frantic yelling and scattering as two uniformed attendants waded into the crowd and drove it back with heavy swagger sticks.

With the crowd dispersed, one of the attendants approached Slade, and with a glowing smile, offered him the club.

"You must beat them, suh! Beat them or they will give you no rest!"

Slade hesitantly reached for the heavy club, taken aback by the prospect of beating street urchins. Noting Slade's pause, the attendant's smile became even brighter. "Do not worry about me, suh." He wagged a finger. "I have plenty more sticks!"

Slade took the club, nodded his thanks, and crossed the street already busy with traffic. He noted that although the club didn't prevent children from approaching, it did keep them at a respectful distance.

Head swiveling, Slade walked the broad, garbage-strewn sidewalks of downtown Nairobi, cataloguing details, observing behavior. Always suspicious, he employed an urban evasion ritual, following a path that randomly changed direction and frequently backtracked on itself. Several times he turned down a dark alley, drew his weapon, and waited in ambush—only to find that he was being hunted by nothing more than ghosts.

Continuing on, a convoy of vehicles lumbered past in a rush of diesel smoke and rough-running engines. As the final vehicle in the convoy passed, Slade squinted after it through the billowing dust. There in the rear window, a girl with her hands pressed against the glass. A tear-streaked face framed by black hair.

Elizabeth.

A bolt of adrenaline so intense as to cause pain. Slade erupted into a sprint after the receding bus, bowled over a vendor's cart, flattened a vagrant, and charged ahead unfazed. He was frantically hailing a tuk-tuk when his gait stuttered and then slowed to a walk.

There had been other faces behind the glass, beside the girl.

Abe Howard.

And his own dead son.

Slade slowed to a stop and stood confounded, grasping at the threads of his unraveling reality. Had it been her?

No, he was seeing what he wanted to see, what he needed to see. He was losing it, coming unglued. Slade cursed himself and ground his teeth. Three days in town, and he was running around like a nutjob. He had to get his shit wired tight or he'd end up as dead as the Judeans.

Fuming, Slade pushed back the intruding doubts, found his line, and turned back toward his original objective. He still had a shopping list to fill.

CHAPTER FORTY-EIGHT

EXHAUSTED, HUNGRY, AND covered in a gritty film of sweat, Slade entered his hotel room with his weapon raised and targeting light on. He flicked on the ceiling lights, cleared the room, then brought his bags inside. He checked the room for signs of entry. There were none, and the intrusion alarms that Kraven had given him indicated that all was well. He went to the lockbox and punched in his code. His equipment and cash were undisturbed. Satisfied, he brought his shopping bags to the table, pulled up a chair, and unpacked the gear he had purchased at the street market.

He started by unwinding the power cords to a battered laptop and a satellite phone. Then he set them both to charging. Unlike the laptop, the sat-phone was top of the line and came with the latest programs, apps, and wireless access features. It had obviously been stolen from a careless foreigner. Moving to the window, Slade set the sat-phone on the sill. With a bit of adjusting and fidgeting, he was able to get a strong satellite signal. Lastly, he reached into his pocket and pulled out a newly purchased, prepaid debit card.

With his system in place, Slade powered up the laptop, connected it to the sat-phone, accessed an Internet service provider, created an account, paid for a week's worth of service, and was searching the Internet within ten minutes. For the first time in months a feeling of control flickered to life.

With anonymous global communications sitting in the palm of his hand, Slade's thoughts turned to his sister and the pain he had brought upon her. More than anything he wanted to let her know that he was well, but even if he routed his message through multiple servers and concealed its origin, a cryptic e-mail from overseas would give the authorities a thread to pull on. And if they found enough interesting threads they might be inspired to reopen his case. Given enough time, Slade would contact Summer, but for now, the best thing he could do was eliminate the man who threatened her.

Kraven.

And Elizabeth? To find her, he had to find the blood cult. And who could give him the resources to do that?

Again, Kraven.

Focusing, he tapped on the tablet's touch screen and activated its verbally directed web crawler. "Computer, perform web search for information on a person named Kraven, probable spelling K-R-A-V-E-N. Male. American. Approximately fifty years old. Caucasian. He holds the rank of colonel in the United States Army."

The computer worked for several minutes but could find nothing of interest. Slade tapped a fingernail against his teeth. He needed to refine his search. Kraven would have commanded various units and attended numerous military schools. There would be promotion orders and command selection lists published by Army media centers. There would also be paper trails at the Army's professional development schools, graduation programs, alumni associations, and Master's thesis published in military journals.

Slade started digging, eliminating false trails, and pointing the computer in new directions as required. After twenty minutes' work and a few hits to his debit card, Slade had the measure of his man: Gary M. Kraven, Colonel, United States Army. Graduated magna cum laude from West Point with a major in political science. He'd gone on to command an infantry platoon in the 82nd Airborne, then moved on to the Rangers and Special Forces where he'd earned a silver star. He was a fast burner that had checked all of the boxes and moved up the command ladder as quickly as he could.

Kraven was also a family man. He'd married his high school sweetheart and fathered five children, two of whom were still living with Mrs. Janet Kraven at their home outside of Washington, DC. Slade then downloaded aerial, street-level, and interior photographs of Kraven's house, complete with backyard pool, gazebo, shade trees, and stainless-steel BBQ grill.

Slade leaned back from his computer, rubbed his eyes, and stroked his beard. Kraven had balls but was no war horse. When the doors to the staff office had opened, he'd run through them. Kraven's tour at the Pentagon working for the Joint Chiefs of Staff meant that he was well connected in Washington. So why would somebody who circled in the highest of orbits give a damn about a blood cult shooting up campsites on the far side of the planet? And why did he need Slade? . . . Was he handcuffed or just hiding his trail? And the blood cult . . . Who was controlling them? Why did Kraven need to know?

Slade shook his head. He'd reached his limits of deduction, was bone tired, and pissed off. In short, it was time for some R&R. Turning, he grabbed some cash from the safe and headed for the bar.

CHAPTER FORTY-NINE

SLADE SAT IN a darkened corner of the bar with three security contractors, their heads inclined inwards as if joined in conspiracy, a small forest of empty glasses littering the table between them. Their eyelids drooped and tongues wagged with liquid ease. It had not been difficult for Slade to penetrate their small circle; he looked the part, walked the walk, and spoke the language with the best of them. All it had taken was a few carefully dropped phrases and a round of free drinks.

His new drinking mates were former New Zealand SAS and were in-country providing protection for UN construction teams. Slade had worked extensively with the British, Australian, and Kiwi SAS during his military career, and to a man, they were disciplined, mission-driven professionals cursed with dry throats and balls the size of full-grown koalas. Slade had told them he was new in town, looking to secure a contract, and that his name was Tom, no surname required.

As much as he felt a natural affinity with the Kiwis, Slade kept his true motives concealed. Elizabeth had been right; well-balanced men who had their lives in order would be someplace other than Africa. Every man here was running from something. These cowboys had motives and morals unknown to Slade. They could be as deeply involved in the flesh or weapons trade as anyone else. Trust was not an option.

The shaggy redheaded Kiwi leaned in closer. "Thing is, mate, Nairobi is a piece-o-piss gold rush for blokes like us. The UN is shoveling money out the window like it's on fire for piss work sitting on your arse. Its money for jam! I'd feel guilty taking the green from anyone else."

"Sounds like my kind of show." Slade swigged a gin and tonic then sucked on the lime. "What about the local boys? I was expecting Mogadishu and Monrovia rolled into one, but they seem pretty tame."

"That's the funny thing," the second Kiwi, a Maori giant, said. "They go meat-axe out in the countryside." He punched his fist into a cupped palm. "All horror show like you'd expect. But 'round these parts, they're soft as kittens."

"Why's that?"

"Piss off if I know. Carry a short stick an' you'll be alright 'round these parts. Just don't go too far east. Past the Asoobi all this posh plaid comes to an abrupt end and the real Africa starts."

"Past the what?"

"The Asu—the Asubu—you know, mate, the big tower. Go east of that and things get real in a fast way."

The third Kiwi, a well-seasoned gent who wore the gaunt look of a death row convict, leaned across the table, wagged a scarred finger at Slade, and ejaculated an unintelligible stream of tortured vowels, imaginary words, and AWOL consonants. He raised his hands and mimed a recoiling rifle. "Tap! Tap! Tap!" He ended his tirade with a sharp slap against the table that sent empty glasses skittering and the Kiwis into peals of laughter.

The curly redhead pointed a thumb toward the convict. "What Bert is trying to say is that the good times is ova though."

"How's that?"

"First we got here a year ago, this place was Mickey and Donald for shootas like us. Got the lead out a couple times a day. Times is changed though, and we's tired of sittin' around. Might be time to up and vacate."

"Where would you go?" Slade asked.

"Someplace that still bleedin'."

Slade nodded in understanding. "So . . . What's your go-by?"

"Me? They call me Sideshow."

"Sideshow? How's that?"

The Kiwi set down his drink, tousled his hair, pulled it away from his scalp, and made a face.

Slade looked at the mess of tangled red locks, the tall, thin face, and the jutting upper lip. "Ahh . . . Sideshow Bob!" He laughed.

"Right you are, mate. And we call that chap Kai," he said, pointing to the dark-skinned hulk. "Kai means food in Maori. As you'll notice he's always stuffin' somethin' down the hatch." Sideshow then pointed to the convict. "And that's Bert over there, our resident senior citizen."

"Why do you call him Bert?"

"Cuz that's his fuckin' name!"

Laughing, Slade held up his palms in surrender.

As the night wore on, Slade found that pumping the Kiwis for information required nothing more than frequent hand gestures toward the drink hostess. The three men proved more than eager to help out a like-minded bloke who was new in town and looking to get green. Within an hour he had a first-rate intelligence report delivered by men who knew their business, and knew it well. But it wasn't merely information that Slade was after; he needed a team. And so, with a degree of earned trust and the judicious application of currency, the Kiwis might well prove to be powerful allies.

CHAPTER FIFTY

THE NEXT DAY Slade chased down another hunch; the Penitents had been firing newly manufactured Serbian ammunition from their AK-47s. Perhaps they had obtained it from somebody here in town.

A quick Internet search uncovered the UN military contingents that had served in Nairobi over the last year. Slade scanned the list: France, Germany, India, Canada, Pakistan, Hungary, Saudi Arabia, and Bangladesh. He drummed his fingers against the table, his eye zeroing in on the Pakistanis, Bangladeshis, and Hungarians. Only those three countries equipped their soldiers with weapons that could fire the Serbian bullets. The Pakistanis and Hungarians were still in town.

Slade walked the streets of Nairobi for the remainder of the day, approaching UN guard posts, striking up conversations, offering cigarettes, and smiling broadly. Eventually the conscripts would relax and warm, and eventually Slade would steer the halting conversation toward weapons. Slade would offer his CR-30 for review, and they would inevitably submit their rifles for his inspection.

But three hours into the routine, tired of the fake smiles and glad-handing shtick, Slade would approach the soldiers with cash in hand. Two minutes later he would leave, their weapons' serial numbers and ammo stampings recorded.

CHAPTER FIFTY-ONE

"YOU'RE CERTAIN THAT the weapons and ammunition came through the Hungarians?" Kraven asked.

"That's not what I said," Slade replied. "Yes, they have the same ammunition and their AKs are the same make and model the Penitents are using, but it doesn't prove anything."

"I understand, but in your professional opinion, are Hungarians supplying the Penitents?"

"I won't say that. But I will say that somewhere in their supply train someone is siphoning weapons and ammo off to the side. It could be happening at a depot in Europe, or it could be a corrupt quartermaster here in Nairobi, or it could be a make-believe gun-walking sting run by the Attorney General of the United States. That's something that you'll have to figure out on your end." Slade knew that Kraven already understood all of this; the old man had just been ruminating, bouncing ideas around as they came through his head.

"And another question," Slade said.

"Go ahead."

"What do you need me for? This is Cub Scout–level intel. NSA or NGA could have told you the same thing with ten minutes of research. Hell, you could have called the embassies and just asked them for the info. If their supply lines are being raided, they would want to know."

"Stay in your lane," Kraven warned. "And stand by for further taskings."

The line went dead.

Slade grinned. The exchange proved beyond doubt that Kraven was handcuffed. The information on the Hungarians was chump change for any intel agency. That meant that the colonel was unable to request the information through official channels.

Kraven was running an unsanctioned operation.

And that meant he had limited access to the instruments of power. Every time the colonel employed a military asset he was exposing his ass and taking a tremendous risk. The colonel was weaker and more vulnerable than Slade had hoped. As much as he longed to exploit Kraven's weakness, he had to remain patient. Destroying the relationship would dry up his access to Kraven's resources. Slade would drip-feed the colonel information, milk him for what he could until he found Elizabeth. But when the moment came to break free, that would also be the moment of maximum risk. For if Kraven realized that he was about to be exposed, he had every incentive to erase the key witness. At that moment, the chess match would turn into a gunfight.

CHAPTER FIFTY-TWO

Slade spent the evening poolside, drinking with the Kiwis, but he found himself repeatedly eyeballing the containment wall and the world that lay beyond it. Each second spent inside the wall was a second where Elizabeth moved further and further to God knew where. He needed to be out there searching and digging up intel, but a solitary white man wandering the back alleys after dark without aim or support was suicide. If he could put a team together, he would have options. But to get a team he needed trust . . .

Slade turned toward Sideshow. "You boys here in Africa during the big collapse?"

Sideshow shook his head. "No, but Bert was here for the whole show. Bloody tosser loved it so much he quit his contract when they tried to bring him home."

Bert looked up and rubbed a hand across the salt-and-pepper stubble that ringed his head. "Whassat?"

"I was just telling the seppo about your time in Warri."

Bert's face showed the barest flicker of a smile.

"Warri, where's that?" Slade asked.

"Niger Delta, oil country, right on the riva," Bert said. "I ran security for the big refinery there."

"How'd it go down, the collapse?"

Bert leaned back and took a long drink as his eyes focused on a different place. "First, was as you'd expect, typical clan war. Locals had been at a low boil since the President and 'is family got hit.

Churches and mosques was hashin' it up, takin' pokes at each other. Most nights some part of the city was burnin'. Government couldn't stop shit, mostly just picked sides and settled political scores.

"Then things cranked up when NATO bumbled into the mix and started bombin' an' handing out weapons like welfare." Bert locked eyes with Slade to ensure that he had his attention. "But things got real interestin' after all the fuel ports and refineries got hit; one week later, the fuel was gone. All of it. Power stations stopped running, lights went dark, coms and Internet went out. No commerce, no water, no transpo, stores empty. Then came all-out clan warfare as they fought for the scraps.

"Now, before I go further"—Bert paused to wet his throat—"let me give ya some perspective on what skinnies can achieve when they set their minds to it . . . 'kay?"

"Okay."

"During World War Two, the Americans lost roughly four hundred thousand troops over four years. So, the combined efforts of Nazi Germany and Imperial Japan killed roughly one hundred thousand Yanks per year. Follow?"

"Yes."

"In 1994, the Rwandans turned on each other and slaughtered almost a million *civilians* in *three months*. That's one hundred thousand killed every *ten days*! It was neighbor against neighbor, and they did their killin' with machetes, shovels, an' buckets of gasoline. You see what I'm getting at? Ain't nobody on God's red earth as good at killin' skinnies as is the skinnies. They's bred for it."

"Sounds like hell on earth."

"That it was, mate. Hades in the flesh." Bert released his drink just enough to level a finger at Slade. "All the best bits from the Bible: the Flood, Gomorrah, Ten Plagues, Herod killin' the kids. All of it."

Slade nodded, urging Bert to continue.

"There was 160 million skinnies in Nigeria, and within two weeks of the fuel running out, there wasn't a scrap of food to be had—160 million—Christ—the Niger River's a thousand meters across—couldn't see the water for all the bodies in it. They'd come floatin' down all puffed like black balloons, rollin' over each other an' standin' up in big piles on the riva' bends. An' the crocs was there in the middle of it all, rollin' and threshin' about. Even the sharks started swimmin' up riva' to get their cut, tearing at the bodies." Bert reached for the Grey Goose and stiffened his drink. "Me an' the mates was turtled up in the refinery. Plenty o' beans an' bullets. No problems there." He lowered his voice. Slade could not tell whether out of caution or reverence. "We'd hop the fence at night and go into town—each man kitted out with nothing but five hundred rounds an' a bottle o' Johnnie Walker. We called it 'Walkin' with Dante'—right through the nine circles of hell. Dispensing justice, getting our kill on like we was the right hand of God, like ain't been done since Moses and Passover.

"After a month, you couldn't travel cuz the streets was filled knee-deep with blood, bodies, and raw shit. Then came the cholera. I was out by the time ebola hit. Good for that as they had to quarantine the whole bloody continent."

"What about the spark that started it all? When the Nigerian President and his family got hit? Were you there?"

"No, but a lot of me mates was on his security detail. Lost some good ones that day."

"What's your take on it?"

"The hit?" Bert's anger was evident. "First off, it wasn't no Boko-fuckin'-Haram that did the job. Kidnapping teenage girls was more their speed, not pullin' a hit on the First Family. Boko's nothing more than a mob o' illiterate bush thugs that paint a light coat of jihad on their crimes, makes 'em feel godly. That, and raisin' the black flag opens a pipeline of green from Saudi and Qatar."

"You're saying it wasn't Boko Haram that did it?"

"That's exactly what I'm saying. Nigerian First Family had top-shelf security, mostly ex-SAS, likes of you and me. The guys that done the hit staged a complex attack on two targets *simultaneously*. They had intel, drone reconnaissance, overwatch snipers, squirter containment, a command center, electronic surveillance, and assault elements that coordinated and changed plans as the action unfolded. It would have required months of planning and rehearsal. Sure, the nobs who tortured and killed the Pres on the Internet was Boko, but the pros who grabbed him off the street—They was Tier One, mate. Tier One."

"Really?" Slade failed to hide his doubt. "That sounds odd. What's the motive?"

Bert sat up straight, put his drink down, and got both of his hands into the operation. "Okay. I'll explain some things, in very small words. Ready?"

"Yup."

"It was a fucking setup. The entire thing. The hit on the President was used to spark the civil war, which opened the way for the NATO intervention, which then led to the larger war, which then led to the collapse."

"I still don't get it," Slade said. "*Cui bono?*"

Bert's eyebrows rose in wonder. "A Latin-speakin' seppo . . . now I seen everything."

Slade touched his hand to his chest and bowed his head in mock humility. "*Quaeso redona me.*"

"Well . . ." Bert raised a finger, struggling to find a retort. "Well . . . Fuck you then. How ya like that?"

"Ha! Seppo owned ya." Sideshow laughed. "'Bout time. My head hurts from listenin' to you spout off again."

"Alright, alright, settle down," Bert said, struggling to regain momentum. "I'm almost—"

Bert's monologue was interrupted by a deafening chant emanating from the crowd at the bar. The three men glanced over and saw Kai standing at the center of a ring of security contractors who were hoisting their drinks to the raucous chant, "Ha-ka! Ha-ka! Ha-ka!"

Slade leaned toward Sideshow and tapped him on the shoulder. "What's that all about?"

"That?" Sideshow shouted through the din. "Kai played rugby for a few seasons with the All Blacks. Used to lead the team when they performed the Haka. These blokes want him to do it."

"The what?" Slade asked, unable to hear over the noise.

"The Haka! The Maori war dance!"

Slade's memory snapped back to a day fifteen years removed from this one—Papakura Military Camp outside of Auckland, New Zealand. The second week of a joint training exercise with the Kiwi SAS. The day had been cold with a leaden sky that promised rain. The morning training scenario had been canceled and the entire SAS regiment called to formation in their dress uniforms. A white hearse had passed slowly in front of the formation on its way to the regimental cemetery, bearing a trooper killed in a training accident the previous week. Suddenly, one hundred fifty throats erupted in a war cry summoned from across the centuries. Slade had stood in awed silence, watching the Kiwi warriors as they channeled the spirits of their ancestors and said goodbye to their comrade, offering Slade a glimpse of an ancient race that had once charged into battle clothed in nothing but the bones of defeated enemies. One hundred fifty men, knees bent, backs straight, advanced toward the hearse, chanting in unison, fists extended, teeth bared, stomping their feet, striking their chests and thighs in time with the cadence. The men had struck themselves with such violence that the thudding of fists against flesh echoed across the courtyard, across the years, and now years later raised goosebumps on the back of Slade's neck.

Slade watched to see what Kai's response would be, but the Maori deferred politely, smiled his appreciation, and returned to his circle of friends. The crowd groaned in disappointment.

As the chant died away, Sideshow leaned back into Slade. "Good thing there, mate. Kai will give you the shoes off his feet if you need 'em. But when that gent puts on his war face—someone's gonna end up bleedin' buckets."

"I'll keep that in mind," Slade replied.

Kai regained his seat, then pointed a thumb toward the bar. "Too many tossers here. I'm headin' for a long one at the Can-Can Club." He turned and slapped Slade on the shoulder. "You in, mate?"

Slade shook his head. "Gonna have to disappoint. I've got other plans."

A broad smile bloomed across Kai's face. His eyes swung toward the ladies seated at the bar and gave them a thorough scrubbing. "Gonna let the ferret out for a run, eh? Which one?"

Slade laughed, leaned back in his chair, and laced his fingers behind his head. "Sorry, friend, but OPSEC is the key to victory."

CHAPTER FIFTY-THREE

ALTHOUGH UNBURDENED BY heavy surveillance equipment, the tower stairs proved no less painful the second time around. Carrying his weapon, water, and supplies, Slade sloughed up floor after endless floor, maintaining his security ritual—pausing, listening, and looking for tracks other than his own. When he reached the observation post, legs trembling, Slade deactivated the motion detectors and trip mines. He then cleared the entire floor, room by room. Satisfied that he was alone, he settled into the business suite and began checking the health of his surveillance system. All was in order.

Donning the VR goggles, Slade began to replay the visual and electronic surveillance files. Across his view of the city, red dots and data tags indicating electronic activity popped in and out of existence. "Computer, present the three-day file in a continual loop. Display it at three thousand times normal speed."

By setting each day to flow past in thirty seconds, Slade would be able to see Nairobi's pattern of life—the ebb and flow of people, vehicles, lights, and electricity. By watching Nairobi's beats and rhythms, he hoped to uncover its hidden heart.

Watching the recordings, Slade saw the flickers of the first morning cook fires, the fading of the stars, and the sun vaulting into the sky. He saw the blurred hustle of people rising from their homes and converging on foot toward the central business district and the vehicles flowing like blurred water along shimmering grime paths.

With nightfall came a sudden bloom of neon lights. Then a sub current of Westerners moving from their hotels to the nightlife district and the gradual fading of activity into the early morning hours.

Slade kept the loop running and remained in his chair long into the night, like an astronomer staring endless hours at indecipherable patterns, at a multitude of beings, their purpose and orbits unknowable. He marked the places that never dimmed, their electricity uninterrupted. He marked the places that maintained a constant flow of vehicle traffic day and night. He watched clusters of cell phone activity blinking in and out of existence.

Patterns coalesced and rhythms formed.

A vast compound in the eastern slums drew his attention—a pool of light in a sea of darkness. It was a cluster of electronic activity—with regular vehicle traffic. Cigarette coals stood sentry on its walled perimeter. Vehicle patrols left every five hours and prowled the eastern wastes.

Slade watched the cargo trucks that entered the compound, noted their arrival times, then placed the video in reverse and watched as the vehicles were sucked inexorably backward, back to the very origin of their journey. He plotted their positions, gauged their speeds, mapped their routes, pulled on the facts, and unraveled the cloth of their camouflage until at last their truths were laid bare.

CHAPTER FIFTY-FOUR

"THE UN IS using NGO vehicles to supply the Penitents with weapons," Slade said. "Every evening a small convoy departs the Nyayo Sports Stadium then drives onto the UN base, Camp Annan. They depart Annan an hour later and drive to a Penitent compound in the eastern slums. Thirty minutes later they depart the Penitent compound and return to the stadium, circuit complete."

"So, whose trucks are they? Which NGO is involved?"

"I don't know. The trucks are unmarked. Red Cross, Doctors Without Borders, USAID, and about a dozen other NGOs are using the Nyayo sports stadium as their motor pool. It could be any of them."

"You think this is the weapons smuggling outfit?" Kraven asked.

Slade switched the sat-phone to his other ear. "I can't see what's in the trucks, but based upon their acceleration profiles I can confirm they're picking up something heavy inside of Annan then dropping it off in the Penitent compound. I doubt it's baby formula."

"And the compound?"

"Fifteen-foot containment walls, elevated guard towers, barracks, random patrols in the surrounding area, electrical power 24/7. It's the strongest concentration of emitters in the city—cell, satellite, Wi-Fi, and radio."

"How do you know it's the Penitents?"

"Last night a sixty-vehicle convoy left under cover of night and shipped out to the south: fuel tankers, troop transports, gun trucks, supply vehicles, command and control antennas. I was able to identify Penitent graffiti on several of the vehicles. Nairobi appears to be their supply depot. It's a slick operation, similar to the ISIS-Turkey logistics system we saw in Syria."

"Copy. And your assessment of the UN . . . Are they a willing partner in this op?"

"I can't say. But losing twenty truckloads of supplies every week is pretty hard to overlook."

"And Camp Annan itself, what's your take on it?"

"It's huge. They're building infrastructure and hard barracks for over fifty thousand people. Looks like the buildup at Balad back in the day. They're also running a squadron of long-distance ISR drones."

"What kind?"

"Israeli Heron TPs. Twenty-five-hour endurance, full suite of electro-optics, Ground Moving Target Indicators, all military grade. UN press releases say they're being used to locate remaining pockets of civilization for the relief effort."

"Copy. Good work, Slade. Now we just have to dig into the guts of this operation. I need concrete evidence the UN's shipping arms, and I need to know *who's* doing it. Get me the names and identities of the people involved."

"Copy. Out," Slade said with manufactured confidence as he hung up. In truth, he was steaming, because what the colonel was demanding was little less than suicide, far beyond the capabilities of a single man. But now, more than ever, Slade needed to be the good boy and play along. For he'd found something else inside the Penitent compound, something he hadn't told the colonel about: cargo trucks identical to those that had rounded up the Judeans.

And a solitary building that had its windows barred from the outside. He hadn't told the colonel about the slender, pale arms that dangled from between the bars, cigarettes smoldering. Nor the laundry lines with colorful women's clothing fluttering like forlorn prayer banners.

Slade didn't have direct proof that Elizabeth was being held there, but his gut told him that she was. She had to be. The best thing that he could do was gather intel for Kraven, then parlay it out in return for more resources. With more resources, he could perform an up-close recon of the compound, and ultimately, find Elizabeth.

Slade rose from his chair, stretched his back, and paced the hotel room. So how could he prove that the smugglers were moving weapons? How could he get the players to surface and show themselves, electronically or physically?

The Penitents undoubtedly used cell phones to stay in touch with their NGO smuggling network. Slade could easily download a contagious eavesdropping virus into the phones of the smugglers. It would require nothing more than positioning himself next to their delivery route. As the smugglers drove past, Slade would activate Kraven's comm gear and upload a virus into their phones. The smugglers would then go on to infect their Penitent handlers. From there the eavesdropping virus would spread throughout the entire Penitent network in Nairobi. Then all Slade would have to do was shock that network—shock it hard—and watch it react.

CHAPTER FIFTY-FIVE

SEATED AT HIS work table in the crown of the Asubuhi Tower, Slade donned his VR goggles and spun his chair until he was facing southeast. He checked his watch, then activated the magnification function on the surveillance system, zooming in on the northern gate of Camp Annan.

Exactly on schedule, a convoy of two cargo trucks and a fueler left the gate, the blue-helmeted guards waving them through. Slade watched as the convoy rumbled north on the Nairobi beltway, took an off-ramp, then worked its way deep into the eastern slums. He checked his watch again.

Thirty seconds.

Twenty hours prior, Slade had approached the Nyayo sports stadium on foot, a small duffel bag strung across his back.

Twenty seconds.

The guards had been asleep on duty, and Slade had walked past them without so much as a pause. The parking area had been unlit, the NGO cargo trucks covered in shadow.

Ten seconds.

He'd crawled under the cargo truck, installed his equipment, then made it back to the hotel bar in time for last call.

Five seconds.

High in the Asubuhi Tower, Slade Crawford rose from his chair, crossed to the window, and folded his arms over his chest.

One second.

Slade's thumb depressed the send button on a satellite phone. Five miles across town, its companion phone received an incoming call. As programed, the phone's processor closed a micro-switch directing a ten-milliamp electrical current to the phone's speaker assembly. Amplified by a nine-volt battery that had been hotwired into the circuitry board, the electrical impulse traveled down the speaker cable, jumped onto a spliced electrical wire, passed outside of the phone and into a blasting cap embedded in the explosive charge of a BR-45 anti-vehicle mine.

Inside the blasting cap, the electrical current vaporized a micron-thin bridge wire, initiating a chain of energetic, ever more explosive reactions. Twenty milliseconds later, the mine, and the cargo truck that it was attached to, experienced a high-order detonation, creating a series of brilliant white flashes that for a brief moment held the whole of the city and its surrounding lands in stark relief.

Slade blinked his eyes as roiling balls of smoke and flames rose through a constellation of glimmering sparks then faded to blackness. There was a long, empty pause, then a deep bass *k-crunck* slapped through the tower, shaking the windows and setting dust afloat. Slade then activated the electronic overlay on his VR goggles and watched as the cell phone traffic in eastern Nairobi went berserk.

CHAPTER FIFTY-SIX

"I SHOW YOU secure."

"I show same. Send it."

"I've got more info on the smugglers. They're an NGO called Global Food Justice, a small nonprofit out of Italy, bunch of nobodies. But whoever they are, I've got proof that they are smuggling UN munitions. I'm sending the video now. You'll see I touched off one of their cargo trucks. Enhanced imagery shows the primary detonation followed by a much larger secondary detonation, followed by thirty minutes of residual cook-offs. Frag pattern, collateral damage, and crater analysis confirms that the vehicles were carrying large-caliber ammo and military-grade explosives."

"What? How many vehicles!"

"There were sympathetic detonations in a second cargo truck and a fueler."

"Jesus." There was a long pause as Kraven downloaded and reviewed the video. "Slade?"

"Yes?"

"Christ almighty, do you know what *covert* means?"

"I did the best I could with the limited resources I have." Slade paused to let the statement sink in. "If you want this done right, I need a team of men, intel, surveillance, and logistical support. I—"

"What else do you have for me?" Kraven interrupted.

"Colonel, I need to have more—"

"You've got everything you're going to get, Crawford." Kraven's tone indicated that the discussion was over. "Now what else do you have for me? You map their cell network?"

"Yes." Slade hung his head. He'd made his pitch and come up with exactly nothing.

"Good. What kind of structure are we looking at?"

"Classic vertical pyramid with highly centralized execution. Whoever is at the top likes to push all the buttons himself, doesn't give his subordinates much freedom of action. Very similar to US models."

"You get voice prints on the players?"

"Yes. But it's too much for me to diagnose on this end. Many are speaking Swahili. I've isolated the primary control node, but I can't ID who that person actually is. You'll have to send the voice print behind the green door and see what the intel wienies can spit out."

"Copy all. I'll have it digested then pass the product down to you. And, Slade, in the future . . . use more discretion."

As Slade broke the connection, a flicker of hope sparked inside of him. When Kraven told him who the primary control node was, he would have the identity of the Big Chief.

* * *

High in the tower, running low on food and water, Slade spent the next day mapping the eastern slums and recording the Penitents' security procedures. Planning a ground reconnaissance of the compound, he charted ingress and egress routes, identified population centers, and designated hole-up points. But even as he went through the ritual and constructed a plan, he knew that he was living a fantasy. He had no idea how to enter the compound undetected, locate

Elizabeth, break her free, and then evade pursuit. He was living out a fantasy—one that ended with his own death.

* * *

A message from Kraven arrived. His intel troops had identified the primary control node. Slade eagerly opened the files, skimming over the text and pictures in front of him.

Graeme Mujuru: 78 inches tall, 260 lbs, 58 years old with acne-pocked skin and large pouches beneath his yellowed eyes. The son of a wealthy Zimbabwean politician, Graeme had received a commission in the Zimbabwean Army, rose to the rank of general, and commanded the National Intelligence Agency. His time at the agency had been marked by savage repression of local dissidents, and he'd retired when evidence of war crimes surfaced. Subsequently, he was appointed to Zimbabwe's chair on the UN Human Rights Council. He'd remained at the UN for two years, but since the big collapse, his fate was unknown.

With the Big Chief's identity confirmed, Slade's spirit's soared, right up until he read the attached message from Kraven.

Voice print analysis indicates with 97% probability that the primary control node is Graeme Mujuru. You are directed to geolocate subject, establish persistent surveillance, confirm suspect's identity, and ascertain his level of involvement in the smuggling of UN arms.

Dossier indicates that Mujuru is implanted with a data chip in his left wrist. Perform remote download of the biochip data, then determine operational details of the smuggling organization to include the identity of deputies and operatives and financial records. Continue to detect and evaluate organizational structure and vulnerabilities that could present opportunities for future exploitation—

Slade stopped reading. He activated the sat-phone and hit speed dial. The line opened after a lengthy ring. He tried to control himself, to keep playing the game, but couldn't. "Is this your idea of a joke?" he spat.

"I am not given to humor, Mr. Crawford."

"You want me to establish *persistent* surveillance? Then get close enough to download the data in his biochip? Christ, what do you think I have down here? My own battalion? I've got a shitty hotel room, a gun, and a horse."

"Make do."

"He'll have shielding on his wrist. I'll need to—"

"I'm aware of that. The e-snoop I provided you is capable of circumventing the shielding. You'll be able to perform the data extraction by positioning yourself within approximately ten feet of him."

"Ten feet! What you're asking for is not a one-man oper—"

"I'm not *asking*, Crawford."

Slade felt his composure crumbling. "Colonel, this is absurd. You've got an entire task force at your disposal. If you need this info so damn badly, then commit the necessary resources to the problem."

"How I employ my resources is not your concern."

"Sending me on a suicide mission—that's not my concern?"

"Mr. Crawford, I don't like where this conversation is going . . . If you find the terms of your service unacceptable, need I remind you that your sister and her family aided and abetted a known fugi—"

"Terms of service!" Slade shouted. "As if I signed up for this! You know goddamn well those charges against me were the wet dream of a tick-turd bureaucrat looking for a promotion. And knowing that, you're still more than happy to bend a fellow warrior over a barrel for the sake of whatever game you're playing! I'll choke the life out of you if you ever show your face down here! You got that? I will choke you until your eyeballs pop out of your fucking skull!" Slade paced back and forth panting, red faced.

"Are you quite done, Mr. Crawford?"

Slade wasn't. He raged full-throated, face sweating, his free hand alternately clenching an invisible throat or stabbing ragged holes in the air.

The colonel waited until Slade was raw and spent, then continued as if the tirade never happened. "You have your orders," he said, then hung up.

Slade sat on his bed struggling to control his breathing. More than ever he felt like a rat being played with by a petulant lab technician. The maze was getting tighter, the ceiling lower, and the floor hotter. The small advantages that he'd gained had proven to be just like his chances of success, a vanishing illusion.

CHAPTER FIFTY-SEVEN

THAT NIGHT AT the bar, Slade's sullen mood didn't pass unnoticed. Kai broke from the crowd and took a seat next to him.

"Somethin' troublin', mate? Looks like ya got the bloody world on ya shouldas." He handed Slade a tall drink. "Here's a little handle to freshen things."

Slade took the drink and smiled his thanks. "Just got some problems need chewing on."

"What sort of problems, mate? Chick back home givin' grief? Wants you back 'er way, no doubt."

Slade shook his head and decided to take a small risk. "I'm looking for someone . . . someone here in town, and I'm not sure how to go about finding him."

"Oh?" Kai's eyebrows lifted and his voice lowered till it was barely audible over the music. "What sort of tosser we talkin' about? Would he likely wannabe . . . be found? By the likes of you?"

Slade looked Kai directly in the eyes to gauge his reaction. "No. No he wouldn't."

Kai nodded and took a long pull of his drink. "I see." He chewed on an ice cube while gazing at the constellations. He chose his words carefully. "This chap of yours . . . what sort is he? Big fish . . . Small fish . . . African or import . . . Soft or hard?"

"Big fish . . . African . . . Hard . . . With lots of friends."

"I see . . ." Kai chewed some more ice. "Lives in a hole . . . or swims about?"

"Got himself a deep hole, over on the east side."

Kai offered a low whistle and began kneading his chin, running scenarios and stacking odds. "Paying 'im a visit at home is out . . . You'll have to meet 'im while he's strollin', I imagine. It'll be dodgy, them eastside boys carry big juju 'round these parts. They ain't the kind you wanna trade insults with, know?"

Slade did.

Kai glanced over his shoulder, confirming no one was within earshot. "You alone on this fishin' trip, mate?"

Slade nodded.

"Christ, you like to hang it out, don't ya?"

"No, actually I don't." Slade's displeasure was clear.

Kai drummed his fingers, gears turning. "What you needs is to find the right fishin' hole an' then wait up for 'im. This chap, he thick on money?"

"Yes."

"Park yourself at the Pred, and he'll come 'round."

"The what?"

"The Predator Night Club, third alley off Kenyata Road. Down where the lights end. You're serious about catching a big fish with money, that's the place to set your hook."

"Why's that?"

"Everything there's top-shelf. An' the girls got talent. With those chicks . . ." Kai chuckled at a memory. "An hour into it, you still won't know if you're fuckin' or fightin'."

Slade nodded in understanding.

"Oh, and one other thing, mate. If ya gonna go to the Pred, dress posh an' get yourself some new threads."

"Why's that?"

"Cuz you smell like horse shit."

CHAPTER FIFTY-EIGHT

SLADE SETTLED INTO a darkened corner of the Predator Night Club. The lighting was dim, the décor lavish, the air smelled of strong perfume and cigar smoke. The African hostess who had seated him spoke with an impeccable British accent and looked as if she had just stepped from the runways of Milan. The door security that had taken his sidearm and searched him with a metal detector looked as if they'd just stepped from the Thunderdome.

Slade ordered a drink while his hands unconsciously smoothed his new clothes. He was seated on a leather couch, back to the wall, overlooking a maze of plush recliners and a raised stage that was showcasing some of the local talent. On the far side of the room a waterfall bar served high-priced drinks to a pressing throng of patrons and scrambling waitresses. The clientele tended toward the older and softer side, with corporate softies outnumbering the odd roughneck out on a spree. The prostitutes were well dressed, classy, and exclusively African. At regular intervals, couples and trios exited the lounge through a curtained alcove. They generally returned within the hour.

Slade refused an offer of company and spent his time watching the crowd, the help, and the security. He took a turn through the different rooms, halls, and chambers, checked the bathrooms and noted the exits. He talked with no one, stayed for another hour, accepted an obligatory lap dance, then took his leave, recon complete.

CHAPTER FIFTY-NINE

SEATED BEFORE HIS computer, combing through maps and collected imagery, Slade cursed in frustration and shattered a bottle against the wall of his hotel room. In regard to mounting a recon or rescue mission against the Penitent compound, he'd reached a dead end. The compound was protected by not only highly disciplined troops, but by its surrounding environment. A solitary white man had no chance of traversing five miles of unfamiliar, populated urban terrain and remaining hidden. He had no intelligence unit to plan his route and identify threats, no fire support to neutralize enemies, no helicopter extraction to escape pursuers. A one-man assault on the Penitent compound was suicide, and suicide was failure. He needed to attack the problem from a different angle. Slade had no clue what that angle would be, but it better present itself soon.

Sick of spinning his wheels on a dead-end tactical plan, Slade turned to confront the bigger unknown: Nairobi, in general, and Kraven, in particular. The key lay with Kraven . . .

Kraven was a political warrior . . . Handcuffed by politicians . . . His war was political.

Who were the political players in Nairobi? The United Nations . . . Mujuru.

Who were the foot soldiers? Global Food Justice, the gunrunning NGO. The Penitents and Slade.

"Computer, create a list of all first- and second-order associates of Graeme Mujuru. Perform the same procedure for Global Food Justice. Then compare the two lists for any overlap."

Slade stood, stretched, and began to pace the hotel room. It would take the computer a while to populate a list that big. He dug through the crumpled paper bags on his dresser, mauled the brittle remains of a sandwich, then finished off a wounded beer.

The computer chimed a happy chime. It had found an overlap. Slade examined the withered face displayed on his screen: Frederick von Helm, Austrian billionaire, champion of socialist causes, globalism, and open borders. Second-order benefactor of Global Food Justice, second-order associate of Mujuru.

Von Helm had no direct ties to the African General, but he knew people who did.

Von Helm had no direct ties to the gunrunning NGO, but he gave money to people who did.

Slade bit into a mango wedge then wiped the juice that dribbled down his beard. "Computer, search for any ties that Frederick von Helm has to Africa."

Slade recoiled—there where thousands of hits. Von Helm was the primary benefactor of the OneAfrica charity, an NGO that was currently performing humanitarian, reconstruction, and political advocacy work throughout the sub-Sahara. It had ongoing relief operations running out of Dakar, Nairobi, Monrovia, Kinshasa, Pretoria, and Abuja. The NGO was also running a massive public relations push with celebrity endorsements, campus outreach, benefit concerts, and webcast specials. Slade scrolled through numerous pictures of student rallies and concerts, complete with dreadlocked white kids flashing peace signs and wearing OneAfrica t-shirts.

Von Helm was also the primary champion of United Nations Security Council Resolution 2288, a UN resolution that would unify all of collapsed Africa under the UN banner.

Slade tried to place the facts in context, to bring it all together. Von Helm was working to save the continent and unify its people under a single government, but at the same time, he was connected with people who were trying to burn it all down. Slade shook his head in frustration.

Nobody acted within reason . . . Motives and actions lay in contradiction to each other . . . It was a world of madmen.

Suddenly, an idea surfaced. Somebody at Camp Annan was in deep with the Penitents. Somebody with enough swagger to cover up a massive smuggling operation. To have that kind of pull, Mr. Somebody would be a high-ranking UN bureaucrat assigned to an official duty station at Camp Annan. Mr. Somebody was a UN softy.

"Computer, check the roster of UN personnel stationed at Camp Annan. Highlight any that are associated with Frederick von Helm."

A profile popped up: Phillipe Lefleur, a career UN bureaucrat currently assigned as the Senior Director of Logistics at Camp Annan. He was also a member of von Helm's immediate social circle.

Slade smiled. Phillipe Lefleur was overseeing the weapons smuggling op. He would have numerous connections with the Penitents.

The plan crystalized. Slade would arrange for his and Phillipe's paths to cross in an intimate setting. With a brick of cash in one hand and a pair of pliers in the other, Slade would be at his most convincing. Phillipe would find it within his heart to locate and extricate Elizabeth via fiscal means, no tactical shenanigans required.

All that remained was the making of proper introductions.

CHAPTER SIXTY

"Would you prefer your usual seat this evening, sir?" Miss Milan asked in her crisp accent.

"Of course. Please." Slade's lips thinned. He'd spent so much time on stakeout at the Predator that he'd been recognized.

As soon as he took his seat, a large African woman approached, straddled his lap, removed her sequined bikini top, and pressed her naked chest forward. "Hello, Tom. I meesed you yesterday."

"Sorry, Karleen. Got caught up with some things," Slade mumbled through the flesh mask.

"Dat's okay, I saved myself. Just fo you!" She laughed.

Slade smiled up at the girl. He'd cultivated a professional relationship with Karleen because her presence provided both situational and physical cover for him to operate behind. Her lack of looks kept prices low and her faltering command of English kept the chatter to a minimum.

Slade took his usual drink. The same music thumped. Karleen began her awkward routine. The johns came and went on a normal schedule. Time passed.

Until something changed.

One of the door guards touched his earpiece, rotated toward Miss Milan, snapped his fingers, and pointed. Slade watched as the stunning hostess fast-stepped it across the room and greeted a knot of men who had just entered the lounge. The newcomers included soft, well-dressed foreigners as well as a few Africans. Maintaining his lap dance slouch, Slade peered from behind Karleen's girth, watching the new group with laser focus.

Miss Milan's body language was overly gracious and accommodating as she led the group across the room, pulled back a velvet rope, and gestured for them to be seated. There was an immediate migration of dancers toward the newly arrived party. Even faithful Karleen glanced over her shoulder, calculating her chances. Slade produced a clutch of bills to keep his cover in place.

The new group was loud and obnoxious. Bottle service arrived, corks popped, women were pulled into laps, men cackled like hyenas, bills disappeared into crevasses, and thinly veiled sex acts passed in trade.

"Hey!" Slade rapped on Karleen's flank to get her attention. "Hey!"

"Yah?"

"Those guys that just came in. Who are they?"

"Who?"

"The ones in the VIP. Who are they?"

"Ohh, dat's da Boss an 'is yoo ehn friends."

"Boss and who?"

"The yoo ehn."

"The UN? The people from the airport?"

Karleen nodded.

Karleen had said "Boss." Was that the Big Chief that he was looking for? Perhaps it was Mujuru? Slade kept watch but was unable to identify any faces through the gloom. In time the VIP table grew a crystalline forest of empty bottles and drifting tendrils of ganja smoke hung throughout the lounge. Slade's lap began to chafe.

But there, back among the shadowed duvets and hanging silks of the VIP sat a hulking shadow. A pair of charcoal black hands became visible as they reached for a bottle. There was a thick metal band around the left wrist. Was it shielding for a biochip or simply a large bracelet?

The man rose to his feet, his back toward Slade, brushed at his slacks and straightened his white silk suit. He beckoned for one of his friends to join him. The companion rose on unsteady legs, wobbled, then plopped back into his chair. The tall African laughed, pulled his friend to standing, and slung an arm over his shoulder. They leaned into each other and a joke passed between them. The African then extended his arm and swept it back and forth, clearing a path through the crowd. The two worked their way out of the VIP section, across the room, and through the archway that led to the brothel's private bedrooms.

Slade rose, paid Karleen for her faithful service, crossed the lounge, then followed the two men down a long, torch-lit corridor, the pounding lounge beats fading behind. As he made the passage, Slade reached into his jacket pocket and activated Kraven's e-snoop. If the man he was following was Mujuru . . . And if he could get close enough for the e-snoop to penetrate the wrist shielding . . . And if he could remain there long enough for the device to download the information . . . And if he could do it without getting his dumb white ass noticed . . . Slade gritted his teeth—there were too many *ifs* for this to work.

He brushed his hand against the short ceramic knife hidden inside his sleeve, the only weapon he'd been able to slip past the metal detectors. He might need it in the next few minutes.

Slade exited the hallway and entered what had once been a hotel courtyard. From within the surrounding rooms came the sound of loud music and vigorous fucking. Up ahead the two men stumbled across the courtyard and through another curtained archway. Their laughter receded as if growing in distance. Slade crossed the courtyard and made a pass by the archway. Dammit, it was another hallway, one he'd missed during his initial reconnaissance. Heading into an unmapped area raised the risk level another notch.

Twenty meters later, Slade emerged into another courtyard with a bubbling fountain in the center. In each of the surrounding alcoves, the curtains were drawn back, a woman on display. They sat on plush couches, reclining in various stages of undress, bleary eyed and passive. Slade kept his eyes averted and focused on the target ahead where the two men were browsing the stalls, leering at the girls, talking at them, laughing at them. Slade shuffled along, feigning interest.

Five alcoves ahead, the two men stopped, whispering and giggling. The tall African clapped his friend on the back, broke away, then passed into an alcove. The drunker man tried to follow but was pushed back out, giggling into his drink. He wobbled precariously, glanced about, then turned and began shuffling toward Slade, beckoning and laughing.

Slade could not permit the man to get close enough to see his face. Tucking his chin, he ducked into the nearest alcove, pulled the curtains closed and waited, listening as the uncertain footsteps approached. The prostitute seated on the couch behind Slade shifted nervously in the candle gloom. He glanced toward her and gave a quick shushing motion. The footsteps paused directly outside the alcove. The curtains jumped; the man was trying to enter the alcove.

Slade grabbed the curtains and held them closed. "Occupied!" he barked.

The man pushed harder and began muscling forward. "No, sss-he's fur me, she's mine," he slurred.

The prostitute startled and stood up. Slade stood firm, placed his hand on the curtained head lump, and shoved it back. "Occupied!" he barked again.

There was a thump and the sound of breaking glass as the man hit the floor, swearing profusely. "She's mine!"

Slade stayed at the curtain and held it closed, marveling at how quickly the operation had gone to shit. Drunk Man was making another attempt at the curtain when two guards arrived. After a few minutes, they were able to coax him away from the alcove.

When it was finally quiet, Slade backed away from the curtain and lowered himself onto the couch. He glanced toward the prostitute, grinned, and apologized.

The girl shied away from him, hand over her mouth, seemingly terrified. She was in her late teens with porcelain skin, Indian-ink hair, and a sharp, angular beauty.

"Slade? Is that you?"

"Oh, God . . ."

CHAPTER SIXTY-ONE

Elizabeth Brightman cowered like a trapped animal in the rear of the alcove, knees pulled up against her exposed breasts, her face turned away.

For Slade, there was no elation at having found her, only shame. Shame like a knife as he beheld what he had done to her, his failure manifest. He reached out his hand but pulled back. He looked for something to cover her, pulled the sheet off the bed and draped it over her naked shoulders. She shied away from his touch, but he persisted. He lifted her up and carried her back to the couch, light and frail as autumn leaves. She covered her face. He kept his arm around her, head bowed, saying nothing. In time her shoulders began to quake, and the sobs grew and moved freely through her body. Slade sat unspeaking, lacking the words to calm her soft weeping.

Eventually, she raised her face and her bloodshot eyes found the ceiling. She answered the questions he couldn't ask.

"The night you left, we escaped alright. We thought we were free." She wiped at her nose and smeared away the snot. "But then Mantis and his people started arguing that we should go back to Lake Malawi. They got in fights and even shot someone. Then they left and they took all three of the Cougars. And . . ." She fought back a growing sob . . . " and then the raiders found us again. We fought, but there were too many of them." She looked toward Slade, her face contorting with anguish, her voice tipping toward hysteria.

"And I lost Isaac . . . And . . . And then they killed *everybody.*" She wilted downward, hands over her mouth, voice strangled through her fingers. "Even the babies!" She broke into a scream but Slade clamped his hand over her mouth, forced the pain back into her, and held her close as each of her strangled shrieks drove a spear through his chest.

"I'm sorry . . . I'm sorry . . . I'm sorry," he repeated.

Long after his mantra had faded to nothing, Slade continued to mouth the words without sound, his head filling with a sonorous buzzing . . . the buzzing of flies. Flies, moving in an amorphous cloud across a field of prairie dress corpses, and covering in a glistening pelt the impaling forest, the piled families, and the solitary children still sprawled in their hiding places, fingers clasped in unanswered prayer. Slade clamped a hand over his own mouth to silence a moan of shame.

In time, Elizabeth stilled and quieted. She pushed away from him and stared through the wall. Slade's mouth moved but issued nothing. He tried again, his whisper too harsh, his words useless. "I'll get you out. Right now. Tonight. I'll get you out. I can do it. I can do it right now." He repeated the lie again and again, unable to stop himself.

She looked up at him as though apologizing. "I can't. They'd torture the other girls if I ran away." She was wracked by another spasm of grief. "Oh, Jesus, I've seen them do it."

After her breathing slowed, Elizabeth straightened herself, wiped her face, and brushed back her hair. "So, you're here . . . in this place." Her lips pulled tight and her eyes hardened.

Slade got her meaning and shook his head vigorously. "No. I'm not here for that. I've been trying to track you down. I was following somebody." Slade leaned in close to her ear and lowered his voice to a whisper. "The men who walked by, outside the curtain, I was follow—"

"Those two? Boss and Phillipe?"

Slade pulled back. "Phillipe? Phillipe LeFleur? You know him?"

Elizabeth's face contorted in mock pride. "Why yes . . ." Her throat bobbed like she was about to vomit. "I'm one of his favorite pets." She pointed to a mottled yellow bite mark on her neck.

Slade regretted pushing the drunken man away, wished instead that he'd pulled him inside the curtain and buried the ceramic blade in the wattled throat. He lowered his voice to a barely audible whisper. "Do you know if there's a way to get you out of here?"

She shook her head. "We're never alone, there are always guards. If someone makes them angry . . . They do things." There was raw fear in her voice.

"Where's your room? Where do they keep you?"

"Room 1026." She pointed upwards then shrugged, her face drifting down into her hands, still not believing.

Grudgingly, Slade accepted that she was correct. He had no plan, no weapons, no intel, no backup, nothing but a stubby knife and a track record of epic failure. Ego aside, he couldn't get her out tonight.

"I'll figure something out. I'll come back, get you out of here." He reached into his pocket and pulled out his satellite phone. "Do you have some place you can hide this?"

She looked at it. "Yes."

"Do you know how to work it?"

She flashed him an annoyed look, a spark of life flickering still, like a candle glowing defiant in the darkness of a mine.

"Okay, I don't know exactly when but I'm going to get you out. I'll contact you on this phone. Understand?"

"Yes." She took the phone and pushed it down into the sofa cushions.

Slade then pressed his ceramic knife into her hand. "And take this, too. If you ever need to use it, get close, keep it hidden, then slice here . . ." He drew a finger across his jugular. "Then keep sawing till he's done."

Slade stayed with her for another hour. She darkened his shoulder with her tears, thin limbs clinging to him. He spoke of hope because there was nothing else to speak of and loathed himself for doing so. When he left her there, alone in that place, his throat burned as though scalded with lye and his vision tunneled with rage. He paid a Madam for the girl's time with thick, fumbling hands then stalked back into the lounge. Physically ill, hate stoned, Slade's eyes found the cackling men of wealth and power. He looked through the crowd at their low-slung bellies, lewd howls, and bejeweled high fiving.

His eyes searched for the two men, Phillipe and Boss. He found them back in their corner, lounging and talking. But he stood there too long and was noticed. The tall African looked at him, paused, then broke off his conversation. The man rose from his couch then slowly walked past Slade on his way to the bathroom. They eyeballed each other.

The man had stained, heavily bagged eyes, a massive domed forehead, and acne-pocked skin. Old gunpowder burns freckled his face and there was a poorly healed wound slashed across his scalp, florid and raw.

It was Graeme Mujuru.

It was the Penitent Priest.

CHAPTER SIXTY-TWO

SLADE TURNED FOR the exit, not looking back.

Graeme Mujuru, the Penitent Priest, turned to watch Slade leave, head cocked, gears turning.

As he made his way across the lounge, Slade had just enough time to piece together how deep the shit really was; the Penitent cult was not a backwoods freak show. The sect was armed and led by highly placed UN officials. And whatever the cult's political ties and agenda, it had bedfellows in Washington, DC with enough power to shackle the US military. And whatever was at stake, it was enough to drive a decorated war hero, Colonel Gary Kraven, to risk hard prison time by running an unsanctioned operation.

Slade was standing at the epicenter of a struggle that spanned three continents and had caused fractures between the US government and its own military. He was beyond his depth—and badly.

At the weapons check desk, Slade reached into his pocket and pulled out his claim ticket, but the ancient clerk moved with agonizing slowness retrieving another man's pistol belt.

Slade glanced over his shoulder. Mujuru was pointing frantically toward him; men were moving in his direction.

No time. Slade shouldered forward, spun the man standing at the desk, cold-cocked him, and caught his pistol as it fell from his hand. Wracking the slide, Slade turned and sprinted toward the exit, pistol rising, the startled door guards diving away.

Out the door and into the street, Slade waved frantically at a passing tuk-tuk. The tri-wheel skidded to a stop. Slade was moving for the passenger seat when he saw the driver's eyes widen and lock onto an object to his rear. Slade rolled to his left and dove for the street as gunfire slapped his ears and bullets tore through the tuk-tuk. Rolling to his feet, firing cross-body under his arm, Slade bolted into traffic, hunching low, crossing the street, and sprinting down the sidewalk, gunfire popping behind him.

He glanced back. A dozen men had flooded out of the Predator in pursuit but were caught in a gunfight with random passersby. Bodies lay limp on the sidewalk. Two men rushed from the Predator cocking automatic rifles; they bloodily ended the confused disputes.

Slade continued his flight, barreling down the sidewalk at flank speed, pushing straight into the night, knowing only that he had to put as much distance as possible between himself and the lights of central Nairobi.

He rounded a corner, and bolted past a UN checkpoint, blue helmets bobbing nervously behind its sandbag walls. Slade continued thirty meters past the checkpoint then threw himself behind a burned-out kiosk. Turning, he crouched and leveled his pistol back the way he had come.

The pursuers rounded the corner, arms pumping, the blue UN helmets prairie-dogging above the sandbags.

Slade waited until the cluster of sprinting men reached the UN checkpoint, then leaned from his cover and fluttered off half a dozen shots at the blue helmets. The pursuing pack scattered and rolled in all directions, their own weapons clapping. The terrified UN soldiers lit off in the thick of it, their panicked machine-gun fire shattering storefronts and spalling off the sidewalks. As the gunfire grew behind him, Slade fled from the light.

CHAPTER SIXTY-THREE

MOVING IN THE day's first dim light, his new clothes tattered and holed, Slade limped down the shaded and overgrown streets of an abandoned country club neighborhood. A solitary cheetah lounged in a bay window while Ibis fowl and Lapwing birds morning-called in the cool, still dawn. Reading addresses like a wayward paperboy, Slade found the dilapidated colonial, entered through the unhinged door, climbed the creaking stairs, headed for the children's bedroom, and flipped over the playpen, revealing a blue nylon duffel bag that he had cached ten days prior.

Kneeling, he unzipped the duffel, reached inside, and pulled out a well-maintained AK-47. He extended the folding stock, fed in a magazine, chambered a round, and set it aside. Then he extracted the battered 1911, checked the chamber, and holstered the heavy pistol on his belt. Next he pulled out a Rhodesian chest bandolier equipped with four AK magazines, donned it, and cinched the straps down tightly. Lastly, he took out a small backpack and checked its inventory: sat-phone, spare battery and solar charger, two money bricks, med kit, water bladder and filter, knife, headlamp, batteries, compass, and energy bars.

Slade pulled out the water hose and drank till it was near empty. He then downed two energy bars that tasted like wet sawdust spiced with pet dander.

Rising, backpack resting in place, AK in hand, he paced the room, staying away from the windows, weighing his options.

The Predator would have surveillance video of Slade's face. Phillipe and Mujuru would distribute Slade's image among whatever networks they had—shopkeepers, guards, waiters, concierges, taxi drivers, and hotel staff. Someone would recognize Slade and point out his hotel room, perhaps Big's location at the stables. The hotel room was burned. Slade's weapons, electronics, and half of his money was gone.

But worst of all, they might make the connection between him and Elizabeth. Mujuru had just recognized Slade from their encounter at the Ngongo slaughter. Would he realize that Slade had just visited the last surviving Judean girl? If he did, Elizabeth was now in grave danger.

A sense of impending failure gripped Slade. The mission was collapsing. Elizabeth languished in hell. The freedom of his sister and her children hung by a thread. And he, the man responsible for righting those wrongs, possessed only what he wore.

Slade powered up the sat-phone and dialed Kraven. After a long wait the lines opened.

"Who is this?" a synthetic voice asked.

"It's me. I show you encrypted."

"I show same. Why are you calling from a different phone?"

"The other phone was compromised."

"How?"

Slade grimaced. This was going to be a painful conversation. "Who exactly do you think I'm playing with down here? They aren't Girl Scouts."

"What happened?"

"I was recognized."

"Recognized? By whom?"

"By the target. I confirmed it's Mujuru. I tracked him down at a local brothel, but he recognized me and the op is compromised. Lost everything. Gear. Money. Weapons."

"The target *recognized* you? What do you mean?"

"Mujuru is the Penitent Priest that I had a run-in with last month. I didn't make the connection because he was wearing face paint. I already sent you video of the Penitent procession. Look at it closely, you can tell it's him."

"You saw the Penitent Priest in Nairobi? *And* he's the target I assigned you? Graeme Mujuru?" Kraven's voice was rapid fire, his tone rising.

"Yes. And he's deep in bed with the UN bubbas at Camp Annan. This is a huge operation."

"Mujuru's in a direct leadership role." Kraven's voice was almost inaudible, talking to himself. "Incredible."

Slade waited.

"This is fantastic news, Slade. Resume the mission ASAP. Use whatever means necessary to achieve—"

"They have my face. I just spent ten hours evading groups of armed men in trucks. I have no freedom of movement, no safe haven, no cover, no resources, no team."

"Damn it, Crawford! You just don't get it, do you?"

"You're damn right I don't—" Slade's rising anger transformed into a flash of hope. He'd just found true leverage. "Actually . . . there may be one possibility," Slade continued, formulating a plan. "I can put a team together. I know the right men. But—"

"But, what?"

"I'll need something in return."

Kraven raged. The telephone speaker distorted from the volume of his tirade.

Slade hung up, eased himself into a chair, and crossed his legs in satisfaction.

The phone chimed. He answered after a lengthy delay. "Go."

"What do you want?"

"I need you to exfil an American girl from Nairobi, get her to the nearest embassy. State Department will take it from there."

"Negative. Her appearance will raise too many questions."

Slade stood up. "She's the only survivor of the Judean convoy. The people you refused to protect. I need—"

"Negative. She'll be interrogated by State. The involvement of my assets will be exposed."

"She's in a brothel, being used as a *sex slave*. I'll get her out of the city then you send in the Ospreys for the exfil. When you arrive, I'll hand over the info from Mujuru's data chip."

"Can't be done, she'll compromise the entire op. Wait . . . You said she's confined in a brothel?"

"Yes." Slade had landed his barb. There was a sliver of humanity in the old bastard after all.

"Is this the same brothel where you encountered Mujuru?"

"Yes. I'll need more equipment for the op, enough to—"

"Get her involved. She can generate opportunities for you to exploit."

Slade's mouth hung agape. "No. Not a chance. She isn't an option." He had underestimated Kraven and played his feeble cards too far.

"She's the natural choice, Crawford. As a prostitute, she'll be able to gain a private audience with him. She'll be able to administer narcotics, read his biochip, she'll—"

"*Private audience*! It's not a fucking conversation club! You saw that video I sent you. Mujuru flayed the skin off his own people. What's he gonna do with a teenage girl?" Slade was frothing with rage.

"We've gotten off track. This isn't a negotiation."

"Sir, if you want Mujuru's biochip, you will get this kid off continent."

"Negative. You will do as instructed."

"This is me." Slade's finger stabbed the air. "Telling you. That you will never see that data unless you exfil the girl." The threat hung in the stifling air.

When he spoke, Kraven's voice was dead calm. "I'm giving you one more chance. If you refuse, I will imprison your sister. Don't force me to play my hand, Mr. Crawford. Now, one last time, get me the data."

Slade paced the room furiously, sweat beading down his face. "Negative, sir. Not without—"

"That's your final answer?"

"Yes."

"Then you are no longer a functional asset. We're finished," Kraven said.

"Don't do this!" Slade shouted, grasping for a solution.

The phone went silent as Kraven moved to break the connection.

"Four-thirty-nine Maplewood Street," Slade spat.

Static hissed over the line, unending, unbroken.

When Kraven finally spoke, his voice was unnaturally soft, barely audible. "What did you say?"

"You heard me," Slade hissed. "Four thirty-nine Maplewood Street, Alexandria, Virginia." He paused to gain control of his voice. "The bay window of your bedroom looks out over a forested stream. Your wife, Janet, drives a silver G550 Mercedes. Your oldest daughter, Wendy, just pledged Delta Phi Epsilon at Georgetown and she wore black to this year's homecoming." Slade waited for a response.

None came.

"I'll walk across this damn continent if I have to. Then buy my way to Central America. Then work north through Mexico and walk across the border. Forty-eight hours later, I'm in your neighborhood, your daughter's campus, or your son's apartment. Think this through, Gary. Because if you imprison my sister, I have absolutely *nothing* left to lose. And I will cross this world—to end yours."

Slade broke the connection. He hurled the phone down, wiped the sweat from his face, and clenched his hands into fists to prevent them from shaking. He'd just prevented a checkmate on Summer, but the gambit left Kraven with only one logical course of action.

Kill Slade Crawford.

CHAPTER SIXTY-FOUR

IT WAS ALMOST nightfall before Slade stopped running, putting as much distance as possible between himself and the conversation with Kraven. Slade didn't know what kind of hellfire Kraven could call onto those last coordinates, but he wasn't about to find out.

Holed up in the basement of an abandoned factory, he reached for his sat-phone, powered it up, and dialed Kai.

The line opened. "Kia ora, who's this?" Kai asked, his voice barely discernible over a background of music and laughter.

"It's Slade."

"Who?"

Slade winced, realizing that he had given his real name by accident. "It's Tom. Tom the Yank."

"Well why didn't you bloody well say so?" The background noise died away as Kai moved to a quieter corner of the bar. "Where ya been, mate? We're havin' a bun-fight down here at the pool. Got some lady friends here dying to have a go at ya."

"Sorry, buddy, but I can't make it. Gotten myself into a bit of a jam."

There was the sound of movement, the clang and chatter of night-life died to nothing. Kai's voice lowered and lost its usual holiday cheer. "What's up, mate? You ain't soundin' like a box of budgies."

"Yeah, things are a bit . . ." Slade searched for words to sum up just how deep the shit had become. He couldn't find any.

"How's that, mate?"

Slade hesitated. "Remember that fish I told you I was looking for?"

"'Course."

"Turns out he's a shark. Didn't take kindly to me at the fishing hole. Been after me since."

"Shit, mate, was that open slather all for you? Every skinny in town went meat axe last night. You stepped in it and deep now, didn't ya?"

"Yeah. I did." Slade didn't include the part about the renegade colonel who wanted him dead . . . Or the teenage girl condemned to a rape machine . . . Or the fact that it was his failures that sent her there. Slade's chin sank toward his chest. "Yeah, I stepped in it pretty deep."

"You're soundin' low, mate. Where're you holed up?"

"Outside of town."

"Need any scroggin?"

"What?"

"Scroggin! Food, mate! You had any bloody food?"

"No, not much."

"Any extra holes in ya?"

"What?"

"*Holes*! Little round places where there ain't anything. Anybody put extra holes in ya?"

"No."

"Brilliant. Send me your grid."

"Sorry, I can't. My phone is compromised. And so is yours now."

"Now ya making me feel all important. Where ya at?"

"You remember the fishing hole we talked about?"

"'Course."

"Plot a 285 radial from that location, then—"

"What?"

"285 radial from the fishing hole—"

"You tryin' to give me a range-bearing?"

"Yes. Get something to write with."

"Christ—" Slade could hear the giant Kiwi fumbling and cussing as he located a pen.

"Ready? Now for range, in klicks, double the total number of people in our drinking group. Then subtract two. That's my range on the 285 radial. Think you can handle that math?"

"Christ, mate, don't get astro on me."

"Sorry, but I've got some world-class dicks looking for me. And when I say world-class, I mean world-class. So—"

"No need to get all big-headed." Kai laughed. "Fuckin' seppos. Just sit tight."

The line went dead.

*　*　*

The full moon was directly overhead when the three Kiwis arrived. Slade had expected them to park their vehicle at a distance and cover the last kilometer on foot, using stealth to mask their approach, but the Land Rover SUV parked at the rendezvous location, headlights on, horn blaring, suggested otherwise. Sideshow stepped from the passenger seat and shone a flashlight through the windows of an abandoned building. "Come out, come out, wherever you seppos are!" He was not visibly armed.

Slade stepped from cover and approached. "Evenin', gents."

Kai squeezed himself from the vehicle. "Evenin', mate."

"Thanks for coming. Anybody follow you out here?" Slade knew it was a stupid question, but he wanted to underscore the fact that people were hunting him.

"Not likely after that tiki tour," Sideshow replied.

Bert rabbled an unintelligible slur, spiked with profanity and laughter.

Slade examined the newcomers. "Are you guys shit-faced?"

"It's night, init?"

Shaking his head, Slade led them inside the building to an inner, windowless room.

Once inside, Kai unslung his pack, opened it, and produced two six-packs of beer, the bottles beaded with condensation. "No worries, mate, here ya go. Straight from the chilly bin." He then pulled out a grease-stained paper bag stuffed to bursting with dripping cheeseburgers. Slade accepted the gifts gratefully, then handed the food and beer around to his companions.

The men ate, joked, and drank. In time, Slade found himself smiling and laughing as the coat of despair sloughed from his shoulders.

Kai eventually interrupted the party. "Alright, seppo, enough of the take-away n' suds. What the hell are you really up to, and why are you sittin' out here in the wop-wops? Out with it."

Slade told them who he was. He told them about his imprisonment by the DHS, his escape from America, and his recapture by Kraven. He told them about the Judeans, the Penitent cult, the UN, Elizabeth, Mujuru, and his falling out with the colonel.

The Kiwis listened without interruption.

When Slade was finished, Bert straightened himself and spoke, his voice measured and solemn. "I've seen some men step deep init, but that takes the bloody cake, mate. You're in it heaps." He nodded with deep respect. "What're ya plans?"

Slade shook his head. "I don't know."

"Way I see it, you got two options. Stay down here and tramp about, playin' the sneaky peak till the colonel or the tribe gits ya. Or you make nice wit the colonel, give the relationship a quick fixer-upper, and get on with the job."

Slade shook his head in refusal. "I've got to get the girl out of the Pred before anything else."

Sideshow looked at him askance. "I'm not one to piss in the punch, but your chances of pullin' that alone are slim to hell-no. You willin' to get killed over it?"

Slade leaned forward on his elbows and watched his hands rubbing themselves together. "Yes. Yes, I am." He paused, searching for words. "I was responsible for protecting her. I'm accountable."

"That wasn't your fault, mate. Don't git yourself killed makin' to be the hero."

"It's more than that . . . I don't . . . What about Mombasa?" Slade asked, changing the subject. "I've heard there's port traffic there. I could get her to a ship."

Sideshow shook his head. "If you're thinking about putting her on some ship, slappin' her on the arse, and biddin' her good day, have fun in America . . . it ain't gonna happen. Insurance won't let legit companies dock here. The people who do are dodgy—runnin' weapons, drugs n' slaves. Not the sort to look after a lamb." The other two Kiwis nodded in agreement.

"Nearest you could drop her is fifteen hundred miles south in Johannesburg, or a thousand miles north in Djibouti. Only option you got is to make nice with that colonel chap of yours."

"Not gonna happen. I threatened to kill his family."

"People say a heap o' rubbish when they're mad. Bring 'im some flowers."

Slade laughed in spite of himself.

Kai leaned forward, talking around a mouthful of cheeseburger. "You know, mate, I bet if you went and nicked that Priest, then sent the old rupert some viddy and told 'im no shit—here's your man—bring the trolley 'round—he'd be willin' to forgive a lot more than you think."

Slade shook his head. "Not possible. I'd have to pull a snatch-n-grab on a hard target, then stash him somewhere while I bust the girl out of lockdown. Then get the whole circus out into the countryside to rendezvous with a man that wants me dead. And do all of it while evading the Penitents. I'd need a platoon to pull a job like that, more like a company."

"True, true," Kai said, kneading his chin. "But that bird of yours is chained at the Pred, you say?"

"Yeah."

"And this fella you gotta grab, Mujuru, is in thick with the slave trade?"

"Yeah."

"And how much green ya got?"

Slade dug in his pack and produced two bricks of cash, then lifted his shirt and pointed at his belt. "And ten ounces of gold."

Kai briefly locked eyes with his fellow Kiwis—an agreement seemed to pass between them. The Maori sniffed, then finished off his cheeseburger. "You said you'd need a company to pull off your snatch and grab. True, true. A company of Yanks . . ." Kai swallowed, licked his fingers clean, then spread his arms to their full length. "Or three Kiwis. Your call."

CHAPTER SIXTY-FIVE

BY THE TIME the party slowed, the burgers had been reduced to a pile of grease-stained papers and the beers to scattered shards of glass. Kai and Sideshow sat by the door, headlamps burning, rehashing old engagements, their rapidly moving hands casting a crazed shadow dance on the floor. Bert and Slade sat on the other side of the room, locked in conversation.

"So," Bert said, "what's ya take on all this crazy stuff you been findin'?"

Slade let out a long breath. "It's hard to say. None of the actors appear rational. Kraven has everything to lose, but he's risking Gitmo time? For what? And Mujuru, a wealthy diplomat, goes off the grid and starts running a blood cult? For what? And von Helm funds an arms-smuggling operation in collusion with UN officials? For what?" Slade shook his head. "Nobody has anything to gain."

Bert's voice dropped to a hiss. "Yes there is, mate. You can see for yourself there's a game afoot. Now ask yourself, what's the prize?" He turned his wrist and pointed a single finger down at the earth beneath his feet. "Africa. And after that, the world."

Slade remained silent, uncomprehending.

"Do you think the UN would come in, rebuild things, then hand it back to the skinnies to fuck up again?"

Slade shook his head.

"Right. They're aiming to run the show themselves, top to bottom. And the blood cult is for gittin' rid o' the competition."

"What do you mean? Nobody's competing with the UN."

"Oh? The UN knows it'll take a decade to establish control over the continent. And in the meantime, settlers like your little girlfriend and all them gooks is pouring in an settin' up camp. Ten years from now, the UN don't want to find a hundred million people livin' in New China, New India, and New Alabama. Would those happy drongos submit to UN rule? Follow its laws? Pay its taxes? Not bloody likely. And starting a fight with those nobs would spoil the show, make the UN look like the bad guy.

"So to avoid that, they've commissioned a wild injin tribe to run around and keep things clean. That way, when the UN does roll through, it'll be nothing but rose petals and cheering crowds to put on the tube. Everybody's happy, it's for the greater good, and everybody goes along easy peasy."

Slade was nodding unconsciously, adding things up, whispering to himself. "The surveillance drones at the airport . . . They're equipped with a radar that detects moving vehicles . . . They've been using those to track the convoys . . . locate the settlers . . . then they feed that info to the Penitents. That's how they were able to converge on us so quickly." Slade's head was bobbing, his voice rising. "It all makes sense, but why would they want to take over? That's not the UN's charter."

"The hell it ain't! The UN's always been about One World Government. Africa's the stepping-stone."

"I don't buy it. It's just . . . too . . . too . . ."

"Too human? You ever study history?" Bert sat forward, opened one palm as if it were a book, then began stabbing it with the finger of his other hand. "Alexander. Huang. Mohamed. Khan. Tamerlane. Kamehameha. Napoleon. Zulu. Stalin. Hitler. Cheney. Hilla—"

"Alright, I get it."

"I don't think you do. Do you imagine that world conquerors no longer exist? It's in our DNA! They still walk among us and they still want the world. A unified Africa is the first step. It gives them control of populations, resources, taxes, tariffs, armies. Turns the UN into a T-Rex overnight." Bert swung his arm in an arc as if to cover the entirety of the ruin that surrounded them. "They know they can't build a new world without first destroying the old. So, they put out a professional hit on the Nigerian president and his family. Made sure it was so horrible that it would spark a nasty civil war. Then they brought in NATO to make things worse and spread it across the continent. The chaos then provided perfect cover for them to bomb the oil refineries and fuel terminals. Boom!" Bert threw his hands up into the air. "Ring-a-bloody-rosie, it all falls down."

"You really think so?"

"I was there, Slade, guarding the Warri refinery when it got hit. There wasn't any fighting going on. We weren't under attack from any rebels. It was an airstrike that did it. You know that sound just before a JDAM hits? Like there's a freight train coming down on ya at five hundred knots? I heard that sound, made me duck—then boom! Four simultaneous hits, dead center on the cooling towers. Made the refinery inoperable but easily repairable at a later date. Same thing happened at all the major refineries. And the fuel terminals at the shipping ports? Perfect hits on the switching valves. Again, made the gear unusable but easily repairable. Don't take my word for it, see for yourself." Bert pulled out his phone, activated the map app, and pulled up recent satellite photography. "Look, Warri refinery—see the craters? Perfect hits on the cooling towers. One meter accuracy." He scrolled the map to another location. "Port Harcourt Refinery, perfect hits on the cooling towers. One meter accuracy."

He scrolled the map. "Look, the fuel terminals in Lagos, perfect hits on the switching valves. One meter accuracy. You want me to go on? Because I can . . ."

Slade sat back, his mind reeling. "But it's so damn obvious. If it really was them, why wouldn't they try and hide it, alter the satellite imagery or something?"

"Because they don't have to. Yanks lied to the world about WMD in Iraq, burned a nation to the ground, and nobody gave a fuck.

"You lied about Libya, turned the most prosperous country in Africa into a failed state, and nobody gave a fuck.

"Your State Department bragged about overthrowing the government of Ukraine, ignited a civil war that killed tens of thousands. Nobody gave a fuck.

"You started arming *Al-Qaida* in Syria, half a million civies died, no fucks were given.

"NATO member, Turkey, was proven to be funding and arming ISIS, and once again, completely fuckless. And you think people will get upset because of a few craters in Africa? Jesus, seppo, wake the hell up." Bert sat back, breathing heavily, his tirade finished.

"Holy shit . . . They did do it." Slade's eyes took on a glassy stare as he strung the pieces together. "And now the UN General Assembly just floated von Helm's resolution to place Africa under UN stewardship. Christ almighty, it's the Hegelian Dialectic . . ."

Bert's face puckered with suspicion.

"Hegelian Dialectic: You intentionally create a problem . . . which requires a solution . . . that benefits you. Politics 101. Get with the program, Bert."

Bert shrugged. "Fair 'nough."

"A lot of it fits," Slade continued, "but I'm having trouble swallowing it. I've seen dozens of UN ops over the years. They're inept and corrupt . . . but hundreds of *millions* of people just died. You think it was on purpose?"

"Just like your government, the UN is controlled by the uber-wealthy. An' if you've been paying attention to rich folks, they openly say the human population has to go down below two billion. So, do I think they would kill a couple hundred million carbon-emitting skinnies to save the world? Yes, I do. And in fact, I think they's just gettin' started."

"Oi! Bert!" Kai interrupted. "If you and the seppo is finished kissin', we're dry as a bone over 'ere. Let's get back to the crib an' scull a few handles. Seppo, you got what you need?"

Slade rose, stretched his stiff legs, then moved to thank them. "Yeah, I'm good for now. I can't thank you enough for the resupply. I'd be in a world of shit otherwise."

"No worries, seppo." Kai stood and slapped him on the shoulder. "You serious about bringing us in on this job of yours?"

Slade produced his two money bricks and tossed them to Kai without hesitation. "That serious enough for you?" He then lifted his shirt and began to unbuckle his money belt. "I've also got my belt here if—"

"Easy now, mate, need a few more handles to get me swinging that way." Kai laughed. "Keep your trousers on. This's more 'n enough."

"Okay. But I'll need you to see me through till I get Elizabeth off the continent. And I'll need more kit: clothing, armor, vest, rifle, night vision. Comm."

Kai ran his thumb along the edge of the money brick, fanning the bills. "No worries, this'll get you topped off. You run a CR-30, right?"

"Yeah, ten-inch barrel. Suppressed."

"Done." Kai extended his hand.

Slade extended his and shook hands with each of the Kiwis, his belly filling with the heady cocktail of one newly committed to a dangerous course of action.

"No tears, stay in touch," Kai said as he turned for the exit.

As the Kiwis passed, Slade grabbed at Sideshow's sleeve. "One other thing. What the hell is a seppo?"

"Ahhh, don't take it personal, mate—all Yanks are seppos."

"But, *what* is a seppo?"

"Seppo: short for septic tank."

"Septic tank? Why that?"

Sideshow drained the last of his beer then let the bottle drop. "Because yer full of shit."

CHAPTER SIXTY-SIX

SEATED ON A filthy couch in the basement of an abandoned building, Slade worked on the message to Kraven, typing and retyping on his sat-phone. Three times his finger paused above the "Send" button, but three times he balked. He breathed deeply, reread his message, then hit "Send."

The current situation benefits neither of us. I propose a solution. I've assembled a team. If you arrange for the exfil of the girl, I will deliver Mujuru to you. Alive.

A day passed without reply. Slade found himself checking and rechecking his sat-phone like a lovesick teenager.

The world hung in the balance.

His phone warbled. He snapped it to his ear. It wasn't Kraven.

"Mr. Crawford," Elizabeth said, her voice frighteningly cold and devoid of emotion.

"Yes? Elizabeth, how are you?" Slade flinched, profoundly aware of how obscene his greeting was.

"I'm fine." The words were delivered in a flat monotone, like a robot reading from a script. Slade had heard that tone before, spoken by a friend of his, one hour before his friend blew his brains out.

"Elizabeth? What's going on?"

"I don't want you to get hurt. You don't have to come for me."

"Elizabeth, I'm going to get you out. You got my last text, didn't you? We're just waiting on a few details to come through." Slade hung his head at the lie. He'd not heard back from Kraven nor formed a credible plan that would allow him to snatch Mujuru and Elizabeth in quick succession. "Don't do anything stupid, okay? I'll get you out of there and—"

"I've got enough pills saved up. It won't hurt."

"Goddammit, Elizabeth! I promised I would get you out. Just hold on a little longer," Slade begged.

"Goodbye, Brother Crawford. Thank you for trying."

Her thanks sent another blade through his chest. "Elizabeth, I'm coming for you tonight," Slade blurted. He looked at his watch. "I'm coming for you in six hours. Do you understand? Just hang on for six more hours, and I'll have you out."

There was a long pause.

"Elizabeth. There will be men coming to get you. It might not be me, but we are coming. Hold on a few more hours."

When the connection finally broke, Slade bolted for the stairs and took them three at a time, his finger mashing on the button that would summon his Kiwis.

CHAPTER SIXTY-SEVEN

"You sure you wanna pull this jobber right now, mate?" Kai asked.

"Yes. I'm sure." Slade spoke with the halting cadence of a man deeply unsure of himself. "If she kills herself while I sit here looking after my own skin . . ."

"Fair 'nuff," Kai sniffed. "How we gonna go about it? Gettin' her out, that is."

"I don't know. But that place is made to keep the women in, not to keep us out. We could create a diversion outside the front door—a few propane tanks in a car. I enter through the loading docks while everybody is evacuating and then you—"

"Whoa, whoa there, mate! That's pretty astro stuff." Kai shook his head in mock disgust. "Keep it simple. Something like the old Eastwood flicks, eh? Bring the horses up to the back of the jail, tie some chains to the bars, giddy up, and off they come."

"You're kidding."

Kai narrowed his eyes and wagged a finger. "If you eva got a look at my cock, you'd know I'm not the kiddin' sort."

"That's right, mate, he ain't the kiddin' sort and then some," Bert added.

"So how 'bout this . . ." Kai spread his hands as if framing a picture. "Bert and Sideshow goes in the front door, cocks in hand, looking for a good time. They toss a little cash, knock back a few handles, then buy a ticket for some alone time with your girl. Follow?

"Then they book a room at the back of the hotel on the lower floors. Then, as they take in the lovely view of the city, they just so happen to notice that you and I have parked a lorry beneath the window. Still with me?"

Slade nodded.

"We throw 'em a chain, they tie it to the bars, we yank 'em free, they hop down, off we go, and Bob's ya uncle, we're home and hosed!" Kai leaned back, arms crossed, a look of supreme satisfaction spreading across his face.

"Bloody 'ell, mate. That's a right propa job there," Sideshow agreed.

Bert slapped his hands together. "You're tellin' me it is! That's straight-up Eastwood."

Slade leaned forward on his elbows, eyes closed, and rubbed his temples. "Oh, Jesus."

"Whatsa matta, mate? You got a better idea?"

"No." Slade pressed his temples until it hurt. "No, I don't."

Kai's satisfaction was complete, but his face turned serious. "I gotta tell you though, mate, as fun as this'll be, after we muddy the waters with this stunt, there ain't a chance in hell any of us can go back to the Pred lookin' for your big fish."

Slade nodded.

"And you still gotta catch him if you want the colonel to get your girl back to America, right?"

Slade nodded.

"And you ain't gonna just be losing the Pred. Bert and Sideshow will hafta skip town 'bout five minutes after 'lizabeth's off the stage."

"I know."

"And she can't stay in the city. So, you'll be babysitting 'er in the bush while you go about tryin' to catch a shark, without no fishin' hole."

"I know."

Kai released a deep sigh, leaned in close, put his hand on Slade's shoulder, and looked him in the eyes. "You sure you know what you're doing, mate? I've seen some dodgy plans in my day, and this is the worst of 'em. I'd put hard money on this going down the gurgler."

"I know."

"So why ya doing it?" Kai asked. "Not to pry, but when me and the mates slap our sweet meats on the barbie, we like to know what the chef's aimin' to cook."

Slade lowered his eyes, struggling to expose that part of himself that he could barely look upon let alone put into words. "I've failed at everything a man can. Let down every person who ever put their trust in me." He pressed his hand against his eyes. "My wife . . . My son . . . My sister . . . The Judeans . . . And now Elizabeth is in the Pred because I fucked up." Slade pulled himself erect and returned Kai's gaze. "My life has to mean something . . . I can't let her down, too," he finished.

Kai squeezed Slade's shoulder with undisguised affection. "I know it sucks, mate, but if we pull the trigger now, she'll likely die in the bush waitin' on a ride home."

Slade wiped his nose and composed himself. "That's better than dying tonight. In that place."

"And you're willin' to go all in for that?"

"Yes."

Kai nodded solemnly. "You're a straight hooker, mate. A damn straight one." He stood, a smile cracking his broad face. "Jock up, lads. It's kickin' off tonight!"

CHAPTER SIXTY-EIGHT

THE LAND ROVER idled smoothly, its engine purring, the interior smelling of rich leather and rank man. Slade shifted nervously in the driver seat. Rivulets of sweat broke from his hairline and ran beneath his armor in spite of the hissing air conditioner. His eyes found his watch, glanced outside at the pressing darkness, then found the watch again. He tightened his gloves, reached to the passenger seat, and set his hand on his new rifle. He checked to ensure that the magazine was secure, a round chambered, the suppressor locked, and the optics activated. He reinspected his vest, checking the buckles and magazines.

It had been an hour since Bert and Sideshow entered the Predator. They should have made contact with Elizabeth by now. Slade keyed his transmitter. "Bravo, what's the status?" He immediately regretted making the call. He was acting like fresh meat on his first op.

"All shiny and chrome. Just sit tight," Kai responded from his position behind the Predator.

Parked two blocks away, Slade sat in the Kiwis' Land Rover, waiting to kick off the dumbest op he'd ever been party to. He hung his head just thinking about it. It was undermanned, underequipped, childishly simple . . .

But it was going to work. It had to. He would not get another shot at Elizabeth. His face was known around town. Kraven was stalking him. He was down to his last dollars, and Sideshow and Bert were leaving town before dawn.

And even if they were successful tonight, he still needed to find a place to sequester Elizabeth. Then he needed to bag Mujuru alive, an impossible task in itself. And then he needed to convince Kraven to extract them all. The chances of everything coming together was nonexistent. It simply wouldn't happen.

The feeling that constricted his throat brought back memories of a time he'd gone sledding as a child; of hurtling down a rocky gully too fast to stop and too blinded to steer. All he could do was hang on, hold his breath, and hope there was something left to salvage when the violence stopped.

"Heads up, Alpha," Kai's voice interrupted. "Two vehicles just left the Pred. Headed your way."

Slade glanced at the dashboard and ensured that all his lights were off. From the direction of the Predator, headlights swept the darkness revealing gray and trash-strewn streets.

Slade pulled his weapon into his lap, reclined his seat, and lowered himself from view as the two vehicles approached. The first SUV passed in a blaze of neon running lights, flashing rims, and the tectonic thump of hip-hop beats.

Slade angled his head and eyeballed the passing vehicle as it slowed and made a turn. For a moment, its interior was illuminated by the headlights of the second vehicle. In that brief flash, Slade saw a woman fawning . . . A man laughing . . . Mujuru.

As the SUVs passed and the hip-hop drone faded, Slade rose in his electric seat, hand coming to the gear shift.

Kai's voice crackled in his headset, "Alpha, lamb's in the bag. Bring the trolley 'round."

Slade blinked, looked at the receding SUVs and back toward the Predator. "Negative. Kill it. Abort. I've got a VID on the Priest. Abort."

"What?"

"In the vehicles that just passed. I got a VID on the Priest. Abort and regroup. We're taking the Priest right now."

"What? You sure? I'm looking right at me mates. They're standing in the window with your lamb."

"We'll never get a chance this good at the Priest. Fall back to my position. You and I'll take the Priest, then we'll come back for the lamb. Do it all in one night."

"That's a negative, Alpha—"

"Why?"

"I ain't leavin' till me mates clear the objective area. We'll press with ya, but it'll be five minutes before they're out."

"I can't wait that long. It's gotta be now."

The neon taillights blinkered out of view. The chances of success were diminishing by the second. Slade heard one of his teeth crack.

"Sorry, mate, I ain't—"

"Fuck it. I'll take him alone."

"Alright, mate, we'll—"

The rest of Kai's transmission was drowned out by the roar of the Land Rover's engine and the sound of its tires biting the graveled street. Accelerating, Slade swung the heavy vehicle after the vanished taillights and barreled after them, directly into the eastern slums.

With his headlights off and the dim sky-glow suggesting only a darkened path, Slade turned down the street Mujuru had taken but saw only darkness before him. He'd already lost his quarry.

He braked to a stop at the first intersection, rolled down the windows, killed the engine, and listened.

The guttural hip-hop thump came from the road to his left. Turning the engine back on, Slade hammered the gas pedal, swung the wheel, and accelerated down the trash lane at full throttle, crouched forward over the wheel, watching dim shapes rush past in the dark. Headlights were not an option, nor was patience. He had to complete the intercept before they reached Penitent territory.

The neon light pool of Mujuru's convoy hovered into view. Slade stayed on the accelerator, pushing faster still, the engine howling as wind battered through the open windows.

Guided by the trail vehicle's taillights, he closed on his target. A dim shadow crossed the road, obscuring the taillights for a blink, and Slade's window went spiderwhite with a cannon boom as an old woman, newly dead, spun over the truck and into the night.

Slewing and skidding to a stop, Slade pulled and punched against the staved-in window, its spiderweb cracks matted with hair and blood.

With the crumpled windshield half collapsed into the cabin, Slade got back on the accelerator and closed on the trail vehicle. Coming abreast his quarry, he clicked on his high beams then veered and accelerated into the SUV's flank, breaking the rear tires free from the pavement. The SUV slewed broadside, tires screeching and smoking, the driver frozen in headlights screaming mutely as the vehicle left the road, rolled twice, and disappeared into a storefront.

Back on the accelerator, Slade closed on Mujuru's vehicle and maneuvered to come abeam, but muzzle flashes illuminated its interior and bullets slapped off of Slade's hood, bloodying his face. Responding, Slade raised his own weapon and set it to chattering through the empty window space.

The two vehicles collided, locked at the bumper, then struck a parked car while spattering at each other, then careened onward, windows fogged with bullet strikes. Suddenly, Mujuru's door opened, and a terrified woman dressed in gaily colored clothes was pushed onto the road. Slade swerved, but too late, and the bump threw the wheel from his blood-slicked hand. The Land Rover overturned, sliding in a blizzard of glass until it stopped.

Slade unbuckled and wormed his way out of the wrecked Land Rover. He found his rifle, reloaded it, shouldered it, placed the sighting reticle between Mujuru's escaping taillights, then held the trigger down until the stuttering gun became still and the night went silent save for the delicate tinkling of brass.

The distant taillights wavered and slewed and tumbled and the sound of crumpling metal echoed through the night. Slade levered himself up from the street and limped toward the crazy canted headlights, reloading his weapon. A figure stumbled broken-legged from the wrecked SUV, weapon cracking. Raising his own, Slade tapped the figure to the ground.

He closed on Mujuru's overturned vehicle, weapon shouldered, the targeting light casting stark shadows. The man crying and worming on the ground was young and fit, definitely not Mujuru. Slade's muzzle tracked toward him and coughed once, the metallic crack of the rifle's mechanism louder than the actual gunshot. He knelt and scanned the interior of the overturned SUV. The driver hung in his seat, inverted, mewling pitifully. Slade's weapon cracked again.

He circled the vehicle, found a thick blood trail, and took after it at a broken trot. The blood lay in long streaks, lost from a running wound. A footprint in red. A palm scrape along a wall.

Slade rounded corners at full speed, ignoring the possibility of a trap, weapon up, kicking over trash piles, probing corners, alleys, and storefronts with his light. But the light revealed no Priest, only ragged scarecrow shapes that blinked their yellow orbs and scrambled from the glare while snarling in animal tongue.

There was shouting one street over.

Slade closed on the sound, a new blood spatter pointing the way. He rounded a corner. A figure limped along the sidewalk one block ahead. The figure turned into Slade's light, snarling, eyes shining like a feral cat. Mujuru raised his arm, clacked a shot off, then took to flight. Slade closed at a run, but Mujuru was yelling now, motioning, pointing back toward Slade.

Yelling to whom?

Movement up ahead. A trashcan fire flickering and men rising to their feet and lifting weapons as they called to each other.

The patter of naked feet on concrete.

A loose gang of Penitents sprinted into Slade's light pool, their weapons rising. He met them on the run, upending them in rapid succession until they lay in their numbers upon the street, silent now save those gagging and retching on the last of their lung blood.

Slade pushed into a sprint, knowing that he had to take control of Mujuru and get him off the street. Seconds mattered.

Mujuru, hobbling and wheezing, looked over his shoulder just as Slade hammered into his back. With a slap of colliding flesh the two men rolled in a tumble, but Slade came out atop the flailing mass. Mounting the Priest from behind, he wrapped his arm around the man's throat, placed his other hand atop the bald scalp, knurled his fingers down into the wet eye sockets, then heaved backward, dragging Mujuru across the sidewalk and into the interior of a burned-out store. Still struggling, they tripped over an unseen something and toppled to the ground. Screaming for help, the Priest pushed away, freed an arm, and swung his chrome pistol toward Slade's face. Slade caught the arm, yanked the Priest off his feet, then straddled his chest, pressing him into the floor. Still struggling with the Priest's pistol arm, unable to silence him, Slade bent the chrome pistol back toward Mujuru's face, then bore down with his entire weight, forcing the barrel between Mujuru's lips, pressing and pressing until the front teeth hinged inwards with a sucking sigh and the screams dampened to a gurgling hiss and all was still.

Panting, Slade heaved and dragged the unconscious body further into the burnt-out store, his head filling with the smell of wood ash, melted plastic, and fear. He glanced down at his prize—the Priest lay motionless, not breathing. Crouching, Slade rolled Mujuru onto his side, then repeatedly jackhammered his knee into Mujuru's diaphragm.

He cupped a hand over the ruined mouth as the Priest sputtered back to life, wheezing raggedly. Seeing the Priest's eyes flutter open, Slade pressed the muzzle of his weapon to the temple and leaned into it. "Shhh," he breathed, as one would to a baby. "I know you speak English. The next sound you make will be your last."

The Priest nodded, rigid in his agony.

Slade knelt on the man, pinned him to the floor, then turned his eyes to the street. Outside, men were arriving, calling to each other. A truck growled past, its headlights blooming the interior of the ash-black store.

The Penitents were collecting the bodies of the slain night guards. One babbled and coughed in his dying, pointing up the street. Others motioned and called. Men began searching, pushing back the night with torch and flashlight.

Two dozen men were now milling in the street. One jabbered into a radio issuing orders. Another truck growled into view, its bed spilling over with AK-armed men and boys. Slade rose, set himself deep in the shadows, braced his rifle tightly, took aim, and dropped the radio man. Next, he sighted on the speeding truck, stitched three holes in the driver's windscreen, then emptied the magazine into the packed truck bed. Turning to the Priest, Slade hauled the man erect and pushed him toward the back of the store as screaming and gunfire erupted wholesale in the street outside.

Slade gripped Mujuru by his collar. "They find us, you die."

Mujuru shuffled through the ankle-deep cinders, wheezing from his free-bleeding mouth. He threw a glance over his shoulder and offered a pitiful, gap-toothed smile. "I'll pay whatever you want," he said, his words sodden and liquid.

Slade answered with a muzzle strike to the side of the Priest's head, opening a coin-shaped gash in the fatted flesh. Mujuru righted himself and hobbled forward, clutching at his skull, sobbing.

Deeper in the building, Slade used his weapon light to navigate through the ashes of the back storerooms until he found an exit. Leaning into the alleyway, he found it empty, then shoved and clubbed the Priest across. When they were deep in the bowels of the next building, Slade pushed the Priest down into a corner and turned his light full on him, blinding the cowering man. Reaching into his vest, Slade drew a set of handcuffs, clacked one manacle onto the Priest's arm and the other to an exposed pipe. With the Priest secured, Slade checked his wrist computer and thumbed the transmit button.

"Bravo? Bravo, you up?"

Static.

"Bravo, this is Alpha, in the blind. Jackpot. Footrace. Danger close."

No response.

Failing to contact the Kiwis, Slade drew his sat-phone and dialed Kraven. The call went straight to voice mail. Slade broke the connection and tried again but with the same result.

Frustration growing, he activated the sat-phone's video feed and put the camera in Mujuru's face. "Here's your man, Colonel. You want to talk to him, you better call back ASAP. I don't know how much longer I can keep him. I'll leave my sat-phone on. Vector all assets to my location if you want this guy." Slade broke the connection but left the phone on, hoping that Kraven would take the bait and send someone to assist. It was a gamble, one that could get him killed, but it was all he had.

Slade turned back to the Priest, kicked him, and motioned for him to rise. "Interview's canceled. On your feet. Time to move." But the Priest remained on his haunches, shook his head, and sobbed. Disgusted, Slade began to reach for his blade; few things could motivate like naked steel. But before he could draw his knife, a lone Penitent ambushed forward out of the ashen shadows, machete drawn back, eyes like murder burning.

Slade flinched away from the charge and raised his rifle to block the machete's killing blow. Deflected away from his face, the rusty blade skinned off the side of Slade's scalp and embedded itself in the shoulder of his armor as he reeled backward, arms flailing, blood spraying from his half-severed ear. Foundering dumbstruck, his rifle knocked away, Slade tried to fend off the charge but toppled over backward. The Penitent stayed on him, pressing forward like an enraged bulldozer, hands snapping closed around his neck. Slade brought his feet up kicking, trying to worm away, but the Penitent blitzed past Slade's boots in the spinning darkness, raised a fist, and brought a sledgehammer blow that popped Slade's nose to splinters and turned his vision red with pain. As the man drew back for a second blow, Slade caught at the strangling wrist with both hands, thrust his hips upward, and scissored his legs closed around the Penitent's upper arm and shoulder. Bellowing, the man jerked and bucked to free himself, then levered himself up to standing. Slade maintained his scissor grip, clinging to the Penitent's arm as the man thrashed and struck at him. Suspended there, Slade released one of his own hands, drew a steel talon from his sheath, and scrolled it across the Penitent's naked belly, opening a series of obscene gills through which coiled viscera spurt. The man wilted with a scream, and Slade rode him down, his blade still tilling flesh.

Slade rolled away from the gurgling heap, gasping and choking on their comingled blood, numbed hands scrambling for his rifle.

Snatching it up, he swung it wildly. Its light revealed a panicked Mujuru thrashing and yanking against his manacle, scrambling in place, feet slipping over concrete, a bracelet of raw meat growing on his wrist as the handcuff stripped away the flesh.

Slade swayed on his feet, panting and coughing, pressing at the gouts of blood that flowed from his scalp and nose. He glanced toward the growing clamor of searching Penitents. He had captured Mujuru but could not keep him. This path was at an end . . .

He slowly lowered his rifle, bent and picked up the dead Penitent's machete, tested its heft, then advanced toward the struggling Priest.

CHAPTER SIXTY-NINE

SLADE MOVED THROUGH darkness and fled from the lights that followed, lost in the eastern slums where nothing grew save towering trash piles, tin-roofed shanties, and sewers of whim.

Charging through the gutted bowels of a factory, then across a train yard, he plunged into a labyrinth of alleys headlong, hands in front of him, blindly kicking through knee-high trash. He continued at a run until his lungs caught fire and his legs flooded with concrete. Slowing, he kept a staggering pace, stopping now and again to retch and glance down side streets before stumbling across.

Finally halting his flight, he withdrew into a sagging doorway, searched the street behind him, and tried to listen, but all he could hear was the rushing of blood and his uncontrollable lung spasms. Something moved beneath a pile of trash, flashlights swung and jumped in the distance, parties of men shouted and called to each other back the way he had come. He gave himself fifteen seconds then took flight again with a stumbling jog.

Up ahead, a burnt-out city bus lay across an intersection, its innards aglow with a fire around which unformed shadows sat motionless, staring blindly into its depths.

He moved on, heard the sound of stereos thumping and trucks prowling the streets, their beds laden with laughing children who fired into the trash heaps and cut down the shadows that ran.

Cornered, diving, covering himself in trash, Slade lay breathless beside a glass-eyed old man, gagging on the reek of him as a truck sputtered by, spotlights stabbing. The old man beheld the alien intruder with an unblinking God-calm and said not a word.

When the truck had passed, he slithered on, away from all motion, noise, or spark of life and held himself as though dead while shadows stalked his wake. For the remainder of the night, he wormed his way south, crouch by measured crouch, as his clothes took on a thick slicking of mud and his boots a rich polish of man-shit.

With dawn growing in the eastern sky he was discovered and stalked by a pack of feral children. Mud-painted, stone-eyed, and draped in the skins of their dead, gripping bone clubs and skull totems they called and hooted through the ruins, flanking his path, hurling stones and spears, laughing as they brandished their bald boy-cocks.

Surrounded, his exits blocked, Slade found the pack leader among them, set his rifle sight on the boy's forehead, and fired, sending him jackknifing backward, end over end. The pack scattered in terror.

Moving on, he found a collapsed building no different from any other, crawled into its dusty innards, and lay motionless beneath its heaps. He stayed there, stilled and empty, through the next sun's rising and inevitable setting, stirring only to lap at the rain that guttered down through a crease in the roof. Cupping his hands, he ladled the drippings onto his wounds and tended to them with his sparse medical kit. Then, with night full upon him, he set forth again, limping deeply, strength fading.

CHAPTER SEVENTY

"Kai! Come in, Kai. This is Slade. Jesus, I need some fucking help."
Stumbling down a coal-black alley, pressing the location data burst
on his radio again and again, Slade Crawford was spent.

Discovered soon after he left the collapsed building, he had spent
the night fleeing down rat alleys and scrambling through gutted
buildings, hiding in filth sewers and sour bone piles. Each time
he was discovered, he would drop the yellow-eyed shadows, his
weapon cracking, then stagger once again into the night.

He drew up short in a dead-end alley, panting, lungs heaving
and caustic. He wiped the free-flowing blood from his hands and
checked his pistol. The suppressor was hot to the touch. The chamber
was empty. He had no fresh magazines.

He holstered the pistol then reached into his dump-pouch, drew
the expended rifle magazines, and scavenged the last odd rounds,
consolidating them in the palm of his hand. There were two rounds
remaining.

Slade lowered his head in defeat. He was out of ammunition, options, and was utterly alone. The whole of his life's reward was a
world without family, friends, allies, or country.

The one thing that he did have . . . was two rounds. Laughing,
he dropped the bullets to the ground. The rifle fell to the end of
its sling, his hands fell to his sides, and his head lolled backward.
His eyes found a narrow strip of stars hanging between the building

tops. He stayed there for long moments, taking in their incredible silence. He listened to the Penitent huntsmen as they combed the alleys and called to each other, their gunfire thundering at random.

Walking with a zombie stagger, Slade reached for a stairwell door, pulled it open, passed through it, then set to plodding up the stairs, hands on his thighs, levering himself up, step by painful step. Five stories later, he came out onto the roof, leaned against the door, and shoved it closed against shrieking hinges. He then shuffled about, back bent, stacking what debris he could against the door, the metal banging and scraping as he tipped and shoved it into place.

He would go no farther.

* * *

When he finished the barricade, he shuffled away from the door and sat down heavily, the last of his will draining down his side. He was tired. So damn tired.

From his pocket, he pulled the threadbare flag. The false altar upon which he had sacrificed his life and the people that loved him. Running his thumb over it, he could not recall the world in which those colors had meant something. Now, those colors stood for nothing but lies and meaningless words that were hackneyed punchlines for fools and the blind. Slade snickered—the foolish and the blind, that pretty much spelled him out.

Snorting, he tossed the flag away.

Liberated, he reached to the billfold strung around his neck and drew the small stack of photographs, now sodden with sweat and blood. He turned on his flashlight and leafed through each in turn, studying them, smiling at them.

Other memories came . . . He saw his sister and her daughters. He saw Isaac, Elizabeth, and the Judeans. He saw Mike Albertson and their comrades, all dead these many years. He saw his son waving to him as he returned from deployment. He saw his wife and the last time that she ever smiled.

He saw his life.

From the street below came the howls of a Penitent pack, hounding up his blood trail. Then came the pounding drumline of naked feet hammering up flights of steel stairs. Then came laughter, shouted taunts, and the metallic boom of shoulders driving against the barricaded door. An arm wedged itself through, bucking the door open.

Slade held the pictures to his mouth, kissed them, set them on the ground, then removed his fingers from the pile. A great wave of peace washed over him.

He drew his two grenades, straightened the arming pins, and rose to meet them.

All of them.

* * *

From behind the door, the shouts and taunts veered into panicked screams. The arm was withdrawn. Then came the metallic cracking of silenced rifle bolts and the meaty thud of bullets slapping through flesh. Slapping. Slapping.

Then came silence, deafening silence, while the stars turned overhead in their nameless millions. Slade listened to the pitter-patter of blood beading and dripping from his hands.

The door was pushed open. A dark form advanced and approached Slade cautiously, heavy boots crunching over roof gravel. It was Bert, his form scattered and wavering ghostlike through the heat waves climbing from his weapon. He strolled toward Slade and leaned in, his face spattered with blood though he bore no wounds.

His lips cracked in an asylum smile. "This is planet murder, my friend. Planet fuckin' murder."

Slade stared dumbstruck, uncomprehending. Another shadow appeared, this one a giant. The grenades were lifted from his hands and the safety pins bent back into place. Kneeling beside Slade, Kai unlimbered his pack, flashed a faint light over the American, then probed gently at his face and scalp.

"Looks like you got a good one, mate, right down to the bone." He poured water over Slade's wounds then wiped at the blood grime with a cloth. Tearing open a pouch, he tipped Slade's head to the side and poured a powder over the yawning gash. The pain was instant and excruciating. Kai took the flapping ear and pressed it back into place, covered the wound with a fresh bandage, then bound the entire production in place with a length of duct tape drawn repeatedly around Slade's head. When he was finished, Kai leaned back and inspected his handiwork.

"That's top doc right there, mate, top doc. I just don't want to be around when you take it off." He laughed, slapped Slade on the shoulder, and passed him a canteen. Slade drained it. Kai then produced a small plastic bottle and held it to Slade's mouth. "Just a little nightcap to get you right as rain."

Slade gulped down the sweet liquid, which settled into his belly then seemingly blossomed into a charcoal fire that quickly spread to his chest and limbs. Slade felt the crushing fatigue lift like a veil, and heard his heart accelerate in his chest. He sat up blinking, energy surging, the pain fading and evaporating. He lifted himself up, wiped his mouth, inspected his hands, and tried his voice. "Hot damn, that's good stuff."

"The best."

"What is it?"

"Hell if I know. It's the stuff kids take for clubbin' now days. Keep an eye on Bert though, he's had three of 'em. Get in front of 'im, he's likely to either kill ya or fuck ya. Possibly both."

Slade glanced over at Bert, who was peering over the edge of the building, weapon raised.

"Noted. Where's Sideshow?"

"Bottom of the stairs, lootin' the bloodies."

Turning to inspect himself, Slade glanced over his kit. "Got any spare mags?" he asked.

"'Course. Mum raised me right." He handed Slade four magazines. "Here's some sub-sonics."

The small party joined up on the second floor. Bert held security at a window. Sideshow approached, smiling broadly, stepping over piled bodies. "Kia ora, love. You're lookin' rough as guts this mornin'." He pointed toward a pile of spears, machetes, and AK-47 magazines. "Take what ya need."

"Elizabeth, did you see her! How is she?" Slade demanded.

Sideshow shrugged. "She wasn't so chuffed with us leavin' an' all, but she'll get by. Told her we'd be back after dinner."

"Did you get the pills away from her?"

"Got 'em."

Slade let out a breath as the tension bled away; he'd bought Elizabeth more time. He looked at the three men that stood guard around him. "Thanks for coming back, gents."

"No worries, mate. You ready to leg it out of here?" Kai asked.

"Ready." Slade knelt and took six more AK magazines from the pile. "I'll stay with you till you're out of the city and in the clear, then I'm going to cut away, double back, and go after Elizabeth. I'll figure something out."

"You misunderstand, mate," Kai said. "We're all in for another go at your lamb."

Slade's shoulders drooped. "I'm sorry. I've only got a little gold left. It's not enough."

"You're not graspin'." Kai smiled as one would at a dim child. "It was neva about the money, mate. We're more than willing to help a lad who's doin' what needs be done. Whateva you're up for . . . we're in, too. Full tit."

Slade fell mute, lacking the words. Minutes before he'd been utterly alone, lost in the void. And now he was surrounded by brothers, shoulder to shoulder, back on the hunt.

"Once we're out of the city, we'll take a gasper, regroup, and come up with a plan for your lamb. Sound good?" Kai continued.

Slade nodded his head in agreement, still not able to speak, not quite believing.

"Alright, but now's time to leg it. Bert, you're up front with me. Seppo, you and Sideshow cover back. We'll bump in pairs, standard sweeps on the rooms, stack tight on the corners, caterpillar the streets, watch me for cues."

"Got it."

As Kai and Bert moved to the door, Sideshow sidled in next to Slade. "Looks like it's you an' me, love." He brushed the curls back from his face. "But rememba, redheads got plus-five retard strength. Gonna have to work hard keepin' up. Don't go piker on me."

The first hints of a smile twitched Slade's mouth. "Will do, mate."

Standing at the door, Kai gave the signal. They nodded, then entered the night on the run, flowing as a line unbroken, the streets and alleys their trail and their cover. They moved without sound save for the soft scuffing of their boots on concrete and a labored panting broken now and again by the metallic slap of a rifle bolt, a soft vegetable splatter, and the final sigh of a life forgotten.

* * *

An hour into the sprint, Kai signaled for a rest stop and motioned them into a building. Kai and Bert went first. Slade and Sideshow covered their movement, then followed.

Boots crunching over glass, Slade moved to a defensive position. Kneeling, he brushed against a body. It was living warm, its leg twitching slowly like a spent clock winding down its last empty turns. It was a filthy old woman, her face as pitted and wrinkled as a dried apple, her forehead cratered inward from a vicious muzzle strike.

Slade glanced toward Bert and fixed on the dripping blood and hair that clung to the Kiwi's muzzle. He glanced back again at the crumpled woman.

He felt Sideshow's lips touch his ear. "Home court rules, mate. Home court rules."

"Yeah, I know."

Panting, Kai struggled with a whisper. "We can't keep this game up much longa'. Them skinnies is gittin' thicka' and thicka'. At this rate, we'll run out of ammo 'fore we clear the city. We gotsta get off these legs and onto some wheels."

"And we been leavin' a stout trail of bloodies, makes for easy trackin'," Sideshow said.

"We've got to grab a vehicle now," Slade injected, "while we still have enough ammo to pull it off."

"Right."

"So how do we go about jackin' a lorry without drawin' in the whole lot of 'em?"

Slade offered a complex plan that used himself as bait.

"Classic seppo." Sideshow chuckled and shook his head. "Alright, listen up, mate. When it comes to gettin' the job done, there's a time for sleight of hand, talkin' sweet, an ticklin' the girly bits. But times like this . . . you just gotta pull out the lumber and set to the bad business."

"He's right there, mate," Bert added.

Kai locked eyes with each man in turn. "All right then . . . cocks out, lads."

The four men left the building and took to the center of the street, line abreast, weapons raised, then advanced at a run directly toward the lights of a distant cargo truck. As Penitents rose to meet them, their rifles coughed and their targets crumpled to the street, flashlights rolling crazy from newly dead hands.

The cargo truck veered off the road, over a curb, then crashed to a halt, its driver now dead at the wheel. Those in the cargo bed scattered in panic, falling and scrambling, clinging to—and then hacking at—each other as darkness itself rose and sent them gibbering from this world.

CHAPTER SEVENTY-ONE

Twenty kilometers outside of Nairobi, the cargo truck labored and ground, its engine skipping like an arrhythmic heart, a steady fog of oil smoke coughing behind it. Inside the cab, Sideshow jockeyed the stick shift and maintained a steady stream of profanity against the failing machine, repeatedly slamming his fist against the steering column, setting off a steady cadence from the truck's horn. The anemic mechanical bleating only served to enrage him further.

"Sounds like this lorry's about to pack a sad. Gonna have to leg it soon," Kai said. Standing in the bed of the truck, he glanced toward the yellowing east into which they drove. "And in daylight, no less. Brilliant."

"Let's get this heap into cover," Slade said. "If she dies right here in the highway, they'll know our starting point, make it a hell of a lot easier to track us."

"Right." Bert sighted on the pack of trucks that pursued them in the distance. "The skinnies are five minutes back. Take the next turnoff then—"

The discussion ended with a massive backfire, a mechanical shriek, and the awful silence of a dead engine. The truck wobbled to a stop, leaf springs creaking.

"Like I was saying, let's just stop here and leg it straight away."

The four men gathered their kit, dismounted, and took to ground, running across the high grass of an open field. They fled through forests and crossed hills at a run, pushing and dragging each other onward. They drank the last of their water, took the last of their drugs, dropped the weapons that were empty, and knew only panting, breathless flight.

As they crossed a ridgeline, Slade glanced over his shoulder. A half mile behind them, a gypsy convoy of vehicles had braked to a halt and the Penitents were dismounting in their hundreds.

In time, an unerring arithmetic took hold; those in flight were old and spent, those in pursuit were young and fresh. Slowly the gap narrowed, the distance that stood between them faded, and the four men were run to ground.

* * *

They made their stand in the remains of a stone and tile mosque. The mosque's construction was unfinished, but its courtyard walls were high, its gate strong, and its minarets covered. Gasping, they staggered into the courtyard, pushed the gate closed behind them, then collapsed to their haunches, gagging on fatigue.

Kai was the first to speak. "Bert . . ." He rose to his feet and pointed to a minaret. "Bert, rattle ya dags up that tower and get ya scope on the skinnies. You two slags help me barricade the gate. Pile everything you can find. That rubbish over there will work propa. Go with the rocks, bricks, the bones, the whole lot of it. Most of them skinnies is barefoot—anything sharp will slow 'em up."

"Brilliant." Slade staggered to his feet, pulled Sideshow with him, then bent to the task of barricading the gateway. Grunting and straining, they moved scaffolding, a cement mixer, a wheeled generator, and welding equipment and piled it against the wrought-iron gate. Slade checked the pressure gauges on the welding bottles, but they were empty.

Next, they kicked together heaps of moldering bones and wheel-barrowed them into place. Kai stood atop the bone pile, smashing it beneath his feet, issuing a shrapnel of shattered ribs, crushed skulls, and split femurs. Slade and Sideshow gathered up the sharp-edged splinters and scattered them outside the gate.

Satisfied, Kai squinted up at the minaret where Bert, drawn back in the shadows of the gallery, glassed the terrain with his rifle scope.

Kai cued his wrist computer. "Whatcha got, Bert?"

There was a long pause. "Skinnies. Lots of 'em."

"Okay. What kind o' kit they humpin'?"

The older Kiwi remained glued to his scope.

"Bert! Pssst! What kind o' kit those skinnies humpin'?"

"The usual."

"Any MGs?"

"A few."

"How many long guns?" There was no reply again. Kai frowned, shaded his eyes, and looked up at his friend. "What's eatin' ya, mate?"

Bert lowered his rifle and spoke into his wrist computer. "They got poles."

"What?"

"Sharp wooden poles."

"Spears? So what?"

"No. Poles. Four of 'em. Big long ones."

"Oh . . ."

Bert's voice was barely audible. "They got the ending all planned out, mates."

CHAPTER SEVENTY-TWO

THEY HELD THE Penitents off for an hour, fighting as best they could, burning through their ammunition, turning to their work with the raw energy of those giving their last.

Bert, inside the minaret, snapping off single shots, dropping the leaders and riflemen.

Sideshow, atop the walls, heaving bricks and stones.

Kai, in the courtyard, knifing and gutting the squirming Penitents as they were pressed helpless against the gate by their surging peers.

Slade, armed and tossed his grenades, scattering bloody clouds of flesh as the mob surged over the sagging fence.

"Bert, the gate's collapsing! Get down and fall back. Fall back!" Kai yelled into his wrist computer.

Slade, Kai, and Sideshow fell back across the courtyard and into the blue-tiled prayer room, firing bursts from their rifles and calling for Bert to clear the minaret. The Penitents hammered through the last of the iron gate then surged across the yard in a flood, surrounding the mosque, beating on its doors, lifting each other up to smash through its windows, catching themselves on the broken glass, then tumbling slain and gushing, their falls deadened by the lush carpets within.

The final door was caving in, breaking free from its hinges.

The three men turtled up, weapons raised.

"Where's Bert! Where the fuck is Bert!" Kai yelled.

Slade knelt, leaned from cover, and snapped off a series of shots. "I thought he was on your side!"

"No! He neva made it in!" Kai fired till empty then performed a magazine change. "Last mag! Last mag!"

"I thought he did! He came to cover your side—" Caught by a charging boy, Slade toppled backward, his muzzle jammed into the child's chest. His grenade launcher triggered, lifting the child to the ceiling where the grenade detonated in a concussive rain of debris, blood, and atomized plaster.

* * *

Slade found himself lying on the floor, immersed in a world that had fallen strangely silent. He struggled to his feet, legs weak, straining to see through the smoke and dust, his weapon rising to meet the final charge.

It didn't come.

Turning, looking, staggering, he found Kai still alive, blood flowing. Slade leaned over him, swept the debris away, slapped him awake, and hauled him up, the Maori's face a kabuki mask of blood and dust. Slade shouted in his ear to be heard, fetched him his weapon, then did the same for Sideshow.

They waited, blinking in the silence.

Still nothing.

And more nothing.

Till a screaming rose gently in that concussed, ringing vacuum. The screaming, long and liquid, sharp and mortal.

It was Bert. Screaming through his death.

The three rose and staggered across the prayer room to the doorway, which held view across the courtyard. They stopped beneath its arches, stood blinking in the sun, and beheld the death of their friend, hoisted skyward on a wooden pole, in that moment, the world's newest ending.

Surrounding Bert, the grinning, the leering and jumping mob, laughing like children in the shadow of their blood rite, cutting and tearing at the body, bedecking themselves in colorful flesh garlands as would merrybegots dancing 'round a maypole.

Stone mute, the three men beheld their own inevitable end.

But then came a hoarse bawling—rising and swelling.

It was Kai. Face contorted in pain, screaming to his lost friend, blood tears painting tracks down his dusted face.

Some in the mob paused and glanced toward the new sound, laughing, brandishing their trophies.

Kai's rifle clattered to the stone. He reached and slowly unstrapped his chest rig. His armor slumped to the ground. Then in a single abrupt spasm, he tore his shirt from his chest. In another motion, he slipped from his shoes, then his pants. Now naked, he prepared for death in the manner of his ancestors.

Breathing deeply, the Maori giant lowered himself into a half crouch, feet spread, back straight, neck chords standing like exposed guy wires. He loosed a full-throated scream and built it to an ursine roar, eyes bulged and mouth yawned, tongue protruding as a broad flat blade. He swung his arms and landed brutal slaps against his thighs and chest in time with his rhythmic scream. The slaps and strikes echoed through the courtyard, spalling fans of dust and his own running blood into the air.

Ka Mah-te, ka Mah-Te! Ka oora, ka oora!

He uprooted his feet and advanced slowly, stomping, gesturing violently at his enemy, at his dead friend, at the rising of the sun.

Ka Mah-te, ka Mah-Te! Ka oora, ka oora!

Tenei te tangata puhuruhuhu!!!

The Penitent mob stilled, shocked into silence as they beheld the gore-spackled giant that stalked toward them, blood flowing, raising clouds of dust, immense cock swinging pendulous, arms punching and slapping. The mob began to mill and founder, making signs, calling for powerful witchcraft, brandishing totems, and invoking their own animal spirits.

Kai advanced fearless, head up, spat murder, and beckoned them closer.

Nana nei i tiki mai whakawhiti te ra!!!

A upane! Ka upane!!!

A, upane, ka upane, whiti te ra!!!

The mob shied back in a crescent before his advance. Their leader appeared at the fore, tried to lash his boys into attack, and pushed the nearest forward. Instead, the boy turned and fled, sparking a roil of confusion and panic. The man raised a trembling pistol at Kai, fired and missed, fired and missed, fired and missed. Seemingly impervious, Kai bellowed one last time then exploded forward into the teetering mob.

Slade and Sideshow burst upon the flank of the crowd, firing the last of their magazines at point-blank range before wading into the scrum, swinging their rifles as clubs. The three men attacked forward—braining—cracking—gouging—biting—splitting—

Within seconds, the mob was turned to panicked flight, dropping their spears and machetes, pushing, trampling, and climbing over each other as they fought to escape through the narrow gateway.

Slade saw himself from afar, a predator loosed in their midst, berserk, blood lusting beyond reason or sating. The three men wolf-packed the fleeing mob, dragging down the slow and wounded, slaying, then springing to the next. As the last of the Penitents escaped, the men found themselves staggering and retching like blood drunkards among the filth and flesh till at last they collapsed and lay dreamless among the dead.

CHAPTER SEVENTY-THREE

SIDESHOW WAS THE first with the strength to stand. He found and helped the others to their feet, collected fallen weapons, and scavenged ammunition. He found them water, then bandaged their wounds with clothes pulled from the dead. They gathered themselves.

In time, they lowered Bert and wrapped his ruin in a pulled curtain. Kai wept openly and spoke gently to the spotting bundle. They spoke of leaving, of continuing on though not knowing how. They were spent utterly and without reserve. The Penitents would return. The three had only to choose the place of their dying.

They waited.

*   *   *

Slade saw the soldier first, up where the courtyard wall joined against the minaret. The man was equipped with full battle armor, a short carbine, suppressor, laser, and optics. Blinking through a haze of exhaustion, Slade looked elsewhere and saw other camouflaged soldiers ringing them from above, coming over the courtyard walls, surrounding the mosque, two dozen or more. The weapons . . . the uniforms . . . the gear . . . they were Americans. And if they were Americans . . .

Kraven.

Slade called a warning to Kai and Sideshow. They rose and stood in the courtyard, those three, looking upwards, uncaring, unspeaking, gripping their own pathetic weapons.

A voice called out, commanding they drop their arms.

They did not.

The voice demanded again.

Kai motioned for them to come and take his.

None accepted.

"Put the weapons down, Crawford!" a new voice shouted.

Slade looked to the courtyard entrance where Colonel Kraven, covered by a phalanx of soldiers, was stepping over the piled bodies. Slade judged the distance to his target, the dozen men with weapons trained on him, his own blurred vision and numbed limbs. He wouldn't get a single shot off.

"Put the weapons down, and my PJs will see to you and your men," Kraven said.

Swaying on his feet, Slade swallowed thickly and tried to speak. Failing, he tried again. "Send the Js over, then we'll talk."

"I could end this right now, Crawford." Kraven raised his eyes toward the soldiers on the wall.

Slade leaned and spit a gobbet of blood. "Go fuck yourself, Gary."

Kraven halted just inside the courtyard.

"That your rupert?" Sideshow asked.

"Yeah. That's him."

Kraven's eyes narrowed as he took measure of the battered men and the charnel house upon which they stood. After long moments, he motioned toward his rear and called the PJs forward. Two heavily burdened men broke from Kraven's group and approached the trio. When the pararescue jumpers were within touching distance, Slade dropped his weapon. Kai and Sideshow did likewise.

The PJs led the three survivors inside the prayer room, seated them, then opened up their medical kits. They put oxygen monitors on their fingers, cleaned their wounds, and started IV drips. They cut away the duct tape encircling Slade's head, sterilized the ear gash, then secured the flapping lobe with surgical glue. They irrigated and bandaged his broken nose and administered meds for the pain. They tended to the Kiwis' injuries, gave all three men antibiotic injections, then applied time-release med patches to their abdomens. As a final measure, the PJs unwrapped painkilling narcotic lollipops and taped them to the men's thumbs.

Seeing the Kiwis' enquiring expression, the PJ mimed pulling a lollipop out of his mouth. "We tape them to your thumb so you won't choke if you pass out."

"Bloody seppos can't help going astro." Sideshow shook his head in disgust. "See, Down Under we avoid all that by givin' 'em as suppositories." With that said, he licked his lollipop, toppled Kai onto his side, and attempted to deliver the narcotics.

Slade turned away from the Kiwis as Kraven approached.

"Where's my Priest? You said you had him," the colonel said.

Slade shook his head. "Lost him."

Kraven's skeletal face hardened further. "I find that unacceptable."

Slade looked away to conceal his anger.

The older of the two PJs glanced up at the colonel. "They're stable for now, sir, nothing critical, but I'd like to get them back to the Ranch, let a surgeon work on this ear and nose." He then pointed at the Kiwis. "If not, I can patch these guys with fluids and stitches."

"Good. Do what you can." Kraven turned to Slade. "You able to stand?"

Slade nodded.

"Walk with me," Kraven said as he turned and strode toward the courtyard.

The PJ helped Slade to his feet and unhooked the IV line from his forearm. "Soon as you finish up with the colonel, I'd like to get another IV in you. You've lost a lot of blood."

"Alright. Will do." Slade motioned toward the two Kiwis. "Look after my guys while I'm gone."

"Already on it, Senior Chief."

Slade thanked the PJ then followed the colonel out of the prayer room and into the sun. Outside, Kraven strolled across the courtyard as if alone, stepping over bodies and waving away flies.

Kraven's radio crackled. "Talon Six, this is Zulu 4-3, we have approximately three hundred indig massing four hundred meters to the north."

Kraven keyed his mike. "Cleared hot."

"Roger."

The staccato chatter of suppressed rifle fire came from the minaret.

The colonel continued across the courtyard, exited through the gateway, then moved to a place where he had a clear view across the Nairobi plains. The towering mirrors of the city shimmered in the distance.

Slade drew up beside Kraven, fists knurled, knuckles white.

Kraven motioned toward the bloodied shambles. "Looks like you and your men had a rough go of it." He crossed his arms over his chest and raised his chin. "But you failed to complete your mission. I don't tolerate failure."

"Life's full of disappointments, Colonel."

Kraven placed his arms akimbo and issued a stillborn chuckle. "Funny. But you've pushed me into a difficult position. You disobeyed my direct orders, broke the agreement we had, and—"

"You call that an *agreement*?"

"—*and* failed to get Mujuru's chip, *and* threatened my family."

"It wasn't a threat," Slade replied softly.

Kraven turned toward Slade and held him in regard: the bandaged scalp, the smashed nose, the blood-stained hands, and the narrow eyes of a killer come fresh from the slaughter. The colonel looked away and released a long breath. "It's clear that our relationship has broken down and is no longer functional. We need a reset. I'm prepared to release you from your obligation in exchange for—"

"Obligation?"

A look of irritation flashed across Kraven's face. "Call it what you want, I'm no longer holding you in my service."

Slade showed no response, for he had none. Words spoken by a man such as Kraven held no meaning.

"But—" The colonel turned and faced Slade directly. "I want to know if you'll work for me voluntarily."

Kraven waited for a reaction but got none. "I know I've given you reason to hate me, Crawford, but I'm offering you a new life—"

"*Hate* ain't the word, Colonel." Slade's finger became a grime-clagged railroad spike that he leveled in Kraven's face. "Give me the chance, and I'll spit you on one of those poles myself." Slade pointed toward a crumpled Penitent body. "You think that flag on your shoulder is any different from the brand on that chest? I'd gut you both just the same."

The colonel watched the horizon. "So . . . is that a 'no'?"

Slade took a step toward Kraven, face contorted, teeth bared.

Distant soldiers moved closer and brought their weapons to full raise. Kraven waived them off. He met Slade's gaze and his voice lost its iron-edge. "Hear me out, Slade. If you don't care about what I can offer you . . . your freedom . . . a new identify . . . a new life . . . at least hear the *why*, so you can understand that—"

"*Why* don't mean a thing. You know how many women and children were in that Judean convoy? You had a chance to help them and you did nothing. I'll go to my grave—"

"And there'll be billions more if I don't do what I must!" Kraven barked, his face suddenly red. "Stop thinking about yourself, Crawford! This is bigger than us! This is for the world, the entire goddamn planet!"

Slade searched Kraven's eyes and studied the deep strain written there. "It's true, then. You're here because of von Helm and the UN."

Kraven looked away and smoothed his uniform, regaining his composure. "So you figured it out."

"With some help."

"What's your take on it . . . How much do you know?"

Slade got the distinct impression that Kraven was testing him. "I know you're opposed to a plan unfolding here. Something driven by the One-World crowd. I think they engineered the African collapse. And they're using the Penitents to keep settlers out of Africa until the UN can establish control."

Kraven wore a look of approval. "You've got the basics down. As for me, the long and the short of it—If globalists gain control of Africa, they'll have taken a quantum leap toward their goal of One-World Government, and One-World Government is a world of slavery that I cannot abide."

"Don't you think you're being a bit dramatic, Colonel?"

"Slade, totalitarianism has evolved over time. In previous decades, tyrants arrived on the backs of tanks and enforced their will through the barrel of a gun. Their methods were crude, transparent, and always inspired violent opposition. But today, tyranny has been refined and perfected. Now tyrants use international trade deals, usurious debt, multinational corporations, central banks, bought legislatures, and impenetrable bureaucracies to enslave us. On the home front, militarized police, welfare states, captured media, and endless entertainment are used to control the populations. In the 1930s the tyrants called themselves Fascists, and we defeated them.

Then they called themselves Communists, and we defeated them. But today, the new name for tyranny is Corporatism and Globalism, and we have embraced it. We have remained asleep as there are no beaches to storm, no jack-booted Nazis to punch in the face."

"Now that's just goddamn depressing, Colonel."

"Have you ever heard of the Domino Theory, Slade?"

"No. But I imagine you're about to tell me—"

"As World War I was winding down, Westerners recognized the threat that the Bolshevik revolution posed to free societies. So, in 1918, America, Britain, France, and sixteen other allies briefly invaded Russia to destroy the Communist revolution. They failed. And because they failed, like dominoes, the rest of the world slowly began to fall. After Russia, over twenty countries in Eastern Europe and Central Asia fell to Communism. Then came China, North Korea, Cuba, Vietnam, Cambodia, and the countless dirty, unseen wars that raged throughout Africa and the Americas. Our failure to stamp out Communism in 1918 resulted in seventy years of warfare, political violence, conflict, and almost two hundred million deaths."

"So what's that got to do with you and me?"

"Because here in Africa, right now, the first Globalist domino is falling."

"I don't buy it. Putting Africa under UN control would be good for the place. Might even get the Africans to stop killing each other. Bring some stability."

"You're right about that," Kraven replied. "But what happens when the Globalists expand their reach past Africa, into the rest of the world?"

"I don't know." Slade shrugged.

"Think about it, Crawford: Truly, what is the enduring legacy of Globalism in the Western world? The last forty years have brought us nothing but the fascist union of banks, big business, and the

State, the rise of the corporate oligarchs, the destruction of the middle class, and the erosion of our freedoms. Once the Globalists have absolute control, the decline will only accelerate, until the last remnants of our freedom and prosperity have been stripped away and *all* of us live in the Third World. A Third World lorded over by a small, ultra-wealthy elite. Poor people are powerless and easy to control, thus we will all live in poverty. It's that simple."

"Agenda 21."

"Yes. And the descent into poverty will not be peaceful. People that oppose the confiscation of their freedom and wealth will be introduced to the secret police, the reeducation camps, the gulags, the killing fields, and the bone ovens. Tyranny and mass murder is the inevitable end of every statist, collectivist movement throughout history—ruin for the masses, power for the elite, death for those who refuse to submit. It is the eternal struggle between those who would be free, and those who would control and compel."

"That's a pretty grim take on things, Colonel."

"Really, Slade? Consider your own experience. First the State came for your privacy. Then they came for your rights and your property. Then they came for you. You think it's bad now? Wait until the laws and taxes are made by bureaucrats in Mexico City, Brussels, and Beijing. Do you think those men will have higher regard for your freedoms and prosperity? The more remote a power structure grows, the more abusive and unaccountable it becomes. They will use the words *justice, equality, race,* and *climate* to excuse their actions and achieve their ultimate goal: *tyranny.*"

Slade weighed the gravity of Kraven's words and judged the truth of their meaning.

"Who exactly are these people?" Slade asked.

"You want names and faces? Look for power players who never have to face an election. Spend time in Davos, Switzerland, and the central banks of the world. Look to the supranational organizations and the corporations that control them: G7, G10, the UN. If you listen, they make no secret of their ambitions. They want the world, Slade. All of it."

"Okay. But why me? What've I got to do with this?"

"After the African Holocaust, the UN declared the continent a demilitarized zone. Supposedly, it was to keep foreign militaries from seizing ground and clashing with each other. In reality, it was to keep us from interfering with the Globalists' plans. I can make brief penetrations from the American base in Djibouti under the guise of 'training missions,' but I can't allow my Ospreys to be seen by surveillance radars at UN bases. And sending in my men is extremely risky—if one of them is caught, it would compromise my entire operation. As for your involvement . . . I needed boots on the ground and your boots were the best I could find. You were my workaround."

Slade shook his head in disagreement. "The boys from the Deep Black unit would be untraceable. You could've used them."

"You're still not getting it, Slade. People at the highest levels are deeply involved in the plan, orchestrating it, in fact. They know that many in the US military will oppose them. Because of that they've assigned *Civil Rights Officers* to monitor all military units, Company level and above."

"Civil Rights Officers?" Slade asked, disbelieving.

"Yeah." Kraven snorted in contempt. "Ostensibly, they keep us from drinking, screwing, and telling dirty jokes. In reality they exist for the sole purpose of reporting *unpatriotic* behavior."

"Political commissars."

"Yes, we've come to that. And because of them, all my normal assets and channels are closely monitored. Every contact I have with you raises the risk level dramatically. And that . . ." Kraven ran a hand over his face and looked away, his voice softening to a whisper.

"That's why I couldn't assist you when you were under attack. Why I had to let the Judeans die." He looked at Slade, measuring the impact of his words. "You saw it as callous disregard . . . But it wasn't . . . It was the cold calculus of operational risk."

"Call it what you will, I'd still kill you for it."

"Jesus! I have five children of my own, Slade! Raised them up! I'd slit my throat for them! I know what I did to the Judeans . . ." Kraven's voice trailed off, acutely aware of the obscenity of offering an excuse. "But I couldn't place them ahead of this operation."

"I could."

Kraven let out a long breath and his shoulders slumped. "I know, Slade . . . I know."

"But I do understand."

"Do you?"

"Yeah, when it's all over . . . Neither of us will be forgiven for the things we've done," Slade said, accepting the colonel's unspoken apology. After a long silence, he looked toward Kraven. "So what's your proposal?"

Kraven filled his chest, regaining his composure. He pointed toward Nairobi. "What I want you to do is kick the legs out from under this UN op and strangle it in the cradle. Fight the Penitents. Kill their leaders. Break their will. Drive them out.

"You'll establish a safe haven and assemble a team, then run a recon and direct-action campaign across the continent. Your first order of business will be to grab Mujuru. If you can get him or his biochip, we'll know the Penitents' plans, finance trails, and who he takes orders from."

"Speaking of Mujuru . . ." Slade murmured. He reached to the cargo pocket on his thigh, opened it, and drew out a severed hand, its wrist de-skinned, the raw end of its forearm a chaotic blossom of bone chips and dirt-encrusted meat.

"I took it off high enough that the chip should still be in there. You'll have to dig it out yourself."

Kraven regarded the hand with something bordering on suspicion. "Is he dead?"

"He won't play piano again, but I figured you'd want to talk to him someday, so he's still alive. If the tourniquets held . . ."

Kraven swallowed thickly. "Tourniquets?"

"I took both off," Slade said, brandishing the hand. "As for this chip, if you want it, you're going to help me free Elizabeth tonight."

Kraven nodded. "Deal. I'll fly her to Djibouti and drop her with State Department."

"Negative, you won't just dump her on State. You'll personally escort her back to the US and see her settled with family."

Kraven sucked on his teeth and eyed his opponent through narrowed eyes. "Done."

Slade tossed the hand to Kraven, but the colonel made no effort to catch it. He glanced to where it landed in the dirt. "That's some fine work, Crawford." He nodded his head in approval. "My men are yours for the night. We'll get the girl out. But the reason I'm here . . . I want to know if you'll join me."

Without hesitation, Slade shook his head. "No. After tonight, you and I are done. Had my fill of your kind."

"Sure I can't change your mind?"

"Yup."

"I'll have to ask you to reconsider." Kraven reached into his pocket, pulled out a scrap of fabric, and offered it to Slade. It was an American flag shoulder patch, threadbare, the colors faded by decades of grime and sweat. "My men couldn't reach you in time. Got to the rooftop five minutes after you left. Thought you might want it back."

Slade stared at the flag, dumbfounded, but then narrowed his eyes. "Jesus, now you're going to wave the flag at me?"

"It's not a flag that I'm asking you to serve, it's an idea."

"Yeah, well that idea is a lie. A lie that you and I have destroyed nations for."

"Slade, if a truth is used in the telling of a lie, that does not change the truth. The ideas represented by this flag are some of the most sacred ever written down by man. I'm asking you to fight for those."

"I'll fight for freedom, Colonel, but I'm done fighting for that flag."

"Why? Because you're pissed at some of the frauds and criminals who wave it? They're as un-America as people can be. If you want to right what they made wrong, then join me and restore the meaning of that flag. The reason we're in trouble now is because good men turned their backs and walked away, didn't do the right thing, the hard thing."

Slade flinched at the comment, then looked away to hide his shame.

"I am not a godly man," Kraven continued, "but I do know this: there is Good and there is Evil, and the nature of our world is determined by the actions of the men who live within it. Men like us must stand up for Good, even if it kills us." Kraven looked into Slade's eyes and saw the distrust written there. He lowered his voice to a gentler tone. "I know I haven't earned it, Slade, God knows I haven't. But I'm asking you to take a leap of faith and trust me. And if you still believe in what you fought for those many years ... then for God's sake join me."

Slade expended a long breath and his chin dipped to his chest. "Do the right thing..." He stared at the earth upon which he stood, as if trying to see through to its very core and divine the terrible truths that dwelled therein. He turned his head toward the colonel, searched his gaze, and found the sincerity of his intent. He looked at the distant towers of Nairobi, thinking of the mistakes that he had made, the people that mattered to him, and the world they might live in.

Kraven waited quietly, the morning stillness torn at long intervals by the ripping of guns in the minaret.

Slade swung his head and locked eyes with the colonel. "First time we met, you made me a promise."

"Did I?"

"Yes. You said that if I broke the deal, you'd kill me."

Kraven nodded. "I guess I did."

"So . . . I'd like to extend you the same courtesy."

"How's that?"

"If you betray me . . . I'm going to kill you."

"Fair enough."

"Alright then . . ." Slowly, Slade turned, extended his arm, and grasped the colonel's hand, enveloping the flag. "I'm in."

CHAPTER SEVENTY-FOUR

THEY CAME AFTER midnight, their drones orbiting quietly over-head, their eyes lit by the phosphor glow of night vision goggles. When they killed the generators and plunged the building into darkness, those inside the Predator laughed, raised their glasses, and shouted aloud, never hearing the soft scuffing of ladders being placed against the outer walls, nor the window bars and glass being silently removed, nor the soldiers as they entered on soft-soled boots. The johns and guards stumbled through the halls with arms raised in front of them as though to stop the gunfire they could neither hear nor see. They dropped soundlessly, without complaint, and lay in heaps in the corridors, stairwells, and bedrooms, bub-bling out their last.

Slade found Elizabeth, covered her with a blanket, and led her away. There was no gratitude or relief in her expression for she lived in a world devoid of both.

They searched the compound and herded over two dozen cow-ering girls down to the loading dock where a stolen delivery truck waited. Sideshow leaned from the driver's window. "Where to, mate?"

"Drop them at the Grand Regency, right at the pool-bar." Slade checked his watch. "The newsies will still be there. Give them a scoop. It'll give them something to report on for a few days."

"Chief!" the PJ called from inside the brothel. "Got a problem up on the second floor. It's your girl."

Slade turned, looked for Elizabeth, but she was gone. Fearing the worst, he bolted back into the Predator and took the stairs three at a time. A Delta trooper beckoned him into a bedroom. Slade entered, flashlight splaying, dreading what he would find.

Elizabeth stood motionless in the center of the room. A man knelt before her with his hands clasped together, pleading. It was Mujuru's drinking buddy, Phillipe Lefleur.

Slade approached cautiously. "Elizabeth?"

She seemed not to hear. Her face was corpse cold, giving the appearance of one who'd passed beyond the frailties of life and returned in form only. Her eyes never left Phillipe as her right arm slowly raised and extended toward Slade, open palm turned toward the ceiling, waiting. Slade looked at her open hand, at the way her thumb was spread and the index finger slightly extended. There was only one thing that could be placed within that grip.

"You sure you want to do this?" Slade asked.

The granite weight of her unshifting gaze was her only answer.

Slade looked at the wrinkled worm begging wet-eyed at her feet. He looked at the bite marks and bruises on Elizabeth's skin. Relenting, he nodded, reached to his belt, and drew the 1911.

"This is something you won't be able to undo," he said softly.

There was no reply.

Slade placed the pistol in her palm and watched as her fingers curled to accept it. He paused, allowing her to feel its weight, its gravity, the invariable consequence of its purpose. She waited motionless until Slade released his grip on the weapon.

He then stood beside her and bore witness as she took her vengeance.

When the pistol was empty, Slade put his arm around her, turned her away, and led her from that place.

* * *

As they passed through the main lounge, stepping over bodies, feet crushing glass, Slade did a double take and paused at the weapons check desk. The ancient clerk stood blinking in the light of Slade's helmet lamp. Slade then rummaged in his pocket, pulled out a crumpled claim ticket, and handed it to the old man. Moving with agonizing slowness, the clerk walked to the row of lockers, fumbled within them, and returned with Slade's Sig.

Slade thanked the clerk, checked the Sig's chamber, and holstered it. As he turned toward the door, Elizabeth's cold gaze stopped him in place.

"You'll be needing that," she said softly.

"Why?" Slade asked, disturbed by the complete absence of fear or anger in her voice.

"Because we've got a lot of work to do."

CPSIA information can be obtained
at www.ICGtesting.com
Printed in the USA
BVHW03s1337110818
524180BV00003B/14/P